Glory Be
to The Father,
The Son . . .

13298-STIC

Glory Be to The Father, The Son . . .

Richard Stickann

To order additional copies of this book, contact:
Xlibris Corporation
1-888-7-XLIBRIS
www.Xlibris.com
Orders@Xlibris.com

TO CATHERINE

PART I

I

It was a muggy Wednesday evening in June when Edward first detected a serious flaw in his father's family affiliation. It was not a minor defect a child might witness when a father has a momentary lapse of family loyalty or a transient decline in time spent with a child. It was greater than that, greater than anything Edward had experienced in his eight plus years. But as he grew, the episode languished somewhere in the bustling mind of an adolescent, then teenager, then young adult until it had been absorbed, or maybe supplanted, with thousands of other thoughts that never included his father. But it also grew as Edward did. Hidden away, ready to bolt from its hiding pace in his brain when the appropriate circumstance presented itself; when it was most convenient to displace Edward's agreeable thoughts with those that had been impermissible for so long. And it grew exponentially.

The summer sun, still warm on Edward's neck, was beginning to set. It was a city sun spurring it to disappear earlier than the country sun. The city offered no horizon to watch it dip below, no flat farm fields to allow a person to savor its glow until the last ray disappeared. Once it hit the tops of the trees and the houses in the city, twilight quickly covered the neighborhood. And besides, the haze that frequently covered the city like a tattered strip of gauze, made the sun always seem distant, as if it recoiled when threatened by the earth it warmed.

Edward's mother rested her stomach against the sink, the top of her head was barely visible through the kitchen window. She looked up for a moment as she washed a freshly peeled carrot. Edward waved. She didn't see him. She was looking beyond the neighborhood, beyond the noise, the traffic, slicing a carrot, placing it in a bowl with other sliced carrots, celery stalks cut in half and Spanish olives, the kind that Edward thought tasted both rancid and savory, alternating those hostile flavors as the salty orb moved over his tongue. His mother drained a jar of dill pickles as she searched for something out of the normal realm she inhabited. Edward wondered what. Praying maybe. Like she does day in and day out. She always seemed to be lost in another world whenever she prepared for the arrival of her husband's poker pals. The sausages were in the frying pan, Italian and Polish. The sandwiches, liver sausage, ham and cheese and corned beef were in the refrigerator. Three dozen cans of Busch Bavarian beer had been shoved into the refrigerator that morning. Dad liked them ice cold. Edward's sister, Roberta, had washed the tumblers after lunch and placed them upside down on the kitchen counter, in readiness for anyone who may ask for a highball.

Inside, Edward's father, between counting out the poker chips, stacking them neatly in even piles of white, red and blue on the dining room table and setting up the bottles of bourbon and gin, kept checking to see if the beer was cold. Outside, Edward and his brother, Kevin, rode around the neighborhood on Kevin's bicycle, him pedaling, Edward, eight years old, sitting on the back fender, his shoes resting on the axle bolts, arms wrapped around his brother's waist. They headed up the side street parallel to their house swerving to miss the gaps and holes that had been created in the sidewalk from years of traffic and bitter Chicago winters.

Kevin, changing his mind at the last minute to avoid Mrs. Patrowski turning the corner with her shopping cart in tow, cut across the vacant lot next to their house. That's when Edward waved to his mother and speculated on what she was staring at. The lot was criss-crossed with paths grooved out of the dirt by walkers or bicycles seeking just such shortcuts to Avalon street. Since Edward could remember it had been overgrown with weeds and small trees. Isolated piles of litter and a few discarded tires decorated it as if someone had dumped the trash in a pattern.

Just when Edward lowered his arm after his unsuccessful greeting to his mother, the front tire of Kevin's bicycle bumped something solid buried beneath the weeds. The jounce, for that's all it was, tossed Edward slightly sideways, like a person's rear end might make an almost unnoticeable variation in the passenger seat of a car when the vehicle makes contact with a small rut in the road. He shifted his butt back to the center of the fender but lost his balance when the bicycle jolted over something else, something more solid this time, hidden in the tall grass. His left foot became wedged in the spokes of the back wheel. He screamed, first from the pain, and then for Kevin to stop.

When the memory of that incident intrudes into the active part of Edward's brain after thirty years, it enters in black and white, no red blood, no green grass, no blue sky. The memory is vivid even without the hues of a summer evening. His father stands colorless against the pale bricks of the house, bricks Edward new were deep burgundy. His back is slightly hunched , his face pale, everything around him without luster or life while he stands on the porch chewing on a polish sausage, waiting for his poker buddies to arrive, looking down upon the carnage while a neighbor, a neighbor neither Edward nor any member of his family had ever spoken to or even acknowledged as residing anywhere in the vicinity, cuts Edward's leg loose from the bicycle spokes. The obscure neighbor takes Edward to the hospital in his car. Edward's mother follows, but only after the sandwiches are made, covered with aluminum foil and shoved in the refrigerator. His father plays poker. Maybe they make side bets on how many stitches will be needed to close up the wound. Maybe on how long it takes to get to the hospital.

For the week after the accident, after the poker game, after the leftovers of sausage, potato chips, peanuts were put away and the beer cans discarded in the trash, Edward lived on the back porch of his house while his ankle healed. The porch swing, pockmarked from years of Edward, his friends, his brother and sister and their friends, using the porch as a fort, a road rally for toy trucks and cars and a safe haven for tag or hide and go seek, was the only place where Edward felt comfortable resting his injured limb. After ten days the stitches, thirty of them, were removed and he was able to limp to the playground just down the alley next to the public elementary school, but could only watch the basketball or softball games his friends played. No running jumping for at least three weeks after the stitches are removed, the doctor told him. After the three weeks passed, no more and no less, Edward managed to be the catcher in the softball games and still hit the ball deep into left center near the swing set when he batted. He hobbled to first base and then either Bobby or Bruce or one of the other guys ran the rest of the bases for him.

Edward immediately discovered that limping gave him a stature with his friends that normal walking never would no matter how much he tried to strut or swagger. Even the girls gave him a sliver of attention, another bright spot in the course of his recuperation. But like anyone who is given attention by others because of an injury, the excuse for what precipitated the attention lingers on long after that justification is gone. His limp remained a distinct part of his outward presentation to his friends far longer than the healing process required. The other kids brought him RC Colas or orange Nehis from the store because he tired easily from favoring his injured ankle. He got to sit on the top step of the entrance to the elementary school that bordered the playground, the steps where Ted Galinski always sat because he was the biggest. Nobody questioned Ted's right to the top step. Everybody asked him how he was getting along, told him how that must of been some cut. Did it bleed a lot? How big is the scar? You think you'll always have that limp? "As well as can be ex-

pected," he told them. And, "Yes, it was all the way to the bone."
It wasn't. And, "I hope not," although he knew that the limp
would vanish as soon as he saw that it's use no longer had value.

Edward limped home every evening and fell into his normal
gait as he entered his back yard from the alley. He had thought
seriously about continuing the limp even in front of his family.
Maybe his father would pay more attention to him if he exaggerated a disability he did not have. Maybe his father might say as
he noticed the limp, "Wow, you really did yourself in. How ya
gettin' along?" And Edward would reply, "Well, it's coming along.
"I think a few more weeks might just do it." And he would reply,
"Hey, I'm really sorry I didn't come out to help you out of that
mess, but . . ." And as Edward grappled with those visions of his
father actually saying those words to his son, showing even the
most minimal amount of concern, he always stopped in mid fan-
tasy and realized how deceiving those delusions were. He turned
to wherever his father might be at the time his imagination wandered into those illusions of a father-son connection, down toward
the basement, out toward the front porch or the living room in
front of the television or north toward downtown Chicago where
his office was and he wanted to say "Fuck you, Dad. You weren't
there." But he didn't say that. He did not use those kind of words
then. He only thought them. Using them came later, but he was
on the verge.

At those infrequent times when visions, or maybe they were
wishes, of his father being his father got the best of him, he felt
closer to the rag man than he did to his father. It was an affection
he would never admit to anyone. Perhaps it was more of an empathy than a feeling of fondness. Even so, he could not disclose
it, especially that it was the rag man he felt a closeness to.

The rag man collected old clothes and rags in the neighborhood. There were many occasions on Saturday mornings when
no one was at the playground, on cold or dreary days in particular, or on summer mornings when no one got up past nine o'clock.
On those days Edward sat on the back porch swing, his legs

across the seat of warped unpainted boards, his back against the arm rest reading a Superman or Archie comic book. Sometimes he sat on the porch stairs next to the cellar door. In either case each time he turned a page he looked up to see if the rag man was about to turn down the alley behind his house precisely at any time the rag man felt inclined to turn down the alley.

The rag man did not appear to follow a set route. Sometimes it was nine o'clock in the morning and sometimes as late as three o'clock in the afternoon when his truck rambled down the street and into the alley. He never came before nine o'clock lest his business suffer. Waking people in a working class neighborhood such as Edward's on Saturday morning was not recommended and it would have certainly eaten into the rag man's ability to collect the rags that filled the back of his dilapidated truck. The fact that he was black would not have helped his cause either. In the fifteen years Edward lived in that neighborhood, besides the garbage men who came every Tuesday, the rag man was the only black person who was able to enter the neighborhood and leave it without a scratch.

It was not every Saturday morning that Edward was able to wave to the rag man, or run up to him with a handful of rags or his father's old undershirts or T-shirts his brother or he had outgrown or talk to the rag man about things Edward had done that other people did not care to hear. During the summer most Saturdays were devoted to baseball games at the little league field. Occasionally Edward was called to serve mass at a wedding or a funeral, usually a wedding on Saturdays, rarely a funeral. So in the summer it was a rarity that he saw the rag man drive down the alley, hearing his gravely voice in the distance "Rag man, rag man. want yo old rags."

People up and down the alleys that criss-crossed the neighborhood stood at the alley's edge and flung their rags in the back of his truck. The rag man wouldn't pay any money for them; he just offered a toothless smile from a gaunt black face covered with gray stubble. Sometimes a "thank ya." The truck then rumbled to the next house where someone else waited to toss their rags and old T-shirts into the truck. After a few minutes the faint calling of "Rag man, rag man . . ." was lost until another Saturday when Edward found himself lounging on his back porch or in the yard with nothing to do. He watched the rag man's truck enter the alley. Edward's mother always handed him the rags she had and he took them to the alley and tossed them into the back of the rag man's truck. He stood there and watched until the rag man was out of sight. He watched the people at each house on the rag man's route waiting for him, dust feathering down on top of them when the rag man pressed his squeaky breaks and rolled to a stop, throwing their rags into the back of the truck, the younger kids darting back to their house because they were frightened of the rag man. He was probably the most gentle man anyone could meet. He never got out of his truck and never said any more than "Rag man, rag man, want yo old rags," and "Thank ya." Except to Edward.

. Two Saturdays after Edward caught his ankle in the spokes of Kevin's bicycle, he was on the back porch swing when he heard the rag man turning into the alley. Edward's mother came out the back door with a hand full of rags. He pushed himself up from the swing and asked her if he could take the rags down to the rag man. "Are you up to it," she asked. "Yea," he told her. "My muscles are getting a little stiff anyway." She handed her son the rags and went back inside. Edward limped slowly to the alley. The rag man saw him coming toward him and he stopped his truck.

The dented door gave up a piercing squeak as the rag man got out of his truck. Edward's eyes widened. He had never seen the rag man get out of his truck. He was short, not much taller than Edward. He wore a white shirt buttoned all the way up to the collar and baggy pants that were in no better shape than the rags he collected. He took the rags from Edward and tossed them into the back of his truck. "Looks like you got some banged up there," he said in a drawl that jumbled his words together and made him hard to understand. Edward didn't answer right away. He was still surprised the rag man was out of his truck. "How'd it happen?" he asked. Edward told him. "Well, you really did yourself in. How ya gettin' along?" And Edward replied, "Well, it's coming along. I think a few more weeks might just do it." "Well, you take care of that leg," the rag man said with a sympathetic grin. "Can't play ball with a bum leg." And he was back in his truck and heading down the alley yelling "Rag man, rag man, want yo old rags." Edward watched the rag man's truck trudge down the alley until it was out of sight. What he said to Edward, those few seemingly insignificant words, that's what Edward's father should have said to him. Instead he got them from the rag man.

Edward never knew where the rag man came from, where he went or, what intrigued him the most, what he did with those rags. When Edward was six Kevin told him the rag man took the rags home and had his wife sew them into clothes for his thirteen kids. "Did he wash them first?" Edward asked his brother. "Nah, she just sews them up and puts them on the kids." Wow, Edward thought. How could anyone do that. That was disgusting. Edward believed that story for a while until one of his friends, not his best friend, Theodore (Ted) Galinski, told him "He gives them to all the niggers down in the projects and they wear them." "Do they wash them first?" Edward asked Ted this time. "Nah, why should they, that's how they live."

Ted hated black people. So did most of the other people in the neighborhood. So did Edward for a while. They tolerated the rag man and the garbage men. But no one else. Kevin was a racist, His father even worse. On the other had, Edward's mother was on the fence, if that was any better than being on the wrong side. Edward admired his mother for several reasons. The most notable was that she put up with his father. Another was that she did not appear to be as much of a racist as his father and brother. Edward's mother was a "compassionate" racist. She taught him what Edward at that time thought was the fully reasoned principle: "You leave us alone and we'll leave you alone, as long as you stay where you are." She instructed her children that white people were different from black people, Mexicans and Chinese and, "Well son, every other color out there," they were all different. Granted the black people had been enslaved at one time but they have been free for quite some time now and, well, son, they just don't seem to care about themselves. You, know, like the rag man. Pray for them, son. That is the best we can do. That was her answer to help them. Pray for them.

But Edward suspected that, despite her belief that everyone was a child of God, she didn't pray much for black people. She prayed a lot, but it was highly questionable that any of her prayers went for any group of people not comprised of white folk. Edward was a teenager when he discovered her racism was not really of the complacent variety. He discovered this not by himself, for a discovery like that was never accessible in a neighborhood such as his, but with the help of Father Healey, the assistant pastor at St. Clement Church.

Racism is not an innate quality of a human being, Father Healey preached to the children at St. Clem's. It is not something that is passed down to us biologically but mentally, through the habits and beliefs our parents have and pass onto their children. Kevin, on the other hand, taught Edward how to throw bottles and rocks at black kids if they dared to come near their neighborhood or their parks. Edward's father taught him how to yell at them and block their way and threaten the parents who attempted to move into their neighborhood, or the children who tried to enter their schools. Edward's mother taught him how to be complacent about what other white people did to black people. They did not teach him directly but by example. He followed that example for a while, throwing a few rocks and bottles, calling them "nigger" and other names when the opportunity arose and he was in a place or a position where the chances of reprisal from them were slim. But even with the neighborhood he lived in awash with racism, he never had his heart in the rock and bottle throwing or the name calling. Very few of his classmates at St. Clem's listened to Father Healey. Those who did never admitted to anyone else that perhaps what he said made sense.

After three years at St. Clem's, Father Healey was transferred to a parish near the projects, his punishment, Edward guessed, for preaching tolerance, for encouraging diversity, a term he used frequently but one that would not be in vogue for at least two more decades. Father Healey was moved to an inner city parish because he told the children of St. Clem's that it was wrong to use the word "nigger." He was driven out of the parish because he devised a plan to bring poor black kids from the ghetto to St. Clem's, to give some of them the opportunity to be properly educated. That move was what sealed his fate. Within a few weeks after word got out that "Healey is gonna bring niggers to our school," he was gone. No good-byes, no forwarding address to write for the few who felt a closeness to him, a bond that, although reluctant to display when he was around, they were destined to carry with them as adults.

It was from that point on that Edward began to develop a distaste for those people he knew and didn't know, including his father and brother and mother, who had defined their lives with either outright hatred or complacency. It was a difficult transition for Edward and it came in small parts over a period of years. The passage was laborious because those inclinations toward blacks, Hispanics, Asians and Jews he had learned in the neighborhood, those feelings of hate passed down through generations of European whites, were the only sentiments he had access to. And even after he had removed himself from that climate he found it to be pervasive everywhere he went and not easily invalidated and dismissed.

But it was not just blacks that stirred Edward's father's intolerance. Any color or nationality, and most religions, brought out the best of his biases complemented by the applicable vocabulary that further emphasized his bigotry. He frequently used the derogatory terms to describe the Irish (although never in the com-

pany of Edward's mother or her relatives for they were Irish),
Chinese, Italians, Jews and Hispanics. Niggers, spics, kikes—
the words easily and without hesitation flowed across his lips.
The expression of loathing flooded the air around him without
him looking around to see if anyone in the room or anyone on the
street or in the barber shop, or in the restaurant, might be offended. Even in the vestibule of the church as people dipped
their fingers in the ornate bowl of holy water, touched it to their
forehead, shoulders and heart in the sign of the cross as a tribute
to God, he opened conversations with "We'll have more niggers
than we can handle if Healey gets his way." He said this as the
holy water on his finger tips still glistened when the huge church
door opened and the late morning sunlight poured in.

When word got out that Father Healey was planning to "force
upon us inferior people and do harm to our school and our neighborhood," Edward's father attended the meetings that were held
late on Saturday nights in neighbors' homes, where his father
and the fathers of his friends developed their strategy and eventually gave an ultimatum to the pastor of St. Clem's, Father
McMann. "Healey goes or. . . ." Edward never found out what
the "or" was. He suspected it had to do with financial support for
the church as well as for the school that Edward and most of his
friends in the neighborhood, at least the Catholic kids (and that
was most of them), attended. Father McMann would never hesitate to do anything the parishioners wanted if they threatened to
withhold their tithes. He liked his big Buick bought for him by
the parishioners. He liked the remodeling of the church sanctuary paid for by the parishioners. He liked the new windows in
the rectory, and the new furnace, and the housekeeper, all paid
for through the generosity of the parishioners. Money talked for
Father McMann. The Parishioners talked with their money. Three
weeks after the ultimatum was given, Father Healey was gone.
After their Saturday night meetings, these generous parishioners
went to church, received communion from Father McMann in
the new sanctuary warmed by the new furnace and prayed for

the souls of the dearly departed, the souls of their loved ones and their own souls. But they never uttered a word for those upon whom they piled suffering and injustice.

So after Father Healey left, the only black voices Edward still heard were the garbage men every Tuesday, the black kids yelling at the white kids as the white kids threw bottles at them if they came too close to the white kid's neighborhood and "Rag man, rag man, want yo old rags."

II

Bacon and eggs, French fries and Mary Jo Bandera's breasts. Every time Edward thought about the time of his growing up in South Chicago, the three most vivid, most graphic recollections that first entered his mind were Bacon and eggs, French fries and Mary Jo Bandera's breasts. Nothing else. Nothing else seemed important as an adult, though he was certain that there were more recollections stored somewhere where access had been lost. He often felt that perhaps nothing else seemed significant enough that he felt compelled to burden himself by reflecting on it. Even when Edward's mother was dying, died and was being buried in a vast Catholic cemetery in Phoenix, Edward never once abandoned the present (except for those two foods and breasts) to reflect on the past. For him there was little of his past that he was able to remember, or perhaps, little he had not blocked from his memory because he did not want to remember it.

That all changed after he walked away from his mother's grave. It was not his mother's death or burial that dug up the past he wanted to keep buried. It was his father's meagerness of life that brought it all back. Once his mother was officially started on her way to eternity, the thoughts of gulping down bacon and eggs, chewing on French fries and nudging against Mary Jo Bandera's breasts, or any breasts for that matter, quickly grew, and were enhanced by those alarming memories people have of their childhood, memories that become intolerable to recall soon after they advance from real life to dreadful recollections. His father chewing on the polish sausage while Edward's ankle stained the weeds and trash with his blood in the yard next to his house. How the rag man showed more interest in his injury than the sausage man.

A few hours after his mother died in February 1990, Kevin, Edward's older brother, said to him, "Every life has its watershed and this is Mom's." Edward presumed he was right. At least to some extent. Of course, Kevin never said if this watershed their mother had reached as a result of her death was a positive thing, and Edward didn't ask. Kevin was prone to say things he thought were astute and penetrating. If someone asked him to elaborate on his keen insight, he wandered off to grab a beer or smoke a cigarette because his thought processes quickly became overheated after only a few moments of use.

Edward thought about what his brother said, nonetheless. He figured that in most circumstances, when a watershed occurs in a person's life, it's a positive development. For some, though, it's simply another stumbling block in an existence that serves no other purpose than to benignly pass through life from mortality to eternity. Some people have multiple watersheds that periodically alter their lives as they move through their existence. Kevin was one of those who had numerous life altering events: two divorces that put him deeper into debt and heavier into drinking after each nasty split. With each divorce the potency of his life dwindled dramatically and his spirit was critically damaged. Also, a stint in Vietnam in 1964 made him quiet and aloof except when someone asked him about his divorces or when he was drinking.

Edward's sister, Roberta, had her watershed too. There was only one the brothers were aware of and one they thought was a defining moment in her life. It happened early in her life, when she was sixteen and became pregnant. In and of itself, pregnancy is a significant life altering event. To also be forced to marry the man responsible, the man who was chosen simply for sex and not for his family instincts, adds a great deal of misfortune to the event, as it did in Roberta's case, and that, in Edward's view, and perhaps Kevin's too, although Kevin said little of the event, became an affliction that they thought would last until Roberta reached that same eternity their mother had grasped.

As Edward stood beside his mother's grave after the casket had been blessed and splashed with holy water, Roberta sobbing, his father staring off into the hazy desert air beyond the cemetery, Kevin examining the wheel covers of the hearse, Edward realized, reluctantly, that Kevin was right; her only watershed was her death. For the sibling's father, his watershed would probably be the same, although, until he died, Edward, at least, would give him the benefit of the doubt.

The old woman who laid before them in that hospital bed, her body punctured with tubes that passed into every crevice of her tiny frame, was to have only one notable event in her life, and she was nearing that event. Edward was certain of that, based on his knowledge of her existence, For this old women who barely filled half of the bed where she lay, her youth had been uneventful , her middle age had been tedious, her old age had been frightening, but death was, for her, the ultimate fulfillment. Her life, and her approaching death, was revealed in her hollow cheeks and sunken eyes. She lay motionless in the intensive care unit of that hospital in Phoenix. Her posture was fetal. Her body emaciated, forty pounds quickly shed in the short time it took her to get from feeble health to a terminal condition.

Death had been the consummate mission for her, for with it she ascended into heaven, her final resting place. She was a devout Catholic who prayed her entire life of eighty years for just this moment. She wore out scores of rosaries and prayer books; she eroded deep gouges out of the kneeler at church, the same kneeler, the same pew, the same church for twenty-five years until she moved to another city, lay claim to another church and quickly marked her territory, her kneeler, her pew, and again inscribed her legacy of perfect faith to everyone around her. She wore out the confessionals and the priests who dwelled in them. Every week those priests heard from her the most trifling of venial sins, for how could she commit anything but the most insignificant of sins when she was the most spiritual woman in the congregation?

The death she sought was her life, the watershed she welcomed with open arms and eager heart. It was suddenly close, closer and sooner than she had believed, closer than her family had predicted, but that was okay with her. Without warning she was on the verge of moving on to wherever the spirit she grasped when she died took her. Her religion told her heaven was her final destination. After she died, Edward saw her body lowered into its grave. There her body would stay for eternity. Her soul? He didn't know.

The Southwest was unusually warm for February, a sharp contrast from the blistering cold and snow Edward left in Missouri when he was called to be a witness to what he knew would be his mother's demise. By Midwest standards it was like a sizzling summer day without the flood of sweat that a Midwest summer heat can drain from a body. Arizonians thought it was barely mild. Nevertheless, for Edward it was hot.

The air conditioned hospital room, stainless and antiseptic, brought Edward and Kevin and Roberta and their father little relief from the desert heat. Even so, the heat they had to endure for three days wasn't as oppressive as the disquieting death watch they were forced to observe.

Edward had arrived in Phoenix from his home in Missouri the evening before his mother went into surgery to repair leaking heart valves. Her chances were slim, the doctor had informed Edward's father. His father didn't care, for he was also told the odds were slimmer without the operation. Go ahead with the operation, he told them. He needed her. He could not bear to lose her. Don't worry about the cost. Operate! Operate! Edward's mother agreed, though, he thought reluctantly. They operated. After the operation, when she was moved to the intensive care unit and tubes were crammed into her body, her chances became even slimmer. She died three days later.

The morning she died, Edward's father was at his home. He, along with Roberta, Kevin and Edward, drove to their father and mother's apartment in Tempe. Roberta insisted their father needed to freshen up after three days of sleeping in a hospital bed in the room next to where his wife lay, and to eat something besides hospital food. It was difficult for Roberta to persuade her father to leave his wife's side. The doctor had encouraged him to take some time out. She was resting comfortably and a few minutes away wouldn't make a difference. So they left the hospital.

They had taken little time away from the hospital. The three children watched their mother die in shifts. Their father was there day and night, holding her hand when he was not sleeping in a chair or on the hospital bed. He ate little, mostly hamburgers and pork tenderloin sandwiches, always with a pickle and a bag of chips. Each evening, before he crawled into the bed next door and the three children went back to the apartment, he enjoyed a dish of vanilla ice cream with chocolate syrup.

For the few moments he was not by her side, for the meager thirty minutes it took them to go home so the restless father could change his clothes and get a decent bite to eat, a scant passage of time in a life waiting for death, she died. The call came from the doctor. He had looked for the family in the waiting room and then in the cafeteria. He had paged them over the hospital's intercom. When he could not find any of them, he called the apartment. Roberta took the call. She said nothing recognizable into the receiver after she answered, just a grunt, as if the caller had hung up before any contact had been made. She gently laid the phone back into its cradle and, before she could walk the five feet to where her father sat, she broke down and fell to his side. In a voice that resembled a robotic dialect from a science fiction movie, monotonal and coarse, she told her father not that his wife had died or that their mother had died, but "My momma is dead."

Edward's father sat rigid at the kitchen table as Edward pictured he sat every day at lunch time since he had retired fifteen years earlier. Coming to the table exactly at noon, waiting for his wife to enter the room and prepare his lunch, him sitting upright, hands clasped together, thinking wistfully of the previous evening's *Wheel of Fortune*, Vanna's revealing neckline and comely, though hackneyed, smile.

He sighed and his stomach followed with a growl. There would be no lunch prepared and served by the old woman today or ever again. His sighs became more pronounced, more frequent. It was a mixture of impatience and mounting grief that failed to stir this man at the news of his wife's death.

His thumbs twitched. An odd response, Edward thought, to bad news. He called to her. "Mother," as if she were only a room away and she might appear suddenly, open the refrigerator door and begin the daily task of preparing a ham or corned beef sandwich, laying a dill pickle and some chips next to it, dropping ice cubes into a glass and pouring a Coke over the top until the bronze tinted bubbles poured over the rim, and sitting across from him to work the newspaper crossword puzzle as he ate. He let another sigh slide past his clenched lips. Then he rose, placed the chair neatly in its space under the table and walked back to the bedroom. When the reality of her death hit him, the impatience faded and the grief swelled. He lay on the bed and sobbed.

There is no comfort in watching someone die. People look for distractions. They perform insignificant behavior that had never before been a part of their spare time. Like playing solitaire and burying their face in crossword puzzles. They ponder. The only redress are the walks about the hospital grounds; the only rest the brief naps taken in the harshly lit waiting room. There is no sleep at night, only fitful dozing between visions of the old lady and the tubes and the constant comings and goings of doctors and nurses and people whose jobs the family did not know but assumed, hoped, they were moving about the room and the patient for same valid reason.

The final relief came after three days of pacing, sitting, card playing and planning. It was the planning, how morbid it may be to some, that was the most beneficial activity of the vigil. When the moment of their mother's death arrived, Edward's father, sister and brother had already come to a consensus as to where she was to be buried, the color of the casket, the headstone and the dress she was to wear.

A consensus in such a disconnected family, however, was fairly easy to gain. A consensus simply meant that Edward and Kevin had wearied of arguing with Roberta. Their father, the noncommittal, indecisive man he was, always deferred to Roberta. She had for many years controlled the hearts and minds of Edward's parents. Granted, she was there when they needed someone. He wasn't. Neither was Kevin. She wrote the letters; she visited often. She was also the hardship case in the family, always financially distraught and emotionally disabled, and she was always the most adept at eliciting the most sympathy. They needed each other, Roberta and her parents. They complimented each other.

She had the first grandchildren, notwithstanding they were born before, during and after wedlock. While she gradually and consistently reaped the rewards of being absolutely dysfunctional, Edward and Kevin quickly, albeit for the most part voluntarily, gradually and consistently fell out of favor. The two boys quietly became at-will outcasts and sometimes partners in the battles that would ensue.

The funeral for Edward's mother was Catholic in all its splendor. Edward thought, and Kevin concurred, that the Mass lasted longer than was spiritually necessary. The holy water alone their mother had spread on her forehead in her eighty years should have been enough to float her to heaven. It was spiritual overkill, a profusion of pious mumbling, annoying sobbing and noxious incense fumes exacting from the mourners the intensity they brought with them to see Edward's mother off to her eternity. Most of the two dozen grieving relatives and friends were the same age as the woman they came to send off. They were the bridge partners she had spent time with every Wednesday afternoon talking more about their grandchildren and their neighbors than playing cards. They were the elderly widows who shared an apartment next door and who occasionally took Edward's mother shopping with them. When her vision began to fade, she no longer drove, although it had been a battle that raged for years before Roberta was able to take away her keys. So the two neighborly octogenarians, with eyesight no better than Edward's mother's, shoved her into their Cadillac DeVille every Saturday and squinted their way to the mall.

There was Mrs. Conipher or Doniphan, Edward never knew which because she apparently visited a dentist who had finished at the bottom of his class and had never learned the correct way to fit dentures. Whenever she introduced herself, which was about every fifteen minutes at the visitation and before and after the mass and once again at the cemetery, her mouth seemed to move in a circular motion like a cow delighting in its cud. He always clearly heard the *ph* sound but never quite mastered what came before and after.

There was a group of women from the church auxiliary, veteran mourners who attended just about every funeral whether they knew the deceased or not. They filled the first two pews on the left side, a half dozen elderly spinsters and widows sitting upright as if in a robotic trance staring stone faced at the coffin. Rosaries in every pastel color poured from their entwined fingers like a waterfall of painted beads. There was Edward's mother's brother, Uncle Jerry, a quiet, cantankerous widower who sat silently at the visitation, at the church and in the car when Edward drove him to the airport for his return trip to Milwaukee. The trip to attend his only sister's funeral seemed like an ordeal for him. He was impatient at how the services droned on, how the priest dawdled saying the mass and how the auxiliary ladies doted on him.

In the last pew near the stark white baptismal font sat an aged white haired man, wearing dark olive trousers like a custodian would wear while mopping faded tile floors in an equally faded building, a shopworn white dress shirt that appeared to have never been ironed and a paisley bow tie. A wooden cane hung from the side railing of the pew. Edward asked his father who the stranger was. "Don't know," he answered gruffly without looking around to identify the mysterious mourner. Roberta shrugged her hunched shoulders when Edward queried her on the man's identity. His father's odd behavior when Edward asked about the man prompted him to muse on the notion that maybe his mother had another life that none of them, except maybe his father, were aware of. No, that could not be right. His mother? Really! Was it something she had confessed to the priest on a Saturday morning only to rendezvous with this stranger after she left the church and then return to the same church, the same confessional, the same priest the next week and many weeks thereafter to confess the same sin again and again. Is it why she prayed so much? If Edward's father did know, when did he find out and is that why he had not shed a tear since that one fit of sobbing he had on his bed when he was told his wife had died? Edward smiled what he knew was an impish grin. His mother? He didn't think so. Edward dismissed the thought, but it was a question he would occasionally review the rest of his life. And each time he would grin and wonder.

Edward's mother was laid in her grave next to a bishop, an important prelate no doubt who rated a black marble slab with an extensive epitaph of gold inlaid lettering covering his entire grave. A holy man who had been dead nearly as long as Edward's mother had lived. "She would like that," Roberta sobbed. Close to a bishop, separated by only three feet of dirt and a seventy-five year head start in eternity. Roberta and, as a result, her father, faithfully believed the proximity of Catholic royalty would be a saving grace for wife and mother. It was a closeness more consequential for them than any family bonds had ever been.

For Edward and Kevin, the sudden death of their mother softened the disagreements they had endured in the past, strife that had disrupted their relationship often, so much so that their new found brotherly connection caused Roberta to become alarmed. Once outcasts, Edward and Kevin were now, in Roberta's conniving mind, co-conspirators, renegades that unexpectedly became a coalition, scheming against Roberta and the vengeful walls she had constructed to protect the reign as family matriarch she was creating for herself out of the loss of her mother and the vulnerability of her father.

Edward did not know how Kevin felt about it, but being an outcast was an arduous burden to carry. Essentially it meant Edward had no family. It was a label so often pointedly emphasized overtly by Roberta and surreptitiously by his mother. At least now as a co-conspirator, he felt he had an acceptance by one quarter of the remaining family members, and perhaps in the intervening years between his mother's death and his father's he could extract a fraction of recognition from another quarter, his father, however dubious or precarious it might be. His father had neither the guts to challenge Edward's mother or Roberta nor the paternal instinct to correct their misdeeds, or his, committed against Edward and Kevin. Edward knew that as soon as Roberta began manipulating her father's thinking and preying on his liability of being halved by the death of his wife, any recognition of Edward's standing as a family member that seemed to be balancing on the brink would tumble off and become as departed as the old woman they had buried.

The funeral entourage consisted of twenty-four people, including family members, packed into five automobiles. Most of those people were at that stage of their lives where they knew more people that called the cemetery home than they did outside the graveyard. After the metal casket was lowered into the ground, and while Roberta hugged all the people who had followed the family to the cemetery whether she knew them or not, and while Kevin stood by the limousine smoking a cigarette, Edward strolled over to other headstones pretending to investigate epitaphs and names. Actually, he was trying to rid himself of the sickening feeling that everything was not right with his father. Granted, he had just buried his wife, but Edward sensed in his demeanor, in his glazed eyes and tight lips that there was more than just the emotional dilemma he had found himself in with the loss of a lifetime companion. Edward sensed a devastation that reached far beyond death.

After the burial, the procession followed the black hearse back to the church to eat a meager lunch of cold cuts, potato salad, cole slaw and brownies prepared by the church's ladies' auxiliary. Roberta's eyes, still swollen from crying, looked like they were being sucked into their sockets. A dark ring encircled them. Makeup, Edward surmised. A white handkerchief, saturated from tears and whatever she had extracted from her runny nose, seemed to weigh down the sleeve where she stuffed it. It kept falling to the floor and she picked it up each time it fell, wiped her eyes or nose again, and stuffed it back into her sleeve.

Roberta hugged everyone who entered as if the hug she bestowed on them at the cemetery had worn off in the intervening ten minutes and had to be replenished. She formed a one-person receiving line while Edward, Kevin and their father filled their plates and were nearing the time for a refill before she was even inclined to eat. As she broke each embrace, Roberta supplied to the hungry mourners, whether they cared to listen or not, maudlin anecdotes of her mother's life, the woman's enormous faith, her virtuous qualities as a mother and wife. After everyone had entered and made their way to the buffet, Roberta cornered those who were not engaged in conversation and replenished their stock of already forgotten reminiscences. When she finished with one she moved on to the next, but not without giving the last a hug, or a squeeze on the shoulder if they were sitting, before she moved on. Edward noticed people who were quietly enjoying their lunch quickly strike up a conversation with the stranger next to them when they saw Roberta approaching.

Edward watched his father stuffing into his mouth a dangling piece of bologna that had tried to escape his gnashing dentures. His face appeared distorted, a combination of discomfort and gratification. Edward bent down and whispered to the old man, "Are you okay?" He looked up at his son and returned an earnest look. "My bowels are back in business," he replied. "Couldn't get them to cooperate for the longest time. I guess your mother's passing cured me." Edward tried to smile in understanding or delight or empathy or whatever sentiment might be appropriate for his father's enlightenment, but he could not. He was afraid to laugh. Everyone else in the room was so serious, so sedate. He was afraid laughter might show all in attendance that, yes, he was certainly as disrespectful as he had been portrayed by Roberta. The errant son showing how he had become so aloof, so uncaring. Edward patted his father's shoulder and went to find Kevin.

In any circumstance that had to do with family, Kevin had trouble showing emotion. He avoided any conversation that might have even the slightest relevance to what was going on around him. Whenever anyone approached him and began to offer condolences for the death of his mother he offered them his version of despondency. "You'd think the goddamn church, as rich as it is, could give us a goddamn decent meal. Cold cuts. Goddamn it."

His abhorrence of anything religious intensified exponentially later in the day when he discovered that it was not the church, the rich church, the wealthy and opulent church, as he portrayed it, that provided the meal, but his father who had to foot the bill. Ninety-four dollars and eighty cents for the food, fifty dollars to rent the room at the back of the church and a small donation of fifty dollars to the auxiliary for their time to spread the bologna, turkey, salami, bread and side dishes on the folding table covered with a paper table cloth. The lunch was at the insistence of Roberta, a way to get as much mileage out of her mother's death and, at the same time, intensify her power over her increasingly depressed father, a depression seemingly lessened by his functioning bowels.

The rite of death begins with the last breath and ends with . . . with what? Is the final event of a person's life when the coffin is laid into the grave and all the people who thought the deceased was important in their lives, or that they were important in the deceased's life, stride wearily away mumbling about how hungry standing out in the open air at a cemetery has made them, or how sickly that old Mrs. Langley looked, or complaining how standing for so long has made their bunions flare up? Or is it when the final paper plate from the post burial meal hosted but not funded by six little old ladies from the church auxiliary is tossed in the twenty gallon trash can partially blocking the exit? Or does it really occur much, much later when the person who died and left loved ones behind is no longer remembered every waking minute of her husband's remaining years, and her children have trouble recalling when it was that she let them cross the street alone to get an errant ball, or when she held an injured arm in her lap in the back seat of the Ford Fairlane on the way to the hospital while pressing on the wound with her fingers trying to get it to stop bleeding.

Whose perspective determines when that final event occurs? Is it the beginning of that rite of death when the mother no longer has feelings for her son, no longer considers the son part of her life and therefore looks only toward death? Was it when, at fourteen years old, the son made a decision that, at least for the son's mother, signaled a loss of the relationship between her and her youngest son?

For Kevin, was it the first time he was arrested, the second time? Was it after his first divorce, his second? For Edward and Kevin, the final event occurred long before their mother's death knell sounded. For Roberta, it probably never ended. For their father, it would not end until his rite of death began.

However relative it might be to each of them as the remaining family members, the physical end of their mother's event was over, the burial complete, the meal half eaten, and the four of them congregated at the father's apartment: a cramped, four room dwelling on the east side of Tempe that, like the parents' hearts and souls, held nothing that suggested there were three children in this family. Roberta and her children's faces were plastered conspicuously all over the starkly white painted walls and cluttered around the maroon cookie jar table lamps that sat on the end tables in the living room. They spilled over on to each mismatched table in the place. Even the bathroom was not immune to Roberta's domination. Her photo was center stage over the stool. An appropriate site, Edward and Kevin agreed. The number of photos of Roberta and her children in the apartment nearly matched the number of pictures of Jesus and the Virgin Mary. Edward quickly began to grow weary of it all.

He searched for something, anything, in the apartment that was not Roberta, but nothing emerged. Only the vestiges of his mother's religious zealotry and his sister enshrined on every available space in the place. He closed the door to the bathroom and sat on the edge of the tub. His elbow nudged the shower curtain. It sprinkled him with droplets of water that remained from the last shower taken. Above the door was a plaque with the standard picture of the Catholic's impression of what God looked like: flowing cape, long, smooth hair and beard, his arms outstretched hovering over the multitudes and showering them with his blessings. Below the picture were the words *Glory be to the Father, the Son and the Holy Ghost*, words that made Edward wince as he brushed the beads of water from his arm.

III

Glory Be to the Father and to the Son and to the Holy Ghost.
Glory Be to the Father and to the Son and to the Holy Ghost.
Glory Be to the Father and to the Son and to the Holy Ghost.
Sister Mary Hortense, Edward's sixth grade teacher, stood over the three boys, Ray Martinelli, Jesse Martinez and Edward, her yard stick in hand ready to whack the snot out of any one of them or all three of them if their eyes should stray one inch from the paper upon which they wrote those words. Stood over is perhaps the wrong description. Even when standing next to the sixth graders, Sister Mary Hortense's protruding whiskered chin barely rose above their foreheads. If stature was an indication of domination, Sister Mary Hortense was an anomaly. Perhaps she once was a very tall lady who had shrunk over the years from some unknown cause, most likely from swinging that yardstick at boys one-fifth her age but twice her size.

Edward went to St. Clement grammar school. There the priests were Irish, the students had parents or grandparents from every European and Central American country and the nuns, since they did not have last names once they covered themselves with those black habits with the white bibs and took their vows, had nationalities that were undetectable, except maybe in the rare circumstance where a particular nun had an accent. Even then some accents were difficult to place with an identifiable country. In every other circumstance the students never knew what the nuns were.

They did know that Sister Mary Hortense was mean. Mean not in the sense that she said mean things to her charges. In most instances she spoke to them in a very considerate manner. When she was intent on punishing someone she did not have to speak. She always carried that yardstick and when it was not resting securely in her folded arms it was smacking the back of someone's legs or neck or arms. She used it regularly to mete out punishment whenever a rule was broken. Except in church. Breaking a rule in church was altogether different for Sister Mary Hortense. If the students talked in church or acted up in some manner she felt was insulting to God, she pulled the perpetrator out of the pew, marched the recalcitrant sinner to the back of the church, yardstick in hand, acted like she was going to whack you on the head and then, as the quivering child closed his or her eyes and waited for the yardstick to make burning contact with the scalp, Sister Mary Hortense would kick the offender in the shin or some other part of the leg with her pointed black boots.

But wielding her yardstick was not the only punishment she doled out, although it was the most painful and the most dreaded. Whenever someone broke a rule in class the unfortunate student stayed after school and wrote. Sometimes, if the infraction was very serious, the child felt both the sting of the yardstick and the hand cramps from writing. They wrote *Glory be to the Father and to the Son and to the Holy Ghost* as punishment. One hundred times on paper ripped from their ragged notebooks, thin strips hanging from the edge where the page had been pulled from its attachment to the notebook's coiled metal spine. They wrote line after line of words that Edward thought should be reserved for giving praise to God and the rest of his family but, instead, were used to cramp the hands of sixth graders and spur them into a monotonous exercise of penance. It did not teach them to be remorseful or penitent, or even more religious. God knows if writing prayers, or parts of prayers, as many times as they had written them in similar circumstances since second grade made a person more religious with each line put to paper, Edward, and many of his impish compatriots in grades second through eighth, should all have been able to take turns being Pope.

For anyone who had the notion to sit down and write one hundred times *Glory be to the Father and to the Son and to the Holy Ghost,* simply because they had time to kill and enjoyed the tediousness of such an exercise, it should be completed in a short period of time. Say fifteen minutes. But for Sister Mary Hortense, the essence of the punishments she meted out was not to do it, get it done, say your sorry and out the door. Sister Mary Hortense was obsessed with subtlety when punishing a ten year old.

Actually, one hundred times of anything was not a punishment for a serious offense. It was for minor infractions like throwing spitballs in class, talking in the cloak room, or talking in class the first time. Students in Sister Mary Hortense's class who committed the crimes of fighting, cheating, lying, any of the transgressions that were on her list of major venial sins, were given punishments much greater than Jesse, Ray or Edward had experienced. Usually it was writing longer prayers like the *Our Father* one hundred times, or the *Hail Mary* or any number of prayers that sometimes Edward thought Sister Mary Hortense made up simply to aggravate him and his classmates. Students who committed offenses she thought were greater than a major venial sin, but not as great as say a mortal sin or students who were repeat offenders and who, she thought, could not easily be rehabilitated by repeating a prayer on paper, or who might slip into a mode of wickedness and even lure themselves into a life of evil and be forever shut behind bars because of their immoral ways (several did, including Jesse) were told to *Go to the priest!* No one in the school wanted to *Go to the priest!* They were subjected to the priest's vilification in the confessional and they did not care to listen in person, face to face, God's personal representative to God's lowest creature, to his indignation for the young sinners. They had enough of the priest on Saturday afternoons when they confessed their sins to him. They did not want any more of the priest.

It was not the one hundred lines of *Glory Bes* that gave them concern. It was how Sister Mary Hortense wanted them written. In their best handwriting with the dips and curls and swirls and loops that, to her, and to every other nun at St. Clem's, and, they had concluded from the first day of first grade as they had ground hundreds of pencils to the nub, every nun in every school in every part of the world, were the signs not only of a good writer but of a good person. Sister Mary Hortense stressed over and over to her students that good handwriting made a person closer to God. Edward figured that he wanted to be closer to God so he practiced his handwriting every chance he got. What did he know? To his amazement he discovered that one residual advantage of practicing his loops and swirls and dips and curls was that he finished his *Glory Bes* first with the least erasures, and Sister Mary Hortense allowed him to leave earlier than the other boys because his handwriting was better and he didn't have to spend the time erasing misplaced loops and dips. Ray, Jesse and the other boys Edward shared penalty time with did not care about being close to God. So they weren't. And their handwriting showed it.

As they wrote, Sister Mary Hortense paced up and down the aisle, stopped at each desk as they toiled over their punishment, checked their handwriting and demanded perfection with an unpretentious, even benevolent whack on the head and a command to erase and begin again. If the loop was gnarled, she announced in her squeaky, raspy voice to erase it and showed them on the blackboard the proper way to write an *l*. If a curl was too wide, erase it and redo it. If the erasing tore a hole in the paper, get a new sheet and begin again even if one of them was on the ninety-ninth line of *Glory Be to the Father and to the Son and to the Holy Ghost.* If her correction of a loop or a curl or her command that a new piece of paper be used because of all the erasure holes elicited a moan or a sigh or even a roll of the eyes, the yard stick cracked mercilessly on the students back with a sting that forced the trembling child to wipe the single tear he accidentally let seep from his eye so he could see the paper to start all over again with the *Glory Bes.*

Edward was never a big enough sinner in Sister Mary Hortense's class to have to write anything but *Glory Bes* one hundred times. He did, in Sister Mary Norbert's seventh grade class, commit an offense that was not on the venial sin list but on the next list up somewhere between venial and mortal. For some reason, the nuns weighted differently the sins that were on their lists. The sins were the same, but committing the sin brought different punishments from different nuns. Edward suspected there were several levels, at least as Sister Mary Norbert saw sin, but she never told any of her students how many levels there were or what might be on those in-between levels. It would have compromised her authority, her power over elementary school students. Since the priest was out of town on the day Edward committed his grievous offense, he thought he had gotten a re-prieve from meeting face to face with him. Instead, he thought sure he would be required to stay after school and write maybe the *Hail Mary* one hundred times, or maybe even one hundred and fifty. That was not as bad an alternative as *Going to the priest!*

Sister Mary Norbert was a tall woman with a pie shaped face and skin that made it look like Dutch apple left in the oven too long, a little brown and crisp around the edges. She was about six feet tall and her arms hung low almost, it appeared to seventh graders, to her knees. She was a large woman, big boned as they say, and the black nun's habit that covered her from head to toe, except for that apple pie face, made her look like the right tackle for the Chicago Bears.

Compared to Sister Mary Hortense, Sister Mary Norbert was humane. Her ruler was shorter—twelve inches compared to thirty-six, and kicking shins or any other part of the body was not in her arsenal of weapons to be used for infliction of punishment on seventh graders. Instead, she had the glare. The eyes of chastisement discharged a deluge of reproach and reprimand from her dark and doughy face that seemed to place a paralyzing hex on anyone the glare was aimed at. And those eyes were often upon her students .

She seldom used the ruler. When she did it hurt. Unlike Sister Mary Hortense who utilized corporal punishment quite frequently, the glare of Sister Mary Norbert seemed, at least for a room full of eleven and twelve year olds, a more severe reprimand for any of their misdeeds than any thrashing Sister Mary Hortense could have heaped upon them. Over the years of being a nun she had developed the capacity for conveying to anyone who stepped beyond the standards of behavior a sense of foreboding and misery through a look, a look that flowed from beyond her eyes like a deadly laser.

Despite her reluctance to distribute physical punishment, or rather her preference for what her students saw as a more severe form of discipline, Sister Mary Norbert also had in her storehouse of punishment a penalty that was far more harsh and unmerciful than any experienced under the other nuns first through eighth grade, even more severe than sending the wayward student to the priest. She called parents. Not just one parent but mother *and* father. If no father was around, an uncle would do, or a brother as long as he was mature, or even a male neighbor. Sister Mary Norbert was certain the presence of a male had a profound effect on the student who was being castigated. She did not merely ask that the father or some uninterested male figure be present, she demanded it. She explained to the mother, who usually was the one at home who answered the phone when Sister Mary Norbert called, that it was for the benefit of the student, that a man has the strength and force that a woman does not and for the meeting to be successful the student must see that strength, must realize that he or she will have to face the intensity of that strength that only a male can project.

Edward received plenty of glares from Sister Mary Norbert as he trudged his way through seventh grade. He was luckier than most of the other boys in that class. He was able to get away with some of the antics that others in his class could not and who thus were subjected to a parent meeting. It was not a talent Edward had for evading the ultimate punishment. It was just pure luck. He was lucky that is, until late February of that school year of seventh grade. It was a dreary February day when Edward crossed the line, Sister Mary Norbert's line, clearly drawn in the sand, a distinct boundary that allowed no deviation. He crossed that line in a big way, a huge way, a way that, once it was executed and discovered (and it was easily discovered because every girl in the school wanted to be the first to run to Sister Mary whichever and snitch on a boy), there was no way out, no turning back, no do over.

Edward hit a girl. A boy hitting a boy was also an offense but not a capital offense like a boy hitting a girl. It did not matter to Sister Mary Norbert that the girl might have hit the boy first, or that, whether she hit first or not, she deserved to be hit. A girl hitting a boy was overlooked by the nuns who were, as fate would have it, girls. The former was a misdemeanor, the latter a felony. A girl hitting a boy extracted a glare, a whack and correctly written *Glory Bes* (Sister Mary Norbert was a stickler for perfect handwriting too). The number of *Glory Bes* the perpetrator wrote depended on how severe the hit was, if the reason for hitting was warranted and sometimes on the number of hits.

Fat Debbie, the girl Edward hit, deserved to be hit on numerous occasions. But knowing the penalty, the boys were reluctant to take a swing.

Fat Debbie had taunted all of the boys at one time or another. She was a large girl, a girl who appeared to have known and practiced meanness all of her life. Freckles coated her pudgy cruel looking face, like enormous birthmarks that bred indiscriminately and took shelter on every inch of her cheeks, forehead and nose. Only her chin had resisted the onslaught. The orange dots of varying sizes flowed down her arms, on her legs, and where else the boys had no desire to see. She had contempt for all of them and did not discriminate between age or national origin. Perhaps it was her weight, of which she had plenty, that provoked her to be nasty. Or maybe her parents were the same way and she wished to emulate them. Or maybe it was the freckles. It seemed that freckle faced kids who went to elementary school with Edward had a wretched disposition. Whatever the reason, on that particular day in February, a cold and dreary winter day, recess was nearly over when Edward suddenly and indiscriminately became the target of fat Debbie's wickedness.

Several of the boys were sitting on the concrete steps leading into the church. They were resting from a short basketball game they had just finished. They had to rest and let the perspiration that had accumulated evaporate before they went back to class. Sister Mary Norbert did not like sweat.

Fat Debbie lumbered over to them, displaying her usual smirk that seemed to flatten her lips and at the same time widen her speckled nose. Edward saw her out of the corner of his eye. So did Jesse and Toad, Edward's friend who was given that name because his face, well, it resembled the face of a toad. They started to scatter, not wanting to face the wrath of a massively speckled and immensely fat, treacherous girl. But she cornered Edward between the propped open door and the steps.

She looked directly into his eyes. He avoided looking at her at all. "I hear your brother got arrested last weekend." she said disdainfully.

"Yea?" Edward replied with as much indifference as he could summon. "Who told you that?" Kevin had been arrested on the previous Saturday, but it was a result of guilt by association, a justification frequently used by the Chicago police at that time on the South Side of the city, and he was quickly released.

"My mother. She said it was for stealing cars."

Edward looked at her despite the revulsion he felt from her looks, her manner, even her odor. He was repulsed not only by her but by her accusations. Sure Kevin had been arrested. Sure he ran with people who stole cars and did a whole lot of other things that went way beyond any punishment Sister Mary Hortense or Sister Mary Norbert might see fit to bestow upon them.

"He didn't steal *anything*." Edward could feel the eyes of his friends watching him, waiting for something, anything that might once and for all put this chubby slug in her place.

"That's not what I heard. I heard . . ."

Edward cut her off. "I don't care what you heard." She raised her voice so all in the playground could hear her. "I heard that your brother . . ." Edward slapped her, not hard so as to knock her down or even cause her to move from her perch in front of him. It required much greater force than what he wielded to move Fat Debbie. But he hit her hard enough to redden her cheek. Hard enough so he could not distinguish between her pale skin and her freckles. She stood there for a moment, then ran inside followed closely by every other girl who had witnessed what to them was a revolting display of cowardice, even if it was Fat Debbie who no one, not even the girls, liked. Edward knew where she was going. Everyone knew where she was going. The boys gathered around Edward, slapping his back, shaking his hand and then, each in his own way, offering their condemned friend sympathy for what was to come.

That afternoon, because he hit Fat Debbie, Edward's mother arrived at school just as the bell rang at three o'clock. She looked peeved. At age fifty-one his mother's hair was nearly all white and thin like strands of thread had been placed indiscriminately on her scalp. Her hair aged her tremendously. Her seasoned hair along with the wrinkles on her cheeks and forehead and around her small narrow eyes made her look even madder than she was. In the classroom they sat next to each other in two front row desks. His mother wiggled back and forth trying to fit a middle aged body in a desk made for a twelve year old. She did not say much to Edward. She knew he must be in big trouble for her to be called to school.

Sister Mary Norbert entered the room stern faced and irritated. She sat at her desk in the front facing mother and son, her back straight and rigid against the chair, her hands folded neatly in front of her, each arm at the same angle to her body, her head cocked slightly up so she was looking down her nose at them. Her first words to Edward's mother were not about what he had done (he was proud of what he had done) or about what should be done to him (he was willing to take his punishment for what he had done *because* he was proud of what he had done). Her first words were "Where is the boy's father?"

"He is at work," Edward's mother responded. "Downtown."

"He should be here," Sister Mary Norbert said acidly. "When I called you I requested that he be here also. I feel it is important that . . ."

"There is no way that he could get here from downtown in time to meet with you." Edward's mother had interrupted her. Not a good idea for anyone to interrupt Sister Mary Norbert, or any nun for that matter.

Sister Mary Norbert stared at both of them for a while without showing any emotion or giving away her thoughts. Then she said, "Is there an uncle?"

"No."

"A brother?"

"He is out of town." He was not out of town. He was at home asleep because he worked the late shift at the mill. Edward's mother lied. He could not believe it, his mother not only interrupted a nun but lied to her as well. Even if Kevin was available, Edward's mother certainly did not want Kevin here especially as an example for his younger brother.

"Any neighbor that. . . ?"

"No." Again the stare, that stare that appeared far away and at the same time went right through a person. She told Edward's mother what he had done, but he could see she was reluctant to go on without a man present. Then she told Edward's mother that her son would be required to stay after school every day for a week and write, and that she was to make sure her son went to confession the next Saturday so he could tell his sin to the priest and ask for absolution. She also told her she wanted to schedule another meeting with both mother and father present. Edward's mother simply nodded and Sister Mary Norbert left the room. Mother and son went home in silence.

When Edward's father arrived home from work that evening, the boy's mother told him what he had done and what Sister Mary Norbert had said and how Edward was to go to confession and confess his sin and beg for absolution and that they were to meet again with Sister Mary Norbert. *Ask* for absolution, Edward thought. Sister Mary Norbert did not say *beg* for absolution. Edward's father laid the evening paper on the table in the hall. He just glared at his son, staring at his face for what seemed like forever, a glare not as substantial as Sister Mary Norbert's but strong enough to get across its meaning. His lips moved as if he was forming words. But he did not speak and then he just walked into the other room to change his clothes. Not another word was said about the incident. The next Saturday morning Edward was reminded by his mother to go to confession which he dutifully did. His father told his mother to call Sister Mary Norbert and tell her that he was not going to waste his time meeting with a nun. That nuns didn't know how to handle children, and that no nun was going to tell him how to raise his children. She never called. His father never met with her. Edward thought maybe he should have. Just maybe Sister Mary Norbert might have had some good advise for him, like pay some attention to your children, give them some time. Even punish them once in a while. Tell them to write a *Glory Be*.

IV

Edward dabbed the last droplet of water from his arm, rose from the tub and headed to the living room to confront whatever had been gnawing at him since they left the cemetery and he had witnessed the panic that suddenly emerged from what had been a blank stare on his father's face.

Before her death, Edward's mother held a place of honor and consequence in a unquestionably disabled family. It was, Edward presumed, because his father had been infected with the handicap of weakness. Because of this deficiency, his lack of competence at confrontation, his unexpressiveness, the scarcity of anything resembling a personality, the father was inferior to the mother. It certainly was a situation Roberta relished now that the mother was dead, but one she had no part in creating. Edward's father did that all on his own. Roberta just took full advantage of it.

Throughout Edward's life as a full-fledged family member, up until he was fourteen, he realized his father had multiple deficiencies. He was dominated first by one female and then, as Roberta was mentored by her mother to follow her lead, by two females; and he never cried foul, but only whimpered his concession. Edward had never realized how subjugated his father was until the family had moved from memorializing a dead women to suddenly having to resuscitate a man who appeared inept at every daily chore, every routine social and economic task that most people execute with little thought and minimal exertion.

At his father's apartment, Edward and his siblings glumly sat at the counterfeit wood grained Formica table in the center of what real estate agents call a "breakfast nook." It was actually an extension of the paltry section of the apartment that had been designated as the living room. They sat at the table like poker players eager for the dealer to begin tossing cards their way. Edward's father became the holder of a hand that Edward, nor any other respectable gambler, would ever have bet on. He would never have bet on it because he grew up in a family where he truly believed that his father was in charge, however silent the old man may have been. Based on what he thought he knew about him, Edward would have lost the bet. As Kevin cleaned his fingernails with the tine of a kitchen fork, and Edward stared at the vacant eyes of the old man who sat across from him, Roberta tossed a stack of bills on the kitchen table. What the old man offered back to her and to his sons was a blank stare, a true poker face.

"What's this?" he finally asked Roberta.

"Bills!" she answered curtly, a little too brusque considering what the man had been through over the last five days. "Bills that need paid, she added with even less compassion." She picked them up again, in fact snatched them from the table just as the old man began to reach for them. She tossed them back on the table in front of him one at a time. It looked like she was dealing cards to him, five card stud, and he was examining each card as it hit the table in front of him. He contemplated the hand dealt him with what appeared at first to be uneasiness, a look of inner turmoil, as if his bowls recently repaired suddenly were in flux. Roberta rattled off the contents of each bill as she tossed it toward him. "Utility bill, hundred and four seventy-five, telephone bill, nineteen twenty-five, doctor bill, one fifty-five . . ." and on and on. My father looked meekly at her. His empty stare turned to fright. His right hand shook; it vibrated like a hula doll on the dashboard of a dump truck.

"What's the problem?" Kevin asked him. The tremor increased. He looked around the table at his children, his frightened gaze imploring one of them to help him. But to help him how? What was so disconcerting about these normal everyday bills that everyone gets and no one wants to pay but they pay anyway? These were not bills that were outrageous. They were not huge credit card bills for expensive jewelry or trips or furniture that most people cannot pay off for ten years. What was it about these bills that he appeared on the verge of collapse?

He picked the envelopes up off the table, holding them as if they gave off a toxic goo that might seep through his skin and poison him. He solemnly stared at them. "I cannot pay these bills," he announced in a quivering voice.

"What do you mean you can't pay them?" Roberta asked in her most prosecutorial way. "You have plenty of money. What's the problem?"

"Yea, Dad," Kevin echoed. Kevin was a man of few words, and those he used invariably mimicked those of the people around him. "You're in good financial shape. What seems to be the problem?" They intently glared at the old man waiting for an answer none of them could possibly have contemplated.

"I don't mean I can't afford to pay the bills," he explained, still shaking, the table still vibrating. "I mean . . ." He stopped here. His hand again shook. He looked at the questioning eyes of his children one at a time, staring sheepishly for a moment then turning to the next child, then turning away. He gazed glumly at the bills. Finally, he reluctantly admitted, "I mean I don't know how to write checks. I've never written a check. Your mother always took care of that. In fact, I've never written a check, never paid a bill, ever, in my life." He rose from his chair as his children sat dumbfounded. He shuffled to his bedroom and closed the door.

Kevin rose and quickly moved the three steps it took to get to the kitchen. He fumbled for something in the refrigerator. A tab popped. He drank his beer while leaning against the stove. Edward picked up a deck of cards moved to the couch and began dealing solitaire on the glass top coffee table. Roberta rose and walked to the patio door. The brothers heard sobbing.

They removed themselves one by one from the bizarre and, at least Edward thought fleetingly, somewhat humorous event that had occurred at the table in the breakfast nook. Each took their disbelief elsewhere, to ponder it and maybe calculate the next step in this bizarre turn of events. Edward and Kevin simultaneously shook their heads at what had occurred. Edward laughed to himself, overwhelmed at how sadly funny it was. This characteristic of his father, Edward recalled from his childhood, had suddenly once more appeared to him. It was one small scrap of a moment when he was a child noticing, but never registering as a memory he wanted to permanently log away, that his father knew barely enough of life to get by and he did not care to know any more. And now his lack of direction, lack of passion, absence of motivation that was his whole life had pooled together in a vast sea of inadequacy and ignorance.

He stayed in his room for a long time, probably lying on the bed he had shared for fifty-five years with the woman he had just buried, contemplating not only how lost he was now that he did not have her to do everything for him, but how utterly lonely he would be the rest of his life. He had been lonely from the beginning whenever that beginning was, that beginning of his loneliness. He was lonely with Edward; he was lonely without Edward. He was lonely with his wife; he would be lonely without her. The loneliness had not changed, only the way it had been created had changed. Nothing, tragic or cursory, could alter his state of loneliness.

Kevin was probably snickering in his beer also. Roberta, Edward knew, was not laughing because her sobbing increased and her shoulders quivered. Roberta, because of her quest for dominance over her widowed father, without warning was thrust into the position of educating her father in the finer points of writing a check. She also knew that, if he was so inept at life that he could not accomplish the simple task of writing a check, there certainly had to be more he could not do that would require tutoring.

With her mother around, Roberta's choice as the beneficiary of her mother's whim and will was secure. The mother was the supreme ruler; the daughter the heir apparent, waiting in the wings for the demise of the queen mother. Not that Roberta wanted her mother to die. On the contrary, she relied on her financial and moral generosity and protection so heavily she had no desire to see her mentor's death thrust Roberta into the unknown, the unexplored, undiscovered recesses of her father. Edward suspected his father had long ago ceded to his mother any authority he may have had over family matters, if he ever had any. And now, with the evidence of that surrender before them, Roberta no longer felt that she would have to battle against her father for supremacy. Edward suspected her sobbing was not a result of commiseration for her father's awkwardness at life skills but sympathy for herself that she was abruptly forced to correct some of his shortcomings so she would not have to care for him and be his nanny, cook, housekeeper and accountant. Edward also suspected that she was also crying for joy because, in his pitiable state, she would have total control over him. Roberta was delighted that her father was so helpless. At the same time, she recognized the daunting task she had before her. In essence Roberta had been the heir to the throne. Now with her mother's passing she reigned. But as she accepted the throne, she realized that monarchs should not have to teach an old man how to write a check.

Roberta continued sobbing while staring forlornly through the sliding glass door that led to the patio. Her breath made little round patches of fog on the glass like wet warning signals blinking on and off. Kevin still leaned against the stove, flipping the tab on his second beer. Every few seconds he shook his head as if his mind had trouble grasping what had just occurred at the table. Edward wondered how many other things his father did not know how to do.

It had been evident for years that the father's social skills, in fact his proficiency for living as a normal human being, were in default. That is why, in their fifty-five years of marriage, the mother had been deprived of any social life. She had her bridge club, but that was the extent of her socializing. Was Roberta now also responsible for instructing her father in how to meet people and, once he had completed that training, must she also train him in getting along with them? Must he also learn how to dish up his evening bowl of vanilla ice cream, pull a beer from the refrigerator, fix dinner? What about cashing in the meager life insurance policies he had taken out on his wife? Are making bank deposits and withdrawals skills he had never mastered? Will he be able to pay his rent on time or will one of the children receive a call from him late one evening explaining in that tone of his that makes him sound like he just can't understand why all the fuss, "I'm being evicted and I don't know why." "Did you pay your rent, Dad?" "My what? Pay my what?" "I guess you didn't, Dad." Then one of the children, maybe a son but probably the daughter, must call the landlord and make arrangements for the back rent to be paid—one month, two months, six months, however accommodating the landlord had been for an old man recently widowed. Roberta had her hands full, and Edward certainly had no sympathy for her. Neither did Kevin. For her entire life she maneuvered herself into position to take control. Death was the strategy. Her scheming while doting over her parents was as much designed to keep mother and father as her allies as it was to prohibit the development of any relationship between the parents and their sons. Now she was forced to teach her father minimal competence where there had been none. It was rather amusing for Edward and Kevin to think how her contrivances rewarded her.

Edward shuffled the cards for the fifth, maybe sixth, game of solitaire and then decided he was tired of playing a card game he had not, after four tries, or maybe five, come close to winning. He was also tired of listening to Roberta play out her role as compassionate and sympathetic daughter. He was also thirsty. He rose from the couch. As he walked toward the refrigerator Kevin nudged it open, brought out a beer and tossed it to Edward. He rolled his eyes toward Roberta then looked back at his brother. Edward flipped the tab on the beer can. Their concurrent grins were evidence that they both saw great humor in the situation before them. They made no move nor uttered any acknowledgment to Roberta that they were prepared to help in this endeavor at remedial banking or bill paying or cooking. Kevin nudged Edward, "You think he knows how to bathe himself?"

Edward motioned to the door. Kevin followed him out. Edward felt on his back an icy stare from his sister. Had she the opportunity, she would have committed a grizzly murder right there on the spot, with no remorse. They didn't care. She had maneuvered herself into this corner. The boys were going shopping.

It was shopping as much as two grown men who rarely patronized more than a convenience store could contrive. It was more browsing than buying. Kevin found a steamy novel at a local used book store. Edward selected an unpretentious piece of Navaho pottery for his wife, Teresa. They ate French fries and burgers at a corner cafe in downtown Phoenix while they talked about the funeral, the meager meal afterward, and how astounded, as well as baffled, they were by the deficiencies their father had displayed at the kitchen table. They never knew. When they were children their father did little for them or with them. They always thought it was because he had no interest. Now, as Kevin spread mustard on his burger and Edward gnawed on a French fry, they experienced an uneasy suspicion that maybe their father never had the skills to raise children. After leaving the cafe, they rummaged through some sale racks of men's shirts, not because they were attracted to the styles or the prices, although either one of them may have bought one had they found something worth buying, but because they were out in the mall simply to kill time until they thought it was safe to return.

Even for the two hours they were gone, it was a treat to get away from the helpless old man and his sinister daughter. True, they were both grieving, but the father's grief appeared genuine although it was difficult to distinguish between his sorrow and his customary ill-humor. Roberta's grief seemed contrived.

When Edward and Kevin returned to the apartment, their father had apparently regained his composure, come out of his bedroom and taken his seat at the kitchen table. A dinner plate holding crumbs of bread and a half eaten dill pickle sat near him. Unwilling teacher and uncomprehending student were still deeply involved in the elementary points of paying bills: figuring where to find the total, writing the check, filling in the check register, learning which part of the bill to send with the check, and putting the bill in the envelope correctly if it was a window envelope or filling out the address properly if it was not.

"Don't forget the stamp," my sister said, obviously from her tone, repeating it again. The old man took notes.

The evening went the same way. Kevin drank beer and watched a basketball game. Edward drank beer and played solitaire and watched the same basketball game. Their father learned how to apply for the insurance benefits, how to make a bank deposit and who to call for plumbing or other problems. Roberta organized his newly created files, alphabetizing them by those who were to be paid money, creating a schedule for paying the bills, codifying the do's and don'ts, barking out rules and regulations of household finance and maintenance. "Who do you call to fix plumbing?" she asked, no, demanded. "Uh." "The plumber, Dad." He nodded, still maintaining a confused look. "Who do you call to repair the television?" "The television repairman." "Where do you find a television repairman?" He looked at her with a look of achievement. "Why, in the phone book." "Who do you call . . ." "Ghostbusters," Kevin called after a healthy swig of beer. Roberta ignored him. The old man did not hear Kevin's smug comment. Edward watched his father nodding at his sister's instructions, but his brow betrayed him. He didn't have a clue.

Everyone makes bad choices sometime in life. Except Edward's father. He made no choices except the one that estranged him from just about everybody in the world except his wife and Roberta. Now he was paying for it. Edward watched Kevin toss back his beers, Roberta drop her head in despair, his father stare into the ether with every word of instruction Roberta uttered.

Edward wanted to believe that he was an anomaly, maybe even adopted. Everyone likes to think he or she is an exception. But as he compared his life with that of his siblings and his father, he found himself not conforming to any of the patterns he saw before him in that apartment in Tempe. Maybe Edward did not stand extraordinarily far out, but he was unmistakably at a distance that distinguished his life of some consequence with their lives of none.

"Do you know how to get to church, Dad?" Roberta continued her interrogation. A nod. "The doctor?" Another nod. "The grocery store or pharmacy?" He appeared annoyed. "Roberta, I have done all the driving for your mother. I know how to get to those places." Questionable, Edward thought. He may have been at the wheel, but mother always was the navigator. She always told him where to go, when to go and how to go. Edward had a vision of him driving all over town from early morning until dark looking for one or another place on the list Roberta had just ticked off, only to become exasperated in that gruff, almost feral way he did when he could not locate his favorite bowl, open a sealed envelope or screw in a light bulb.

Edward recalled a time when he was fifteen years old and went to a dance in a seedy part of Whiting, Indiana, about a forty minute drive from their home. An easy drive with few turns and on main streets. When the dance let out at 11:00 p.m. his ride had ditched him probably to score with the Whiting girl he had picked up earlier in the evening. Whiting girls were known to be easy. At least for everyone but Edward. He was the only one left waiting outside the dance hall. He called his father but he told

Edward he was unable to come and get him. He didn't know the way. His mother picked him up.

The anxious children asked their father what plans he had for the future. Will he live in the same place? Yes. Was he sure he could handle everyday tasks? Yes. Was he able to fix his own meals? Yes. Will he make sure he eats right? Yes. Despite all the positives given in his faint, almost reclusive, voice, they were not persuaded that he could survive more than a few months without some intervention on their part, on Roberta's part.

Roberta made a meager overture to him that he move in with her. Edward was convinced she no more wished him as a house guest than she would seek the plague as a lodger. Edward and Kevin, knowing the turmoil having their father as a tenant in their homes would cause, remained silent. No suggestions, no offers, no guilt.

The old man shook his head. "No, no, I intend to stay right here. I can live on my own. I'll do just fine." He looked at the three of them, their eyes still full of questions and doubt, his eyes showing them that he had been wounded by their suggestions of incompetence. " I don't need any help from anyone. It will take a major calamity before I burden any of you." They were unaware then of how prophetic his last statement was.

The next day was a Saturday. Roberta and her father left the apartment about ten to go to confession. Edward never thought of his father as religious. Far from it. Roberta had insisted the night before that both of them go to confession and then to Mass on Saturday night. His father reluctantly agreed.

To confess what, Edward thought. That he is inept and he asks for forgiveness for that trait that has brought him to this point? That he did not shed a lot of tears for his wife? He was wasting his time. Edward saw confession, especially for a man who had never seen religion as a essential part of life, as an exercise in futility. Confession had always been a burden, a religious rite that seemed to be nothing more than a weigh station to unburden yourself of sins that you begin committing again as soon as you let the confessional door bang shut.

As his father and sister confessed their sins, Edward packed for his trip home.

V

By the time Edward reached seventh grade, confession had become a chore, no longer an honor or sacred grant from God as the nuns and priests of St. Clem's had taught him. It no longer was a gift to gain absolution from God as he and his friends had been indoctrinated in second grade before they made their First Confession.

His First Confession was the day before he made his First Holy Communion. Second grade. At seven years old he had no idea what sin was and may not have known for a long time if the nuns at St. Clem's had not been so kind as to make a list for him and his classmates. Before they had the list of sins, venial on one side of the page and mortal on the other, they did not have any inclination or desire to commit, at least with forethought, any of the sins on the list. After collecting in small clandestine groups, at least the boys did, to pour over the list and then later, having most of the sins, not the ones that had anything remotely to do with sex, explained to them by Sister Mary Genevieve, the principal and eighth grade teacher, most of the second graders, at least the boys, were eager to get at it, except for maybe murder. Edward thought the coveting sounded intriguing.

He did not know how to commit most of the sins that the nuns listed for them as possible candidates for the confessional. Lying. Yes, he had done that. He had told his mother he washed his hands when he hadn't. He had lied to Sister Mary Frances, his second grade teacher and the school's assistant principal when he told her he left his homework on the bus when actually he had not done it at all. Sure he told some lies. But the stealing sin and hate and revenge and envy? Second graders did not do those things. Edward may not have liked someone or maybe was a little jealous of a new jacket someone was wearing, wishing he had something that warm, and he may have even wanted that jacket, but none of those feelings, at age seven, ever became earnest enough to be classified as serious sinning. Even if he might have done some of those things in second grade, it was inadvertent, and he always believed that if a person didn't know it was a sin, it wasn't a sin. Ignorance of the law, be it civil or God's, was an appropriate excuse for seven year olds.

In third grade Edward thought he had discovered another sin that he should confess. It was one he thought might be a sin but, after further reflection, he decided it was not a sin at all. It was when he got his ankle caught in the spokes of Kevin's bicycle and his father stood on the porch with a beer in one hand and a sausage in the other and watched his youngest child bleed all over the weeds and litter in the empty lot next door, while a neighbor his father probably had never talked to and did not know and did not care to know, cut the spokes of the wheel with a pair of wire cutters. Edward felt loathing for his father who showed no interest in his injury. When that incident came to him as he was searching for sins, he thought hatred was a sin that he must confess. Fortunately he thought about it probably longer than he should have and decided that since his father probably hated him, then his father's hatred of him canceled his out his hatred for his father, and therefore there was no sin for either of them. Edward's logic at the time was primitive but it was enough for him.

Edward's First Confession was easy, although a little frightening when he stepped into the confessional for the first time and the priest slid the door that opened up his sins to the man behind the screen. "Bless me father for I have sinned, this is my first confession." That did not seem to electrify Father McMann, the parish pastor, even though Sister Mary Genevieve told the children it would excite every one they met because it was the most glorious occasion for a child. Father McMann just made what sounded like a growling noise, maybe a yawn, or the grumbles from a hungry stomach. He listened to Edward's sins, how intently he could not tell, for the screen that separated them was too thick for Edward to see the priest's face. Anyway, he was afraid to look at the priest because he thought maybe that was a sin, one inadvertently omitted from the list. Edward had only two sins to offer even though he mulled it over for an entire week trying to come up with sins he had committed since his life began. In that whole week he only came up with two (lying to his mother about washing his hands and the homework lie he told to Sister Mary Frances).

After all the badgering on sin he received from Sister Mary Genevieve and Sister Mary Frances, Edward learned how to know if the devil was after him, how to avoid sin and how to confess any sins that might have been unavoidable, and that it was not for him but the priest in the confessional to determine whether or not something was a sin. But Edward began to wonder what it would be like if everyone who entered the confessional had not done a sin analysis like he had before he confessed. If every Catholic who knelt in a confessional inventoried every thing they did that they were unable to put in the non-sin pile because that was something the priest did, the confessional lines would never end. Edward thought it was better to save the priest some time and allow some greater sinner to have extra time with Father McMann.

The day after his first confession was his First Holy Communion. Edward dressed up in a navy blue suit with white shirt and white bow tie and marched down the aisle with all the other second graders, said prayers, sang songs, sat through a long dull mass and finally, toward the end, marched up to the railing that guarded the altar. Their little second grade legs tried to keep time with the music like Sister Mary Genevieve told them to, marching to mournful music that should have been happy music. They knelt at the railing and received the wafer they were told by Sister Mary Genevieve was the body of Christ, another mystery of the Catholic church that a second grader had difficulty grasping. Edward was without sin when the wafer was laid on his tongue. He had been to confession and informed the priest of the nasty little lies he had told and the priest gave Edward his penance and Edward said the three Hail, Marys and one Our Father and he was pure at least until the next time he lied or, as he grew older, felt envious of someone, or hated someone like Fat Debbie. Then he would confess again and he would be pure again at least for a day. Confession was always on a Saturday, the day before he went to mass and received communion. It could not be on any other day because no one Edward knew could last that long until communion on Sunday.

Edward's father did not attend his First Holy Communion. All the other fathers were there, the drunks and the misfits and the wife beaters and the few that were able to sneak around the neighborhood and do it with the wives of the ones that were drunk all the time. His father was busy with something, Edward didn't remember what. That was a sin, Edward thought. One his father probably never confessed. One Edward could never cancel out.

As Edward grew older confessions became more complex. Actually it was not confession that was complicated, that was a breeze, it was the sins that became more convoluted and elaborate. He continued to tell lies as did everyone he knew, and as he grew up he realized that everyone told lies, most of them a lot more involved than his. But for him and, he guessed, for most of the other kids, the list of sins grew longer as they moved through grammar school. By eighth grade there was not only lying and maybe some envy now and then, but Edward also had to confess lust and coveting and, the most difficult for any boy of thirteen, that sin of self gratification that involves lust and coveting but of himself. That was the most difficult sin to confess to the priest behind the screen.

So as Edward matured not only in age, but also in bodily needs and therefore the number and intricacy of sins that were applicable to him, he, along with his friends who had the same problems, was very careful who he told his sins to.

There were two priests in St. Clement parish. There was Father O'Connor, the young priest just five years out of the seminary who took his vocation very seriously and made people feel like they were the lowest people on earth by the time they exited the confessional. When Sister Mary Norbert or any of the other nuns told one of the children to *Go to the priest!* for punishment, Father O'Connor was that priest. Father O'Connor had the looks, the stature and the intelligence to go far in the world, probably business, some sort of executive. And, had he not become a priest, his chances at success in the corporate world were even greater because of his personality. He was sly and vindictive. While the boys at St. Clem's did not like him, the boys' mothers, the girls, the girls' mothers and the nuns adored him. After church or at a school event like bingo, or the Mother's Club, the women, not surreptitiously as one would think a priest should be approached by a woman, openly displayed their attentiveness and attractiveness toward Father O'Connor. On Tuesday and Thursday afternoons when Father O'Connor came into Edward's classroom to teach catechism, Sister Mary Norbert assembled an enormous smile where her students had never seen one appear before. She actually showed her teeth when Father O'Connor entered. She straightened the cuffs of her sleeves, smoothed her habit and never took her eyes off of him for thirty minutes as he regaled the students with the teachings of the Church. Ah, if only Sister Mary Norbert and Father O'Connor had never chosen the vocations that kept them from doing what they had never done but wanted to do.

Since many of the boys either had visited Father O'Connor as punishment or were altar boys for him when he said mass, he knew their voices. No kid wanted to tell a priest who knew who he was that he played with his pecker down in his basement, or that he got his kicks from rubbing his elbow against Mary Jo Bandera's newly swollen breasts in the cloakroom as he was hanging up his coat before school or retrieving his coat at the end of the day or in line to go into church or any number of other times when he had the urge to touch Mary Jo Bandera's breasts.

Then there was the pastor of the parish, Father McMann. After Edward realized that Father O'Connor could easily identify the confessor even with that dark screen between the sinner and the person listening to every foul thing the sinner had done to himself and to others, and after he visualized Father O'Connor leaving the confessional at the end of the day, going back to the rectory and marking down in his ledger all the sins of all the boys so that someday, sometime in the future, if he ever needed to use that information, he would be able to say to Edward or any of his friends or even to his parents or his friend's parents "Remember your sin against the flesh in your bedroom or the sin against Mary Jo Bandera" or whatever other sin he thought may be useful for the occasion, whatever that occasion might be, Edward told his sins to Father McMann. So did every other boy. The girls and the girls' and the boys' mothers went to Father O'Connor. Many of them, Edward was sure, not only wanted to tell him their sins, but probably wanted to try some of them out on him. Edward wondered how a priest who had taken a vow of celibacy was able, without committing what surely was a mortal sin, to listen to all those sins of lust and passion and craving day in and day out and not explode with his own craving to commit a few of those sins. Maybe he did, Edward didn't know.

Jesse told Edward one time about priests breaking their vows when Edward asked him what a priest did when he had the urge to do some of the things the older boys in the neighborhood talked about doing to girls. Jesse said sometimes they just go nuts and go after every woman they can find. Jesse told Edward that his old man had told him about a priest over at Saint Timothy Church who got three women parishioners pregnant. What did they do with the priest? They sent him away. Some island in the Pacific

Ocean somewhere, he said. Never saw the women around. Don't know what happened to them or the babies. He also heard from his brother in Texas about a priest who didn't like women but liked little girls instead. You know what they do to people like that? Edward told him he did, but he really didn't know what they did to people like that. He told him he did because he didn't want to sound stupid in front of Jesse who knew a lot about the world. Jesse laughed then and said he figured it was better than a priest liking little boys. Yea, Edward told him, you'd never hear of a priest going after little boys.

Father McMann was the kind of man who was scarcely noticeable in a crowd, even in a crowd of grade school children. His tone was faint, his words indistinct. The boys attributed this not only to his age—he was certainly in his late seventies, although children have a difficult time distinguishing the age of anyone who is at least a generation beyond them—but also to his stature which, they thought, was why his personality was so meager and constricted. He was short, not much taller than Sister Mary Hortense. If the boys could have seen beyond the square foot of flesh that nuns were allowed to show in public, they were certain that Father McMann and Sister Mary Hortense were twins. In looks only. Father McMann was a gentle person, and he was deaf. That is why the boys clamored to his confessional. He heard maybe fifty percent of what they told him in that box. If they muttered, particularly on the big sins, the major venials, he never knew what they had done. Needless to say the penance was easy. Edward thought the record was for Jesse one Saturday in September of seventh grade; one Hail Mary and One Our Father. Edward's personal best was two of each. No matter how much he muttered Edward could never match Jesse's record. Every Saturday, a person entering the church could readily tell which confessional held Father McMann. A line of boys waited outside ready to mutter their sins to the old deaf priest.

VI

"Am I unfeeling?" Edward asked his wife, Teresa, after returning home to Missouri from his mother's funeral. "Heartless? Hateful?"

"No," she answered to all the dishonorable designations he had conferred on himself. "You are, however," she responded in her most amiable tone, then she paused desiring to offer the most appropriate word and at the same time sound sympathetic, "you are , I would say, mutually indifferent."

Not as sympathetic as he had anticipated, and, in his prevailing estimation of himself, not quite appropriate. When he began to protest, she patted his shoulder and explained, "I don't mean that in a derogatory way. What I mean is, your emotions about your parents have been numbed by years of indifference on their part."

Edward nodded. Yes, that was certainly true.

She continued. "While your mother paid attention to you and mothered you as a child, your father never did. And they paid very little attention to you as a teenager, a stage of life where a person most needs parents. And I don't need to tell you how they treated you as an adult."

He nodded again. She was certainly on the mark.

"As an adult you became indifferent to their needs because of their inattention to you when you were growing up. And they blamed you for all that, not themselves."

His nodding became more intense. She had uncovered his

feelings, and, although accurate, they were not particularly admirable for either side. She had a talent for finding feelings that were deep inside a person. Not bad for a BA in business administration, Edward thought and then kissed her.

Edward didn't sleep well that first night back and he was unable to focus on much of anything the next day. He became so intent on finding reasons for his feelings that he was unable to tell if the lack of concentration was a result of what Teresa had precisely described as his lack of concern and he was experiencing a backlash of remorse, or if the funeral and being sardined for five days in a tiny apartment with his father, sister and brother, and in an even smaller hospital room with a dying mother, had conjured up a need to resolve a long burning urgency to identify exactly when his position in the family had become insignificant. Teresa told him that funerals will do that to a person. Such a help she could be. Granted, Kevin's standing was also tenuous. But Edward had neither the time nor the inclination to make his brother a part of his exploration. Kevin could think for himself (sometimes) and therefore could make the effort to determine why his spot also had been nearly erased (he never would).

Not until Edward was sitting in the airport in Phoenix impatiently waiting for his flight home did he consider as true, although he had toyed with its credibility many times when he was growing up, the notion that his life had a contradictory effect on the maternal and paternal instincts of his parents. It was a not a dramatic realization but simply one he had finally grasped and held onto instead of shaking his head at and denying as plausible.

As he watched little children scurrying around the terminal, some taking their errant behavior to its maximum, he recalled watching his oldest child, now his teenage daughter, take her first steps. The memory of that marvelous experience brought with it questions of his own development at that age. He tried to recollect how his parents had reacted to crawling, first steps, first words. The answers were at first evasive. It was difficult to remember what happened during his first four years of life and sometimes sickening to recall what happened in subsequent years. So for a long time he tried not to think about it. Not until he had witnessed the behavior of his father at the breakfast nook table the day before, did his mind begin to unravel what he had neatly tucked away and forgotten. The post funeral idleness opened the iron gate that had for years held it all in check.

As he recalled events where there should have been involvement from his mother and father but wasn't, he recognized that they had made a half-hearted effort to raise him. His mother tried at first, until his watershed, the one that abruptly changed the stature that he had been trying so hard to build in the eyes of his mother. He became convinced that he had not been a welcome addition to the family, and even appeared to occupy a sore spot, and even no spot at all, in the hearts of his parents. He suspected he put a crimp in their future lifestyle plans. He was six years younger than Kevin, five younger than Roberta. He was unexpected, a surprise. His unanticipated addition to the family developed into a case of benign neglect. The circumstances of his birth or, rather, the circumstances that his birth disrupted, led his parents, particularly his father, to unconsciously default their parental obligations. His father's disregard was evident everywhere, even on Sunday when the coins Edward was given to place in the collection plate were less than what Roberta and Kevin received. As if the amount of spiritual closeness to God tithing was intended to bring to the giver should be less for him than for his siblings.

Of course, a child has no inkling that the treatment it receives from parents is intentional. An adult clamoring for memories of childhood will soon smart from the same acts that as a child were deemed typical for childhood. The death of Edward's mother allowed many memories to resurface, but as swiftly as they filled his head, after he caught his plane back to Missouri, they quickly receded back into the crevices of his mind where they had been hidden away for many years. It would be several more years before they again overwhelmed him.

Six months after his mother died his father moved in with Roberta who lived in an inconspicuous suburb south of Chicago. The prophecy of a calamity, the last words he left with Edward, Roberta and Kevin, and Edward was sure he repeated frequently to Roberta after Edward and Kevin had gone, had come true. The major calamity had occurred, not once or twice but three times.

Within thirty days of his wife's death, twenty-four days after Roberta's departure and her final checklist of do's and don'ts, just four short weeks after the beginning of what they had antici-pated as their father's disastrous self-rule, he drove his four year old Cadillac DeVille into a tree. No injuries, simply out-of-pocket costs of the insurance deductible and a considerable cost in higher insurance premiums.

In a foolish effort to prove to everyone that, at eighty-two years old, he could still drive, to prove himself worthy of a new vehicle, he bought another Cadillac and promptly ran it into a building. A vacant building fortunately. No injuries, again out-of-pocket costs of the insurance deductible, an outrageous increase in insurance premiums.

No sooner had that incident been settled when the old man, with little effort, ran his third Cadillac into the front end of a Chevy Nova. Two injuries, one serious (neither of which was the old man) out-of-pocket costs of the deductible, insurance can-celed.

When Edward heard about the third accident he thought about why his father did not teach him how to drive and, instead, paid what Edward thought then was an extraordinary amount of money for driving lessons. He drove for six weeks, three days a week, an hour each time under the tutelage of a stranger from the Triple A Driving School. It was a paradox he could not un-tangle. Perhaps his father refused to teach him to drive not because he lacked interest in teaching his son, although that sentiment customarily guided his behavior toward Edward, but because he did not know how to drive well enough himself. At any rate, he spent more money on Edward for those lessons than for anything else in his son's entire life. He could have easily said, as he did many other times, that it was a waste of money and just never bothered to have Edward taught or to teach him himself.

Here the brothers and sister had an eighty-two year old man who scarcely knew how to write a check, was unable to ascertain the difference between a light bill and a phone bill, had no friends because he never socialized with people, or, rather people did not care to socialize with him, and could not drive to the bank to cash a check he couldn't write, did not know how to put a check he couldn't write in an envelope he did not know how to mail and therefore had to drive to the power company and phone company which he could no longer do to pay the bill, and could not drive to a place to socialize with people (if he had the ability to socialize with people) because he could not drive and he did not have any friends to mingle with anyway. What were his children to do? Rather, after receiving the details of the Cadillac—Nova accident over the phone from Kevin, Edward and his brother, in a most covert way, as if someone might have been listening in on their conversation, debated the options available and decided the question was, What was a daughter to do?

Edward thought his father's hard-headed resolution to remain in Arizona when he was unable to function in a normal fashion was ludicrous. Despite the absurdity of that decision, his foolish insistence that he would be able to remain there for the duration of his life, his three children had known different. They expected it was just a matter of time before he called one of them (Kevin and Edward knew, or, rather, hoped, he would choose Roberta) and explained in a way that made it sound like he had pondered the advantages and opportunities of living near, or possibly with family, if any one would have him, of course, and made his decision: he wanted to come to Chicago and live with Roberta. But he did not do what they expected. Instead, he wrecked three expensive cars, seriously injured two people, and thus was even less functional than when his children had left him after their mother's funeral.

A week after the last wreck Roberta called him and badgered him into moving in with her. He agreed and told her that, although he had no doubt he could live on his own, perhaps it was wise for a man his age to have some family around and that, despite the fact that his wife was buried in Phoenix, coming back to Chicago may be a prudent decision. Actually he knew it was his only alternative. He sold all his furniture except his television, Lay-Z-Boy recliner and TV tray, packed away all of his wife's china, glassware and those knick knacks that, in Roberta's estimation, had some value or potential value, sent them off to Chicago and caught the first plane out of Phoenix.

By the end of the second week living under Roberta's roof, he asked Kevin to go out to dinner with him. While sitting across from Kevin in a booth at the local Denny's Restaurant, he handed Kevin a check for fifteen thousand dollars and, over a mouth watering burger from Denny's and a piece of carrot cake for dessert, tried to seduce Kevin into buying a car for him—A Cadillac. If you are going to wreck a car why not do it in style, Kevin thought.

A few days before this clandestine meeting between father and son, he had badgered Roberta to do the same, but she would have nothing to do with it. "No insurance company would write a policy," she told him. "And anyway, you'll just run into something and get yourself killed, or kill someone else, or both." Kevin took the check from him. Kevin was not one to turn down money even though he knew it would not be his for long. He put his father off for a while, and when he could no longer forestall the old man's persistence he sent the check back to him, and told him he just could not be a party to what could very well turn into a disaster. Edward conveniently lived four hundred miles away, too much distance to be accommodating.

Edward pondered the situation after Kevin filled him in. Why would he want another car after causing damage, injury and distress to himself, his family, other drivers and insurance agents? Edward surmised he was still attempting to feebly assert his independence, the possession of which he had acquired six months before, but could not manage; the ownership of which he was forced to cede to Roberta because it no longer brought the gratification he anticipated. In relinquishing his short-lived association with being the sole proprietor of his life, he became like a campfire slowly burning out after everyone has crawled off to their tents or RV's to search for sleep in the wilderness, flames intermittently and sporadically flaring from the dying coals, exerting all its energy to again become a flourishing blaze, only to have the park ranger come along and quash the fire with a bucket of water.

Despite his defeats, his scattered efforts at freedom continued for a year or so after he moved in with Roberta. At first it was the persistent whining and conniving for an automobile. When that came to naught, he took bus rides downtown without telling anyone he was leaving or where he was going. At the beginning of his rebellion, Roberta waited for him at the bus stop and scolded him as if he was a child crossing the street without permission, then she called for the police to find him when he did not return after a few hours. When he continued his forays, she firmly told him that she was responsible for his health and welfare and that he no longer was allowed to ride the bus wherever he damned well pleased. He must ask permission to travel anywhere and if he broke the rules he would be confined to the house. She also suggested to him that if he continued to be troublesome the decision might be made to move him to a residential care facility, which he knew as a nursing home where old people are sent to die because their families are unwilling to expend any effort caring for them. He gave up, and in the five years until his death, he never left the house except for the annual trips he made out to Arizona to visit his wife's grave, a pilgrimage for which he had to beg Roberta to allow him to take, journeys that were his last ditch efforts at maintaining any sovereignty he may have attained before his incarceration under Roberta's watch.

For one week in each of the five summers before his death, he caught a plane to Phoenix, checked into a hotel near the cemetery where his wife was buried, and every morning and every evening for seven days he rode in a taxi the five blocks to the cemetery. He sat on a concrete bench set strategically between his wife's grave and the ornate tomb of the bishop, sipping a cup of Dunkin Donuts coffee while he spoke about the past with the old woman in the grave beneath him.

When Kevin phoned Edward to tell him their father was making the trip to Phoenix, the brothers mused over the disasters the old man had initiated out there and wondered if another one might be on the horizon. Kevin said not to worry. Edward did. He didn't know why, but he did.

He had visions of his father hugging with both hands his steaming cup of coffee. Hot coffee, but not as hot as the desert temperature. He'd proudly announce to his wife that he had learned to write checks. Roberta tried to talk him into getting a credit card, but he wouldn't hear of it. In between the consequential news he came to share, the meaningful reports of the progress of grandchildren (Roberta's children, because he had met Edward's children only twice) the condition of his health, that the same Polish guy was Pope but he was getting kind of decrepit, that he still did not like the Mass in English and that the new pastor of the church in Chicago he attended with Roberta didn't look like he was old enough to shave, he also offered news of how the weather had been lately; the Cubs were in the cellar, again; he still watched Jeopardy and Wheel of Fortune, still watched Vanna; Mike Royko died, a Chicago newspaper columnist Edward's mother idolized because he, like her, had that crude way of hanging people out to dry. The difference was that Mike

Royko usually had a legitimate reason backed by fact and aimed at righting some political or social wrong. Edward's mother, on the other hand, saw no need for facts or legitimacy in her attacks. The old man would describe to her the room at the hotel where he was staying. It even contained a refrigerator and microwave, the latter a device the old man was unfamiliar with and therefore would not touch. He'd definitely not tell her about the three cars he wrecked. He had no desire to trouble her with such distressing news.

He'd tell her how miserable his life was without her, how he yearned for the days when just the two of them enjoyed the early mornings of the desert walking in the park down the street from their apartment, how he missed the certainty that came with having her around, the companionship, the sharing, her tolerance of his shortcomings and her patience with his moodiness. He'd never discuss her shortcomings, never utter a dissenting word about her abhorrent treatment of her youngest child, never speak of how she favored her daughter over her two sons, never admit to her that he thought she was wrong in many ways, and refrain from any of the complaints that had filled his mind for so many years about how she had never given her husband any credit for being an intelligent, competent adult even though he knew most of the time he wasn't.

He'd remind her that he had moved to Chicago to live with Roberta, just in case she had forgotten when he said goodbye the morning he left to make that lonely trip east. He'd inform her that nothing on earth had changed. He meant nothing had changed in the family but he would not elaborate. He saw that a lot had changed in Phoenix, but that was not important to him and he was sure it was unimportant to her. What he really meant was that the children had not changed. Roberta was still the intractable, commanding person she had been as a child, giving everyone orders, threatening them with physical punishment just short of murder and promoting herself to everyone as an extraordinary mother and an exceptional wife, and now with her father as a border, a marvelous daughter. She certainly was her mother's daughter.

Admittedly, Roberta could be quite rough, particularly with a person who leaned on her more than she was ordinarily likely to allow. Her crude demeanor, while confined to money matters and mobility when it came to her father, extended beyond a mere coarse deportment to a behavior that was both rude and uncultured. The origin of her unrefined manner was a matter for periodic debate between Edward and Kevin. Edward believed the source of a person's demeanor as an adult, even as an adolescent was a direct result of parental influence. Edward's mother's personality was one of resentment. She readily directed ill will at anyone who had higher income, greater wealth, better behaved children, a more expensive car, better health, a more advanced education (which was most people since his mother never went beyond the eighth grade), a finer wardrobe, thicker hair, polished speech and an opinion—political, social and religious—that was different than hers, particularly non Catholics. She derided those who were in any way different than she was, in any way had opinions that countered her beliefs, particularly her religious convictions, had, in any manner, a lifestyle that was counter to what she had. She lowered them to a position that gave her comfort in her struggle to be more and have more than she had, than she would ever have. She scoffed at them. She found fault with the commodities and circumstances they had and she didn't have.

Kevin, on the other hand, believed that everybody who was an asshole as an adult was born an asshole and nobody had any control over it.

Roberta mirrored her mother in every way, particularly in her feelings toward her brothers. Edward and Kevin had not been disenfranchised simply because they had better cars, or more education, or more success than either woman had ever experienced. They were forcibly ejected from good standing in the family because they had social, religious and political beliefs that directly contradicted those of their mother. Their contrary philosophies wounded her even more deeply because her sons at one time had the same beliefs as she. While she may have given limited acceptance to an insignificant conflict in political opinions (she allowed no deviation from religious doctrine), the reality that the two sons she carried, bore and raised could hold opinions that differed so much from hers, that contradicted what she firmly believed to be the only convictions that any self-respecting human being must hold, was more than she was able to absorb. Roberta, in a style that exemplified every offensive and ignominious trait her mother had acquired and all the slanderous words and deeds she had dispersed, carried on in her image and likeness not only against her brothers but against the descendants of all those who had over the years become targets of her mother's resentment.

The boys were also the same, the old man would probably tell his wife before he left the cemetery for the hotel. Kevin was approaching a third divorce. He still drank a lot, never could commit himself to sobriety or fidelity. Edward, well, he didn't know much about Edward's life. Edward still did not communicate much with the family. He was right. What had always baffled Edward was that his father had no clue as to why. He'd finish up his day at the cemetery with "I love you; I miss you," then walk to the phone to call a taxi.

He'd shed many tears in the hours sitting on that bench. In the indifferent, simple way he had worshipped all of his life, he'd pray for her soul and pray to her neighbor the bishop to help save her soul. Before he left her on the last day he'd tell her he would trade everything, even the transitory freedom he had enjoyed before Roberta stole it away from him and longed to have again, to have her back with him. After each morning visit he'd return to his hotel room to take a nap, watch television and read the *TV Guide* he'd buy at the drug store down the street from the hotel. After each evening visit he'd return to the hotel, turn out the lights, probably sob for a while and then fall asleep.

He had planned to make this pilgrimage every year as long

as he was physically able. Despite the insistence of Roberta that he was in no condition to travel that long distance, he made the trip each year and brought back many I told you so's. He was proud of his ability to make such a trip, particularly at his age.

That is how Edward saw his father when he visited his wife in Phoenix. Maybe Edward was too presumptuous. Knowing his father as he did, he probably just sat at her grave and said nothing, because he never had anything to say.

VII

The tribulations of weekly confession and the annoyance of Father O'Connor changed abruptly four months before the end of Edward's seventh grade. Father Healey arrived to replace Father O'Connor who went on to bigger and better things as pastor of a parish on the north side of Chicago, somewhere near Evanston, where the people were economically sound and where one well-off parishioner's ability to tithe there was dollar for dollar much greater than any ten mill workers' contributions at St. Clem's. He could hear their sins though there probably wouldn't be many. Rich people didn't sin.

At first, though the boys of St. Clem's hoped for the best, they were not convinced that Father Healey was any different than Father O'Connor. As their only experience with priests was either mean and arrogant or feeble and deaf, they figured any new priest had to be one or the other. Father Healey had a severe look to him, taut lines in his forehead and cheeks, his chin like it was stretched to the breaking point. The rigid way he stood and moved, even the way he said Mass made everything around him appear unyielding, uncompromising.

The boy's perceptions changed when, a month after Father Healey arrived, those boys who were told to *Go to the priest!* returned calm and sometimes even remorseful. Imagine that. At recess on those days when a student had been told to *Go to the priest!* and returned with a penitent countenance, he was badgered to tell the others what went on with Father Healey. The most recent casualties told amazing tales of how Father Healey was really nice, a good guy, strict but understanding. Very calm. And this from twelve year olds. Even Jesse, the adolescent criminal who rarely had anything nice to say about anyone, said Father Healey was a pleasant man. Can you imagine, *a pleasant man*, from Jesse.

Edward's first experience, and the most momentous in his young life, with the new priest, was a one on one, or really two on one, that took place when he served mass for Father Healey three weeks after the priest arrived at St. Clem's. It was a seven o'clock mass, the early one, when the sky is still dark, the streets deserted, the church ghostly silent. But even that early in the morning, no matter what day it was, the back door to the church that entered directly into the sacristy behind the altar was always unlocked. Edward never figured out who unlocked it each morning because no one was ever there when he arrived at six thirty.

Edward's on again, off again friend, Frank, who had one of those names that did not have vowels in it, was his partner that day. It was a frigid February day, the kind of day when the January thaw has ended and black snow still sits in piles along the gutters of the streets where the plows had pushed it. The second half of winter had begun with a vengeance. It was on those days that the priest and altar boys and the handful of faithful who defied the early morning cold to seek their salvation were able to see their breath in the church.

The building was old, older than Father McMann, and frigid air seeped though the cracks in the window frames. The pastor started a fund raiser the year Edward was in sixth grade to raise money for new windows in the church and the school that was above the church. The money trickled in and the building still had the old leaky windows after Edward graduated two years later. Steel mill workers didn't have a lot to give to fix a church building. They had there own to take care of. Maybe if they had known how cold everyone would be when they were lying in their coffin at their funeral mass, they may have given more.

Edward's father gave twenty dollars, and that was at the insistence of Edward's mother, not much when he made a hell of a lot more money than the mill workers.

People never took their coats off when they attended mass at St. Clem's in the winter. Fortunately, altar boys had the added clothing of cassock and surplice so they didn't have to wear their coats. And when they lit the candles, they stood close to the flame to get some brief pleasure from its warmth. The alter boys' responsibilities for the first mass of the day were to turn on the lights in the church, lay out the vestments for the priest, fill the cruets with water from the tap and wine from the cheap bottle of vino kept in a cabinet in the back of the sacristy. The candles had to be lit and then they put on their black cassocks and white surpluses.

When Father Healey arrived that morning, about fifteen minutes before mass was to begin, he walked in the door and went directly to the altar. He inspected everything, the cruets, the candles, the floor. He even looked at the ceiling and Edward could not decide whether he was looking for cobwebs or saying a quick prayer. Edward was frightened Father Healey might find something wrong and come in and ban Frank and he forever from being altar boys. He didn't. He came back to the sacristy and began to dress for mass. He was silent, with not even a glance at his assistants. The mass went well, no mistakes, at least none that Edward knew he made. With Father O'Connor the altar boys always made mistakes when he said mass. Even if they didn't make mistakes, Father O'Connor always found something to be annoyed about. And he let the boys know it when mass was over and the church empty. With Father McMann, the altar boys could make all the mistakes they wanted and the old deaf priest never knew. If he did know he never said anything to the altar boys. The people in the church didn't know if mistakes were made. They were sleepy and, if they came to mass that early in the morning, their minds were certainly on other more spiritual things than whether or not the altar boys were screwing up and not giving the audience the full benefit of an early morning religious experience.

When this particular mass ended, Father Healey gingerly removed his vestments, again not speaking or even acknowledging the boys presence until all the vestments were put away and the lights of the church dimmed. As Edward and Frank headed for the sacristy door, Father Healey turned to them and said "Thank you, it went very well." A thank you, from a priest. And then it happened. Something that no altar boy had ever dreamed could occur. Father Healey invited Edward and Frank to the rectory. "Have you boys had breakfast?" he asked them in a very gentle voice. They shook their heads. Normally when Edward served an early mass he skipped breakfast because it allowed him to sleep later. After mass he would run down to the corner store about a block from the church and buy a donut and some chocolate milk and, since he had thirty minutes before school started, he would read the comic section of the *Sun Times* while he ate his breakfast.

Father Healey told the boys to follow him. Edward and Frank walked behind the priest across the play ground, past the garage where the priests kept their cars that were furnished by the parish, and into the rectory. *Breakfast, he's going to feed us breakfast,* Edward thought incredulously, as they trudged behind the priest, all three bundled to the tops of their heads in scarves, jackets, gloves, ear muffs and stocking caps. Once inside Father Healey showed them where to put their coats and hats and he told Mrs. Harmon, the cook and housekeeper, that there were to be two more for breakfast. She looked at the boys with mild disdain, that *they* should even be invited to the rectory, a building she claimed as her domain, *and* that *she* had to fix breakfast for *them*.

The inside of the rectory, at least the part Mrs. Harmon let the intruders see, consisted of an entryway that led either to the interior of the first floor where closed doors offered a mysterious gloom, or to the stairs that led to the bedrooms on the second floor. The first door on the right was the dining room. The walls and floors were old and worn much like Mrs. Harmon, the air musty, so stale that it dominated the slight scent of frying bacon that wafted into the dining room every time Mrs. Harmon went through the swinging door leading to the kitchen. The dining room was dark. In the middle was a blackish colored table with six chairs and along the wall a narrow credenza piled with dishes and utensils. "You can sit anywhere except at that end," Father Healey instructed as he took his seat at the opposite end from where he pointed. "That's where Father McMann sits. When I first came to St. Clement's I made the mistake of sitting there." He chuckled. "Father McMann is very adamant about that being his seat and no one else shall use it." He chuckled again. Edward and Frank chuckled but not as heartily as Father Healey, only enough to be polite. They had to be polite. They owed him now for this meal they were about to receive.

Mrs. Harmon entered the room with a plate of scrambled eggs, bacon and toast in one hand and a glass of juice in the other. She placed the plate and glass before Father Healey and then retrieved a coffee pot from a hot plate on the credenza and filled his cup. Edward and Frank looked at each other, their eyes bright. Bacon and eggs. Edward only had bacon and eggs for breakfast on Sundays after church. His normal breakfast fare was hot oatmeal or cereal and maybe a banana cut up in it or the donut and chocolate milk at the corner store. Bacon and eggs on a Monday morning? He couldn't believe it. Neither could Frank.

As Mrs. Harmon spitefully placed Edward's plate and glass of juice in front of him, he said "Thank you." She mumbled something he could not understand, and then marched into the kitchen. She repeated the mumble when she gave Frank his plate. Later that morning, Edward and Frank debated what it was Mrs.' Harmon said to them when they had politely thanked her for the meal. Frank thought she said "Fuck you, you little shit." Edward said no, she would never say something like that. She is a good Christian woman. She probably said something like, "Fuck you,

you little shit, Amen." They laughed the rest of the day about Mrs. Harmon.

The boys never saw her again after she gave them their plates and juice and went storming into the kitchen mumbling her kind words. Edward thought she would have made a wonderful nun. The boys sat rigid in their chairs. Father Healey picked up his fork and was about to stab at his eggs when he motioned for the boys to eat. "Go ahead," he told them. "Don't let it get cold." "But what about saying grace?" Edward asked. Father Healey thought a moment. "I never say grace at breakfast. I just said a bunch of prayers at Mass and I think there were enough there to cover breakfast." The boys looked at other. They smiled. It was a smile of understanding, one that said this guy is all right. I think he will do just fine. Father Healey swallowed a forkful of eggs and then said, "I think Mrs. Harmon is a little put out with me. We don't usually invite students into the rectory." Then he leaned forward toward his guests and whispered. "She thinks she owns the place." He laughed. They laughed. They ate.

As their plates quickly emptied, Father Healey asked, "So Frank, what do you want to do with yourself?" Edward stared at Frank. He saw the blank look on Frank's face. It was a "huh" look. Edward was thinking the same thing Frank was. Do with yourself? What does he mean, do with yourself? Like they do with themselves in the basement when no one is around, or in the bathroom at night when their parents think they are taking baths. God, Edward thought, he didn't want to answer that question. Why did he have to ask that?

"What do you want to be?" Father Healey said, maybe realizing the boys didn't quite understand what he meant with the first question and wanting to clarify things. How can a twelve year old know what he wants to be. There's the usual professional baseball player, doctor, lawyer, policeman, fireman options. Edward didn't want to be any of those. Although there had been one career he had given some casual thought to, he really just wanted to be a twelve year old for a few more months and then maybe start thinking about the future.

Frank looked up from his plate, a strip of bacon hanging out of his mouth. "Uh, I don't know. I ain't thought about it much."

"You haven't thought about it much," Father Healey corrected. "Yea," Frank said not realizing he had been corrected. "Okay, Frank." He looked at Edward. "What about you Edward?" Edward looked at the ceiling, then at his plate pretending to be deep in thought and seriously contemplating what his future might look like. "Well, I haven't given it much thought either, Father." Edward investigated the ceiling again trying to find something, anything that would impress Father Healey. He suddenly liked the man and Edward wanted the new priest to like him. Edward wanted to be his favorite. Edward looked back at the priest. "A teacher maybe," he finally replied, "or maybe a priest." Frank dropped his fork. Edward looked back at the ceiling, this time not for ideas but because he had frightened himself with his own admission. Did he really say that? Was it a mistake, something that he said to score a point? Or was it something that suddenly rose out of him because there was some truth to it? He knew he had toyed with the idea recently, but to say it out loud now when he wasn't ready, and to a priest. Father Healey set his coffee cup on the saucer. It clattered lightly, spilling a few drops over its rim. *Teacher*, the first choice Edward offered, had been quickly forgotten by Father Healey. What he concentrated on, what his eyes told Edward was the most wonderful thing he had heard in a long time, was that the boy said he wanted to be a priest. Edward didn't really say he wanted to be a priest. He said "maybe a priest." But the "maybe" had been lost too. Edward could see Father Healey had been taken aback, surprised by Edward's astonishing admission. Edward was just as surprised. Father Healey smiled. Edward tried to smile back but it came out as a grimace. Edward quickly finished his breakfast, told the priest that school was about to start and excused himself from the table. Frank smiled lightly and followed Edward.

Somewhere along the line Edward must have decided he wanted to be a priest, or at least thought of it as an option, otherwise he wouldn't have blurted it out over bacon and eggs. But where? It was not a decision that just popped out of a person's mouth when eating bacon and eggs, or as an acknowledgment of gratitude for being offered bacon and eggs on a Monday morning at the rectory no less instead of eating a donut and chocolate milk down at the corner store where it was much colder than the rectory, and where he had to stand to eat and not sit in a comfortable high back chair. But no matter how hard or how long he thought of where it came from, how he became unexpectedly inspired to say what he said in front of Father Healey and Frank, who, by the way, had the biggest mouth in the school, he could not come up with a reasonable explanation.

True, it had crossed his mind before, numerous times. Many times Edward watched the priest say mass and he was mesmerized by how deftly the man, particularly Father O'Connor moved upon the altar, how easily the hundreds of Latin words he had to say each day just rolled off his tongue.

Edward had even pretended he was a priest. Like some boys pretend they are athletes making the big run or scoring the big touchdown, or a soldier defeating a squad of enemy soldiers, Edward had numerous times pretended he was saying mass. He played mass on the ping-pong table in the basement of his home. White bread cut out of a bread slice with a glass was his host; grape juice his wine; a wine goblet from his mother's china cabinet his chalice. He said the whole mass, what he could remember of it. He used an old dictionary as the book the priests use to say the prayers at Mass. He had all the moves, the graceful motion of the arms, the solemn blessing given to the congregation. Edward was a natural priest. Whenever he said his counterfeit mass in the basement on the ping-pong table, it was inevitable that at the moment he raised the piece of bread up to heaven, or just as he blessed the wine or blessed the congregation or read a prayer, Kevin came down stairs and said "What the fuck are you doing?" Edward always ignored him and went on with his priestly duties. Kevin would walk back up the stairs mumbling how his little brother was an asshole.

In fact, Edward had mused over the prospect of the priesthood the night before he had the bacon and eggs. It was the night his sister, sixteen at the time, confessed to his parents that she was pregnant. As Edward's friend, Jesse, often said when he got in trouble with his parents, the shit really hit the fan that night.

Perhaps thinking of the priesthood was Edward's way of removing himself from a family that had no direction. He certainly did not think his contemplation of that particular vocation was the result of some overpowering force that enveloped him when he took his First Holy Communion or Confirmation. It must have come later somewhere between the stinging of Sister Mary Hortense's thirty-six inch enforcement weapon and the menacing glare of Sister Mary Norbert. But as they say, the die had been cast straight from his big mouth full of bacon and eggs, and he was reluctant to change his mind, particularly now that his statement had accomplished the one immediate thing he wanted— he was Father Healey's favorite.

Father Healey had nothing to do with Edward choosing to study for the priesthood but he did have something to do with it's realization. Edward believed Father Healey's role was as a patron, or maybe defender more properly described it. Once Edward had made that single announcement and did not back down from it, Father Healey seemed to be always at his side or shadowing him. Perhaps it was not that he wanted to help Edward along the path to the priesthood but, rather, that he wanted to catch the boy should he stray from that path and quickly guide him back in the right direction. Whatever it was, the priest treated Edward like he was a professional boxer and Father Healey was the promoter.

Edward speculated that how and why he made the decision to become a priest was because the shelter and security the church offered him when he required a safe haven produced inside him a susceptibility, no matter how invalid it may have been, to be obligated to that church and to everything it represented. Edward felt he owed the church something. Maybe. Maybe not.

Growing up on the south side of Chicago was hazardous. Even at St. Clem's there were plenty of clashes between boys at school, particularly when nationality played a part in any conflict that arose. Edward was not a fighter. He was afraid to fight. He despised pain. Fighting produced pain. But he also had an aversion to inflicting pain on someone else. He shied away from conflict not only to prevent his own discomfort but also to avert suffering on the part of anyone who may be caused pain because of him. A noble reason. But one that was not nearly as controlling as eluding that one thing that was phobic to him—pain. So maybe a small portion of his intentions to avoid conflict were honorable but, for the most part, he avoided it simply because he did not like the result of being hit upon, and at St. Clem's conflict usually involved being hit upon.

If a fight broke out between two boys, particularly if Edward was one of them, or if a boy did not like something Edward said or did or didn't do, and threatened to beat the snot out of him, Edward scurried, sometimes scrambled, to the church, kneeled in a pew and prayed. Many times he stayed through the recess or the lunch time, whenever the incident occurred, and prayed and sometimes cried, and prayed some more. He derived pleasure from praying, but he was always praying for himself, usually to keep himself out of harm's way.

There was only one incident that was a deviation from Edward's normal run toward the church sanctuary. During an afternoon recess while he and his friends played "run across," a game where one boy out of about twenty stood in the middle of a grassless field behind the school and tried to tackle, not tag, tackle, the others as they ran across to the other side of the field. As one was tackled he joined the first one and each subsequent boy tackled joined the others until only one boy remained to run across the field trying to avoid the shoves and pushes and dives and bumps of nineteen others trying to tackle him. On one of those days that resulted in many torn shirts and ripped pants, Mickey Bandera, Mary Jo's older brother, spat in Edward's face as Edward tried to tackle him. Edward discovered at that moment that one thing that really pissed him off was to have someone's spit dripping from his forehead and nose. Mickey was just about Edward's size, slightly built and maybe shorter by an inch. But at that moment as Edward felt the spit on his skin, size didn't matter. He was angry enough to even pounce on Evan McAllister, a boy his age but forty pounds heavier and four inches taller. But he didn't because Evan hadn't done a thing to Edward on that day. But Mickey did.

Edward stopped in mid stride and drove his fist into the side of Mickey's head. He fell hard, kicking up dust as his body skidded a few inches along the rocks and dirt. Edward stood over him. Blood ran down Mickey's cheek. He rose and ran toward the school building, but Edward was not finished. He ran after him, grabbed Mickey's neck and arm and shoved him head first into a barrel the school custodian used to burn paper. *Then* Edward went to the church. He prayed for Mickey and he prayed for himself. More for himself because he knew that Sister Mary Genevieve, the principal, would soon be on her way to drag him up to her office for fighting. And she did. For an hour after school Edward cleaned floors in the classrooms, with Mickey Bandera. For another hour after that the two boys wrote *Glory be to the Father and to the Son and to the Holy Ghost* one hundred times.

There were other dangers at St. Clem's and on the south side of Chicago that led Edward to believe his decision to go to the seminary, whether a spur of the moment decision over bacon and eggs or divine intervention, was made just in time. At age twelve in Chicago, on the south side, Edward knew he was on the verge of becoming the type of boy each of his friends was. It wasn't something deliberate, but he could feel himself on the edge, approaching a point where he would begin evolving into something he did not want to be. Perhaps that was not a problem for boys on the north side of Chicago, or in small towns, or in foreign countries. He didn't know about that then, nor did he care. He knew if he was to continue on the same road that nearly every other boy in the neighborhood had taken, he would be consumed by all the sordid and vile habits and vices that preyed on every boy who lived on the south side.

Edward could feel the change coming, much like the changes in his body he had been experiencing since the end of sixth grade. He was beginning to curse out loud. He had cursed plenty of times in his head, at the other boys, at Sister Mary Hortense or Sister Mary Norbert, at Fat Debbie, at his father. Many times at his father, even more than at Fat Debbie. But those curse words he had held in check for some time were beginning to flow across his lips. Not extensively, a damn here, a hell there, sometimes, though rarely, something worse. One time when Jesse had blindsided him when they were playing tag football, Edward said shit. Seldom anything more elegant than those three words.

The most popular thing the boys did was to give someone the finger. Edward couldn't, although he did realize that using the words shit, hell and damn, particularly when directed at some-one, were sins, venial sins, but sins nonetheless. But giving someone the finger, that was like silently saying fuck you, and in his mind there was no difference between saying it out loud and miming it. But as the pressure built, he eventually succumbed to the popular norm.

On a gray May afternoon during recess, Frank with the vowelless last name asked Edward if he could come over to Edward's house that evening and copy a paper that was due the next day. He hadn't even started writing the paper and he knew Edward always had his homework done on time. "No," Edward said quickly. "I don't let anyone copy my homework." Frank just stared at him for a moment then raised his right arm, extended his middle finger and stuck it in front of Edward's face. Frank,

Edward's fellow altar boy, the person he shared bacon and eggs with in the rectory when he made the most significant pronouncement of his young life, gave him the finger. Unlike other times when a middle finger was shoved into his face, he became angry, upset that someone who he thought was a good friend would tell him to get . . . you know. Edward watched Frank walk away. Edward grabbed his right hand and stared at it. Then he grabbed his middle finger. He raised it while holding the other fingers down. It came up halfway then went back down curled against his palm like the other fingers. Again he raised the finger halfway. He was wanting to raise it up but at the same time fighting to keep it from plunging him into a deep moral dilemma. He raised it again, this time all the way up. He felt his stomach tingle like it did when he was caught talking in line and a nun walks up behind him and says his name so everyone else in line can hear, or when he feels like he is about to throw up.

With finger extended Edward raised his arm up and aimed it at Frank, but Frank was already out of sight. It was a wasted finger. Edward scurried into church and prayed. He prayed for forgiveness for all the damns and hells, the one shit and the other words he had used indiscriminately. He prayed for forgiveness for giving the finger to someone, someone who was out of range no less. He prayed for forgiveness for touching Mary Jo Bandera's breasts although he had not touched them in a long time ever since he told Father Healey he was thinking about being a priest. He prayed and he cried, and he prayed again for forgiveness for even thinking about Mary Jo Bandera's breasts. He liked girls during seventh grade, but he never pursued them except for Mary Jo Bandera's breasts. The next Saturday he confessed all these sins to Father McMann who didn't hear anything Edward told him and gave Edward a penance and that was that.

When he started eighth grade, Edward, along with every other boy and girl in his class, impatiently waited for graduation. It was nine months away. He was going to the seminary and he vowed to keep himself pure through the entire year so his ascension to the role of seminarian would be undefiled. His friends didn't help much. They continued to raise their middle fingers in his presence. They added new words to their vocabulary like fuck and mother fuck and others. Mary Jo Bandera didn't help either. She came to school on the first day of eighth grade having matured considerably over the summer. The boys and girls coveted the role of being the ruling eighth graders, overseers of all the lesser grades, but they also could not wait until May when they could give up all of it.

Sister Mary Genevieve, the principal at St. Clem's, was shocked at Edward's choice of vocations since he had never given her, or anyone else for that matter, except Father Healey, any indication of his interest in the priesthood. The coolness toward Edward displayed by Sister Mary Genevieve through his first seven years of grammar school turned miraculously into incessant attention, even doting. The fat old nun ceaselessly slobbered over Edward calling him her "little seminarian" in front of the class. She mothered him until he began to feel the first regret of his decision.

VIII

It is peculiar how a relationship that is as bad as a person thinks it can get can decline even more. Even without either side making any effort to cause further deterioration, an already tenuous relationship can be hammered even lower than anybody involved in it can grasp, than a person's imagination can even contemplate. Granted, Edward and his father had a poor relationship for the entire time their lives intermingled. The old man contributed to the relationship as stingily as he gave Edward money to pay for activities that ordinary kids enjoyed or bought items that might make his family's life and their home more comfortable or tithed to the church. On the other hand, Edward contributed to it, at first as a young child, quite vigorously, making every effort possible to develop that father-son connection. But then, as he grew up Edward realized how fruitless were his offerings. So it was with quite a bit of uneasiness and doubt that, after his mother died and at the urging of his wife, he decided to make an effort to improve that relationship.

During the six years Edward's father lived with Roberta he visited him twice, both times very reluctantly. On the first visit he went to see him as an acutely injured son who was prepared to unilaterally offer an olive branch to, in Edward's estimation, an erratic father who really had no conception of what his lack of interest had wrought in his son's life. His father had lived with Roberta in Chicago nearly four years when Edward decided he should make such a gesture. He knew that since his father was eighty-four years old he had only a few years left. Making an effort to at least soften the animosity that existed between him and his parents when his mother was alive and between him and his father since she died, seemed to be a way to placate any guilt Edward may have had and, in a more selfish sense, to place the guilt on the old man where it belonged, but that he had failed to acknowledge as his.

It was the most difficult endeavor Edward had ever undertaken. It was troublesome because of those years of exclusion when he was exiled from family relationships because of words he had written twenty-five years before, because of a decision he had made to pursue a direction in his life that had not been sanctioned or accepted by his parents, because of his choice of spouse that was not of the same religion, because of whatever other reasons there might have been over the years. Edward had become expatriated, and he was never quite sure of the motive that caused the parents to relegate the son to a status that was outside the family circle, a circle that grew smaller, and a circle that gave Edward no reason to jump back in. But it was not merely those words he, hastily and without much thought for their consequences, wrote on a piece of note paper when he was nineteen; words that became his justification for leaving, for finding a different direction, for severing his intangible and indistinct relationship with his parents that had withered over the years. It was also the acts of repudiation randomly dispersed over two and one-half decades since he wrote that ignominious note.

His parents took an impenetrable position, one that was laden with letters of reproach, scathing tongue lashings on ruled notebook paper stuffed in envelopes without return addresses, spiteful letters issued to the son for not sending a birthday card, father's day card, anniversary card. It continued with the cessation of those same cards, to Edward at first, then later, apparently to intensify the condemnation that they felt had not sufficiently wounded him, to his children, their grandchildren. Edward's wife never received a card or any gesture of acknowledgment that she was even his wife or the mother of their grandchildren. It became even more disturbing when, the Christmas after his mother died, he and his children no longer received Christmas gifts or even cards. It was distressing when, two years after his father moved in with Roberta, he received a large manila envelope full of all the photographs of the grandchildren that he had sent to his parents over the years. No note, no explanation, no "Here's all the pictures you ever sent. Kiss my ass. Sincerely."

Edward questioned if his father was the one who had returned them; he believed it was Roberta who realized those chronicles of his family had no monetary value and therefore were to be given no room in her home. She probably thought they might even cause Edward's father to become teary eyed if he looked at them and then offer his own olive branch to his son. Doubtful, Edward knew, but Roberta's logic was always questionable. Roberta could not take that chance. Her mind always saw in everything the potential for damage to her position.

It was tormenting when, six months later, Edward received a large box of photographs that chronicled his own life from birth to his graduation from high school. Again, he pictured Roberta flinging the pictures into the box with no mention to her father that they were being discarded. But then, perhaps Edward's father never looked at them, never took one in his hands to admire the charm of his son as a toddler or the stature of that same child as an adult. "Where are those pictures of Edward, Roberta," he would say if he ever thought to ask. "Don't know, Father. Must have been lost in the move," Roberta would reply with a smirk.

"At least she, or maybe he, didn't just throw them into the trash," Teresa offered. Not much consolation, Edward thought. It might have been better if they had discarded them in the trash. Then he would never have known that they deemed them unimportant. The misery concluded with his finding out from Kevin six months after it occurred, that Roberta, and therefore Edward's father, moved to another city in another state. The new home was not far from where they had lived previously, just across the border in Indiana. They never told Edward. But then, his father had stopped sending cards long ago, so why should he think he would be informed of anything.

All these things, along with the barren years of his youth, acted with enormous force to prevent Edward from ever wanting to come face to face with his father again, or with Roberta, who he strongly believed orchestrated every act of defiance, every move to once and for all banish Edward from the family and, as a consequence reduce the number of heirs that were available to share in any fortune his father might possess upon his death. It was Teresa who persuaded Edward to make one last effort to regain some standing in the family and, perhaps as a by-product of that effort, sabotage Roberta's attempts at seducing Edward's father to change his will. Edward believed his father's will, that final manifestation of a person's true feelings to those people who think they have a stake in the final bequests, was what gave him the impetus to pay his father a visit.

The first visit, the one Teresa talked him into by using her natural grace and conviction, was requested by a letter Edward sent to his father four weeks in advance of the intended visit date. He figured advance notice offered all the parties the opportunity to consider the consequences of the visit. He had second thoughts every day as he pondered what he was up against. Teresa, the one person who had received from Edward's parents and Roberta what amounted to a demeaning position in the entire human race and had every reason to be offended, even hostile, by her inlaw's words and deeds, became more supportive, almost cheerleader like, as the day drew near. Apparently neither Edward's father nor his sister were inclined to postpone or cancel the visit. Their affability was unnerving although he was positive it never grew to the level of Teresa's. Edward suspected the worse, but Teresa had read differently the response to her husband's request for an audience.

That letter came a week after Edward sent his, typed and signed by his father in his illegible scrawl that had stupefied

Edward since he had learned to read because of its lack of control and purpose. The o's and c's and every other letter that had any kind of curvature to them appeared like black dots on the page as if he had sat down after composing the letter on his typewriter and, with a newly sharpened pencil, filled in all the letters, a desperate act to show his son that he really didn't care how the letter looked, that he wasn't serious about what he said, that while he was thinking whether he really wanted his son to visit he thought long and hard while letting his pencil run amok on the page. It was not signed *Dad*, but *Father*. the salutation simply said *Son*, not Edward, or Dear Edward or even Dear Son. "Sure you can come," he wrote. "I will be glad to see you on that day. If you bring the kids make sure they are not rambunctious. My heart is not as strong as it used to be."

Teresa read in all three sentences a positive attempt on the part of *Father* to try to make some conciliatory gesture to *Son*. Edward reread the lines to his wife as they had been interpreted in his mind. "You can come if you really think it's necessary. I hope you won't bring the kids. My heart will not allow a lengthy visit not because my heart is not strong but because my heart just isn't in it." It was not a weak heart that caused him distress, but a heart that had never been inclined to show any love or caring. It was a heart that was never tender and affectionate. It was a heart that never pumped through his veins a hug or a pat on the back or a palm rubbing the top of his son's head. "For God's sake," Edward said to Teresa, "I am bringing my children, his four grandchildren, three of whom he hasn't seen but one time before, and one he's never seen. Surely he wants to reconcile for them alone. Hell with me, think of the children." Edward had his doubts despite the hope-filled opinions periodically offered by his wife. He had his doubts about reconciliation. He had his doubts about the intentions of his father and sister. He had a lot of doubts.

If there had ever been any desire on his father's part for a settlement of the hostilities that had gone on for so long, the effort would have come sooner and the effort would not have been unilateral. It should have started at the old woman's funeral, but all Edward got out of him then was an assurance that his bowels were moving again. Perhaps they had plans to ridicule him face to face, to do battle and once and for all eliminate him from the fold. What was he walking into? Was it worth the effort? Would it provide an explanation to the lunacy that had consumed this family for the last thirty years, or provide a clarification as to why one letter, one lousy missive could disenfranchise a child for so long? Was that letter he wrote twenty-five years before so abhorrent, so offensive, did it wound them so badly that they felt it necessary to throw away that many years, to throw away one of their children, to wound so badly in return? Did they derive any benefit from their actions? Was it worth it to them?

Perhaps that letter of one hundred thirty-three inflammatory words Edward had written twenty-five years before had more meaning for them than it did for its author. Edward saw it then as a young adult's attempt at autonomy, dominion over self, control of his fate and, if it came to it, his doom. His father did not understand those concepts then. He may have understood them to some minor degree twenty-five years later because he had wanted them so much after his wife died and they were confiscated by Roberta when he moved in with her. For Edward, twenty-five years later he saw it the same way he did then. Perhaps the letter was not the most sensible method to convey those feelings to his parents, but it should not have been the cause of such dreadful behavior on their part. It should not have become Edward's curse. But the letter was in the past, the upcoming visit was what concerned him.

When the day arrived, rumblings assaulted Edward's gut. His entire GI tract was like rush hour in the big city, traffic wanting to get out on clogged roads but finding very little movement. Edward, Teresa and their four children drove up to Indiana the morning of the visit and checked into a hotel about two miles away from Roberta's house. Too close for Edward's comfort. He stayed in the hotel room, afraid to venture out and perhaps run into Roberta. Even the hotel lobby might be dangerous. He thought she might be out stalking him, trying to find a way to derail the visit. Teresa thought he was acting foolish but he had not yet fully prepared himself for the prospect of coming face to face with Roberta.

After ordering an early dinner he could not eat and scanning a newspaper that seemed to have no words, the family walked to the car. It was nearly five o'clock and time for the showdown. Edward stood next to the car door unable to open it, incapable of making the simple movement of pulling the handle. He did not want to do this. Teresa knew it, his kids knew it, but no one said a word to him. They waited patiently until he gathered the nerve to get into the car, start the engine and extend what should have been a five minute drive into a ten minute dawdle.

As they drove up the street of well manicured lawns and lots considerably larger than most residential areas, Edward felt the heat of dread consuming his body. When Kevin told him that Roberta had moved to Indiana, he described the inside of the house—four bedrooms, two and a half baths, family room in the full finished basement, formal dining room, immense living room and a kitchen that was equipped for the great chefs of Europe. Kevin had a knack for embellishment, Edward thought. But when Edward entered the house, he realized how Kevin had, if anything, left out some things in his description. It was a home, he was immediately convinced, that carried a lofty price tag, much more costly than Roberta could afford on the salary of an police officer. How much had his father contributed to the purchase of this manor? Teresa and Edward traded glances that simultaneously conjured up visions of Roberta brow beating her father into paying for most of the house he had insisted he share with her. In her name, of course.

Edward knocked, lightly at first, then again with barely an increase in force. Teresa rang the doorbell. Edward scowled at her. "Thank you very much," he grumbled. The door was answered by Roberta's oldest son, Edward's nephew Eric. A boy, once a boy, now a man, a boy when Edward saw him last. A kid with little ambition, scattered direction, suspect intelligence and a meager grasp of the world around him. He was an inconsequential kid, the kind whose performance in any occupation often is described as ordinary, who eternally lived at home with his mom, the kind of kid whose name was always on the tip of someone's tongue and was always known as what's his name. Inconsequential, unremembered.

"Hi, Eric," Edward said cordially as he and his brood entered the well appointed living room. "You here visiting grandpa, today?" "No," he responded with a look of dismay, "I live here." "Oh, sorry," Edward said consolingly. "What are you doing these days?" Again the look of dismay from Eric, as if Edward should even be asking such a question. *I should know this*, Edward thought, *shouldn't I?* "At the steel mill," Eric answered. "Been there sixteen years." He looked at Edward as if to add, *You stoop, don't you know anything? If you'd keep in touch, you'd know. If you wouldn't have been such a fuck for thirty years, you'd know what was going on in the family. You'd know that my brother, Willy, lost an arm working at the mill and has been on disability for six years.* Edward did know that, but had forgotten. *You'd know my sister, god damn it, you probably don't even know her name, has three kids and been divorced twice.* He knew of one divorce, but was not surprised it happened a second time. *You'd realize that there's more to life than being a selfish fuck. More than giving up your family.* He would have said all that the same way Roberta would have said it, in a mean, belittling manner. Edward could see in his eyes he wanted to say it. He had Roberta's eyes. But he didn't say it. He's lucky he didn't say it, Edward mused.

"Where's grandpa?" Edward asked, ready to make his escape before Eric could say anything Edward had anticipated him saying. Before he answered Edward actually thought that maybe he should prod him into vocalizing his feelings of loathing. Then he could react, he could counteract, and before long Edward would be banned from his sister's house and not have to go through this agonizing, and what will probably turn out to be, meaningless, event. "Upstairs," he said rudely and pointed vaguely into a void that existed somewhere in the upper most reaches of the house. If anyone had the keen ability to take any word, just one word was all he needed, in the English language and make it sound uncivil, it was Eric. And Roberta. Edward did not ask Eric if his mother was around. He figured she was either at work, working an extra shift to avoid a confrontation, or hiding somewhere in the immense house for the same reason. If she wanted to see her brother or challenge him, she certainly had the opportunity to make her presence known.

Standing at the bottom of the stairs Edward sensed immediately the general location of his father's room. The television blared Pat Sajac's mousy voice from a room somewhere in the blackness of the second story. The sound was so deafening it sounded like Pat was up there in person yelling at the top of his lungs, introducing the contestants, preparing them and millions of viewers for the amazing competition of cerebral inertia and manual proficiency.

He trudged up the stairs, his family in tow. He immediately spotted the door to his father's room as he turned the corner; the glare from the television lit his way. Edward stood at the door a moment surveying the room and the back of his father's scabbed and mottled bald head as he gazed at Vanna White marching back and forth delicately exposing letters to the applause of contestants and audience. Edward's family, as apprehensive as he was, maybe more so, stood behind him peeking into the room over his shoulder or under his arm. The decor was barren, impotent, devoid of any of the pictures or furniture Edward remembered from his parent's place in Tempe or from the high rise on seventy-fifth street in Chicago or the home on Avalon street also in Chicago where he grew up. Where had all his father's belongings gone? All the possessions he and his wife had shared at all those places? Had he sold them, stored them some where? Had Roberta prohibited him from bringing any of his self into her house? Had she sold his goods and pocketed the profit? Edward noted the absence of anything belonging to his father except the recliner, a La-Z-Boy he bought on sale in Arizona, the television, an old one that was beginning to lose some of its tint and hue and a TV tray, the kind Edward's mother played solitaire on when her back no longer allowed her to bend over the coffee table. If this was all the material goods that remained, when the time came for negotiations as to distribution to his heirs, a few moments and a flip of a coin would be adequate.

Teresa nudged Edward forward. He slowly walked around the recliner and positioned himself at an angle, allowing equal distance between the television and his father. At first the old man did not notice his son's intrusion into his space because his stare was so transfixed on the hypnotic medium before him. The television seemed to soothe him, to remove the loneliness that had overwhelmed him. Because of it he appeared detached from everything else around him as Vanna and Pat and the personalities he worshipped consumed him. Edward was sure that single piece of electronic equipment was his refuge from Roberta who, he was also sure, when she was not at work, terrorized him, pestered him, mishandled his needs which she had no inclination to understand and, had she even had the disposition to address those needs, Edward was positive she quickly claimed she had no time.

Before Edward spoke, his father cocked his head toward his son as one would when they sense movement out of the corner of the eye and turn abruptly to catch a glimpse of whatever it was that sped by. He sat up slightly in the chair barely decreasing the slump that had defined his posture his whole life. "Son!" he said in a voice of subdued surprise. Then he saw the rest of the family. Edward's children, one by one, stepped up and gave him a hug, brief and undefined. His return embrace was also vague, as if to an old acquaintance met briefly with uncertain remembrance as to what type of relationship had existed with that person many years before. Teresa stood next to Edward and waved to her father-in-law. He smiled weakly.

"How are you, Dad?"

"Oh, oh, fine son, I suppose."

"How do you like being back in Chicago?"

"Oh, it's okay, not like when I lived here before." He turned back toward the television. One of the contestants was buying a vowel, an "e" Edward thought.

"Has it changed a lot?" Edward asked. He watched Vanna walk from one letter to another. Pat watched Vanna, the contestants watched Vanna. The audience, everyone riveted to this show watched Vanna, but no one watched Vanna more than his father watched her. Edward saw his eyes lock onto every movement, every step, every clap of her hands. Edward's father was hot for Vanna.

"Dad, has it changed a lot?" Edward repeated with barely increased volume. He did not want to be forced to compete with a television. He had clashed with the volume of the television every night as he was growing up. His home work against the Wednesday night fights; his telephone calls against the Gary Moore or Lawrence Welk or Ed Sullivan shows; his questions to his father against hours and hours of television, the volume always accommodating to his gradually worsening deafness.

Teresa nudged Edward again. "Can't he turn that thing off?" she asked.

Edward shook his head and sardonically murmured. "That's Vanna White your talking about."

"Can't he at least turn it down."

Again Edward came to his defense. "He's deaf. If he turned it down he wouldn't be able to hear Vanna."

Teresa gave her husband her standard bullshit look. "She doesn't say a damn thing until the end, then its some insipid response to Pat Sajac's pointless remark."

Edward considered his wife's argument. Although logical and well presented, no argument in the world, no matter how analytical and sensible could pull his father away from Vanna White.

The second puzzle was on the board. Vanna was ready to work her magic when a correct letter was called or to pout with disappointment if the letter called was not on the board. The first puzzle, won by a mousy young woman who clapped as if her hands hurt each time the wheel was spun, was a place. The second puzzle, a thing, was already full of six consonants and a vowel. Edward stared at the four word phrase. A thing, he wondered, a thing.

"I got a set of drums last Christmas, Grandpa," Edward's oldest son, Phillip, announced. "I'm taking lessons."

A commercial. The old man turned to Edward. "What did you say, son?" Edward pointed to Phillip. Phillip repeated his announcement. "Well, that's nice," the old man responded pleasantly but with little interest. He checked the screen, then turned back to his guests while there was still time, before Vanna returned, to ask questions of him.

They had run out of questions. Three questions and two statements and they were finished. The children found insignificant ways to display their discomfort. Phillip stared out the window periodically exhaling a barely noticeable sigh, a sign to his parents that he was ready to depart, that there was no compelling reason to stay. Edward thought so too but he was inclined for reasons he could not determine to try one more time, to stick it out just a little longer. Edward's daughter, Rita, stood to the other side of her grandfather, her vacant stare shifting like windshield wipers on intermittent, to and fro from television to grandfather, as if she were trying to make the best choice. Which one was more interesting, which one more likely to respond. It was a tough decision. Edward's middle son, Richard, looked at an old copy of *TV Guide*. Edward wasn't sure if his father allowed others to handle the periodical he revered. Edward moved in front of Richard to hide his transgression. He hoped his son did not leave it mutilated in any manner. Edward's youngest son, Peter, four years old, showed no interest in a man he had never met who paid no attention to him and had never, in any way, even acknowledged his existence or ever acted like a grandfather to him. He never acted like a grandfather to any of them any more than he acted like a father to Edward.

"I hear you just got back from Phoenix. Out there for a week, were you?"

"Huh? Say again?" He cupped his hand over his ear but never averted his eyes away from the television.

"You went to Phoenix. How was it?"

Too late. Pat returned with a special prize on the wheel. Edward knew he should have spoken louder the first time. There were many times he should have spoken louder, when his words were not heard, even before his father became old and deafness was his excuse.

"Dad." No response

"Dad!"

"I'd like to buy an 'e', Pat."

"Dad, we're going to leave now."

"There are three 'ees'."

Rita had made the right choice. The television responded

In the car driving through the south side of Chicago toward Interstate 55, heading south to St. Louis and then home, the children made no comments about the disastrous visit that began and ended in less than fifteen minutes including unloading and loading the car of six people, and the near showdown with Eric. Teresa fumed. She was disgusted with her husband's family, not so much for how Edward had been and continued to be treated, but for the disrespect they paid to his children, her children, the old man's grandchildren. Silent since they left the old man, she opened up as they headed down the ramp to the highway. "That's not normal."

"What's not normal?" Edward asked not knowing if she was

referring to his father or the ruts, grooves and bumps that were, and continue to be, an integral part of an Illinois interstate.

"Your father, the way he treated your children, the way he treats me. How a television show is more important than his family, never mind that there have been problems with the relationship. I've had problems with my sisters and brothers, but I never, ever treated them that way."

"You've got to remember, that was Vanna White on the screen. It might have been different if it was *Jeopardy*," Edward said in jest. She was not amused. "Anyway, it is normal."

She gave her husband a quizzical look. "How could that be normal; how could any reasonable person think your father's actions were normal?"

"Believe me, it's normal. When I was a kid, as far back as I can remember, he very seldom spoke to anyone unless it was to give a direction, ask for something, or discipline one of us. Even those occasions were rare. I can remember times, uncommon though they were, he was a great believer in public transportation, when he drove me somewhere before I had my license and not one word was spoken between us. Even if I asked him a question he answered it in the most economical way he could. He always left for work before I woke. When he got home dinner was on the table. We ate in virtual silence. If I, or my brother, when he was there, or my sister, asked a question or made a comment, my mother answered or responded. The only time he spoke is when the three of us, usually my brother and sister, got into an argument at the table. Then it was 'Quiet!' in a loud gruff voice usually with a mouthful of food. The food spewed out of his mouth and we all looked at our plates trying not to laugh out loud. He continued to eat his dinner with specks of food scattered on the table cloth around his plate."

Teresa shook her head in disbelief. Edward continued his harangue. "I always wondered why he didn't talk. But, then, he was never there to talk even when he was there." Teresa looked confused. "When he was there, at home, his face was always plastered on the television or in the *TV Guide.* Where could I have talked to my father? What was the best location? Not a baseball game or a football game. If he had ever taken me to one it would have been too loud, too many people around. Not at the barbecue in the backyard. He had to concentrate there. Too much in and out of the house to get more sauce or salt or a beer. Not in the living room in front of the television. Definitely not in front of the television. Too much distraction. Too much competition. Maybe on a fishing trip. He enjoyed fishing. So did I. It was not a problem to bait a hook, flip it in the water and just sit and talk while waiting for a bite. No problem, I could wait. But he only took me fishing twice. When he became elderly, during those rare occasions when he and I were 'in the same room together, particularly when my mother died, I'd watch him talk to himself, not loud enough for me to hear the words, but in a mumble too low to understand. Perhaps he was letting out all those words that had built up over the years." Edward considered his last statement. "Or maybe not. Maybe he just never had any words."

"Did he ever talk to your mother?" Teresa asked Edward, not upset like she had been when the trip home began, but now rather intrigued that a father could act so indifferently toward his children.

"More often than he talked to his children," Edward said with what sounded like the beginning of resentment in his voice, an inflection that he was surprised had not become apparent immediately after they exited his father's room. "Usually at night. I could hear their muffled voices in their bedroom. I seldom heard what they talked about." Edward thought a moment about how, as a child, he was intrigued how grown up voices sounded from his room. Only a hallway separated his room from his parents but the deep gruff voice of his father and the soft, almost dainty voice of his mother had an echo quality as if they came from a distance and went through dramatic changes in pitch and tone by the time they entered Edward's room. Did they ever talk about him? Or was it Roberta, or Kevin? Dad's job? National Affairs? Did they wait until the children were asleep before they discussed the state of the economy, the political situation in Africa, the ramifications of Sputnik on our country's ability to maintain military parity with the Soviet Union? No, their conversations most likely never became that serious. Edward's mother never gave a shit about anything beyond her religion, her bridge club and her crossword puzzles. His father would never have been able to glean significant details about world affairs from his *TV Guide.*

Were their muffled dialogues, offered in the privacy of their bedroom, about intimacies that they shared after the lights went out and the children were asleep, or at least thought to be asleep? Doubtful. Edward saw little interest in intimacy between them, vague kisses goodnight, no hugs, no looks of affection. Affectionate behavior toward Edward and Kevin were non-existent. The only time Edward recalled his father touching him was when he peed in his pants in church when he was six because his father did not let him out of the pew to go to the bathroom. When he saw the wet spot in Edward's lap and the puddle forming on the pew between him and his son, he jumped up, grabbed his son's arm and hauled him outside. They silently sat in the car until mass ended, and when Edward's mother and brother and sister got to the car, they drove home in silence. The only word his father uttered in that ordeal was "damn" but he waited until he got out of the church to say it.

"Who taught you the facts of life?" Teresa asked, thus breaking Edward's concentration, thankfully, on one of the most dreadful moments of his life, being dragged out of church with his pants full of pee.

"Bobby O'Connell's dad. He gave me and Bobby *Playboys* and other magazines with naked women in them. And some books that didn't have pictures but were written in such a way that the reader could easily construct his own visions.

"So that's where you learned about sex?"

"There and at the barbershop."

"Where?" she asked with disbelief and amusement.

"The barbershop. My barber, my father's barber too, was a guy named Vinnie, Vinnie something. An Italian guy. Real short and squat. Like that guy who played on *Taxi*, you know, what was his name.

"Danny DeVito."

"Yea. He looked just like him. You know, all legs and chest with no midsection." She nodded, still smiling. "Anyway, he gave me *Playboys* too. Every time he cut my hair he shoved one in my face and, as he was snipping with the scissors, he'd point to a picture and say, 'Ya like that?' or 'How'd ya like to do that one.'" Teresa nudged Edward in the ribs and motioned to the kids. He looked in the rear-view mirror. Two were asleep, the youngest and the oldest, the other two were reading and were oblivious to what was being said in the front seat. "He even told me some of the things he did to women. That's where I got most of my ideas." Edward raised his eyebrows up and down for effect. Teresa ignored him.

"How old were you?" Teresa asked incredulously.

Edward thought a moment. "Let's see. I was probably twelve when the *Playboys* started. The next year I went away to the seminary, but when I came back, Vinnie was still there and still passing out the magazines to all the good little boys who sat in his chair."

Teresa shook her head. "Unbelievable." She laughed out loud. "Do you think Vinnie did the same thing with your father?"

Edward didn't answer. He just smiled. A seditious thought entered his mind. He thought of the stranger sitting in the back of the church at his mother's funeral.

"Why do you think your father never talked to you?" she asked.

"About sex?"

"About anything?"

Edward had pondered that question for years but he was never able to arrive at an acceptable answer, not even a reasonable speculation as to why his father stayed silent all those years while his children were growing up, getting into trouble, getting pregnant and moving away. It was not only his family members he neglected verbally. He spoke to no one, had no friends, maybe a few acquaintances like the men he played poker with, and seldom ventured out of the house to have any contact with people. Edward was baffled as to how he became as successful at his work as he was. Communication was not his strongest point. In fact it was not and, as far as Edward could tell, had never been, a part of his being, yet he had a position with some authority and responsibility, made a good salary and, from Edward's one visit to his father's office in the Sun Times Building in downtown Chicago when Edward was eleven years old, his father had a telephone on his desk which implied that he was obligated to demonstrate some communication skills.

After dinner each weeknight, his father set himself in front of the television and watched whatever caught his interest that particular evening. It there was a boxing match, that was his primary medium of entertainment. The Ed Sullivan Show, the Lawrence Welk show, the Garry Moore show. At ten o'clock, the news, then the monologue of Johnny Carson, then to bed. On weekends, the agenda was the same only stretched over more hours. Two nights a week, Wednesday and Friday, he went out on his own to O'Malleys, a bar on the far south side, where he sat on a bar stool until midnight, sipping beer, munching peanuts and saying nothing to anyone except "another beer" or "more nuts."

When Edward asked for his allowance each Saturday, five dollars a week to cover everything a teenager needed in life, his father simply reached for his wallet, pulled out a five dollar bill and handed it to his son, no "Here, son, have a good time," "Don't spend it on anything foolish," "Here's an extra five for something special you might want," just an exchange of currency as if he was paying an unwelcome invoice, a weekly bill that quieted his obligation for seven days.

When Edward was young, preadolescent, he had questions that most children of that age had assembled inside their minds, and an earnest appetite for answers that, if answered correctly and thoroughly, would guide him through the troublesome and abstract paths of life. At first they were questions about the stars (the few he was able to see in the middle of Chicago), or why do they have stop lights or what keeps the moon up in the sky or how many people live in Chicago. The answers were consistent, "I don't know." No discussion, no effort to find an answer or guide his son to some person, some book, some resource where an answer might be found. Edward truly believed his father did not know the answers nor did he care to know the answers. He only knew what he read in the *TV Guide* and Edward's questions went far beyond the trite and useless information found in that publication. As Edward grew older his questions turned to more practical concerns. *Can I use the car tonight? Can I have more allowance? Can I stay out past curfew? Can I go to Wisconsin for the weekend with some friends?* The answers changed to "No." No discussion, no effort to compromise, but still consistent. Unlike the inquiries of his earlier years, he knew the answers to Edward's questions asked as a teenager, and only had to wait for the questions so he could repeat his one word denial.

After a while Edward stopped asking questions when he realized how absurd his monologue had become, how laughable it was. When the questions ceased, the silence became more intense. The "I don't know's" and the "No's" vanished, not even a shake or a nod of the head. Any link the two may have had, however inadequate and incomplete it may have been, was gone and the cessation of speaking to each other clearly prophesized the estrangement that was to come.

Maybe the words simply could not flow from his mouth. Perhaps he had a physical or mental defect, a technical error in his biological makeup that impeded dialogue, that disallowed his thoughts turning into words or affirmations of feelings. Maybe his father and his father's father had the same aversion to exchanging words and handed down that aberration to their son. Or maybe he simply did not like people. What misery may have sullied his life to form such a dark cloud of absolute quiet over the man?

When he became elderly the lack of talk appeared to contaminate his character even further. Whenever Edward noticed him talking to himself, the discussions he had in this manner appeared serious. Was he talking to someone or just to himself? Or was he merely saying all the words that had been captured inside himself for so many years and all at once expressing all the opinions he had had, answering all the questions that had been asked of him, responding to expressions of resistance or opposition that had flooded his life. It was too late, for although Edward and others around him caught the mutterings, Edward did not care what words were now gushing forth from this old man.

Edward looked at Teresa. "I don't know," he answered.

The second visit to his father, one year later, was no different from the previous one. Except that instead of his family walking in on *Wheel of Fortune*, which Edward deliberately avoided this time, the old man was sitting in the same chair, in the same position, head cocked to the side, one arm hanging down toward the floor, watching *Jeopardy*. Roberta was again indisposed, probably spying on Edward from some adjacent room. Edward received the same steely stare from Eric, the look of revulsion nearly knocked him over. He endured the same lack of interest from his father. They stayed five minutes longer awaiting some sort of response, but found none was coming. They left. Edward was wrong. It didn't make any difference if it was *Wheel of Fortune* or *Jeopardy*.

In the car Edward answered Teresa again, the same question she had asked him last time, the same question for which he had been searching for an answer for the years since his mother died. He gave the same answer, the only answer he had. "I don't know."

PART II

IX

Edward's final year of grammar school, one year away from his leaving for the seminary, was the most dangerous. At least it seemed that way for Edward. It challenged him to keep on the right path. Perhaps it was just that now that he was sure where his life was going and of the path he had chosen (or at least he thought he knew where he was going), it was as if the sins and temptations that had always been there instantly became more apparent and had chosen him to invade at a time when he was most susceptible. He was exceedingly busy in the confessional that year.

He was also busy sorting out other dilemmas that confront twelve year olds. Actually, no matter what a person's age, that person has heroes who bring some definition to the person's life. For a twelve year old living on the south side of Chicago those heroes were people whose lives Edward wanted to imitate and to have the same results they did but whose lives he knew he never could even come close to living. People like Mickey Mantle and Minnie Minoso, Roger Maris, and Father Healey. They were his heroes when he was a boy growing up on the south side of Chicago.

There were boys in other parts of Chicago who had a greater opportunity than Edward to grow up like their heroes, even be heroes themselves. On the south side of the city it was different. The boys on the south side watched their heroes on television and then went outside and found that no matter what heroes they had, those heroes were never able to keep them from getting into fights, throwing bottles at the black boys that daringly road their bicycles through the white boys' neighborhood, sniffing glue or vandalizing a few homes, particularly those of the Hungarians and Czechoslovakians that lived in the neighborhood.

The Hungarians and Czechoslovakians were the best targets because when a rock was thrown through their windows or dirty words were painted on their doors, the police came but could not understand a word these people who had gotten off the boat from the old country a few months or a year before were saying. The cops nodded as if they understood, drove around the neighborhood once to look like they were hot on the trail of the culprits and then drove off. The cops were Irish or German or some other nationality and they didn't really care for Hungarians or Czechoslovakians or anyone else from those Eastern European countries. It was not that the cops liked the boys who were not immigrants and could speak English, they just liked the Hungarians and Czechoslovakians less.

There always were cops in the neighborhood. They drove up and down the streets next to the playground where the boys hung out. They parked at the corner and watched them play softball. They turned the corner as the boys pitched pennies on the sidewalk, and they took the boys' money because they said the boys were gambling. They drove up at night and took the beer away from the older boys who drank at the playground. They took the beer with them and the money from pitching pennies and probably used it to buy more beer. If they found hard liquor and weapons they took the boys away too. If the boys in the neighborhood had real heroes, not the ones on television, the cops might not have come down on them so hard. But they didn't have real heroes and the cops just knew the boys were always about to do something felonious. If they had real heroes they might have kept most of the men, and the boys who were on the verge of becoming men, from going to work in the steel mills for the rest of their lives and living in shabby houses in South Chicago.

On the south side of Chicago heroes changed when the young boys crossed that threshold from fourteen to fifteen. Edward didn't know who set that threshold or why it was set, but, for whatever reason, when the young boys turned fifteen they suddenly were accepted by the older boys and they garnered from the younger boys respect for their new position. The younger boys looked up to the older boys more for protection than anything else. The older boys didn't have much more than that to offer, but the younger boys felt secure with the older boys around because when trouble lurked in the neighborhood, which it invariably did, it was the older boys who brought out the baseball bats and chains and razors to protect their turf and give the younger boys peace of mind. Actually, it was *their* turf they were protecting and Edward doubted that, if the younger boys were ever threatened, the older boys would have lifted a finger to save their small asses. Nonetheless, the younger boys admired the older boys for protecting their turf too.

They called themselves the Sinners, the older boys. That was the name of the white boys' gang. On the west side of the neighborhood, the black side, it was the Blackstone Rangers. On the east side, the Hispanic side, it was the Saints. Mixed in were various smaller gangs that tried to make a name for themselves by insulting the girlfriend of a member of one of the main gangs or insulting a Saint or Sinner or Ranger gang member himself and forcing a confrontation in some neighborhood park or school yard. If there was no insult or no other clear reason to fight, gangs, out of boredom or maybe to keep themselves tuned up, fought each other just for the hell of it. Sometimes, when the younger boys believed it was safe, they tagged along behind (at least a block away) the Sinners whenever they took off to another neighborhood for a rumble with a rival gang. The younger boys remained safely hidden behind someone's porch or hedges while the older boys, the gang, rattled their chains or beat their baseball bats or ax handles against a light pole or trash can or children's' swing set, shouted insults at each other as a warm up to the main event and, if the cops had not arrived by then, swarmed at each other with weapons and fists flying. When the cops did show up, the younger boys watching the melee from a safe distance, hastily retreated back to their neighborhood followed closely by those older boys who had not been collared by the cops. For most of the younger boys, following the older boys to a rumble, or watching them and cheering them on when they assaulted strangers of a different color or nationality who invaded the neighborhood, was to see what it was going to be like when the younger boys turned fifteen, how they should act, how the older boys avoided danger, what were the best moves and the best weapons. For Edward, he was going to the seminary and, even before he had made that decision, he realized he was not tough enough or brave enough or mean and treacherous enough to spend his teenage years boasting of how many rival gang members he pounded or how many scars he had collected. Edward hated pain.

In the neighborhood where Edward lived, most of the other boys, particularly the older boys, those who were fifteen, sixteen and seventeen, had their hero but he wasn't anything like the heroes Edward wanted. For the younger boys their heroes were the older boys. For the older boys their heroes were themselves, and Gary Costello.

Gary Costello did not live in the neighborhood when Edward was on the verge of becoming an older boy. He did at one time but his address changed when he was sent to prison for stealing cars. When he got out of jail he didn't come back to the neighborhood to live. Instead, he instantly had money, a lot of money, a Cadillac, a big black Cadillac, and he lived on the north side of Chicago in a high rise apartment overlooking Lake Michigan, pretty close to where Father O'Conner's new parish was located. How he suddenly made all that money after sitting in jail for five years the younger boys didn't know. In fact, they had no inkling as to where all that money came from. Nor did they really care because he never spent any of it on them. The older boys knew where it came from and most of them wanted to know how they could get some of that kind of money too.

Gary Costello came back to the neighborhood one afternoon in June a few months after he was paroled. The older boys were laying on the grass under the huge cottonwood trees that bordered the grammar school playground where the older boys and younger boys hung out. The younger boys were playing a pick up game of softball, sixteen inch softball, the kind found only in Chicago. Real softball, with bare hands played on asphalt. When playing sixteen inch softball they were high spirited boys who always checked their sportsmanship at the gate.

After he parked his big Cadillac under the tree where the older boys were, the younger boys played their softball game with reduced interest as they watched the older boys flock around Gary Costello and his big black Cadillac. The younger boys didn't know Gary very well because they were only in the third and fourth grades when he went to prison, but they had heard the older boys talk of him in admiring tones. He had become a legend to them. He had become their hero.

He wasn't the kind of hero most people think of when making a list of heroes who had an impact on their lives. He wasn't a football or baseball star, not a great political celebrity or one who had discovered a breakthrough in cancer therapy. He certainly was not a saint. In the neighborhood though, to most of the boys, particularly the older boys, he was what they identified as their hero. The older boys identified with Gary Costello's big black Cadillac and the clothes he wore and how he had managed to purchase such an expensive car and such nice clothes, especially for just being paroled after five years in jail. They identified with where he lived and how he flashed his money around and how sometimes he had a very attractive woman sitting with him when he drove up. They identified with the pints of whiskey he pulled out of his trunk and handed out to the older boys. They identified with him especially when, as the sun began to set on summer evenings, the older boys and Gary Costello sat around his Cadillac parked under the cottonwood trees next to the grammar school playground and sniffed glue.

On summer nights the younger boys sometimes sat on the playground equipment and discussed girls and baseball and what it would be like when they were older and able to sit under the cottonwood trees as one of the older boys. They watched the older boys pull their white handkerchiefs out of the back pocket of their tight jeans, squeeze airplane glue from a tube into the center of the handkerchief, neatly fold it up, hold it against their noses and inhale deeply. After several deep breathes they laid down on the grass and sniffed some more. Then, when the airplane glue that made their handkerchiefs stick together was no longer potent, they opened bottles of whiskey, leaned against Gary Costello's Cadillac and passed around the bottle, then they sat on the grass and passed the bottle, then laid on the grass and passed the bottle. After the bottle was empty, they got in their cars and drove off to buy more whiskey or glue or look for trouble in some neighborhood where trouble was easily found.

The older girls who hung around with the older boys sniffed glue with them. After about thirty minutes of sniffing or drinking or sniffing and drinking, an older boy or two walked off behind the school building with one or two of the girls. Those who were not quick enough to claim one of the older girls laid down under the cottonwood trees and mumbled to each other about what they would do if they took a girl behind the school building. Gary Costello never had to take a girl behind the school building. He had plenty of women he took to his fancy apartment on the north side. If Edward had not heard their boasts, had not listened to them describe where they might put their hands and their lips and other parts of their body, he would never have known what the older boys were actually doing with the older girls behind the school building. Edward and his friends never saw any of the older boys and girls return from behind the building because the younger boys' parents called them home for the night and the only thing left for them was to lie in bed at night and imagine what had transpired.

Gary Costello was not Edward's hero. Neither were the older boys. They had their own heroes none of whom were people Edward wanted to emulate. He was forced to look for his heroes elsewhere.

As a younger boy in the neighborhood, Edward searched for his heroes in places where no one else thought to look. Father Healey was his hero until he was bounced out of the parish on the charge of being a person who actually cared about everyone.

Ronald, the choir teacher at St. Clem's, was his hero for a short time. The choir that Ronald led was composed of all those male seventh and eighth graders who had the slightest propensity for carrying a tune. There was no choir for girls. For a long time Edward thought it was because they could not sing. Boys could do things girls could not, they all knew that. Singing must have been one of those things. Of course, at that time, the conventional wisdom was that women were only good for six things: keeping house, cooking, being a secretary, but only before she was married and ready for number four, having children. Number five was being a teacher but the limitations for a secretary also applied here, and number six was to perform her wifely duties for her husband. Of course, the older girls who hung around with the older boys in the neighborhood were good for other things, but, until Edward was older, he wasn't quite sure what those things were. He had some vague notions, but he could only imagine. All the younger boys knew that the younger girls before they became older girls were really not good for anything, except maybe Mary Jo Bandera. So the girls at St. Clem's simply lost out. No choir.

Those boys who were chosen for the choir had a lot to be thankful for around Christmas and Easter. Those two holiday seasons were the only times during the year that the choir sang. It was much like being an altar boy. When there was a wedding or a funeral on a weekday and Edward and his friends were of the elite to be chosen to serve as altar boys for that occasion, they were excused from class for at least two hours, an hour to prepare the church and get dressed and an hour for the mass itself. Sometimes, if they could get the priest involved in some conversation about sports or a religious rite that they appeared interested in, they could extend that time by thirty minutes.

It was sometimes difficult to figure which was better at Christmas and Easter, altar boy or choir boy. In either case they were all festooned in white surplus, white cassock and red bow tie. They either sang the Christmas carols or the Easter hymns or were out on the altar answering the priest in Latin, moving the big book from one side of the altar to the other, pouring the water and wine into the chalice, or pouring the water over the priests hands and offering him a linen cloth that was slung over their wrists, ringing the bell at Consecration, kneeling, holding the shiny gold plated patent under people's chins when they received communion, feeling important that, should the Body of Christ fall from the priest's hands or slip off someone's tongue, they were there to catch it. It was a grand responsibility. It was important and it made them feel important. But so did standing in the choir loft singing their hearts out, everyone in the standing room only church watching them, smiling at them, feeling spiritual as the choir intoned those sacred songs.

About the first week of November choir practice began in earnest for the Christmas program. For Easter it was about a month before Easter Sunday whenever that would fall. For the first three weeks the boys in the choir were excused from class for an entire morning one day a week. Then it was two days a week. The week before Christmas they had choir practice every morning. If they were lucky they could·combine that once a week or twice a week practice with serving a funeral or wedding. If they were extraordinarily fortunate, they were chosen to serve midnight mass on Christmas eve so that during the last week prior to Christmas they had choir practice every morning and altar boy practice for

Christmas mass every afternoon. In eighth grade Edward missed an entire week of class the week before Christmas. He was chosen for that honor because he was going to the seminary. He sang for twenty minutes with the choir before mass began and then served mass.

To be chosen for the choir each boy had to audition. If an eighth grader was in the choir during seventh grade he was automatically in. So each September, about a week after school began, every seventh grade boy and those eighth grade boys not in the choir the previous year but who were interested in being in the choir, headed down to the choir loft in the back of the church and sang for Ronald. It was just Ronald and the boy whose turn it was. The others waited outside in the unheated entry way that went from the school to the church. Their ears clung to the door so they could listen intently to the screeches and squeals of the boy in the loft. They entered the church alphabetically and as each individual entered, the others stood outside the door shivering from the cold, each waiting his turn, and telling jokes and listening through the door and making fun of the nuns and talking in whispers about Mary Jo Bandera's breasts, in order to keep their minds and their stomachs calm.

Edward didn't know what criteria Ronald used to choose his choir boys. When a boy sang alone each one sounded like the one before him—high pitched and shrill. Together the choir sounded magnificent.

No one in the choir knew Ronald's last name nor from where he came. They knew he had an extraordinary voice and played the organ brilliantly. Other than that he was an unknown quantity. Edward's friend Jimmy Plecker had one time tried to trick Ronald into revealing his last name. He told him he wanted to send him a Christmas card but he didn't know where to send it. He figured if he got Ronald's address he could find his name. A stupid logic to begin with but his friends could expect no less from Jimmy. Ronald looked at him suspiciously knowing what Jimmy was up to. Then he smiled. "No problem," he said to

Jimmy. "Mail it to 9301 Commercial Avenue, Chicago, Illinois." After choir practice that morning Jimmy Plecker thought he had scored the greatest coup as the boys filed out of the church and made their way back to class. "See, I told you I could get it," Jimmy boasted. They all laughed. "You stoop," Frank with the vowelless last name said, "He gave you the address of St. Clem's."

After the end of the school year, Ronald always treated the eighth grade choir boys for a whole day of fun. There were eight boys from eighth grade in the choir that year which was half the male population of the eighth grade class. The day they chose for their outing, a Saturday, was cool, especially for June, and overcast. They went to Pizzeria Uno on Wells Street on the near north side of the city, for an early lunch and then after lunch planned to head to Riverview amusement park. When they walked out of the restaurant the overcast sky that had greeted them that morning had been replaced with dark rain clouds that began spilling thick rain drops on the concrete. They all looked at Ronald for guidance. Riverview was certainly out of the question now, at least until the rain stopped. Ronald thought for a moment and then told the boys to follow him. They ran through the rain stomping their feet down hard in each puddle they came to like the eighth graders they were, eight thirteen and fourteen year olds following a middle aged man in a trench coat down a back street of Chicago in the rain. After two blocks they came to a high rise apartment building.

"What's here," Edward asked. "This is where I live," Ronald announced. The boys smiled at each other. They finally knew where Ronald lived. But what they thought was their fortune and theirs alone was short lived. They discovered from Ronald that he had brought other eighth grade choir boys here in the past when similar circumstances of inclement weather occurred. He unlocked the front door and the boys followed him in.

As they entered his apartment they scoured the walls and rooms in anticipation of what each of them had at one time in their own minds imagined his apartment to look like. Edward did not know what the others had imagined. He had pictured something altogether different than what lay before him when he entered. Ronald's apartment on the fifteenth floor was eclectic before that word had come in vogue. The couch was leather, the two chairs sitting at angles to the fake fire place were thick upholstery, one like the velvet dress Edward's sister wore to Uncle Harry's wedding (his second), the other scratchy and rough like sitting on a cactus, or at least that's what he imagined it felt like because he had never sat on a cactus. Next to the window was a straight back chair with its seat covered in a red oil cloth like the booths in the restaurant on Commercial Avenue Edward and his friends sometimes went to early in the morning while waiting to transfer to another bus on their way to school. The end table was slate set in a dark wood while the coffee table was glass set in a metallic frame that shone like a freshly buffed car bumper. The dining area contained a square table made of metal, and what looked like linoleum, with soft cushioned metal chairs at each end. That room sat off the kitchen which Edward figured, for whatever reason, was off limits to the choir boys because when Jesse told Ronald he was going to get a drink of water and headed for the kitchen, Ronald jumped up from his seat and almost tackled Jesse. "No, no, I'll get you a drink. You sit down." It sounded more like a command than an offer from a considerate host. He called from the kitchen to ask if anyone else wanted anything to drink while he was in there. "No," they all called at once almost singing it like the choir boys they were.

Eight choir boys easily filled up the small indiscriminately furnished living room, sitting on the couch, the chairs, the arms of the chairs and the floor waiting for the rain to stop. Ronald told them they could look at his books in the black enamel bookcase that filled one entire wall of the room. Most everyone else failed to stir at that suggestion preferring to sit catatonic and mope that they could not be at Riverview Park. Edward rose from his seat made from his sister's velvet dress and strolled nonchalantly to the bookcase. He didn't want to appear too anxious to show an interest in books. Jesse and Frank got up and followed Edward. He knew they had no interest in books. They only had an interest in anything that belonged to other people. While Edward's interest was intellectual, or at least he felt like it could be, their's was purely to snoop. The three boys scanned the books that were crammed on each shelf, thick paperback novels on the lower shelves and fat tomes on subjects like history and anthropology on the top. One entire section was devoted to music: Broadway musicals, church music, the history of jazz, the history of blues, the history of every kind of music. Sheets and sheets of organ music, some yellowing on the edges, lay flat on the bottom shelf. At the very top at the end of the bookshelf near the dark corner of the room were a dozen thin volumes with shiny black covers titled *Erotica*. Jesse saw them first. They were barely within reach. For Jesse, though, anything was in reach. Jesse stood on his tip toes and slid one of the *Erotica* books off the shelf. He hugged it close to his chest and sneaked off to sit by the window with his back to everyone. Ronald was on the telephone and was involved in some low voiced secretive conversation with whoever was on the other end of the line. Frank decided not to take a chance of being caught snitching another *Erotica* from the shelf. He walked over to join Jesse at the window. Edward continued to examine the books on the lower shelves keeping his eyes averted from what might demand an extended visit to the confessional next Saturday should he chance a glance at them.

In a few minutes Jesse was back with the book. "Shit," he said. "What? What is it?" Edward said with a rather furtive glance at the book as Jesse raised it to its place on the shelf. Jesse motioned his eyes over to where Ronald sat, the receiver snugly tucked between ear and shoulder while he examined his finger nails. "He's a goddamn queer." "What?" Edward repeated. Jesse pointed to the book he had just looked at. "Those books, they're full of queers, naked guys doing it with each other. He's a goddamn fairy."

Frank stood by the window rolling his eyes. Jesus Christ,

Edward thought, Ronald, a queer. No way. He wanted to grab the book to see if Jesse was on the level but just as he raised his arm to the shelf, Ronald replaced the telephone receiver in its cradle. He walked right past Edward, Jesse and Frank and headed toward the window. Jesse followed behind Ronald, his left hand on his hip, his right hand held out limp and his hips swaying back and forth. The other boys looked up at Jesse's antics. Edward turned away.

Ronald, a queer. A fairy. Edward had never met a queer before, at least not anyone he knew was queer. In an instant he had lost a hero. Ronald walked back toward the group. Edward could not look at him. Frank just rolled his eyes again. Jesse was going from boy to boy whispering in each boy's ear that Ronald, Edward's hero Ronald, the greatest organ player he had ever known, Ronald who gave Edward a solo part in *Adeste Fideles* two Christmases ago at midnight mass, was a queer. Edward saw them all staring at Ronald, wiping their hands on their pants to obliterate any queer germs they might have picked up in his apartment. Ronald stood at the door to his apartment and slipped on his trench coat. He announced that the rain had stopped and they could still have plenty of time at Riverview if they left immediately. Queer or no queer the boys ran downstairs and caught the next bus. But the day was not the same. Edward's hero was a queer.

It is not as troublesome to a person's soul, to a person's well being and equilibrium to want a person to be your hero and never have them as one than to have a hero and lose him. Father Healey was Edward's hero, and when Father Healey left St. Clem's Edward found himself weighted down by the realization that his hero had been banished from the church and school where he had gained Edward's trust and admiration. Banished by nearly everyone, whether vocal or silent, in the parish. Had Edward made an error in judgment? Were his standards for choosing a hero wrong?

Ronald was his hero. Where did he decide, or was it decided

for him, that sexual orientation was a bar to being a hero? And that is if Ronald was actually queer. Edward depended on Jesse for that information. Not a reliable source. Edward had the perception that he was the only kid at St. Clem's that thought of Ronald as a hero. Ronald was intelligent, talented, kind and patient. He listened and seemed to genuinely care about his choir boys. He was an individual who appeared sincerely happy with his life. So why did his being a queer, or assumed by a group of moronic thirteen year olds to be a queer, turn Edward away from someone who had actually induced him through his admirable traits to look up to him?

Edward had two heroes and lost them, one because he had been cast aside by others and his second hero, because he had cast him aside himself because his peers passed judgment on him and Edward, at thirteen years old, was guided by what his peers thought and not by his own heart and mind. He had no one else to place in the hero category. The south side of Chicago was a piss poor source for heroes.

Edward had never looked to his father to be his hero though he longed for him to be. Edward always had the notion that a boy's father should be a hero to his son so that the son has someone close to him to point the way so that when the father passes on, the son can remember all the things about his father that gave him hero status and, if the son learns something from the father, the son can raise his own children with a little less effort expended.

Sadly, Edward realized, his father had a trait that caused some of Edward's neighborhood friends to raise his father to hero status. That trait was his flatulence. Edward's father was not in the least embarrassed by this trait of his. It wasn't a periodic social faux pas, not something that accidentally leaked out on occasion causing him to cover his mouth in embarrassment and maybe giggle and say "oops." His breaking wind was a constant barrage of gas that never seemed to bother him and never elicited a comment from him, as if every person on earth simply lifted their rear end and broke the silence with a fart. They were loud and rough and always caused embarrassment for Edward's mother . She would mildly scold her husband and he would say "Well, mother, I just can't help it." and go on with life. But Edward knew he could "help it" if he really wanted to. He could have muffled the sound instead of letting the rumble come screaming from his raised butt. Just the fact that he deliberately raised his butt up in the air to fart showed how premeditated his action was. Over time Edward got used to it and never even batted an eye when it happened even if other people not used to it were in the room. Edward figured he did it because he was not a social person and his farting was a defensive strategy to keep people away.

He had the ability to sit motionless for a long time, an inert quantity of breathing matter. From the time he finished dinner at around six thirty-five each and every evening to the end of Johnny Carson's monologue at about ten forty-five—over four hours of mental and physical immobility, the only perceptible movement was to change which leg was crossed or to raise up slightly on one elbow, lift his hip and fart; the only words spoken were to call to his wife to fetch him a beer from the refrigerator which she promptly did and then she went back to fingering the clicking beads on her rosary while she intently worked the *Chicago Tribune* crossword puzzle. Edward wondered how intently she was saying her rosary as she scribbled letters in the boxes.

His father was a still life. Like a canvas of fruit that had softened and looked colorless in its drab bowl or a vase of dull colored flowers setting forlornly on a table waiting to be daubed on to a canvas. But nobody ever picked up a brush to paint life into him and the fruit or flowers remained a still life, never to be embellished with bright colors that give spirit to what was a still life before the brush met canvas. His life was still while Edward's was moving. He could have moved with his son, even a little, maybe just a shove in a different direction than where Edward was heading when he thought his son's direction was a little off center or askew from where he thought it should be. But he never thought about where Edward should be; he never thought about where he should be. That's why he was never where Edward was.

As a teenager Edward feared he would end up like his father when he became an adult, immovable, unyielding to everything in the world that, in normal circumstances for a normal human being, forces movement. But his father was not a normal human being. Children are patterned after their parents more than they know. More than they might want to be. Not just in how the hair lays or how the corner of the mouth slants or in the gait. Edward didn't want to pattern after his father. He knew that early on. He made a powerful effort to not be like him and he was stonewalled by his father and his mother every step of the way.

Gary Costello exuded darkness—black clothes, black hair, like he was flaunting his evil. Where was Edward's father when, for a few fleeting moments in his young life, he thought Gary Costello was cool. Where was his father when Edward got his first hard on from a girl named Arlene and didn't know what to do? Where was he when his son ran into church all the time crying? Where was he when his son was looking for a hero?

X

The eyes of Edward's father rarely looked his son's way, and when they did he seemed to be staring toward the outskirts of something that had skimmed off his mind's atmosphere, far enough away so he was not forced to take in more than he wanted to; those eyes never focused on what was worthwhile in a son's life. His hands never touched his son or pointed in directions Edward should have gone. His gestures subtly revealed his lack of interest in anyone's life, even his own. His few words showed the scarcity and vague expressiveness of his voice. He never spanked Edward, never smacked him, shoved him, grabbed his arm, cuffed his neck. While other boys in the neighborhood often had the belt taken to their backsides, Edward was never touched, not once. Edward was jealous of the other boys, the one sin of envy he never confessed. A spanking once in a while, a cuff on the back of the head, even an occasional belt to the butt would have told him his father had some interest in his son. He never hugged Edward. Jimmy Bertels, Edward's on and off best friend in the neighborhood, did not have a father. His father died in a mill accident when Jimmy was five. Jimmy had no father to hug him or spank him. Jimmy really wanted a father. Edward thought about offering him his but then, it would not have changed anything for Jimmy.

Growing up and as an adult Edward avoided reading books, memoirs usually, where the authors wrote about their fathers describing them in terms that caused Edward to respect, even feel an intimacy for, a man he never met. In those books they told of great feats their fathers performed, of enormous odds they over came, of inspiring words they offered to their sons and daughters in exchange for nothing more than a mutual offering of the love they gave their offspring. Those writers described how their fathers sacrificed even the slightest pleasure to help bring the lives of their sons and daughters to fruition. Were there really fathers like that?

Ted Galinski lived around the corner on the street that intersected the street where Edward lived. His side yard, what there was of it, bordered the same alley that bordered Edward's backyard. But there was a tall wooden fence that separated his back yard from the alley and so Edward had to always go through the alley and walk around to the other side to get to Ted's back yard to call him out to play. Ted's father, when he was around, drank heavily, usually sitting on their front porch when the weather was tolerable. When he was done drinking he tossed the empty pint whiskey bottles into the grass where they sat until Ted's mother or one of his older brothers came out the next morning and picked up the one or two bottles Ted's father had finished off the night before, put it in a paper sack and then dumped it into the trash.

Ted's father worked at the steel mills like many of the fathers that lived in the neighborhood. He worked his normal shift plus a lot of overtime. When he wasn't working or sitting on the front porch pitching whiskey bottles, he was gone, no one knew where. He was gone for sometimes a week at a time. He went out to a bar on Sunday evening and did not return until Friday night when he handed the cash from his pay check to his wife minus enough to buy whiskey for the week, gave his sons a slap on the back and walked out to the front porch to open his first bottle. He never missed work when he took these mysterious leaves of absence from his family. Ted's mother knew that he never missed work because he always had a paycheck on Friday, enough because of the overtime, to pay the mortgage, feed and clothe the family and buy a paper sack full of pints.

It was rare to hear Ted talk about his father. When he did, he referred to him as "my ol' man" but always showed a nervous respect for him to his face, saying "Yes, sir" and "No, sir" whenever his father took the time to pull the bottle from his lips and say something to his son. Ted never said much to his friends about his father's lengthy absences, probably because he did not know any more about where his father had gone, or why, than did his mother or anyone else in the neighborhood. But in spite of all the drinking Ted's father indulged in, Edward never saw a bruise on Ted, nor on his mother or older brothers.

Then there was Ricky O'Connor, the kid who lived a block away across the street from the grammar school and whose father drank just as much as Ted's but he never left the house except to go to work at the mill. Ricky would have given anything if his father had been like Ted's and took some short vacations, especially after a few hours of binge drinking that was common for Mr. O'Connor, and hazardous for Ricky, his mother and his brother.

Edward met Ricky right after he and his family moved into the neighborhood. They moved from Milwaukee where his father had worked at a brewery. Edward had just turned nine. Ricky was nine and a half, a full seven months older than Edward. At that age when a boy's only goal in life is to become a teenager and to be able to do what teenagers do, seven months becomes significant. Ricky attended the public elementary school located just across the street from where he lived, the one where the kids of the neighborhood spent most of their waking hours when not in school, where the older boys sniffed their glue, drank their whiskey and took the older girls behind the school building after dark and where the younger boys played softball, basketball and tag football and watched the older boys sniff, drink and take the girls behind the school building.

While most of the kids in the neighborhood, the younger kids (the older boys went to high school or didn't go to school because they dropped out and went to work at the mills), at least the ones Edward hung around with, went to St. Clem's where they were able to forge lasting relationships because they were together during school as well as after school and on weekends, Edward and Ricky had difficulty at first getting to know each other. In fact, Ricky had trouble getting to know anyone in the neighborhood. When he first moved in, sometime in April, he rarely came out of his house. When he did venture out, he invariably had a black eye or fat lip or some bruise on his arm. The neighborhood kids at first thought he got into regular fights at school. Since he did not go to the same school as the others, and they didn't know what it was like at·the public school, they figured it must really be rough. And since they didn't know any of those things, they had no other reason to believe otherwise. Ricky didn't say anything about his cuts and bruises. When the other boys asked, he simply shrugged his shoulders and said, "Guess somebody got in my way." If he was pressed, he glared at whoever asked and told him "It ain't none of your business."

Edward got to know Ricky that first summer after he moved in. The neighborhood boys, the younger boys, were playing their ultimate summer game of demolition derby with their bicycles. They used old bicycles they found discarded by the railroad tracks or they picked up parts at the dump and put them together themselves. They didn't used their good bicycles because their parents would have killed them. They wore football helmets, some wore football shoulder pads if they had them and gloves. About ten of them, or sometimes more, if enough neighborhood kids were able to find enough parts and the right parts to put a bicycle together, sat on their bicycles against the fence that surrounded the school playground, half on one side and half on the other. When somebody said "go" they rode toward the middle and smashed into the nearest competitor trying to disable the other kid's vehicle. They rode around and around smashing and banging and crashing until one person and one bicycle was still rideable. That person was the winner. There was no prize, only the distinction of being the one whose bicycle made from junk outlasted everyone else's bicycle made from junk.

They played this game once each summer because the bicycles were so bent up and smashed that it took them an entire year to find parts and put bicycles together for the next year's event. No one ever got hurt at the demolition derbies. They were lucky.

That summer, as they prepared for the derby, Ricky asked Edward if he had a helmet he could borrow. Edward let him use his brother's since Kevin hadn't played football in years and wouldn't ever play it again. Ricky's bicycle looked in better shape than any of the others, no old or mismatched parts. The other boys figured it was his regular bicycle, but it was no big deal to them. It was his problem. After the derby ended that day Edward took what was left of his bike to his house. As he was shoving it under the porch until he could figure out which parts might be usable next year, Ricky walked into the yard rolling what was left of his bicycle. "Here's your helmet back," he said in a thankful tone. "I hope your brother doesn't get mad at you for letting me use it." Edward looked at the helmet. It looked no different than when he had handed it to Ricky before the derby. "He probably doesn't even remember he has it," Edward said laughing. "Want a popsicle?" he asked Ricky. "Sure," he answered.

They slowly ate their popsicles, a refreshing treat after a grueling competition on a hot day. They sat on the back porch swing and talked about the derby. They recalled all the slick and evasive moves they made, how Jerry Turner plowed into the back of Ricky's bicycle and put him out of the derby. He bent Ricky's back wheel and frame so it wouldn't move and shoved the kickstand into the spokes. Ricky told Edward he was furious at Turner for doing that and was about to hit him but then Jesse rammed Turner's bicycle tearing the wheel completely away from the frame. So instead of hitting Turner, Ricky just laughed and thanked Jesse for getting even for him. Edward described how Jesse got him too, how he came at him head on seeing if he would chicken out and swerve away before he hit Edward's front wheel head on. Edward didn't. Jesse didn't either. Jesse's bicycle was bigger and heavier than Edward's. The impact knocked

Edward off his bicycle and as the bicycle fell Jesse ran over it
and bent both wheels so badly Edward had to drag it off the field.
They laughed and talked some more. As Ricky described how
he had rammed others and disabled their bicycles, Edward noticed the bruises on his arms and neck. They weren't from the
derby because he never got hit that hard and seldom fell to the
ground. Edward wanted to ask him where he got them but he
knew how sensitive he was about his bruises, so he didn't.

As Ricky came to know the other boys better, Edward and
Jesse particularly, he invited them over to his house to play in
his basement. Every house in the neighborhood had a basement
and whenever the boys played inside, the basement, Edward's or
Ted's or Ricky's or Jesse's or someone else's, was where they were
found. The basements in the neighborhood were all the same. In
one corner was an old coal furnace that had been converted to
oil. Even after years of using oil to heat the houses, the basements smelled like coal and the floor beneath the furnace was
black from coal dust and slippery from oil. Everybody had their
most unwanted junk piled against the walls, boxes of old clothes,
old dishes, old furniture, anything old that, for whatever reason,
was saved but never used. Each house had an attic too, but that
was where they kept the good junk that was sometimes used, like
Christmas decorations, card tables and chairs and winter clothes
in the summer and summer clothes in the winter because they
did not have the space in the main part of the house. Edward's
basements had a washer, the kind with a wringer on the top.
When he started high school his mother got a modern automatic
washer. His family was the first. Clothes lines were strung from
wall to wall where the clothes pulled from the washing machine
were hung to dry in the winter. In the summer every yard had
clothes lines that seemed to always have clothes on them. Edward had a ping-pong table. So did Jesse. Ricky had an old pool
table that slanted at one corner so all the balls rolled to that
pocket. They played anyway. Most of the time they spent in the
basements they played ping-pong, pool, sometimes cards or they

just sat and talked about girls, baseball, cars and what it was going to be like when they went to high school.

The basements were large and open and, when there were more than two boys together at any one time, the parents of the boy whose house they chose that day adamantly prohibited them from playing upstairs. Once they began using Ricky's basement as an alternate place to congregate, it did not take them long to realize that his bruises and bumps and fat lips did not come from fights at school but from his father. Ricky's mother had the same identifying marks from a husband and father who, when filled with alcohol, could not keep his temper in check and filled his drunken evenings with bashing his wife and kids. After a while Ricky found a way to avoid being beat on by his father. He spent quite a bit of time in the basements of his friends, remaining there until late at night after he was sure his father had passed out, or gone out to drink somewhere else. Sometimes he stayed overnight if he had any doubts. His mother was not so lucky. She had no where to go, no one to go to.

One of the basements Ricky frequently used as a second home was Mario Messina's, the only Italian in the neighborhood or at least the only one that was identifiable as Italian since he had an Italian last name. There may have been some Italian women in the neighborhood who married Irish or German or Hungarian men but the neighborhood boys didn't know any for sure and they really didn't care. Mario was only half Italian. His mother was Irish and because of that the other boys cut him some slack. Mario's father was not a heavy drinker. His customary beverage choice was wine, not the beer and whisky that most of the other fathers in the neighborhood felt was necessary for their survival. But Mr. Messina liked women the way Mr. O'Connor and Mr. Galinski liked alcohol. Galinski's pint bottles seemed a mild diversion compared to Messina's collection of women. He threw his prick around like O'Connor threw back a shot.

In one of their many rendezvous in Edward's basement, one where Mario and Ted were not present, the other boys speculated that Mr. Messina was even doing it to Mrs. Galinski, on those nights when Ted's father was out on one his jaunts to who knows where — perhaps over to Mrs. Messina's to get even with the Italian gigolo who was screwing his wife. Probably not, but any opportunity to talk about men screwing women and women's breasts or any other talk, that, in some cases, due to their lack of concrete facts and inaccurate information received from the older boys in the neighborhood, was purely speculative, was, nonetheless, entertaining and arousing. Arousing, that is, for a thirteen year old who, at that age, has no idea what is in store for him when he is grown, and is limited as to how that arousal may be satisfied. Edward was quite fond of these discussions because they gave him a brief opportunity to enjoy the crudeness of boyhood before he was confined to the seminary and forced to rid himself of thoughts of fornication, women's bodies and all the details of the secular life that a priest has no business being part of or pondering.

They never told Mario, or Ted, of their notions about Mario's father's infidelity. Mario was not dumb. He probably knew anyway. Ted? Well, Ted was dumb. He was inclined to believe that his mother could do no wrong. There was enough wrong with his father and he must have figured that since his mother had her three sons she didn't need anyone else. Maybe she didn't. The neighborhood kids were just speculating anyway.

Most of the men in the neighborhood drank, some heavier than others. They usually stopped at a bar on the way home from the mill then at a liquor store to bring another bottle or six pack home. On Friday and Saturday nights they went out to the bars sometimes with their wives, sometimes not. It depended on their moods and their needs. Edward's father drank, moderately compared to Ted's father, or Ricky's. He rarely brought hard liquor home with him, never stopped at the liquor store on the way home. He drank beer mainly, sometimes bourbon and water. On Wednesday nights he went out by himself to O'Malleys, a bar a couple miles from his house. It was classier than the bars most of the men went too, but any bar on the south side of Chicago could never really be described as classy. On Friday nights he went out by himself again to O'Malley's. On Saturdays he took his wife with him, maybe as consolation for the two nights he left her home. Edward's father did not go around screwing other woman. Edward would have been rather amazed if someone had told him his father had another woman. Edward would pity the other woman or wonder if her IQ even came close to her chest size. Edward's father did not disappear for days at a time. He was a stay-at-home except for the occasional night out to the local bar by himself to drink four or five Busch Bavarian beers and munch on beer nuts while he stared at himself in the mirror behind the bar. He had plenty of time to stare but, apparently, he never saw anything.

When a child is young, the image of the ideal father is from the perspective of the child. An innocent child believes that the father is doing what a father should do. The child doesn't know any better; there is nothing with which to compare. When the child arrives at those years where being a teenager is clearly attainable and that is all the child waits for, that perspective changes. Then there is no such thing as an ideal father. Fathers can do nothing right. The perspective changes again, at least in most cases, when the teenager becomes an adult. The new adult contemplates childhood and realizes that the father had tried to do his best but the circumstances that make growing up so difficult and the circumstances of being a father did not mesh and the father and son were unable to engage in some type of consequential and substantial relationship. From the perspective of the father, the child is ideal until it grows to be a teenager, then the child is no longer ideal and the father wonders where he went wrong. That perspective also changes, for the most part, when the teenager becomes an adult. Edward's perspective never changed. He didn't think his father had a perspective of him.

Edward didn't think any of the boys in the neighborhood were able to elevate their fathers to hero status. Unless they admired their drinking, screwing other women, beating their wives and kids senseless, and going off for days at a time maybe to drink or screw or beat someone else senseless. Edward's father's vices were minor compared to the fathers of the other boys, but even Edward could not make his father his hero no matter how hard he tried because, while the other fathers had lives that were forever sporadic, they still had movement in their lives, energy. Mr. O'Connor may have often hit Ricky and Ricky's mother, but Edward also saw him put his arm around Ricky on rare occasions and talk to him and ask him how he was doing in school, and even as he was opening a bottle and Ricky knew what was to come that evening after his father had downed a pint, his father seemed to have some feeling for his son and maybe even was aching inside himself for what he would do to him later. And Mario's father had energy too, although Edward and his friends thought most of it was used on Mrs. Galinski. But even so, he talked to his son, explained things to him, touched him. Maybe their fathers had qualities that the sons wanted to model after. Edward had no hero. Father Healey was gone, Ronald was queer. His father was a still life. He was never present even when he was there.

XI

When it came to sex, ignorance was a curse for all the twelve year old boys in the neighborhood, an affliction that caused misery as a preteen, remained dormant within the person all of his life and only resurfaced when his children became that age and suddenly developed a hunger to know about sex. As a preteen, when Edward should have been sitting across from his father learning about where that thing that dangled between his legs should go and should not go and how it should go and what happens if it does go at the wrong time and so on and so on, Edward instead learned all about sex on the streets of South Chicago where most South Chicago boys learned all about it. And he learned it from Vinnie the barber.

Of course, "all about" was a relative term to boys in South Chicago, its meaning determined by what a person found out on the street about sex and how that figured in to what that person thought there was to know about sex and what that person already knew, or thought he already knew, about sex. When any one of the neighborhood boys got to one of those moments of understanding, moments that brought a new vision every day and sometimes more often, when he thought he finally knew everything there was to know about sex, something new and sometimes quite exotic was brought to his attention and his relativity was suddenly shattered.

When Edward went away to the seminary, he thought he knew everything about sex. He did, at least all the terms and where things go and how they go and when they should and shouldn't go and so on and so on. What he did not know, and what he began to suspect while at the seminary, is that no matter how many terms and ways a person may know, it is something altogether different when that thing that dangles between a boy's legs *wants* to go where it is supposed to go or, at age twelve and a seminarian, where it is not supposed to go.

Edward's father never told him about sex, never offered to, so Edward never had the opportunity to decline his offer. He only asked once when he was twelve years old. After that incident he never asked again and his father was secure knowing that his son would never bother him about a subject he had no desire to explore with his son, particularly a son whom he never explored anything with anyway.

One evening, a Monday night, Edward broached the subject with his father. It was a Monday because every Monday Father O'Connor, and later Father Healey, came into their classroom and, for one hour, taught them about the Church and Jesus and Mary and sin and faith and the entire extent of their religion. On one of those Mondays in eighth grade Father Healey split the class in two, girls and boys, and Sister Mary Norbert took the girls to talk to them about sex and Father Healey took the boys to talk to them about sex. Actually, on Mondays Father Healey spoke to the seventh and eighth graders about other topics too ranging from personal hygiene, a subject that for some in Edward's class was not taught at home (apparently Father Healey realized this and decided to take the initiative because hygiene was a frequent subject), to sports and responsibility and initiative with other common subjects thrown in.

It was a Monday night when Edward's mother was out playing bunco with the women from the neighborhood that he asked his father about hairy hands. When he began to introduce the subject to his father, he tried to be as tactful and discreet as possible, knowing full well that his father would immediately either turn the sound up on the television or tell Edward to go to bed if he knew from the start what it was his son was going to discuss with him, or attempt to discuss with him.

He was watching a boxing match, one of his favorite past times while sitting in his chair. He had a Busch Bavarian beer in his hand and a can of salted peanuts on the table. Edward told him that Father Healey came to his class that day to talk to them, but Edward tried to make his father believe that Father Healey's visit to his class was a special occasion and he came to his class to discuss something that was very significant for twelve and thirteen year old boys.

Edward's father continued to stare at the television as his son described Father Healey's visit. "He talked about something really important," Edward said. "In fact, he told us a lot of things that are really important, but he told us something that I wasn't quite sure about and I wanted to ask you what you thought."

"Uh huh."

Edward saw he was getting no where but pressed on. "You see, he told us that when you, when you . . . you know, when you . . ." His father glanced at him with monotone eyes, even though, from all the yelling and screaming on the television it appeared the boxing match he was watching had gotten exciting.

"What?"

"Well, what I want to know because Father Healey didn't really explain this and he didn't let us ask many questions, so when I was about to ask my question he told us that we were all out of time, so I thought I . . ."

"What! Ask me what?"

"He talked to us about, about," Edward whispered, "masturbation."

"About what?" His eyes were again on the boxing match. The last few punches were much more interesting than any question Edward could ask.

Edward increased the speed of his talking. "Well, Father Healey talked to us about masturbation and how bad it was and how it is just abusing our bodies . . ." He was getting up to turn off the television so Edward talked even faster. "And last week Frankie told a bunch of us that if you do that you get hair all over your hands and I was just wondering . . ." He didn't turn the television off, he turned it up louder. As he rushed back to his chair he said it was time for Edward to go to bed. "But." "Go to bed. Goodnight."

For several years after Edward worried about hairy hands and he always discretely checked the hands of other boys to see if it might be true. He figured that out of all the boys he saw every day there had to be some others who did that to themselves. But he never saw one hairy hand.

Edward's first experience with sex with another person was Peggy Petrazak. Grabbing Mary Jo Bandera's breasts was not sex. It was a game played by young boys just like the other games they played like goosing each other with rulers and pouring ketchup on Kotex pads and leaving them in people's mail boxes. It was fun and they got a charge out of it. They got a charge out of grabbing Mary Jo Bandera's breasts, not because they were aroused by it, but because it made her angry and embarrassed her and that is why they got a charge out of it. It was also a challenge to see who could grab her the most. It would not have been as much fun, or much of a challenge if they had grabbed her elbow or shoulder.

Peggy Petrazak was a year older than Edward. She lived a few doors down from him and they had known each other since Edward was five and she was six. About two weeks after he gradu-ated from grammar school and only two and a half months before he was to leave for the seminary Peggy saw Edward sitting alone under one of the big cottonwood trees at the playground. She walked over to him and asked him if he wanted to walk to Frank's with her, the market about three blocks from the playground across the street from the hospital. Sure, he told her, he had nothing better to do. She knew he was going to the seminary, everybody knew, and she had already told him she was going to miss him. She told him again as they walked to Frank's.

Frank's was more of a meat market than a grocery store. It had a few shelves full of soup and beans and peas and peaches and other fruits and vegetables in cans. There was a small frozen food section, although at that time in the late fifties and early sixties, few people in the neighborhood had a freezer large enough to store a lot of frozen goods. Neighborhood people could get milk at Frank's and butter and eggs. He had candy near the front counter and toilet paper near the door. There was a cooler with Nehi and RC Cola in it. For the most part though, the store was devoted to meat and cheese and for the other dry goods, frozen foods and dairy products people needed, they usually went to the A & P.

Frank's smelled like meat, not like a particular meat but a combination of ham and corn beef and liver sausage and sirloin and pork chops and every other kind of meat that sat on display in the meat cooler behind musty glass that looked like it had been cleaned with a slab of meat. The floors were made of wood like what is found in a slaughter house or on the floor of a back-woods cabin. The neighborhood kids never went into Frank's in bare feet for fear of getting splinters, although Frank wouldn't have minded if they came in with bare feet, and if they got splinters he would not have cared about that either. Frank didn't care about anything but meat.

Behind the counter stood Frank every hour of the day and every day of the week except Sunday when the store was closed. His apron, the color of every meat he sold in his store, some of it sold days before, clung to his bulging belly and was tied in the front. The apron string barely made it around him. No matter when Edward went into Frank's, at seven o'clock in the morning when it opened or seven o'clock in the evening when it closed, Frank stood behind that meat counter cutting chops and steaks for neighbors who regularly bought their meat there, slicing lunch meat very thin, and slicing bacon and wrapping everything, even the ring bologna that was already wrapped, in butcher paper. He could have wrapped a piece of meat in his sleep. He could have done anything to a piece of meat in his sleep. Frank knew meat. Frank did not know cleanliness.

At the cash register near the door stood Frank's wife, Alice, a stout woman, her white streaked hair always pulled tightly in a bun. She had the meat smell too. It permeated the entire interior of the building, and sometimes, on warm summer days, the smell could be detected a block away. If a person stayed in there too long, they too came out smelling like old roast beef. Barry Clark and Brian Katowski, boys who graduated from St. Clem's two years before Edward, were stock boys, but only part time. The store did not require much stocking. Frank took care of the meat and meat was more than half the store. Barry and Brian sometimes swept the floors although the floors never looked swept. For the most part though, Alice cleaned the place to the extent that she moved the meat smell around the store like dust swept off a table only to settle again at another location.

Edward opened the door for Peggy. A string of miniature sleigh bells anemically announced that someone was entering. Even blindfolded Edward would know he was in Frank's, the smell hit him so hard when he entered. Edward and Peggy walked to one of the coolers along the wall. Peggy picked out a grape soda and Edward got an RC. They paid Alice and left. Alice smiled at them. Her teeth were the color of meat. Outside they sat on a park bench that butted up against the brick wall of Frank's while Peggy talked about what she was going to do this summer, how she looked forward to starting her sophomore year at St. Francis De Sales High School over on the East Side and how she was going to miss Edward when he went away to the seminary. Edward didn't say much. She talked on and on mostly about herself. When they finished their sodas they walked back to the playground.

When they got back to the playground, she abruptly, and a little roughly, pulled Edward behind a tree and kissed him. She pressed him against the trunk of one of the big cottonwoods. The bark dug into his back. Edward felt her tongue pressing against his lips like a snake pressing against a bird cage with the door wired shut trying to get in and steal its dinner. He didn't know what to do. He resisted her wet tongue pressing harder and harder, his lips clamping tighter and tighter the more she pushed with her tongue. Finally she gave up. She smiled at her quarry. She licked her lips like she was savoring a meal she had just eaten. "You'll learn," she said. Edward felt a tingle in the thing that dangled between his legs, a quivering that grew steadily until he turned away from Peggy and faced the tree afraid she would see the bulge in his pants.

Why did she kiss him? And with her tongue attacking his lips like that. Edward had heard about that kind of kiss, but he never actually envisioned what exactly transpired when a kiss went beyond the lips. What had provoked her to do that? Peggy had a boyfriend, at least Edward thought she still did. Was she going to miss him that much? Was she what Father Healey had described as the evil that lurked all around waiting to pounce on innocent people who chose to serve God and tried to get them to renounce their vocation? Certainly not Peggy Petrazak. She was known to be a little loose, but not evil. Perhaps she thought Edward was a challenge because he was soon to become forbidden fruit. It was probably the same reason she flirted with the young good looking priests who came into their classrooms in grammar school to talk to them about serving God.

As the swelling subsided, at least partially, Edward told Peggy he had to go. She winked at him and smiled. "Write to me," she called, but he was already to the alley and too far to shout an answer. He wouldn't write. He couldn't write. Not now. Not ever. He ran into his room and shut the door. From the top drawer of his dresser he pulled out his rosary. While lying on his bed, he barely finished the first decade of Hail Marys because his mind kept wandering to Peggy, her tongue and the swelling. He rubbed his lips with his finger, and the tingling feeling that appeared when her tongue wet his lips overwhelmed him by the time he got to the first Our Father.

At night, in his bed, for the next two and a half months he felt Peggy's hand on his shoulder, her tongue searching for a way to get to his, and he still not knowing what it was all about. Nobody told him. It was one of those things a person thinks he knows about sex until someone shows him and then he realizes he didn't really know and wished he had never been shown. Edward had no one to ask except the other boys in the neighborhood. They would have only said how stupid he was for not trying to get to her tonsils too, whatever that meant. Edward would have found no solace in the taunts and ribbings the other boys would have heaped upon him had he mentioned his brief, but enlightening, encounter with Peggy Petrazak.

Edward's second experience with sex before he went to the seminary was one that he was unable to discuss with anyone. Nobody had told him about Charlie McDonald, a boy two years older than him who lived two doors down from Jesse. Probably because nobody knew.

Charlie led a reclusive life. He was smart, really smart. The other boys in the neighborhood had no tolerance for smart when smartness was all the person had. Charlie was inept at sports. He did not know how to ride a bicycle and when he walked he looked like he was about to lose his balance with every step. He did not move his arms when he walked. They hung stiffly by his side. His head wobbled and drifted from side to side when the rest of him was motionless. He always dressed in a long sleeve shirt even in hot summer weather. The shirt pocket was invariably full of pens. He rarely ventured outside except occasionally to walk to the store and once each summer to stand near the playground fence and watch the demolition derby. His father was dead, killed in a car wreck when Charlie was a baby. His mother worked two jobs and spent little time with her son. He was different than the rest of the boys, but he never showed any inclination to being weird. They all acknowledged him at those rare times when they saw him on the street. They even invited him to join in the derby, but he just shook his head and watched from a distance. Edward felt sorry for Charlie. Maybe some of the other boys did too but they never said so. He didn't know for sure.

That summer before Edward went to the seminary, a few days after he had his encounter with Peggy Petrazak , he was walking to Frank's to get an RC when he saw Charlie coming toward him. Edward smiled a meager smile and nodded his head. Charlie stopped. He had never stopped before in the few encounters Edward had had with him. He smiled, a broad grin. "I hear you're going away to the seminary," he said in a screechy voice that appeared on the verge of changing to a lower octave. Edward said yes, he was leaving in September. How did he hear that? Edward thought Charlie never talked to anyone in the neighborhood. Who might have told him?

Without a lag in the conversation he asked, "Do you want to come in and see my science project I'm doing for school?" School? Edward thought. This was July. School had ended. It was summer vacation. What was he doing working on a school project? Maybe he *was* weird, Edward thought. "Oh, I don't know if I have time, Charlie. I'm on my way to . . ." "Won't take long, come on." He grabbed Edward's arm and led him to the basement door at the rear of his house. Inside, the basement was just like all the others except where everyone else had a ping-pong table or pool table Charlie had a long table filled with bottles and tubes and books and a Bunsen burner. "I don't have a lot of time, Charlie," Edward repeated. He told Edward what he had to show him would only take a minute. He ducked into a room separated from the rest of the basement by a threadbare blanket. When he reappeared Edward nearly screamed. Sticking out of the zipper of his pants was the thing that dangled, a large thing that dangled, larger than any Edward had ever seen although he had to admit he had seen only a few and only in pictures.

"What the hell is this, Charlie?"

"What is what," he asked innocently.

"That," Edward pointed to his thing.

He looked down. "Oh, that. Do you want to touch it?

"No, no!" He was blocking the door, impeding Edward's escape from his huge thing dangling right there in front of him. Edward positioned himself on the other side of the table that held Charlie's science project, if that was *really* a science project he used as an excuse to lure Edward down to his basement. "Jesus Christ, Charlie, what is wrong with you. You're sick."

"Please touch it, please."

Edward ran for the door, scooting around the washing machine, but Charlie cut him off. He grabbed Edward's arm. He was strong, much stronger than Edward had anticipated. "Please touch it. If you touch mine, I'll touch yours." Edward felt like he was going to throw up. He felt a tingle in his stomach, then some rumbling. Not like the tingle he felt with Peggy Petrazak. Not at all like that. Charlie started to move Edward's arm toward his thing. "Charlie, if you make me touch that I'll tell my father and he'll come over here and cut it off and feed it to the dog." Charlie laughed, then suddenly stopped. He realized that maybe Edward was serious. He let go of his arm. Edward knew his father wouldn't do that. All his father would do would be to laugh and tell his son he should have kicked Charlie in the balls. But if he was watching a boxing match or a baseball game he wouldn't have even done that. Edward ran outside and never walked by Charlie McDonald's house again. He always went around the block or crossed the street.

That same summer Edward had another experience, more frightening than his encounter with either Charlie McDonald or Peggy Petrazak, although it was not a personal encounter, it was an event he realized he might have been a part of if luck, or whatever else might be watching over him, had not been on his side.

The first day of August that summer before he left for the seminary, a twelve year old boy was found dead in the basement of a new house being built three blocks down from where Edward lived. He had been strangled and sexually molested. Edward didn't know him because he lived on the other side of the railroad tracks and he was forbidden to associate with the boys who lived on the other side of the tracks. He was frightened. The other boys were frightened although none of them admitted they were. Edward's mother was frightened. All the mothers were frightened. When his father heard about the murder, he shrugged his shoulders and said "You got to be careful these days," and went back to his *TV Guide*. Edward stayed away from where the boy was murdered. If he had to go that direction he walked two blocks over and went around. He didn't go out as much and when he did he made sure he was with someone else. He spent a lot of time inside or at the playground, always with a group of kids around him. Edward was really looking forward to leaving for the seminary because he wouldn't have to worry so much about being murdered and molested.

About three weeks later, two weeks before he was to leave for the seminary, Edward's mother came in the door after shopping at Frank's. His father was watching a Cubs game. He was pondering his class schedule for the seminary. "They caught the person who killed that boy," she said as she unpacked the steaks and chops she bought at Frank's. She looked distressed. Edward looked up. His father glanced at her. "Yea, anybody we know?" he said jokingly. "As a matter of fact, yes. That strange boy who lives down the street, Charlie McDonald is his name I think." Edward went in the bathroom and threw up.

XII

Edward would not experience the kind of sex that involves more than a tongue attack and a hard on or an inconsequential intimacy with another person until he was a sophomore in college, but he had sexual urges long before that first momentous occasion, some so strong that they caused him to reconsider that great vocation he had chosen while swallowing a mouth full of bacon and eggs.

Getting an erection every time he looked at a girl was not, however, the reason he could use when he called his parents from St. Charles Preparatory Seminary in St. Louis in the middle of the second semester of his freshman year of high school and told them he wanted to come home, for good. When his mother asked why, his reasons were intentionally vague. If Edward had given any specifics on why he wanted to leave the seminary, his mother would have stammered for a moment and then promptly hung up the phone, and then, somewhere, sometime in the future, when he was vulnerable for attack, she would use his alibi of the flesh as ammunition against him.

Edward's mother had a knack for making a person feel guilty. She was skilled at impersonating a martyr. Whenever Edward or Kevin (but not Roberta) had crossed the line, by the time their mother finished with them, they were ashamed they had ever made the decision or did the deed that unleashed her portrayal of saint and sufferer. Later, when Edward had time to recall what led up to what amounted to a duel of wits, he and, he was sure, his brother, felt foolish they had ever told their mother what they did and why they did it.

Edward considered telling her the food was terrible at the seminary. "Your vocation demands that you make many sacrifices," she would have said. The manual labor was exhausting. No, that wouldn't work, same answer. "I just can't pin point it, Mom. I have this gut feeling that something is wrong. I have to come home."

"Now?" she demanded.

"Well," Edward sheepishly answered. "Tomorrow would be okay. Mom I get sick to my stomach every day. There is something really wrong here. I don't feel like I belong."

A sigh, a very heavy sigh aimed directly into the receiver so Edward got the whole effect of her disappointment and disdain. The martyr variety of sigh, the kind a person gets from the priest in the confessional when the sinner tells the same sin week after week after week. The variety of sigh that always precedes her ticking off a litany of suffering and sacrifices she has endured making a life for Edward and Kevin and Roberta. But all that did not come. Only the sigh. She never even tendered a sob. No weeping, no self immolation. She did urge Edward to stay and finish out the semester. Then, over the summer, he could consult with Father Quinn who replaced Father Healey. She was confident that after being brow beat by Father Quinn and badgered by her for the three months of the summer Edward might see his error in dropping out of the seminary before he had even given it the chance to work and he would yield to her request. It will work you know, she told him.

But Edward's mind was made up. His body had definitely made it unequivocally clear that the seminary was not for him. He had experienced the wonders of the flesh. Although still at arms length. But as the days trudged on, that distance was getting shorter and shorter.

When Edward returned home to Chicago the next evening,

Kevin met him at the train station. Edward knew he was in for rough treatment by the way Kevin greeted him.

"You're an asshole, you know that."

Well hello to you to, you butt. "What's wrong with you?" Edward asked defensively.

"Not a goddamn thing is wrong with me beside the fact I had to fucking drive out here at ten o'clock at night in a fucking neighborhood I wouldn't be caught dead in, or maybe I would if I stayed around here too long, to fucking pick you up. Goddamn freezing out here." Kevin was unable to form a coherent sentence without half of it containing terms that referred to sexual intercourse, bodily waste or some orifice of human anatomy except the ears, nose and mouth. Well, sometimes the mouth was used in association with one or more of the other three. And for the many years Edward had known him, all Kevin ever asked God for was to damn someone or something.

"Then why are you mad?"

"Don't give me that bullshit."

Edward stared at him across the roof of the car waiting for him to unlock the passenger side door. In the car Edward avoided his eyes. His eyes could be mean. "Ever since you fucking called yesterday, mom's been in bed crying her goddamn eyes out."

"Crying?" Edward asked, puzzled. She was so accommodating when they talked on the phone.

"Yea, tears flowing like a goddamn broken dike."

Edward remained silent for the remainder of the drive home, twenty-five minutes of agonizing over what manner of reception awaited him when he entered his home after his sudden departure from the one circumstance where his parents (actually only his mother because his father didn't care where his son was or what his son was doing) at least appeared to show some respect for him. What would his standing be now? Edward didn't want to contemplate the ramifications of his decision. However, he had no choice. The outlook appeared grim. He felt like a child who had played doctor with the girl next door and got caught. He knew there was substantial punishment awaiting him, but since he had never played doctor with the neighbor girl nor with any other little girl, he had no sense of the punishment they would inflict.

The ride home seemed faster than twenty-five minutes, not enough time for Edward to concoct a convincing rationale for his quick exit from the seminary. Kevin sped through the streets. The hour was late when the car turned into the drive. Their house had the only light on at that hour. A dim light barely radiating through sheer curtains.

The homes of Edward's friends, Jesse and Bobby and Ted and Michael were dark. Everything was dark. At the moment Edward's future also looked dark. He thought about how his friends were asleep, unaware of the peril he was walking into, untroubled by their friend's distress. Of course, they didn't even know Edward had returned home, but when they found out the next day, he was sure they would be most sympathetic. Edward noticed that Charlie McDonald's house was dark too and a for sale sign had been placed in the front yard.

At the door, Edward stopped. He took a deep breath, one that made his lungs ache, before he entered. Before Kevin could reach for the doorknob, Edward grabbed his arm. "Is Dad mad?" he asked.

Kevin shrugged. "You know Dad, he only gets pissed if Mom is pissed."

Then he was pissed, but not in the customary sense. What Kevin meant was that their Dad was pissed because their Mom was pissed because their Mom being pissed demanded that their Dad fend for himself for a while until their Mom got over being pissed. Who would get his beer for him, his late night ice cream sundae?

When Edward entered the front room, he strategically concealed himself behind Kevin. His father turned off the television got up from his chair and told Edward to go to bed. Then he left the room. Ordinarily, when he was angry, which was rare because ordinarily he didn't care, he would leave the television on although at lower volume, and offer up about three or four sentences about how what Edward, or Kevin, and occasionally, but not often, Roberta, had done, (since they never did anything together, there never was a conspiracy, thus they were always punished singly), had really hurt their mother to the point where she had one of her headaches.

This was serious, very serious. Edward had never seen his father turn *off* the television in the middle of Johnny Carson's monologue. This time he not only switched the television off in the middle of a joke, but went to bed without his nightly dish of vanilla ice cream with sliced bananas and chocolate sauce. He was definitely pissed. But he was not pissed at Edward directly. He was pissed that Edward's mother was pissed and thus in a roundabout way he was pissed at Edward.

Edward picked up his suitcase and walked toward the back to his bedroom. He had only been gone a month since he returned to the seminary after Christmas vacation and the house appeared enormous, like comparing the Empire State Building with a Quonset hut. His cell at the seminary was the hut, five feet by ten feet of metal walls on three sides. No comparison to the seven room brick ranch he grew up in and now returned to.

The house his parents and occasionally Kevin, when he was between jobs, lived in, and that Edward was now returning to, was a rental. His father saw no value in investments. No stocks, no bonds, no mortgage. Everyone else in the neighborhood had realized the American dream of owning their own home. Not Edward's father. It was another dream he shunned. Perhaps that was a consequence of his living during the depression. He was in his twenties at the beginning of the depression, certainly an age when such hardship left, in the least, permanent economic scars on a person who was on the threshold of making a life for himself. Edward thought much of his father's life was guided by his frugality. Renting a house instead of buying a home was just one measure of his austere lifestyle. Although Edward was aware his parents had a bank account, he would not have been surprised if he had caught either of them burying their cash in the back yard under the sand pile or stuffing it in the rafters of the garage.

Since the house the family lived in was owned by someone else, they never put much effort into the yard or the inside. Edward and Kevin cut the grass with a push mower and trimmed the bushes with a pair of rusty hinged hedge clippers. The landlord made repairs or improvements with little emphasis put on the latter. Inside the house the plaster walls were harsh white. One entered from a rectangular concrete and brick porch, high enough off the ground to provoke adolescents to see how far they could jump to the ground below. That's how Jimmy Bertels broke his arm. He jumped last and caught his foot on the ledge. Fell head first. His right arm broke his fall. After that the kids were forbidden to jump off the porch. They did it anyway.

The ledges were high enough to empower those same adolescents in the winter to gather an enormous mass of snow balls, seize the porch as their rampart and declare war on the boys who found cover behind the hedge that bordered the sidewalk in front of the house. Sometimes they put small stones in the snowballs and then plastered each other with them and sometimes bombarded the buses with them when they became bored with their war.

The living room, or as Edward's family called it, the front room, was wanting for character. In addition to being small, the room truly reflected Edward's parents' affinity for not spending money. Furniture was scarce and what was available was inadequate when comfort was called for. The fire place, presumably a source of warmth for previous tenants, was bricked up. But the brick work must not have been securely mortared because on cold winter days when the wind became fierce, tiny traces of cold air were felt by anyone sitting too close to the bricks.

Off the front room was a bedroom. It had sat empty for three years since Roberta became pregnant at age sixteen and was immediately ejected from the house and forced to marry the boy who made her that way. The room now contained nothing. It was a room that, for three years, Edward's mother contemplated changing into a guest room, a den, or a storage room. None of her plans ever came to fruition. They never had guests, so the guest room was a waste. Roberta never came back, at least not to stay overnight. Edward's father despised her husband. In actuality, the primary reason Roberta and her husband never came for an overnight visit was that her father was still angry with Roberta because of her lack of chastity. Edward's father vetoed the den idea. He argued that since the floors in that room were wood, the sound from the television would echo. Actually, Edward thought that, again, he felt an aversion to that room because he may have surmised that that was the room where Roberta actually lost her virginity and conceived her first child. The storage room idea was easily discarded because the house had a full basement and a large attic, and the family really did not have much to store. Edward's parents had no hobbies, his mother did not sew, nor did she ever acquire any of those domestic skills that most women of her generation were taught. His father did nothing except go to work, eat, drink beer and watch television. He had nothing to store.

The house had a dining room where the family ate all its meals and a kitchen which undoubtedly was designed for Lilliputians. In the rear off the dining room were two more bedrooms, one for the parents, and the one Edward would again share with Kevin until his brother found a job and moved out.

As Edward lay on his bed, a much softer bed than what he had at the seminary, still in his clothing, Kevin snoring erratically next to him, he contemplated his circumstances now that he had cast himself into this new state of affairs. It was a situation he should never have left in the first place. He could not contemplate beyond tomorrow. There was too much to reflect on now. What will the morning bring? What will be his plight? Will his parents speak to him tomorrow? If so, will the tone be one of disgust, malevolence? Or of leniency, some degree of tolerance, even an elementary grasp of the fact that he did not want to be a priest, could not be a priest and therefore should be respected for his decision? Will there be even a meager attempt at their being parents to him, of being there for him? As Edward lay considering his fate, he suspected that his fortunes, at least his immediate fate, were in jeopardy. He was certain he would be spurned and, in this household, rejection was regularly given as the prize for making his mother cry and therefore forcing his father to miss a boxing match or an ice cream sundae because he made his mother cry.

Edward's parents forfeited access to their son's emotions upon his return from the seminary. The greatest encumbrance on Edward's independence as an adolescent was of his own making. At the age of thirteen, he entered the seminary. The greatest gift he could give her, his mother told him. Being a devout Catholic, she always wanted a priest in the family. Edward surmised her reasons were selfish. She sincerely believed that the probability of her reaching heaven was greater if she had a man of God in her household. Edward's father, well, he didn't say much about it as usual. Actually, he didn't have to. As placid as he was about most subjects, he had definite opinions about priests. They were lazy, irreverent and condescending. Needless to say, his religious faith frequently wavered.

Edward realized that some priests were that way. But so were many nonpriests. For the most part, though, at least the priests Edward knew at the seminary were very religious men. They made well intentioned efforts to make Edward a very religious man. They were certainly not irreverent. Indeed the priests he knew were very spiritual and dedicated to their vocation. As for being condescending, they could be, particularly when theology was involved. Most priests believed they were closer to God than a lay person. In this way they were able to gain control over their flock, particularly the weak-minded. Edward suspected his father didn't like priests because they were always asking for money. Money to fix the windows in the school building. Money to purchase a new baptismal font. Money to purchase a new boiler for the rectory. It was always money for this and that, pleas that grated on his father's sense of frugality. It was unimportant that the appeals for funds were to pay for items needed to conduct the church's business. It was money and his father was convinced it was not money well spent. Father Healey also did not help Edward's father's opinion of priests.

In the end neither his mother's need for the additional guarantee of redemption and eternal life in heaven next to her savior, nor his father's contempt for priests swayed his decision to quit the seminary eight months after he started. Actually it was a very simple consequence of growing up.

St. Charles Seminary was located near St. Louis, on fifty-five secluded acres of grass, trees, a small lake and solemn, tedious brick buildings. There was an all-girls school next door, Notre Dame Academy for Girls. On the weekdays, after classes ended for the day and before the daily manual labor of cutting grass, cleaning sidewalks, mopping floors, scrubbing toilets and doing all the day to day chores that most institutions pay a custodian to do, several other seminarians regularly walked through the thick grove of oak trees to sit near the front gate. Edward accompanied them one day, curious as to why they rushed to the gate each day at precisely the same time. While they sat there, the girls from Notre Dame passed the gate on their way home. For the first few weeks Edward was puzzled as to why this routine was necessary. Was there a purpose to racing to the gate at precisely 3:15 p.m. Monday through Friday?

Suddenly he discovered the reason, the same one that had driven the others to this daily obsession. After the third week, when the girls passed the boys' perch on the wall next to the seminary gate, Edward began having erections each day, and each night he dreamed he was at the gate with another erection. He should not be in a place where much of his time was spent getting erections or trying to get rid of them so no one noticed.

He soon realized something was amiss with his vocation. Why should he stay in the seminary, a place where he obviously did not belong?

Although he never really figured out exactly how and when the decision to study to be a priest was made, he readily surmised what triggered his decision to leave the seminary after only eight months. It was discovering girls. It was that there were more breasts out there than just Mary Jo Bandera's. It was probably a bad decision to go to the seminary in the first place, one made on the spur of the moment to please someone who had fed him bacon and eggs. But he did not realize how bad until he could not stop having an erection each weekday at three fifteen at the gates of St. Charles.

For Edward, within a few months after he left the seminary, he no longer thought about it, no longer racked his brain looking for answers. When he lost that vocation, he instantly needed new answers to different, more secular questions. He needed to rectify his new position in a family whose matriarch had seemingly bet all her chips on her son becoming a priest, and when she lost, she spent her remaining wrath on that same son. Edward had to deal with a father who cared little about his going to the seminary and cared less about his quitting the seminary.

XIII

After again being verbally abused the next day by Kevin for forcing him out into the late night cold to pick his brother up, and after enduring the sobbing that filled the house throughout the night, flowing continuously from his Mother's bedroom, Edward's mother, acting as if nothing had happened, drove her son to St. Francis De Sales High School to register for classes. Even though she was no longer crying or badgering Edward because of his decision, her silence gave away her true feelings. It was a *you let me down* silence, a *no excuses are accepted* silence, a silence that made Edward feel like the drive to St. Francis was a drive to his execution.

It remained that way for several days after his return. The silence. The final long walk to the execution chamber. When she finally began talking to him, every word was strained. From that point onward until she died, their conversations would be forced, constrained by his decision to direct his life toward something he felt was better suited for him.

Actually, at that time he had no direction. The decision he had made was not to direct his life somewhere but to direct his life away from something he no longer wanted to be part of. Something that did not have anything to offer him. Something that did not stir his emotions the same way the girls from Notre Dame Academy stirred them.

The transition from seminary, all boys, all priests, all work, even for only eight months, to a coeducational high school with girls and less work, was disastrous for Edward. The day he began classes there, two days after leaving the seminary because erections had interfered with his priestly demeanor, he began having them again. There were girls everywhere. Edward liked the girls. He wanted to do things to some of the girls that the older boys at the playground talked about doing to the older girls behind the school building. There were no Mary Jo Bandera's tiny breasts here. These were real breasts. Breasts that made blouses wrinkle and gap.

The worst thing for Edward was that in the back row of his algebra class sat Peggy Petrazak. All through class he kept looking back at her but her eyes never made their way to his. He eagerly recalled her tongue trying to get at his, a thought that, when it happened ten months before, was revolting. After class ended, he had to wait to get out of his desk because thinking about Peggy Petrazak's tongue trying to pry open his lips raised him to heights he had never experienced. He could handle a tongue now, her tongue especially. She had developed quite nicely in that ten months. But it was her tongue he wanted to start with.

Edward cornered her at the door. He smiled. "Hi, Peggy." No smile from her, just a vague pursing of her lips.

"Hi, Edward. I heard you were back." She turned away as if she was looking for someone in the hallway.

"How are you doing?" he asked, trying to put some interest in his voice.

"Fine, Edward. What happened, couldn't take the seminary?"

Edward felt suddenly constricted, like Peggy Petrazak was penalizing him for coming home. He touched her arm. She backed away. "I thought maybe you and me could get together after school. Maybe go get a soda at Ernie's." Ernie's was a combination malt shop and drug store a block from the school.

"Don't think so." She waved to someone. "Gotta go. Nice to see you again."

Nice to see you again? What was that? In ten months she

went from wanting to extract his tonsils with her tongue to wanting to extract herself away from him as quickly as possible. This did not look good. And it wasn't good. What for Peggy Petrazak ten months earlier was a forbidden fruit she wanted to pick and peel had now turned into a rotten banana. Edward was no longer someone who was attractive because he could not be touched. And it was not only Peggy Petrazak that had developed an aversion to him now that he was no longer a seminarian, it was all the girls in the school. If he didn't know better, he would have thought his mother had contacted all the girls at St. Francis De Sales high school and told them to ignore her son. Don't touch him, don't look at him, don't talk to him, as punishment for, what, to her, was a serious transgression. A mortal sin. Needless to say, Edward spent his three and one half years at St. Francis De Sales high school on the sidelines of sex. The only date he had was to his senior prom. It was with Linda Kelly, a girl who, despite the braces, the red hair and the freckles that reminded him a lot of Fat Debbie from grammar school, was intermittently attractive. She had good days and bad. Edward liked her though and he thought she liked him. After the prom, she gave him the one and only kiss he had in high school. A tongue kiss, but not like he imagined he could get from Peggy Petrazak.

Edward had left a school and a vocation that everyone he knew, particularly his mother, wanted him to pursue, to succeed, a vocation they encouraged him to follow. He did not regret leaving the seminary. But he ran into difficulty adjusting to life away from being the center of attention as a result of the vocation he had chosen. In the seminary, the future holy men were protected. They knew nothing else but days of rising at five o'clock in the morning, walking to chapel in the dark for mass, eating breakfast in silence, walking back to the dormitory in silence to collect their books, attending class for three hours, eating lunch in silence, attending class for three more hours, finally having an hour to talk and play like thirteen year olds should, performing manual labor for two hours, eating dinner (not in silence), walking to chapel in the dark for an hour of benediction and prayer, two hours of silent study time and lights out at ten o'clock.

This new environment of boys and girls together, of riding a bus to school each morning and afternoon, of not attending mass each and every morning or benediction and prayer each and every evening, and of being able to talk to people just about anytime he wanted, was devastating for Edward. He wanted the girls to talk to him but they barely uttered a hello. The boys talked to him, but what was that. He could talk to boys anytime. It was the reason he left the seminary. Because he discovered girls. He suffered through three and one half years of boys and no girls. He could have done that at the seminary.

The other barrier he ran up against in his miserable expedition through St. Francis De Sales was that only a handful of all the kids he knew from the neighborhood went to that high school. Most of them went to other schools like Mendel or Mt. Carmel or Brother Rice or Mother McCauley or to the public high school. Edward had to make new friends and that wasn't easy for a boy who immediately ran into rejection from the gender he wanted to be friends with most of all.

Because his social life, a life he dreamed about while on the train heading home from the seminary and dreamed about every day thereafter, languished, his grades also suffered. At the end of his freshman year he had four D's and an F. His summer vacation was spent in summer school. He blamed his poor performance that year on Peggy Petrazak. If she had not slighted him, downright ignored him, he would not have gotten off on the wrong foot. His sophomore year was just as dismal. No F's but all D's. More summer school. His mother had a fit. His father? By this time Edward didn't really care what his father thought because his father thought nothing.

By the end of the first month of his Junior year, Edward's teachers and Edward, not necessarily in concert, could see that he was on the downslide for the third straight year. In October of that year he was called to the principals office. He had no idea why. He had done nothing to warrant the long walk to the principal's office. It was like being told to *Go to the priest!* His grades were terrible, true, but what could the principal do. On his way to the principal's office Edward felt a queasiness he had not felt since his days with Sister Mary Norbert. When he entered, the principal motioned Edward to sit down. Crowded around his desk were the football coach, Mr. Schmitz, the basketball coach, Mr. Smizniak and the counselor, Father Packard.

No one spoke immediately. They just stared at Edward. Mr. Schmitz walked over to Edward and asked him to flex his muscle. He did as he was asked but began to wonder what they all really had in mind for him. Was this some kind of sadistic punishment they had planned for him because he was not measuring up? Mr. Schmitz felt Edward's muscle. "You know," Mr. Schmitz said, "I could use a guy like you on the team." Football? Edward never played football in his life, except pickup games of tag at the playground, but never the get ripped apart by a two hundred pound tackle kind of football. Then Mr. Smizniak spoke. "Me too. I think you could be a great basketball player." What the hell was he talking about? Edward thought. He was five foot two. "Edward," the principal said, " what we're getting at is that we think you will improve academically if you get involved in sports here at St. Francis. It's a proven fact. All our athletes do well in class. It's important to us that you do well. It should be important to you." "Yea," Mr. Schmitz chimed in, "we've only played two games so far this season. It's not too late to join the team and at least start practicing with us. Who knows, next year you might get to play quite a bit, being a senior and all." It was Mr. Smizniak's turn. "Basketball practice begins next week. I want you to be there." He pointed his finger at Edward, not a mean point, but a stern one like the army poster with Uncle Sam pointing at the people he wanted.

They were all staring at Edward. It wasn't any lack of athletic skill that brought him to the lowest grade point average in the history of St. Francis De Sales. It was his mother who implied in her every word and action that her son was going to hell because he failed to become a priest thereby threatening her honored place in heaven. It was his father who didn't give a shit about his son or anything else except his boxing, his beer, his beer nuts and his ability to fart louder and longer than anyone in the world. It was Roberta who had the ability to get knocked up enough in and out of marriage to claim every ounce of sympathy from her mother and every pound of cash from her father, because her mother said so, and leave Edward with clothes that didn't fit because his mother said she couldn't afford to buy him any. It was Kevin . . . well, not Kevin, at least not for the moment, because Edward could not think of anything Kevin did to get his brother into this predicament. And it was Peggy Petrazak and Fat Debbie and all the other girls who had teased him and taunted him, who caused Sister Mary Norbert to call his parents and gave him a perpetual erection that caused him more grief than anyone of them could ever know. *Get me a girl, coach,* he thought, *a naked girl with big breasts who loves sex, and maybe, just maybe, my grades will get better.*

The principal said, "Well, what do you say?"

Edward said, "No thanks." And the principal waved his hand at Edward which he took as a signal that he was dismissed. So he left.

In the remaining two years of high school Edward did not get involved in sports. He did get involved in the school play each year. *Sound of Music* his junior year and *South Pacific* his senior year. He did it to meet girls, but it didn't work. Nothing worked. He did, however, improve academically, enough at least to where he graduated without anymore summer school.

High school after the seminary was a series of winding roads that went around and around in circles. Edward never was able to get close to any suitable destination, never even knew what his destination was. Even his religion, the faith that had brought him to these dips and turns, was disintegrating.

XIV

Edward was never able to pinpoint the true source of his decision to attend the seminary, and, even though he attributed his decision to leave the seminary to the common, everyday erection that young boys are saddled with when actually there probably were more profound forces at work, he likewise had no clue where the notion came from that he no longer wanted any more of the religion he had dedicated a large percentage of his young life to, or any religion for that matter. Within a year after he returned from the seminary he decided that fifteen years of Catholicism was enough.

He did not withdraw from the religion he was raised under as a result of his giving up the vocation of the priesthood. The two decisions were definitely mutually exclusive. The former decision, not necessarily arrived at in haste, was made at least a year after his departure from the seminary and was for reasons, if he could ever clearly determine the reasons, that were distinctly separate from his reasons for the latter decision. An erection, particularly an erection that wanted to demonstrate its capabilities, could not be a justifiable reason for renouncing a religion while it can be a legitimate motive for giving up a vocation that requires its members to be celibate their entire lives.

In fact, after Edward arrived home from the seminary that dreadful night in February, he continued to go to church regularly, at least to those masses good Catholics were bound to attend for fear of eternal damnation. He also continued, at least temporarily, to steadfastly adhere to a rather abundant quantity of what was, at that time, earnest praying, but not nearly at the bulk and caliber he managed to generate before the seminary when he spent much of his time in church praying and crying, and certainly not at the level he produced while at the seminary. For the first few months after he left the seminary, he continued to make every effort to live his life in a most humble and spiritual manner notwithstanding that he took more time now in the confessional. But the effort soon faded.

When confessing his sins in that little box face to screen with faceless grunting and breathing coming from the other side, Edward covered most of Sister Mary Genevieve's list of sins as well as a list of sins he had devised for himself since leaving the seminary. But unlike his decision to become a priest, made when he was gulping down a plate of bacon and eggs in the rectory in the company of Frank and Father Healey, Edward made the decision to cease practicing religion not as quickly, but deliberately and cautiously. He was eating a hamburger and French fries at the McDonalds on seventy-ninth street, a popular hangout for most of the teenagers in the neighborhood who went there to meet their girlfriends and boyfriends, or just meet girls, or after a basketball or football game or, in Edward's case, to make one of the key decisions of his life.

He realized that making that decision at the McDonalds was an irregularity in the standard everyday happenings at a fast food restaurant. The kids who frequented that place rarely made any kind of life shattering decisions while under the golden arches, unless it was to go park at the beach and look at life and other, more intimate things while in the back seat of a car, and later to suffer the consequences of that decision.

The decision itself of Edward actually telling himself that he would no longer attend mass, that prayer was no longer a necessary function of his life, may have been made instantaneous while chewing on a French fry, but there was definitely something, some force or forces that drove him to that decision. Like his decision to become an officer in the army of that religion, his decision to discharge himself altogether from that army was based on motivations that have never been correctly identified. After that decision was made while sitting in a booth at McDonalds, chewing on a soggy French fry dipped in ketchup, Edward never felt compelled to believe in a creator, an omnipotent God, all knowing, who was merciful and good and compassionate. There was just no longer any identifiable signs of compassion and mercy that were being distributed around on earth. And, at the same time Edward found the strength to discard what he had been born to and saddled with for fifteen years, he also, between the last French fry and the final slurp of his chocolate milkshake, settled on an alternative. In spite of, or because of, God and angels and Mary and the saints and the entire Roman Catholic Church and every other religion no matter how much it professed love and mercy and goodness and eternal life in heaven, no matter how much all the churches and religions in the world proclaimed themselves the source of God's word and promised salvation, he put his money on nature and random acts of human nature and coincidence as being sufficiently capable and well suited to explain everything he needed an explanation for. Nature and a random act of human nature made him, although he seriously believed that his creation was the result of intercourse gone awry. As a result, after that last noisy swallow of milkshake, he was no longer occupied with the ongoing pursuit of an understanding of God, eternal life or eternal damnation and he hung up his rosary and gave up the fight for those things others on earth regarded as essential to life in the hereafter.

His mother's proclivity for prayer had no positive effect on his fidelity to the true religion. His six months at the seminary had a more profound impact than he had first realized when he cut the ropes that bound him to it. In retrospect that experience, when a year later he thought about his time there, probably made his decision for him because it gave him the opportunity to realize he had questions, many questions, and he felt obligated to find answers to those questions. It took another year to assimilate the experience into a rationale for giving up the Catholic religion.

But, even though Edward no longer fretted or theorized over why human beings were on earth or where everyone went after life ended, he continued to infrequently explore his mind for reasons why he gave it up. As in most investigations where questions linger and a person attempts to find answers to those questions, he went to the most immediate source, his family.

Edward's father was not much of an example when it came to religion just as he was not much of an example for anything else. On the other hand, Edward's mother went overboard. As a model for Edward to find his direction in the morass of religion, particularly Catholicism, he guessed the two extremes canceled each other out and left him with the chore to make up his own mind.

Edward's mother went to mass every Saturday morning and confession every Saturday afternoon and then again to mass on Sunday with her family. If she had not had children to get off to school on the weekday mornings and a job to go to herself, Edward was certain she would have attended mass every weekday. She demanded grace be said at every meal. Not such a big deal but probably necessary considering the quality of the food she prepared. Each of the children took turns saying grace so that each one was responsible for blessing the evening meal once every three days. At breakfast they were required to say grace but silently because they all ate breakfast at different times except on Sunday when the prayer was said out loud by Edward's mother who, for whatever reason reserved that responsibility for herself and never relinquished the Sunday breakfast grace to anyone.

It was the same prayer every meal, said nightly until it became so mundane Edward was able to run through it in quick time and think of other things while he recited it. *Bless us oh Lord and these Thy gifts, which we are about to receive from Thy bounty through Christ our Lord, Amen.* The *Amen* was group participation. Then everyone made the sign of the cross and ate, usually silently, because Edward's father did not like conversation at the table or anywhere else for that matter. He claimed that conversation while eating always led to arguments and arguments gave him indigestion. The evening dinner was the most opportune time to discuss what everyone did that day, at school, at work. But he was uninterested and used the indigestion excuse to avoid being forced to show any interest. After a time, when the excitement of Edward's day was something no one wanted to share and he shared only with himself, silence at the dinner table was okay with him. After Kevin and Roberta moved out, Edward became the primary grace sayer.

His mother's principal rosary sat in an ashtray on the table next to the couch. Another one, a reserve, lay on the table next to her bed. She had others stuffed in drawers around the house. She always had a spare if she did not have access to the main one and an emergency came up. Sometimes Edward would find one of them on the sink in the bathroom. She had brought it in there with her and prayed while she went to the toilet. She fingered her beads every chance she got. While drinking her morning coffee when he was walking out the door to catch the bus for school she read the morning paper and fingered her beads one prayer at a time, perhaps praying for those unfortunate souls reported in the paper as tragically murdered or killed in some horrible accident. Each morning Edward called to her that he was leaving for school and she always muttered a goodbye between Hail Marys. Sometimes he was out the door before she acknowledged his departure, her having begun an Our Father when he called to her and she not wanting to interrupt her recitation of the Lord's prayer. She said her rosary during Lawrence Welk and during a football or baseball game on television. The simple rhythm of the prayers being silently recited bead after bead while the Cubs were up to bat must have comforted her.

Who was she praying for? Herself? Her children? For Lawrence Welk to play her favorite polka or the Chicago Bears to score a touchdown or for the referee to change that penalty call? Or for herself, to make it into heaven when she died. Was she that much under the grip of sin that she had to devote nearly every waking hour to prayer? Maybe she had some insight into the afterlife that the rest of the family did not have. Perhaps there were multiple levels of eternal life in heaven depending upon the ferocity of the praying. The more she prayed the higher the level she attained until she made it to the highest level where she was allowed to sit next to the Almighty. It confused Edward. All through elementary school and in the seminary and at church on Sunday he was taught that a person can be sent to hell with one mortal sin on their soul just as absolutely as with ten mortal sins on that same soul. So he thought, as his mother ran through those beads day after day, won't one rosary recited each day get a person into heaven just as easily as four rosaries?

Or for her children? Was she praying for her children? Were most of those prayers directed at Kevin to keep him out of jail or to diminish Roberta's fertility so she wouldn't overpopulate the south side of Chicago? Or for Edward, early on, to give thanks to the lord for giving him the right vocation and sending him to the seminary, or later on after those prayers had missed their mark, to ask the lord to get him to change his mind and go back to the seminary. He noticed that her praying increased ten fold, if that were even possible, after he quit the seminary.

If most of her prayers were for her children, to keep them out of sin and on the straight and narrow path to eternal salvation, then she said few prayers for her own salvation and she would probably only make it to the first level in heaven, at the most the second level if the criteria for getting into heaven included the number of masses attended. If that was the case, then her prayers for reforming the lives of her children on earth were not answered. Kevin went to jail twice, Roberta continued to propel children into the world and Edward never went back to the seminary. Never even looked back. He also gave up his religion which his mother never knew. Perhaps those prayers were not wasted.

Maybe, since she tried so hard, she was given extra credit and was promoted up a few levels.

Or for Edward's father? Did she devote most of those prayers for her husband to get him to be a father? If so, she failed there too. Failed miserably.

Edward never saw his father touch a rosary or mutter a prayer. He went to church every Sunday, sat with his family in a pew near the back, stood at the right times and kneeled when everyone else kneeled. He took communion but Edward never saw him go to confession. He dropped his tithe in the collection basket, reluctantly perhaps, and then went home after mass to read his Sunday paper and eat his bacon, sausage and eggs.

Edward was surrounded by religion. He grew up with the Holy Catholic Church and all its accouterments dispersed in the bathroom with the picture of the Sacred Heart of Jesus above the stool with its brilliant beams of light exploding in all directions; in the living room and kitchen with crucifixes on the most prominent wall in each room, two more crucifixes in his parents bedroom so his mother could look at one no matter which side she slept on; in his underwear drawer where his mother periodically placed holy cards with pictures of Jesus or the Blessed Virgin or some saint on one side and a prayer on the other, furtively slipped into his chest drawer when his mother felt he needed something to bolster his faith. The religion, his mother's religion, smothered him.

After he left the seminary, he began to lose interest. Church was not a place he wanted to be; Catholicism was not something he wanted to practice. He no longer wanted to be the family poster boy for Catholicism his mother had prayed for him to be. She had her prayers answered, at least for eight months. Maybe she felt that it was all her fault; maybe she didn't pray hard enough or didn't divvy up enough prayers toward her son's salvation.

For about six months after Edward left the seminary, he attended Sunday mass with his parents. Each Sunday morning at five minutes before ten, the three of them slipped into the pew at church, third pew from the back, the same pew every Sunday. His father insisted they sit at the back for easy egress. His mother sat on the far side, rosary and prayer book in hand anxiously awaiting the start of mass so she was able to double her reserve of praise and prayers by praying along with the priest and fingering her beads at the same time. His father sat on the aisle and Edward squeezed in between them. When mass ended they marched out single file, his father quick stepping it out the door way ahead of his wife and son and nearly to the car by the time his wife and son exited. Back home and then a big breakfast and Edward's father plops his rear end in his chair for an afternoon of scanning the newspaper and watching a game, any game, on television.

When Edward entered his sophomore year of high school, he began sleeping late on Sundays and going to the eleven o'clock or noon mass. Slowly, over a period of about six months, he removed himself altogether from going to church, first sitting in the back pews, then standing in the back of the church near the door, then staying for only half the mass and leaving about the time communion commenced, then for a quarter of the mass, and then just driving past the church in his parents car on his way to the park or the beach or to a friends house or to the McDonalds on Seventy-ninth Street to chew on French fries and contemplate his future.

Those interludes at the McDonalds gave Edward insight he never would have thought could come from a greasy hamburger, greasy fries and a watery milkshake. He began to see what religion was used for, that God had become simply an excuse for defeating someone else, or for ridding a person of troubles they had brought on themselves, sometimes deliberately. People prayed until they were blue in the face, but they only prayed for themselves or for someone who was already dead so that dead person could put in a good word for them and they would be with them in heaven. And when death came for someone they knew, the people still on earth never knew if the person who died went to heaven. Oh, they would say or people would tell them, "Uncle Gus is with the Almighty," but they really didn't know. And then they prayed to get there too. But they didn't know about that either. It was truly a guessing game.

People didn't pray for the things that really mattered. They prayed for themselves and let the rest of the world be damned. And if anyone did pray for what really mattered, those prayers were never answered. Edward's mother prayed a lot. Enough for an army of nuns. What did she pray for? That her older son would straighten up? Never happened. That her daughter would find a good man? Probably never would happen. That Roberta not be so fertile? Not a chance. That Edward would reenter the seminary? No way. That she would go to heaven? Don't know. That there is a heaven? Don't know that either. That there would be no more war or famine or crime, that the hungry would be fed, that children would not suffer abuse or hunger or disease? She didn't have time to pray for all of that. She and millions of others who wore their knees to the bone praying were too busy praying for heaven and other more self-seeking reasons.

XV

Edward spent the summer of 1967 after graduation from high school gazing at the gentle waves of Lake Michigan at Rainbow Beach. He was especially mindful of the women who frequently strolled up and down the beach or lay provocatively on blankets on the sand showing off whatever asset they thought should be displayed. He liked bikinis and especially what was inside them. Most times he just went to sit and watch the people or the sail boats out on the lake. Rarely did he go in the water. On occasion he brought his own blanket and a book to read. That first day after graduation he tossed the blanket in the back seat of the car and rifled through a stack of Kevin's books he had tossed in a box when he moved to an apartment on the East Side. *Giovanni's Room.* James Baldwin. What the hell, Edward thought, he'll give it a try. One line James Baldwin writes in that book, although no more significant than any other line in the book when reading it, came back to him months later after he tossed the book back into the box from where he had retrieved it. "You don't have a home until you leave it and then, when you have left it, you never can go back."

There are two kinds of young adults, those who are reluctant to leave the nest and those who await with longing the day when they can move out away from parents and siblings. Kevin epitomized the former. Except for the two years he served in the army, Kevin lived at home on and off until he was twenty-four. His motives were simple. He found it considerably more cost effective to be exempt from paying rent for his own place, and since his father never demanded rent nor any other portion of the household bills, Kevin was able to sock away quite a bank account and, at the same time, have a maid, laundress, cook and answering service gratis. It was only when he married that he moved out. When he divorced two years later, Edward was amazed, and thankful, that he did not move in with his parents again.

Edward, on the other hand, represented the dissident, the seditious son who not only had a voracious appetite for emancipation, but also craved that independence earlier than most. At seventeen, he was ready to leave home, but he knew that all financial support would be cut off if he jumped ship early. He waited, though not content with what he had to endure, and very uncomfortable with what he was forced to tolerate. To continue receiving allowances and money for college, Edward had to continue attending college, and he had to finish under the terms and conditions set by his parents.

Edward attended junior college his first year, traveling the Illinois Central commuter train to downtown Chicago each weekday at 8:00 a.m., taking three classes each day at Loop Junior College, working as a librarian's assistant each afternoon at the Chicago Municipal Library in City Hall—Mayor Richard J. Daley was his boss, though he never saw the man in the eight months he worked there—and returning home on the train each evening. School was tolerable, work was enjoyable, the travel was monotonous.

His parents became increasingly unbearable. Unbearable not only for the sin he had committed by quitting the seminary but also for the multiple sins and indiscretions his brother and sister became so adept at committing regularly. Despite Edward being assigned second class status in the family because he no longer had the vocation his mother wanted him to have causing her to be miserable and thus transferring that misery to his father, there were other factors that interfered with his development and freedom, influenced considerably by Roberta's and Kevin's disregard for the effect their actions had on their brother's up-bringing.

Roberta got knocked up at sixteen. Consequently, Edward's social life was limited. He tried to explain to his parents that he could not get pregnant, but his pleas unfazed them. He could get someone pregnant, they insisted. Why, Edward wondered, would he want to do that until he was ready. They could not see he had, at age eighteen, developed a more sensible approach to life than Roberta had. Edward did not argue the point further. He could not get a date anyway, so why fret.

When he was a teenager, Kevin ran with a rough crowd that stole cars. He landed in jail once for stealing cars, but he was able to beat that rap, and once in jail for fighting in a bar he and his friends frequented on the East Side. Thus, Edward's privileges were further limited and his curfews were strict. Apparently, his parents believed that Kevin's transgressions might automatically become Edward's if they did not tighten the screws on their younger son's mobility.

After one year of junior college in Chicago, Edward traveled south to the rural backwaters of central Illinois. No sooner had he arrived at Eastern Illinois University in Charleston, Illinois when he was smitten with the neoteric counter culture spreading rapidly across the country. It was rather diminutive where he was compared to other places like San Francisco and New York and Chicago. It was still in its infancy in central Illinois, but it was growing. It appealed to Edward's sense of defiance which, at the moment, was directed at his parents, an attitude he discovered he shared with many others who entered that counter culture at the same time he did. But he thought, as did many of his contemporaries, perhaps his rebellion should be expanded to extend to those issues that were making renegades of many of his friends and many people he did not know.

To a boy who had grown up in Chicago, a city of four million unforgiving people, the shock of encountering country folk who exaggerated the meaning of friendliness, was more than Edward had counted on. From four million population to fourteen thousand souls had the ultimate effect, at least initially, of an alien adventure, a close encounter, a trip to the twilight zone.

He chose the small university in Charleston for one reason. His father vis a vis his mother would not pay for anything else. They could not afford a more expensive school. God knows they could not exploit the funds used to keep Roberta living in the fashion to which she had become accustomed. If, they explained, Edward insisted on leaving the low cost, low quality junior college after only one year, he must pay the price through economy. While his high school classmates were moving on to schools that had better, or at least more advertised reputations, Edward found himself at one that had never actively pursued a reputation. It catered to students within a radius of about one hundred fifty miles, students who had no focus to their lives and students who were required to attend because of abject frugality. Edward felt lost in the wilderness. He also had lousy high school grades which entered into the equation of choosing a school.

The school, while academically sound, was tardy in advancing its social conscience. By 1968 only about one fifth of the faculty had made some level of commitment to the now flourishing defiant disposition that was flourishing in the country, some professors, assistant professors, associate professors progressively shaped by an increasingly obscene war, a sluggish government shuffling at its own leisurely pace toward some consistent policy on civil rights, free speech becoming a diminished commodity and the entire nation in disarray because of a lack of commitment by its leaders except to the economic enrichment of war and their own self preservation.

By 1969, at the peak of demonstrations, marches, sit-ins and take-overs, when the vocal minority in the United States was metamorphosing into an even stronger majority, the administration of the university Edward attended had no clue as to how the winds were shifting and in which direction they were beginning to gust. Soon those winds turned into a gale and the antiquated administration of the school and the equally out-of-date president reacted in a manner consistent with down home middle America. They had been shaped by what had been ultimately identified as an antiquated mindset, fed by the white dominated power structure, that what counts is the control of the purse and control of the purse will lead to power over the people, that what counts is not the rights of the people but the right people, those who have the money and the influence to govern a nation where the people are inconsequential and easily influenced.

They were wrong. The administrators of the university, those men and, in 1969 a trifling small number of women, for the most part, entered the domain of college governance because a) it paid more money and b) they were once teachers themselves but left that field of academics because they were scholastically deficient, lacking the competence required of those who must educate others.

They quickly became immovable objects in a land slide of agitation and discontent. They conceded nothing. They offered no conciliation, no compromise. There was no middle ground, no ground at all but theirs. They had no hint of what was about to befall them. The university was moving into the mainstream of the flow of restlessness and discontent. That was a wonderful year.

Like the minds of the deans and vice presidents and president, the campus was a narrow, elongated rectangle filled with dissimilar buildings of baroque, Greek, late Gothic and modern architecture and odds and ends of designs no self-respecting architect would claim. The homely buildings were spaced among the larger, more attractive, buildings. Many of the structures on campus did not fit the styles that were commonplace on other college campuses. In a broad sense it might have been considered eclectic. Actually it was a result of poor planning and poor taste. A castle guarded the front of the campus, the administration building. Old Main it was called, where the students first concentrated their efforts at advancing their grievances and gauging their strength and the strength of their adversaries. The quadrangle in the center of campus became their staging area especially when their forces grew in numbers. From there they delivered their message to every quarter of the campus. Edward spent most of his time defining the issues at rap sessions, distributing an underground newspaper and listening to outside speakers the university administration claimed were chosen based on the degree of agitation they produced. They focused on the same issues that faced the country through the microcosms of campuses all over the United States. The war had become a convenience for those who had issues. But as their influence of those issues grew, Edward's education faltered.

His budget education. Edward discovered later in life that the shortage of cash to put him through college with one pair of dress pants, two pairs of jeans, tennis shoes that were two years old, steel toed work boots that were Kevin's when he worked at the mill, four shirts, a winter jacket that had seen several winters and underwear that barely covered Edward's ass because he had put on some weight since they had been purchased, was a result of his parents diverting a large portion of their income to supporting Roberta, her three children and a lifestyle that was far more elegant that one could sustain on welfare. It was the same reason Edward was not given money to buy clothes or put gas in the car or go to a dance or the McDonalds on Seventy-ninth Street to eat French fries and contemplate. He had to work for any cash he needed while Roberta, with three children, sat at home collecting her welfare checks and food stamps and the cash and furniture and food Edward's parents carted over there weekly. Edward baby-sat for his sister's kids when his mother and Roberta went shopping for a new outfit for Roberta or a new stove for Roberta or clothes for her children or a new toy for her children or a new battery for Roberta's car which was also purchased for her by them.

He baby-sat when Roberta went to play bunco every other Monday, and when she went to the emergency room after being beaten by her estranged husband. Edward even saved her son, Eric's, life, the one that tells Edward with his eyes to get fucked every time he sees him. He was two years old. He was in the front seat of the car on the freeway after Edward had picked up him and his brother and sister and was taking them to the park. Eric opened the car door and nearly fell out. With one hand on the wheel Edward grabbed him by the leg, threw him in the back seat and then grabbed the door and shut it. So who was the fuck then?

The one consolation of being at a campus that bragged on its backwardness was that Edward was unencumbered. His parents were two hundred miles away. There was little they could do now to influence his new manner of living or to act upon whatever decisions he made regarding what he did, when he did it, how he did it or who he did it with. Or so he thought.

Within one month of his beginning classes at the university Edward's parents came to visit, a surprise visit he was certain was predicated on nothing more than mistrust. They had no sooner entered the lobby of the high rise dormitory where he lived when they commanded that the mustache he started growing the day he caught the bus to the school was to be shaved immediately, the new bell bottom jeans he instinctively knew would be an issue but wore anyway, the ones he bought with his own money earned working as a dish washer in the dormitory cafeteria, were to be pitched. The people with whom he associated, evidenced to his parents by anyone who said hello to Edward or nodded to him when he was in the presence of his parents, were swiftly categorized by dress, hairstyle, and, by his mother the clairvoyant, by morals or lack of. It was not coincidental that the immoral group also was the same group with hairstyles and dress from which Edward had been barred. It was also not coincidental that those same miscreants his mother placed in that category were the people he associated with. The price for disobeying any of their mandates: all financial support eliminated.

This point in time was one of Edward's watersheds in the

already fragile relationship he had with his parents. If his rebellion was in its larval stage before his parents' visit, it abruptly and swiftly was transformed to a new level, one that assuredly induced wounds that never healed.

The absurdity of their demands caught Edward off guard at first, long enough for his parents to seize the moment, befuddle him and swiftly prevail. It was simply a result of Edward being controlled by his parents for so long that four weeks of independence was not enough to provide him with the fortitude to challenge them. Kevin, if he had been there, would have pulled his brother aside and whispered, "No balls, no fucking balls." He would have been right.

Edward's parents spent little time inquiring about their son's classes, activities, grades or anything else related to his academic well-being. "How much you spending?" his father asked. Before Edward could answer he added "Too much, I suspect." His father glanced around the dormitory, then commented, "Quite a few niggers here, aren't there?" Edward didn't answer. Was he eating well, sleeping well? They didn't ask. Did he have enough clothes for the coming winter? They didn't ask that either. Did he have enough money? Edward knew they never had any intention of asking that even if the other unasked questions may have entered their minds for the slightest second. What constituted Edward's well-being and what he needed to keep it fulfilled and appeased was a direct contradiction of his parents' opinion of the same concept.

Once they felt he had been subdued, his mother slapped a sealed envelope in his hand and his parents left to search for beer and peanuts and head for the local motel for the night. As they drove away Edward opened the envelope. In it was a twenty dollar bill. He was flabbergasted that his parents, at least his mother should feel so generous as to give him money for no particular reason. As Edward stuffed the bill in his pocket a note dropped out of the envelope. He picked it up and opened it. It read, "I thought you might need this. You're just fooling yourself

if you think Mom and Dad are going to give you anything. Kevin."
Good old Kevin. Twenty dollars and not a four letter word to be
found on the page. He must have gotten a job.

Edward slept fitfully that night knowing he had compromised
his craving for self-rule. They would be back early in the morning, earlier than he was used to rising, therefore too early to
develop the ire that would consume him once they departed.

And he was right. The next morning, they called at eight
o'clock to tell Edward they were coming by and he should be out
front waiting. He was and the three of them went to breakfast at
Harpo's, a restaurant similar to Denny's, and ate hastily with little
conversation passing among them. The silent eating reminded
him of the rare occasions as a child when the family went out to
eat. It bothered Edward that other families eating at the restaurants Edward and his family went to were actually talking to each
other, laughing at each other's jokes, smiling, while Edward, his
parents, Roberta before she got pregnant the first time, and Kevin
when he felt like joining them, when he needed a free meal, just
sat and ate. Edward watched the other fathers with their children
and how they had animated conversations with them and laughed
with them and tickled them and let them order a dessert. Edward's
parents talked to him only when he did something wrong and in
the harshest terms. Eventually the family stopped going to restaurants. Edward didn't know why. He was glad they stopped
going. He wished they had not initiated the uncommon ritual for
this one encore.

After they finished eating, they walked to the parking lot
dutifully saying goodbye to each other with pretended hugs and
forged smiles. There were mild threats made, reminders that
Edward's clothes and hair length were to abide by certain standards and there was to be no facial hair. Any deviation and all
funds would immediately cease. They drove off presumably confident their son would abide by their demands. After all, Edward
had been docile up to now, for the three and one-half hours they
spent with him. It was fortunate for them they had paid their son

a visit. They were able, in less than twenty-four hours, to save him from an abominable and obscene life style. Edward watched them drive off in their new Ford Fairlane, purchased about the same time it was announced that there was not enough money to send Edward to a college of his choice, about the time his unemployed sister acquired a new dining room table and chairs, about the time he was given only fifty dollars to buy clothes for school. Edward raised his arm and then extended his middle finger. It was so much easier now than it was in seventh grade when he first gave the finger to Frank with the vowelless last name.

Almost immediately upon their departure, when they were no sooner out of the parking lot and the tail lights of their new car were still in view, Edward perceived their demands not as ultimatums but as a dare. He walked back to the student union, ordered some French fries, paid for them out of the twenty dollar bill Kevin sent, pondered his options and by the time the last French fry was eaten, recognized what it was he had to do.

XVI

Within a week the new mustache was noticeable. Three weeks and it was full, even bushy. A beard was started. The hair on Edward's chin grew swiftly but the hair on his cheeks seemed to hesitate at first, though it soon became rather fine, filling his face with earthy reds and browns highlighted with wifts of blond. He fished the bellbottoms out of the trash and bought two additional pair with what was left of the twenty dollars.

Two weeks before Thanksgiving he sent his parents a picture of him in bell bottoms, with beard, mustache and even a string of beads around his neck to heighten the effect, frolicking with his immoral friends in a field of alfalfa. The picture was accompanied by a letter.

> *Dear Parents,*
>
> *I cannot hold my feelings in any longer. You have been unfair to me for a long time now. I have been unable to dress the way I want to, read what I want to, associate with the people I want to, even take certain classes in college* [they had refused to pay Edward's tuition or any other expenses if he took a class on Fidel Castro]. *I have done nothing to deserve this poor treatment. I cannot live in this kind of environment any longer. I am moving down to Charleston permanently and will not come back until you can treat me with respect. It is difficult for me to live in a household where I have a mother who does not seem to*

care about my feelings and a father who cares even less. I
hope you can understand my feelings but I doubt it.

Your Son,
Edward

It wasn't much. It failed to include all the turmoil that had been brewing inside him for four years. He neglected to tell them how he felt about their political convictions, his mother's religious zealotry, Roberta's comfort that they gave to her at Edward's expense, their racial views. He thought it covered what was tearing up his insides at the time he sent it, although in general terms. It was enough to give his parents the reason Edward thought they had been looking for all along to rid themselves of the burden of their youngest child.

After he mailed the letter, Edward felt no revelry, no bravado, not even the feeling of triumph. The revelry never came. In time he boasted to his friends about his independence, but he did not brag on how he achieved it. There was never the feeling of victory and thus no cause for celebration. It took only four days for his parents, surprisingly his father, to answer Edward's letter. The letter must have really upset his mother and deprived his father of a few ice cream sundaes, for his reply was swift and to the point. To reply in that short period of time required his father to actually take time away from the television, his beer and peanuts, his *TV Guide* and sit down most likely in the same chair where he undertakes all his other pursuits that don't require much thought or movement and draft a letter to his son in his untidy scrawl, the spiteful message most likely dictated by Edward's mother in those tearful mutterings she was prone to exaggerate in a crisis, and mail that letter to his son within twenty-four hours of receiving Edward's missive. Not a particularly adequate period of time to decide the fate of their son, notwithstanding the wretched relationship that led up to the estrangement.

Their response was succinct. Too much so. It clearly and

concisely warned Edward that he was on his own now. He would get nothing from them, no money which up to now had been insignificant at best, no moral support, which had been meagerly disbursed ever since that decisive day in his relationship with his parents when he abandoned his religious vocation and jeopardized his mother's ascension into heaven, and no spiritual support which meant they would no longer pray for him, a response Edward found perplexing coming from his ultra-religious mother who repeatedly confided in the pastor of the church she attended that she ceaselessly prayed for all the poor souls on earth. Was Edward not a poor soul? He guessed she figured her son had lost his soul forever and was headed for the fires of hell anyway and no amount of praying could change that. The only way Edward could reinstate himself as a son in good standing, the letter went on, would be to clean up his act, return home and apologize for all the hurtful things he said and did and atone for the wicked lifestyle he had chosen. That was not one of the options he had come up with as he ate French fries in the student union.

So Edward was now on his own. He quickly ran out of money and had a meager income from washing dishes at the dormitory food service. At the end of the semester he no longer could afford to live in the dormitory since he was now his sole source of financial support. Thus he became homeless at Christmas. He slept in friends' garages, living rooms, attics and basements; sometimes he slept on the floor of a dormitory room. The money he made from washing dishes in the cafeteria went to tuition. Food was borrowed or stolen. If circumstances disallowed both methods, he went hungry. He lost a considerable amount of weight—from 165 pounds to 130 in six months. By the end of the second semester of his sophomore year, his body had deteriorated so acutely that his health became threatened. He had no stamina, eating became a burden, sleeping became a blessing. When he slept, all the dissenting forces in his body departed, he slept soundly and long, so long each day that he had little time for classes or any other part of life that people of nineteen take pleasure from.

By the spring of 1969, Edward came to the conclusion that he had a very ambiguous future. When not sleeping, he relieved his depression by sitting cross legged in secreted places, sometimes in friends' living rooms, barely illuminated by flickering candles scattered about the room, or clandestinely in backwoods hideouts, or in attics or basements or old abandoned shanties that sat on the outskirts of town, sometimes passing a joint around the circle of misfits that found solace in each other's company. If no marijuana was available that night, which was rare, a bottle of wine replaced the reefer. On many occasions the wine, instead of a stand in, was the chaser to the deep inhaling of tranquilizing smoke. There was always one eye on the door, securely locked, but easily bashed in by anyone who may find their form of recreation questionable. Before lighting up, everyone identified his or her means of escape. A dubious exercise since evasion from the authorities in their condition was fruitless.

Edward and his friends did not exaggerate their danger. In fact they were always in jeopardy. The town apparently looked the other way when it came to drugs and other infractions that the normal college students committed. It was not the same with the counter culture that was beginning to show a presence on campus and in town. They were not welcome at the restaurants, the bowling alley, the parks or the stores. They limited their activities to the woods, friendly houses and the student union. With so little opportunity to associate with the population of the town or participate in any activities available to everyone else, they found their pleasures in passing the wine and the joint. Edward not only found considerable gratification in that pursuit, but preferred it since it allowed him to wipe from his mind any sense of obligation or accountability toward his parents and, after a while, toward himself.

Edward was in this very frame of mind, a condition he found himself in regularly, when he, along with two girls he had met two hours earlier, left a party and hitchhiked to Chicago. No reason, just a whim to find some excitement away from the burdensome town where there was no excitement. One girl, who called herself Sunday, had become, Edward found out, the object of fondness for most of the other fellows whom he knew. She fully advocated free love and was, at least for the hippies of this small central Illinois town, the champion of the summer of love.

It was the summer of love. You either fucked every girl you could or you boasted you had. You either liked Rock and Roll or you pretended you did. You either took drugs or you said you did. You hated the war and everything it stood for and you really did.

That chaotic summer of 1969 Edward stood for everything his parents abhorred; he abhorred everything his parents stood for. He loathed the government, anything that was government; he despised big business that financed big government and the evil war that big government, at the behest of big business, was using to make big business bigger. Hundreds of people had gotten beaten bloody running from the batons of the Chicago police the year before as Edward watched them on television from the safety of his parent's living room. Edward's father called them scum, bums, commies and more words than Edward had heard spurt from his father's mouth at one time in all the days he lived with the man. Edward's mother reached for her rosary and quietly mouthed each prayer while riveted to the scenes of carnage on the television. Edward never left the room until the news was over and Johnny Carson's monologue filled the screen. He sat glued to reels of film that eerily displayed the growing devisiveness between his generation and that of his parents. It was made clearly visible to all who watched the tragedy unfold and witnessed the swelling hostility and enmity of his generation toward all things their generation held sacred.

Through high school, at least the three years after the seminary, Edward was trying desperately and generally unsuccessfully to make up for the time lost joining an army he drummed himself out of because it fought battles he no longer cared to fight. So in running at full speed to catch up with what he had missed, he let what later became the important things go unnoticed. That is until that night when he watched with dismay and a sprinkling of fear, what that older generation, the big business generation, believed, the generation that had been reared on war and prosperity and educated themselves with the simple equation that war equaled prosperity and that as long as there were communists to fight then the prosperity would continue to swell and that a few lives was a small price to pay for the country's boom and the communists' doom.

During the summer of 1968 Edward did not rant to his parents about the bourgeois lifestyle, the war, their prejudices and biases. They probably thought, because of his silence, he was on their side, or that they had successfully subdued him. But he wasn't and they hadn't, and when he showed his true colors in that letter and the picture that accompanied it, it stunned them. It tore them to pieces.

They didn't have to worry about Roberta being on their side. They were her lifeline. She depended on them for the hard cash that supplemented her welfare checks. Kevin was never on their side so they were never overwhelmed by him having a change of heart because he never had one. Kevin was just for himself.

Edward was watching men and women his age being beaten to a pulp because they protested against something they thought was wrong. It wasn't the war that outraged him as much as it was the indiscriminate swinging of clubs at people who he believed had a legitimate right to do what they were doing. It began a slow burn inside him. He had that right too. He didn't want to lose that right. If it took protesting the war and everything else that required protest to secure that right then that's what he was going to do.

By the spring of 1969, Edward believed his parent's and their contemporaries' ideology was an ideology born of financial ruin and war. They blindly followed those who were glib enough to persuade them that what the government did was right and in their best interests. Edward's ideology was one of questioning, even though he was raised by parents of that generation, was a product of their ideology and lifestyle. He did not originally adopt his new lifestyle because of the war but that became a part of his protestations. He did not adopt it because of the civil rights surge but that became part of it. He did not enter into it to foster women's rights or any other group's rights although he fought for their rights too. He joined the movement for his rights and his only. If he was able to help anyone in the process then that was an added value to the philosophy and lifestyle he chose.

The other in the threesome on their way to Chicago, Becky, became attached to Edward for the simple reason that no one else wanted the risk she carried with her. Edward, on the other hand, felt sorry for her, and in fact sensed a connection between her and him. Becky was a fifteen year old runaway. She left her home somewhere in Illinois because, as she explained to Edward, her parents treated her as a second class child, worth less than her older sisters, who, by the way, had gotten pregnant in high school; who were divorced from their forced marriages and who sponged off their parents at the expense of the youngest. Where had Edward head that story before?

He told Becky his story and they compared notes, only to discover that the more they talked about their circumstances the more depressed they got. Edward and Becky asked Sunday her story. She had none to tell, or none she wanted to tell. She was difficult to talk to. Edward suspected that she was always horny, a true sexual compulsive, that her mind had difficulty focusing on any other subject. Nevertheless, although Becky was trouble for anyone found in her company, Edward felt compelled to be her friend and confidant. He did not ask where she lived, never knew her last name and absolutely made no attempt at affection. Nor did he want to take a chance with Sunday not knowing who she had been with and what her last partner might have given her.

In 1969, hitchhiking was the standard method of travel for those who had no money. It was ten o'clock at night when the three started their spur of the moment trip to Chicago. They stood by the side of the road, a busy two lane heading north straight and flat wedged between fields abundant with corn or thick with soybeans, their thumbs out each time a car neared, then, as it passed, they turned to walk north and await another.

They had no luck until Sunday suggested Edward hide in the ditch that paralleled the highway. The chances were better, she explained, if there were only two women up on the road looking for a ride. When a car stopped all Edward had to do was run up and jump in. It worked. No sooner had he concealed himself in the ditch than a car driven by a lone male stopped. Edward ran up to the shoulder. The girls slid in the back seat and Edward jumped in the front. The look on the driver's face was at first astonishment, then distress and then despair. Edward figured he ruined what scheme the driver had concocted between the time he saw two female hitchhikers and the time Edward plunked his ass down next to him.

The trip took three hours. The driver, who said little in that time, dropped them off on Rush Street near downtown Chicago. It was Saturday night and the boulevards of the city were swarming with every variety of human being. The threesome was exhausted not only from travel but from coming off a fresh high. The energy that came from their indulgence earlier that evening instantly vanished when the high wore off.

Edward scoured the street looking for someone who appeared appropriate for their current need, a place to sleep. But before he could make a choice, Sunday was making her way toward Edward and Becky dragging by the arm her choice for the night's innkeeper. Fortunately, he was someone Edward would have picked to ask for a place to crash. Although Edward was sure the stranger had instantly agreed to providing Sunday a place to sleep, there was reluctance in his voice when he discovered Edward and Becky were also part of the package.

Nevertheless, with hesitation, he agreed to find a place for all three. How was Edward or Becky to know what was really in store? When they arrived at the building about two blocks off Rush Street, Sunday's new found companion motioned toward a door just a few feet down from the elevator. He knocked heavily. "This is where you and your friend (meaning Becky) will sleep," he announced. He said he only had room for one person upstairs in his place. Sunday grinned. She had used what she used best to derive the most benefit, in this case a comfortable bed.

A short round man with gruff appearance, sloppily dressed and smelling of stale alcohol and smoke answered the door. Their guide told him Edward and Becky needed a place to spend the night. He nodded and motioned for them to enter. He acted as if people sleeping in his room was a common occurrence, as if he was customarily brought travelers who didn't fit in with the schemes of his upstairs neighbor. The room was unlit except for a bare bulb above the stove. When Edward's eyes adjusted to the lack of light, he saw a table and two chairs in the corner, on the table was a hot plate, a jar of peanut butter, a half loaf of bread and a television. The rest of the room was taken up by a double size bed and another chair that sat under a window black with the soot and dust of the big city. The murkiness of the room was fortunate. Edward did not want to see what the walls or floors or bed linens looked like.

Edward shared the double bed with their host; Becky slept on the floor. She was frightened. Edward saw it in her face and sensed it most of the night from her fitful sleep. He was also apprehensive until he realized the man next to him was drunk enough that there was no likelihood any harm would come to them. Nevertheless, Edward was prepared to push Becky and himself out the door should the need arise.

But it didn't. The next morning Edward awoke and realized he had slept soundly most of the night. It was 9:00 a.m. His bed mate was still asleep, snoring roughly. Edward looked to where Becky had occupied the floor and found her gone. He rose quickly, put on his shoes and went to search for his companions. At the entrance to the building stood the person who had so ingeniously arranged their sleeping quarters. Edward did not thank him, but asked him where Becky and Sunday had gone. He told Edward he had no idea, but that they had instructed him to explain that now that Edward had guided them to Chicago they could make it on their own. "I guess you're not needed anymore." he said snidely.

Edward asked, "So did you do it with her last night?"

He smiled. "Damn right I did. You didn't think I found other accommodations for you and your little friend for any other reason?"

"Well, you know," Edward informed him, "I did it with her a few weeks ago. Now I got a wicked case of the clap." Edward grinned and walked away. When he hit the street he stuck out his thumb and headed home.

On the way back to Charleston, Edward headed south on Interstate 57 sitting next to a truck driver who liked to sing Tex Ritter songs. He let Edward out at a rest stop just north of Kankakee. He was heading his semi west toward Iowa and he suggested the rest stop was a good place to find another ride south. As he drove away he shouted a reminder down from his towering perch. "Remember what I said. There are no do overs." He drove off waving his baseball cap out the window and shouting like he was riding a bull in a rodeo.

Edward had shared with the truck driver his story of the distressing relationship he had with his parents. "Go back to them," the truck driver advised. "Go back and apologize."

"They're due for apologies, too," Edward responded.

"They will."

"I doubt it. They told me this was all my doing. That I was at fault, and that I could not come back home or receive any support from them unless I came crawling home on my hands and knees and apologized."

"They said that?"

"Not in those exact words, but it was implied."

"That's bullshit. Your parents are probably sitting in their living room right now, trying to figure out what they did wrong to make you leave home, and just waiting for you to come through that door."

"Now that's bullshit," Edward countered.

The conversation proceeded nowhere. It went back and forth. The truck driver trying to persuade Edward to go home, apologize. He might just be surprised how they will react, he told Edward. Edward countering with their words of scorn, Roberta's influence, their German (father) and Irish (mother) stubbornness, and a lot of "bullshits" thrown in to highlight their disagreement.

Edward stood near the rest stop building, pondering the truck driver's admonitions and recommendation. Should he return? Considering the twenty dollars he had in his pocket was all the money he had in the world and the clothes he was wearing just about the limit of his wardrobe, it was tempting. But going back was more than fresh clothes and spending money. Past experience told Edward that no matter how seriously he apologized he would never get either. He felt he had been emotionally mistreated by his parents. For him the offenses they committed were excessive. For Edward to return home and beg forgiveness from two insensitive, uncaring people who he felt had betrayed him was a betrayal of himself. They had given Edward no motive to atone, no incentive to appease them. He could think of no rationale to return home.

Edward caught a ride on a semi heading to Champaign, forty-five miles away. The driver was a talkative older man, about sixty, with thin gray hair parted down the middle and slicked back on the sides. Gray stubble covered his chin and cheeks, and his face looked like he really had been driving the road for the forty years he boasted to Edward when he got in the cab. He made lengthy discourses about his wife (a solid woman that had stood by him through hard times) and his children. The older daughter (a lovely young woman almost out of nursing school), a younger daughter (a senior in high school, a cheerleader, knocks all the guys dead), an older son (the oldest of all the children and now a corporal in the United States Army, going for his second tour in Nam) and a younger son, (heading to be a good for nothing if he didn't get some sense knocked into him). He would do it but he is so often on the road. Edward thought, he had been home often enough to sire four children, why not to give his son some guidance?

Fortunately, the truck driver talked enough for both of them and the subject of Edward's parents never came up.

From Champaign Edward caught a third ride for the last fifty miles from a group of guys his age heading to the same town, college students like Edward who had been to a fraternity party at the University of Illinois. They were drunk. The driver, fortunately, appeared more sober, or perhaps less drunk than the other three. It was nearly dark, the sun just illuminating the tips of the clouds that were scattered about the sky. Edward sensed comfort to be almost home. This *was* his home now, even though he didn't have four walls he was able to call his own. What mattered most to him now and the first order of business in the morning after he woke up in a place he had not yet chosen to sleep for the night, was to find a place to live permanently. For tonight a friends house, or if none were available, the shelter at the city park. The last thing he wanted now was to be homeless.

Knowing his parents would never agree to sustain him financially, Edward doubled his hours in the dormitory kitchen. He was paid monthly and earned enough money to pay his tuition and rent an eight by twelve room in a shabby boarding house only a block from campus. The room contained a metal bed frame, a thin, threadbare mattress and a metal chest of drawers. Rent was thirty dollars a month. The building was dubbed "The Rehab Center" with a hand painted sign over the front door displaying the name. The dozen rooms in the building were rented by a couple of misfits who had dropped out of school but had not found any direction and a group of Pakistani students who banked on an education in an American university to bring them fortune and respect back home.

The money Edward had, though necessary to sustain himself, was barely enough to pay what meager bills he had. Some months he had none left over for food. He scrounged off friends or stuffed his pockets with biscuits and fruit from the kitchen where he worked or stuffed those same pockets with lunch meat and fruit from the IGA. So as to prevent his friends from tiring of his persistent begging, he made serious efforts at alternating among the people in town who were generous enough to supply him with food now and then.

As the days between his sending that letter to his parents and his newly bestowed independence grew greater in number, Edward realized that it was not money that was eluding him as much as it was the emotional support that had for years never been offered to him but that he still yearned for nonetheless. That is what he was searching for, had been searching for at least since he came home from the seminary and probably earlier but had never realized it. He found himself searching in places where the access was easy and noncommittal, but exiting those relationships became an ordeal. Passage out of the mire of searching for succor but finding further distress became a tremendous burden for many people he knew at that time, including himself.

Drugs, sex and Rock and Roll were the forces that carried Edward through one day and into the next but not necessarily in that order. School ran a distant fourth, and sometimes was assigned to fifth place in the hierarchy of his daily life if there was a meaningful political or social issue that demanded his immediate attention. He felt an immediacy to experience those diversions. But in the back of his mind, a mind that was becoming less and less coherent, he had a feeling that some kind of order to his life was close. He hoped it was. Whenever that occurred, he also hoped his values of peace, justice and fairness remained with him, and that the immediate gratification he often sought and regularly demanded from drugs, music and fleeting intimacies swiftly waned. There were others on the campus, a minute number out of the hundreds who sought comfort from marching and protest and indulgence in the hazardous distractions that claimed their bodies and souls, who also wished for distractions that were as perilous and exacting. Although Edward did not recognize it at the time, his lifestyle was merely a detour, in fact a short one, that allowed him to remove himself from a childhood and adolescence he perceived as increasingly wretched the more wretched his independence became.

Seeking an emotional crutch became almost an obsession for him. He inevitably recognized that drugs were leading him away from the object of his search. Random sex, as close to an emotional entanglement as he could find at the time, was actually prolonging the search for his ultimate objective. The women who made themselves available were, for the most part, searching for the same thing he was, everybody was. To complicate matters, the first girl Edward had sex with after he had estranged himself from his parents gave Edward the clap. The second one had an emotional breakdown just as Edward was at the peak of lovemaking, the third one was more eager to order a pizza when they were done than to savor the moment.

Rock and Roll was never intended to furnish emotional strength. It only broke the monotony and briefly concealed the realization that what he and those around him sought was no where to be found.

When Edward came to the threshold of his own peculiar breakdown (he actually contemplated returning to Chicago and reconciling with his parents), he met the girl who one year later became his wife. They met at the student union, Edward with his friends, she with hers. Her friends knew Edward's friends and vice versa, but she and Edward had never met. They met that night and as their mutual friends left the union to explore different interests that might become available, Teresa and Edward talked over coffee. Some of their mutual friends returned, unable to locate anything of interest in that dismal campus town.

They had heard of a party on fourth street. They all went. Teresa and Edward talked over Styrofoam cups filled with cheap wine. For the next two weeks they met and talked over an assortment of beverages. At the end of the two weeks Edward asked Teresa to be his wife. They married one year later.

Teresa was fresh, intelligent and very attractive. And she was not burdened by the unsavory recreations that occupied the lives of those around her. She had a social agenda, particularly a voracious appetite for support of women's rights, an equal insatiable concern for the environment and a very clear opinion as to why everyone should be opposed to the Vietnam War. Edward felt an affinity for those same issues but was unclear as to what he had done to show his support for them. Admittedly he had become lax at setting priorities. When the sex, drugs and Rock and Roll syndrome had taken over his soul, he banished many previously meaningful issues from his clouded mind.

Teresa reversed Edward's ill fortune. She compelled him to focus on those significant issues that were important to him, important to both of them. She cleaned Edward up, dusted him off, even helped him put on weight. At the same time there was a downside, not one that threatened their relationship, but a contrasting view of direction. Edward was content to proceed in a direction resembling the path he had been pursuing for some-time. He was content with having little to call his own as long as he did not have to surrender to the demands his parents or any other representation of authority placed on him. Teresa, on the other hand, while not opposed to Edward's not looking forward, was determined to get him to reconcile with his parents. It was a subject they sometimes hotly debated, and always as a consequence of those sometimes contentious disputes, they ended up in each others arms for the rest of the night.

Although her argument was simple—what did Edward have to lose and there might be something to gain—she arrived at it in a roundabout way. "Your parents are probably as heart sick about this situation as you are." But Edward wasn't. "Sure you are, you're just so numbed by their rejection of you that you feel no connection to them." Edward didn't want any connection; he disconnected himself a long time ago. "Not really, you only think you did. You can never not be their son and they can never not be your parents." There were too many negatives there; Edward never trusted sentences that contained a lot of negatives. He thought it was just that: too many negatives that tore the parent—son relationship asunder. "You're just as much their son as your sister is their daughter and your brother is their son. Without you there are only two children in that family and I don't think any of you want that." Wait a minute. That made some sense to Edward, despite his eagerness to dispel any logical arguments that he might have to accept. If he is on the outside then any benefit that is given to Kevin and Roberta in the future would definitely be beyond his grasp. Finally, an argument that had some merit, but on further reflection, not enough to warrant Edward's one-sided atonement.

In the end it was not Teresa's insight into her new husband's relationship with his parents that coerced him to capitulate, but her potential relationship to them. She wanted to have in-laws. She wanted to get to know her husband's parents, be a good daughter-in-law. She was convinced that once Edward returned and they met his wife, all would be forgiven and forgotten. Edward yielded to her sentimentality, but only on one condition: he would not apologize for anything he had done or said or do and say. After two years of haggling over the details of a reconciliation visit, Edward finally agreed. .

XVII

Since Edward was not certain what the consequences might be when he finally, after four years, faced his adversarial parents, he felt it was prudent to soften the beach head with a volley of conciliation, not the groveling variety but the sort that would make them believe they had an advantage, however slight it might appear to be.

With Teresa's help, Edward carefully crafted a one page letter to his parents. In it he dispensed eloquent philosophies about the importance of relationships particularly between parent and child, how no one should grow old without knowing that their children are always there for them, that, because of the distinct biological and emotional connection that naturally exists between parent and child, there must be the recognition that a child is a person that should be allowed to think for him or her self.

Writing that letter required a lot of endurance on Edward's part. It required more stamina than Edward thought he had. It required more, before, during and after the writing of the letter than he felt the exercise was worth. It required much more than was required of him to write the letter four years before that brought him to this point. Edward felt positive that this letter, in fact any attempt at reconciliation, was probably futile. Just because he assented to Teresa's dogged efforts to write the letter and make the visit, that did not mean he concurred in her assessment of what the final outcome would be.

With Teresa's resolute encouragement, Edward wrote and

mailed the letter, notwithstanding that over the entire week it took him to accomplish that feat, he suffered from insomnia and gas. Actually, he didn't know why he became so distressed over sending the letter. He highly doubted that his parents would agree to his returning to the fold without him providing to them a full and complete written apology for all the things he had said and done and all the things he should have said and should have done and had not said and done and probably some things they thought he had said and done but he really hadn't. Why did he have to worry? There was nothing to be alarmed about. When Edward told Teresa how confident he was that his parents were unlikely to agree to any bilateral reconciliation, and most likely would not even respond to the letter, she smiled and said that if that was the case then there should not be any reason for Edward to be losing so much sleep at night.

A response came within a week. Edward was astounded by the swift reply and sickened by how positive it sounded. Yes, come and visit. Yes, we will be pleased to meet your wife. Not happy, or delighted, not thrilled or even tickled, just pleased. Edward did not expect ecstatic or elated, but a step higher than pleased on the scale of emotions may have removed some of his doubts about this attempt at an armistice. Pleased meant, yes, you can bring her but you should consider yourself fortunate that we are even allowing you to set foot in our house. Teresa told Edward his assessment was full of shit. The letter was typed, not hand written. Surprisingly the letter was signed by Edward's father. Edward suspected his mother wanted no part of this weak effort at an armistice. He was surprised his father did since he had made so little effort in the previous twenty-two years. Edward was also surprised that his father even took the time to sign his name. Had he maybe typed the letter also? My God, what had come over the man? The letter contained a post script, a subtle implication that this journey back to the past that Edward had once rejected was doomed from the start, a statement most likely added after further thought and discussion. "For your mother's sake, please do not visit for longer than two days," his father wrote in his careless scrawl. Two days. That was more than twice as long as Edward had planned anyway.

Edward fired off a quick note suggesting a date. An equally quick reply agreed. The visit was scheduled for August, four weeks from when Edward received the letter from his father. They planned to arrive Friday early in the afternoon and depart Saturday evening. The weekdays were certainly unacceptable because Edward's father worked all day meaning that Edward and Teresa would be alone with Edward's mother to witness the sobbing and malicious remarks she was prone to let trickle out as the beads in her hand clicked in rapid succession. Sunday was out of the question. His mother was insanely Catholic; his father was a tag along, an "I wanna be but I just can't seem to give a shit" Catholic. Since Edward abandoned that religion and all others several years before, he thought it wise to also rule out Sunday. His mother, not knowing Edward was no longer Catholic, would certainly expect him to go to church and that confrontation alone was grounds for Teresa and Edward to be booted out and sent on their way. Besides, Teresa was raised Presbyterian. To Edward's mother, that in itself was blasphemous, but to be in his mother's house on Sunday with a Presbyterian wife was sacrilegious.

A year after Edward sent the infamous letter and was removed from the household, his parents moved to an upscale apartment on Lake Michigan. South Shore Drive, halfway between the projects at 53rd street and the working class neighborhoods where Edward grew up. The street was lined with high-rises, ten, fifteen and twenty story buildings that seemed out of place on that side of the city. Some were opulent and some not so luxurious. The area was mixed affluent. After they moved to South Shore Drive, they bought a Buick because Edward's father thought a Buick was a couple of notches up from a Ford. After Edward cut his ties (or, rather, when his parents cut them) they suddenly had money and moved upscale.

Edward never really knew where their money came from or

what his father did for a living. He knew his mother worked as a secretary for an insurance agent, a meek, unassuming, bald headed man with a big nose and eyes that looked like they were always crying. Knowing his mother, she controlled that business, because her boss was no match for the commanding disposition and conniving nature that directed everything she did and said. With both his mother and father working Edward knew the family wasn't poor. Despite that, they lived frugally in a rented house. Edward's father bought a new car every three years, always a Ford from the same salesman, a short squat Italian man who, oddly, looked much like his father's and Edward's barber who, coincidentally, looked like Danny DeVito. Maybe they were brothers.

Edward felt out of place in this section of Chicago. For twenty years he lived among a concoction of assorted nationalities accumulated from every corner, every nook, every recess of the European continent and all its islands. Now, in this prosperous, quasi-monied neighborhood that outlined the curving shore of Lake Michigan, he found his parents living among people who did not admit to a nationality or ethnic root. They had expunged any connection to the old country if they had arrived from one; if they were second generation American or beyond then their ancestral beginnings had diminished considerably.

Edward knew his parents had a strong loathing to the mix of ethnic blood that occupied the old neighborhood. They, particularly his father, had said as much many times using a few well chosen words. He had talked at length, at least what he might think of as "at length," about moving to a neighborhood that was more in line with their needs and requirements. Translated that meant they had no desire to stay in a neighborhood that would soon become transitional, in other words full of people of color. Those were not his exact words. He could never be so tactful when referring to other races and ethnic groups. They, meaning the blacks, Edward's father moaned periodically, were already eight blocks away. The moans and groans of a man fearing the invasion of black people into his pure white, albeit ethnically polluted, neighborhood began when they were fifteen blocks away and continued regularly with each block they migrated closer. The last lament that the neighborhood's loss of its white sovereignty was imminent came just a week before Edward wrote his infamous letter. When the proximity of a black influx got to within four blocks, they moved.

When Teresa and Edward drove up in their emerald green Volkswagen Beetle, Edward saw the building towering before him as a rigid, resolute bastion of status quo, no social conscience, no political energy beyond voting for those who also had no social conscience. He parked in a visitor space next to a Lincoln Continental. The doorman, a stiff, uncompromising retiree wearing a long brocaded wool coat and hat and who likely had a flask of whiskey in his back pocket to keep the chill at bay in the winter and to cool the blood in the summer, contemplated with obvious disdain Edward's shoulder length hair and beard. He blocked the door while he weighed his options. Edward told him his name and that he had come with his wife to visit his parents who lived on the twelfth floor.

This was not a neighborhood. It was a vicinity, a section of town, a location on the map, a zip code, a spot for only select people. It was a cluster of like minded people who saw economic security as well as personal safety as the absolute objective of life, the be all and end all of their constricted existence. Along with the financial point of convergence came all the adjunct biases, prejudices and intolerance that go along with having money. Edward's parents probably fit in very nicely since they had come to this place with all those same biases already well tuned.

Where Edward grew up, now that was a neighborhood, a true melting pot surrounded by neighborhoods that were boiling pots and that were saturated with distress and ripe for unrest. Edward and his family sat in the middle, a mixture of Irish, German, Hungarian, Czech, and Slovaks with a few Italians, immigrants many of them, in the United States for only a year or two; a few, like Edward's parents, second generation Americans. Being in the midst of potential calamity between warring factions from the surrounding neighborhoods, Edward's neighborhood was always keen to the possibility of being dragged into the center of any clashes that may erupt. For that reason members of the neighborhood supplied security for each other. Beyond that the residents rarely commingled unless it was Irish with Irish, Eastern European with Eastern European.

It was largely a neighborhood of children because, for the most part, the parents had little sense of community in the neighborhood. Their immigration to America had stripped them of any affinity for group dynamics, particularly since many of them were of ethnic origins that had been in conflict with other people of different ethnic origins in the old country and continued to be in conflict with their own political, social and even religious convictions in their new country. The Hungarians were cordial to each other, the Poles talked and socialized with other Poles. The Irish trusted only the Irish and even their own kind mistrusted each other particularly the Irish Catholics and the Irish Protestants. No one favored the Blacks, Hispanics or Jews. They had their own neighborhoods, there own communities, their own attachments. Edward's neighborhood ignored them, they ignored Edward's neighborhood. The only difference was Edward's neighborhood ignored them because the people in it were able to; the other neighborhoods ignored Edward's neighborhood because Edward's neighborhood would not let the other neighborhoods do anything else.

The children, on the other hand, seldom had an inclination to dredge up antagonisms from the old country. They had no old country. They had only a connection to the new. This country they had been born in had relevance; the old country had none. There was no correlation to the old, no bond. And while adolescents normally have a bond with nothing and no one but themselves, an attachment to the neighborhood quickly developed. The parents maintained an affinity for customs of the old country. They perpetuated those customs. The only attachment the parents had to this country was to their church and to the factory where they earned their daily bread, the steel mills mostly, where they worked twelve hour days for wages that supplied enough money to pay the bills and maybe put a little away to pay for a casket when they died. It was a melting pot in the sense that it was teeming with diverse ethnic ingredients, but the original ingredients, the parents, never made the soup palatable.

But the children, the children were the neighborhood. They had the link. There was a kinship that made them all charter members of the neighborhood. They had an affiliation like the Elks and Moose had their alliances. "I'll be in the neighborhood, Ma." She knew the boundaries. "I'll be with some of the neighbor kids, Ma." She knew who they were. Ma may not have known precisely who Edward or any of his friends was with at any particular time, she may not have liked the idea that he was with the Polish kids or the Hungarian kids, but she knew the scores of kids in the neighborhood, where they lived, who there mothers were and their telephone numbers. If she had to, Ma could find her son.

The neighborhood had a broad expanse. It was spacious and the neighborhood kids knew every inch of it. The boundaries were distinct. It extended one mile to the west just to the edge of the black neighborhood; on the south were the railroad tracks. The eastern border was the Hispanic enclave and on the north it was . . . actually the northern border was somewhat indefinite. If a kid from the neighborhood was near the Hispanic neighborhood the northern boundary extended only three blocks. Farther west it was the Jewish neighborhood, about four blocks. Those were the dimensions. About two miles long and the width varied. If anyone ventured beyond those boundaries he or she was taking a risk. The degree of peril that might have befallen them was commensurate with the direction they took. The western edge was dangerously close to the black neighborhood. The distinction was very clear as were the unwritten rules that governed neighborhoods. There was a tacit understanding that the blacks did not venture east beyond their borders; kids from Edward's neighborhood stayed on their side. When, at times, through a dare or to seek revenge for a neighbor wronged, or to use the forbidden territory as a shortcut to another section of the city, someone ventured one direction or the other, there resulted from time to time brief skirmishes that produced some cuts and bruises along with plenty of boasts of bravery and daring, but rarely injuries that required medical care.

The eastern boundary divided Edward's neighborhood from the Hispanic neighborhood. The rules were the same except that both the Mexicans, as they were called, and the kids from Edward's neighborhood were more tolerant of using each other's neighborhood as a shortcut, particularly if the Hispanic gang was planning a daring raid against the neighborhood to the west. The domain south was similar to Edward's neighborhood. Edward and his friends had common characteristics with the kids south of the tracks, the same ethnic, religious and economic mix, same neighborhood pride, but the segregation and resulting implied rules existed because the other side of the tracks was, compared to any other proscribed adjoining neighborhood, enormously more dangerous. The long, dark viaducts burrowing under the railroad tracks connecting one side to the other contained ample hazards to prevent anyone, particularly a child brimming with speculation and curiosity, from venturing through the viaduct to the other side. In those tunnels women were raped, men were beaten unrecognizable and children vanished. Stories of the neighborhood beyond the tracks abounded with hideous murders and molestations, drunks and hobos found in the gutters slashed to death, arsons, and gangs that had no mercy for anyone of any color or national origin.

No one from Edward's neighborhood entered the Jewish enclave for the simple yet never defined reason that they were Jews who lived there and non Jews did not associate with Jews. They were never given an explanation and, as an adolescent, Edward was at a loss as to why the code of segregation applied to other white people. It was easy for them to understand their parents' antagonism toward the dark skinned people beyond their borders. Their color was different, their lifestyle, their economic status. Everything pointed to a lower class that had no incentive nor likelihood of ever reaching the status of white people. But the Jews? True, they were somewhat different. They worshipped differently. They were, for the most part, economically advanced compared to the factory workers that cluttered Edward's neighborhood, and they drove more expensive automobiles and had more expensive homes. Despite what appeared to Edward to be a trivial distinction between white Jews and white Protestants and Catholics, mere idiosyncrasies it seemed to him, he and his neighborhood friends were banned from that part of the city. Since the children and their parents, but particularly the kids, were not bound by nor familiar with logic, they relied on the experience of their parents on matters of race and the dangers that could befall them should they ever venture beyond the protection of their neighborhood. So the Jews were disallowed.

At their parents urging the kids in Edward's neighborhood were inclined to believe that there was something wrong with the Jews, that they were better than the Jews, that they would be tainted from any association with the Jews. As children it was not difficult to accept the trite and absurd arguments of their parents. It was cool to think they were better than other people. It was easy to think they were better than the blacks and Hispanics, but in the back of Edward's mind the question lingered as to why the white Jews were part of that package.

After high school, Edward's attitude and philosophy on just about everything began to evolve into something that progressively clashed with what his parents and the old neighborhood had established long ago. His father became intensely upset when he discovered Edward had once dated a Jewish girl. When his mother found out Edward went on a date with a Jewish girl while in his freshman year at Loop Junior College, she told him that he was just putting another spear in Christ's side as he hung on the cross, and that she felt the pain of that spear also. Edward's father was livid when he found out his son went on one date with a Mexican girl. The latter instance, particularly the words his father used to describe Mexican people in general, gave Edward a thorough insight into his father's precise inclination toward people of other colors and ethnic origins. His mother just picked up her rosary and squeezed those beads harder than Edward had ever seen her squeeze them.

The neighborhood was a dysfunctional creature, a lower order organism that, like every other neighborhood in the city, was a recluse, a self-contained, self-centered solitary beast that protected itself and its denizens from other life forms that bordered it while provoking inner turmoil that was a natural result of throwing together a volatile brew of a dozen different ethnic groups from twenty different countries, who spoke twenty-five different languages and dialects and worshipped in as many churches scattered around the city.

Despite this explosive mixture the neighborhood rarely saw clashes among its own occupants. And when they did occur it amounted to verbal disputes between parents of the kids who could not understand what provoked such a display of antagonism. When those disputes arose there was a feuding period where the Irish kids could not play with the Hungarian kids, or the Protestant kids could not play with the Catholic kids. It wasn't the kids. They didn't care. It was the parents. And until peace was made, and it was always an unsteady peace, the kids just had to make the best of it.

Nonetheless, the neighborhood gave the kids a good life. They played games together at the elementary school playground—baseball, basketball, tag football. They spent night after summer night talking about their futures or about girls if only boys were present while sitting on the swing set and monkey bars at the playground. They made sometimes three or four treks to Frank's corner market each summer day to buy an RC Cola with their allowance, at least for those who got one, or with the money some of them won pitching pennies on the sidewalk in front of Roman Petrowski's house. They sat on front porches guessing the makes and models of cars as they passed by and dreamed about having those cars when they could afford to buy them. They ventured down to the train tracks at dusk to steal flares from the cabooses or at night to throw rocks at the passing boxcars. They walked down the alley to the little league field and stopped to watch Charley O'Connell's sister sunbathing on a blanket in her back yard. They watched the neighborhood gang, the protectors of the neighborhood sovereignty from the gangs to the west and east, sniff glue on the back side of the school and talk about the rumbles they were in and the girls they had humped. If Edward lived in the high rise that his parents had chosen it could never compare to what he and his friends had in the neighborhood.

The doorman rang the bell and announced Edward's arrival to the static filled voice that responded. Edward could not tell if it was his mother or father who answered the bell. The doorman held the door for them and begrudgingly let Edward and Teresa pass. On the elevator Teresa rubbed Edward's back making a gallant but fruitless effort to relieve some of the stress that had been building for the last several hours. When they came to the door of his parent's apartment, there was no one standing there to greet them. They knew they were on their way up, yet Edward wondered if they found it amusing or were simply maintaining what they thought was the advantage by making their son knock as if he had to beg to be admitted?

After the second knock and just before Edward contemplated turning and heading back to the elevator, his father answered the door. He offered only a "Hello, son." All he ever called Edward was "son" as if he had an aversion to his name. Edward repaid his father with a similarly monotonal "Hello, dad." Inside Edward's mother sat on the couch playing what easily could have been her one millionth game of solitaire. It was an obsession, one she had taken more seriously than her parental obligations over the years. There were times as a child when Edward wished he had been a deck of cards so that he would have been handled so deftly and with such endearment, to be so consequential, so cared for, so pleasurable and so tenderly put away each night, safely and securely, or a can of Busch Bavarian beer that his father always lovingly caressed.

"Hello, mother," Edward said from the door. She looked up, ever so slightly acknowledging her son's presence and not missing the beat of putting a ten of hearts on a jack of clubs. "This is Teresa," Edward announced to them. "My wife," he added just in case they had forgotten. She laid another card on one of the piles in front of her, placing it with such force the TV tray that served as her gaming table shuttered.

Edward's father bowed, barely showing the top of his bald head. His mother shuffled the cards, preparing for another game. They sat down. Edward's father guided himself into his easy chair, removing the *TV Guide* from his back pocket and placing it in his lap as he sat. Since the purchase of the family's first television nearly twenty years before Edward had never seen him within viewing distance of the set without some guide to the evening's viewing in his hand, shoved in his pocket or within reaching distance of where he sat. As Edward's mother obsessed on her rosary and the New Testament each and every day, his father was controlled after six thirty each weekday and afternoons and evenings on weekends by the enticement of television. He went through life thinking his only choices were what was listed in the *TV Guide* and in the beer section at the A & P. His most weighty decision was whether to buy a can of peanuts or mixed nuts.

As Edward's mother adeptly shuffled the deck of cards, Edward visualized her wearing a dealer's visor, shuffling the cards with nimble fingers and dealing black jack or stud, a chewed up, unlit cigar hanging out of her mouth, the other players fidgeting and sweating because she had already won most of their money. She could have done that at one time, Edward thought; she may be capable of doing it now. She had that vicious, hard nosed streak in her that could easily bluff anyone into uncontrollably giving up to her their wads of gambling cash. Now, though, at her age, it was the stamina she lacked. She sat with her head bent down toward the cards displaying her sparse white hair. The wrinkles had trebled since Edward last saw her; even with her sitting he saw she had shrunk in stature, appearing on the verge of emaciation. But her eyes, when she forced them in her son's direction, were still potent, the stare of a tenacious adversary spoiling for a fight, her vengeful nature waiting to erupt.

Edward's father sat quietly in his chair, fidgeting with his *TV Guide.* Edward sensed he was preparing for the worst; that, before his son's arrival, they had devised a strategy that he was uncomfortable with executing. Edward's mother was the dominant force as always, his father the disciple. She led the charges; he cleaned up after the battle.

He laid his magazine on the table, then picked it up, rolled it up and held it with both hands. Edward watched his eyes look at everything in the room except his son and Teresa. The most significant feature of his father was not a mole, or scar or repulsive nose. It was his lack of anything notable. Should he have ever committed a crime or some dastardly deed it would have been impossible for the victim to give a description to the police. About the only adjective applicable would be "plain." "No significant features that really stood out, officer." His face, his body, the way he walked, were not any more startling than most men met on the street. He was as absorbing as a test pattern. He had a bald head, which in the dry season became scaly and difficult to look at. His head was permanently cocked to the side away from everything. There were very few gray hairs in proportion to the number of hairs he had. He had the shape of a frequent beer drinker. His penchant for beer along with his weakness for an easy chair and television caused him to wear his pants above the gut with his belt nearly to the breastbone. Otherwise, his pants would have fallen to the floor. His spherical contour was, from the point of view of a child, grotesque. As an adult, Edward mellowed his opinion realizing that many men his age had similar tendencies. Edward had, as a child, vowed to himself that he would never look that way.

No one immediately spoke as Edward's mother nimbly placed each card in its obligatory space. They were at a stalemate before the negotiations had even begun. Edward saw this as an unfavorable sign. Teresa sat primly next to her husband, a sweet smile on her face. Hopeless or not, Edward figured he had no stake in these peace talks. He had a wife now. His parents had not supported him financially for four years, emotionally for twenty-two. What did he have to lose or gain here? Nothing either way. So why not make it quick and to the point.

"Mother, put the cards down." Edward politely ordered. It was meant as half appeal, half command. Her look told Edward she did not hear the appeal part. She stopped in mid-shuffle. His father shuddered. "I've come here to try and make peace. I brought Teresa with me thinking that my being married, and an adult now, would show you that I have some sense of responsibility and somehow validate my position in this family."

His mother glared at him. Edward glared back. Teresa squeezed Edward's hand. His father grabbed his *TV Guide*. "Who do you think you are," she countered, "that you can waltz in here and think that your mere presence can cancel everything you've done to me and your father, everything you've said?"

"You invited us," Edward retorted. She shot one of her looks at her husband, the kind of look that expresses bewilderment along with a smattering of indignation. Edward's father was the one who invited them, Edward suspected, without the affirmation of his wife. She had brow beat him since their visit was announced to her. Somehow he talked her into letting them come but his way now was cautious, even submissive to her implied denial that anything good could come of this meeting. Edward's father, Edward surmised, wanted some means of detente to the chilled relationship they had had. Why he wanted to make peace

Edward could not figure, but his impression, fueled by his father's demeanor and his mother's offensive disposition caused Edward to concede that it was him who looked for some kind of conclusion to this war, probably because he was tired of dealing with his wife's constant complaining of how they had been treated by their son. Edward's mother had no desire to meet her son even a quarter of the way. She went back to her solitaire.

To Edward's left sat a subdued man who had no notion of how meek and obedient he was. Or maybe he did. Edward looked his way and, as usual he reacted in the same unequaled way he responded to any crisis that was unavoidable and unsought. His gut erupted with a turmoil like a washing machine in which the load had become unbalanced. Edward could hear it thump and whoosh. He pressed his right arm against the chair's arm rest, raised his backside and farted. It had a bit of a hollow, windy sound to it, like it was blowing all the gas out quickly. In other circumstances it would get either a laugh where everyone in the group was comfortable with the person's flatulence, or it would elicit stares and *tsk, tsks*, dirty looks and maybe a giggle and a point from a child in public groups where, although everyone else had also experienced gas and let it out in the same manner, they believed such a biological action was a personal matter and not to be shared with strangers.

Here, in this circumstance, neither Edward's mother nor Edward or Teresa reacted at all. Edward and his mother were used to it. Teresa had been warned. It was a common occurrence in this household. After all, it was his father. After the second fart shattered the silence, Teresa, for the first time since Edward had met her, was unable to contain what at first appeared to be disgust but, as she rose and walked to the kitchen, was instead amusement, for Edward heard her giggle as she drew herself a glass of water. "And this wife of yours," Edward's mother blurted without warning after Teresa had left the room. "Is she the one who converted you to such a repugnant lifestyle? Is she the one who persuaded you to write that revolting letter four years ago and then leave as if we had not sacrificed all those years to raise you the best way we knew how?"

Not a good method of attack, Edward thought. She is picking on the wrong person. Edward was not usually aggravated by offensive accusations, especially from his mother. He had learned over the years to ignore them, to classify them as inconsequential. Teresa, on the other hand, was known to occasionally have a short fuse and easily get pissed off when an indictment was aimed at her, especially an unjust and unsupported one. Edward heard the glass slam down hard on the Formica counter in the kitchen. Like a cyclone she whirled around the corner into the living room. She was a capable match for any glare Edward's mother could assemble or any accusatory and malicious posture she could conjure up.

"How dare you! How *dare* you!" Edward's mother was clearly taken aback by Teresa's forcefulness. "Number one," Teresa continued with her usual amount of brusqueness, " I did not know your son when he left home four years ago. I did not have anything to do with the lifestyle he chose, but I can plainly see that what he chose is a damn sight better than what he left. Had I known him four years ago I most likely would have enticed him away from this, this degrading existence."

Go Teresa, go, Edward thought. His father's look of near terror made the rampage even more enjoyable. "And furthermore," she continued, "I am the one who persuaded your son to write to you in order to make an attempt at reconciliation. I'm sorry I did that." She turned to Edward. "I apologize for forcing you to come here tonight." Edward waved away the apology. No reason to ask his forgiveness, he thought. If nothing else Edward was able to substantiate his claims Teresa had doubted were as incredible as he had described.

When Teresa finished, Edward's mother rose slowly, gingerly moved the tray that blocked her exit from the couch and headed toward the bedroom. Teresa and Edward rose also. "I guess we better leave, Dad."

"Okay, son," he said meekly as if he had been rapped in the back of the head. "Maybe some other time, son." Edward nodded. Right, he thought. Another time. Edward doubted if either side would want another helping of what they just went through. Another time will probably be at the funeral of one of them. With Edward's mother continuing to wage this war of closed-hearted unforgiveness there would never be another time. This was the last time as far as Edward was concerned. His father knew that. He knew that negotiations had broken down indefinitely. He knew what indefinitely meant. And Edward really didn't think he cared, except that he still had to put up with his wife.

Teresa and Edward rode the elevator in silence. Now and then she shook her head, thinking how ludicrous the entire affair had been. The door man stood motionless as they passed through the double doors to the outside. He watched them leave making no effort to perform his duty and open the door for them. It was as if he knew they had reached an impasse, that neither side was willing to budge and that he had taken sides and would, after Edward and Teresa left the building, assure Edward's mother that her adversary, her traitor son, would never again be allowed in the building to annoy her in any way or bring her any more anguish.

Teresa kissed Edward on the cheek as he started the car. "I didn't believe you. I didn't think the childhood you described could be real, that your mother could be so, so, I don't even know how to describe her."

"So despicable," Edward offered

"That's one way to describe her."

"I've got dozens more," he said. "All of them describe a woman who, over the last twenty-two years, or at least the last seventeen because I can't remember the first five, treated me as a second class family-member, as if I had been adopted and then she decided she didn't really want me but was stuck with me." Edward described how his mother had metamorphosed into a contemptible person when he left the seminary, how their relationship deteriorated to a point where he became the target for all her animosity, all of her anxieties, all of her emotional collapses, her life malfunctions. How a treacherous conspiracy formed between his mother and Roberta against him. Edward acknowledged to Teresa that the seminary fiasco, although the principal catalyst in the formation of the fracture, was not the sole reason for his reduction in rank. Roberta's promiscuous behavior and Kevin's licentious lifestyle and self-centered demeanor had a very unfavorable impact on any claim Edward may have had on his future in the family. After Edward concluded his discourse on his childhood, they drove in silence until Teresa could no longer contain her amazement at what took place.

"And your father," Teresa said, " does he not have any balls?"

"No," Edward answered somewhat humiliated. "Never has."

PART III.

XVIII

Edward's thoughts seldom dwelled on his father after his parents cut their ties with their son, or, from their perspective, after Edward cut his ties with them. Any thoughts he may have harbored dwindled dramatically after he and Teresa visited them at their apartment on Lake Michigan. It didn't make a bit of difference who did the cutting. Edward's father really had no ties to his family that were worth cutting. His life was rarely a part of his children's when his children were growing up, thus Edward's mind was seldom able to conjure up any feelings for him that might have turned into a reflection of the man as Edward knew him. Occasionally a vague memory surfaced, one that intruded into Edward's mind because of somewhere he was, some smell, some sound that summoned a transient thought of his father. Edward may have caught himself sitting like his father did, resting easily in a recliner, one leg crossed over the other, index finger resting against his temple, thumb next to his chin. That is how his father sat when he watched television. Or Edward might have thought of him when he came across a *TV Guide.* Or when he saw someone drinking a Budweiser, or when dipping his fingers into a can of peanuts. Or when he or someone else farted. There were certain sights and sounds that drew Edward's mind to his father, but those thoughts were brief and only dealt with insignificant memories and never invoked any Edward would want to relive.

When Edward's father left Phoenix to live with Roberta after his wife died and the family buried her next to the bishop, his health was good relative to his age of eighty years. And because Edward never talked to Roberta and she never talked to Edward, the only reports as to his father's physical well-being came from Kevin, who passed along information as if it was that game where one person whispers something into another person's ear until it goes through twenty people and by the end it doesn't sound anything like what it was when it started. And when Kevin's colorful language was added to the mix, each time he called Edward ended up just shaking his head. When Teresa asked her husband what Kevin had told him, Edward could do nothing more than shrug his shoulders. So from the meager and faulty information he got from Kevin, Edward was forced to assume that his father's health was, at the maximum, good, especially considering he was eighty and had just lost his companion of fifty years. Surely Kevin would notify his brother if their father declined or was suddenly struck with a debilitating or terminal disease, or hospitalized because of some unexpected failure of a vital organ.

Surely *not.*

While at work one afternoon in early November, Edward received a telephone call from Kevin. The sound of his brother's voice when Edward said hello immediately led him to the conclusion that something was wrong with someone.

"It's Dad." Kevin's relaxed manner of saying "It's Dad" belied the reason he called. "He's in the hospital. They only give him a few days, maybe a week at the most." Wait a minute, Edward thought. This must be very serious. His style of communication had changed. Their father was not in the "fucking hospital." They had not given him a "few fucking days," not a "goddamn week at the most."

"What's wrong with him?" Edward asked, trying to sound more concerned than he felt comfortable being.

"Don't know. When he went to the hospital last week, it was. . . ."

"Wait, wait a minute. Last week? You say he went in the hospital last week? And I'm just finding out now?"

"Hey, Ed, I didn't hear until this morning. And I called you right away. Dumbshit Roberta thought we didn't have to be fucking told until something was really wrong. Goddamn asshole." That's better; that's Kevin back to normal. It was quite comical that there appeared a difference in his language when he talked about somebody dying he had a marginal fondness for and when he talked about someone he hated and wished was dead.

"And something is really wrong now, huh?" Edward asked, his voice was markedly disturbed by now, not so much because his father was near death, but because his asshole sister had no sense of decency or courtesy to let the two sons know their father was in the hospital. "What exactly is wrong?"

"Well, I don't know exactly. I didn't get much from Roberta." Roberta, a very uncaring, spiteful, self-centered, greedy, unsisterly . . . talked a lot to only those she cared to offer her precious words. You won't get much from her, Kevin, never, ever. "Anyway," Kevin was saying, "I talked to the doctor directly. He said it was just old age and everything was just shutting down."

"Just like that, he's healthy and suddenly everything just shuts down? How can that happen?"

"Don't know, Ed. Doctor said he came into the hospital because he became disoriented and fell in front of Roberta's house. After four days in the hospital, his kidneys started to fail, his liver is not functioning and his heart is getting weaker every minute."

"A few days you say?"

"Maybe a week."

Edward thought of his options. Should he wait until his father dies or should he attend another death watch like he did with his mother? A week. It could be as long as a week. Should he go up there now and maybe spend seven days waiting, within range of his sister's sarcasm and enmity? It could be more than seven days. The doctor could be wrong. It could be ten days, fifteen days. If he went up for five and left it could be the next day; if he went up and he lingered for fifteen days, and he left on the fifteenth day it could be the sixteenth day. It could be tomorrow. It could be now while Edward was sitting at his desk deliberating over his own fate for the next few days, and the fate of his father.

"I'll be up there tomorrow," Edward told Kevin. "I'll meet you at the hospital." A seven hour drive for possibly fifteen days of misery. Shit! Wait a minute. His birthday is in four days. What a time for death.

The imminent death of a parent is the absolute hypnosis. It is therapy, but not good therapy. It is honest but not humane. It is not therapeutic like correcting your well-being or finding yourself, finding your role in life, or discovering your sanity; you are a good mother, wife or husband, you do have feelings that count, depression can be dispelled, your life is valid or, as Kevin was fond of saying, getting your shit together. The death of a parent, a parent that really never was a parent, grants unwanted and unrelenting flashbacks. You lay blame, you find fault, but you never come to conclusions. That's what everyone needs when a parent dies, conclusions, no matter how that parent rates on the child's list of misgivings.

The seven hour drive to Dyer, Indiana was haunting. As Edward's car moved effortlessly on the highway, his mind struggled with memories he hadn't had in many years, memories he did not want to have and memories he never knew he had. There are moments, prolonged and sometimes unsettling, when a person becomes so immersed in thought about some weighty dilemma or uncertainty and, while the mind is absorbed with working out the problem and finding solutions or fretting over the predicament that the mind has focused on, the person misses everything going on within range. Edward's mind had instantly become so saturated with his father that he missed the Gateway Arch and skyline of St. Louis as he sped along Interstate 70 across the Mississippi River and only vaguely caught sight of that huge waterway out of the corner of his eye. He missed the farms and black dirt fields in central Illinois. He missed lunch.

He didn't feel the bumps and worn asphalt of the Illinois road that took him north. He didn't remember the name of the town where he slipped through the drive thru of some fast food restaurant in the middle of the afternoon three hours after his stomach should have warned him that he was hungry. He didn't remember if he bought French fries to chew on as he pondered his father's life. He probably did because he always bought French fries when he did fast food. They are a staple that have always provided fuel for his mental wheels that, this time, were churning and grinding through the seventeen years when he shared the same house as his father.

Edward didn't remember where he stopped for gas and almost forgot to stop until he noticed the needle parallel with the red line on the gas gauge. He didn't remember roads that turned into other roads that were taking him to a place where he did not really want to go.

About the time Edward reached Collinsville, Illinois, just a few miles east of St. Louis, he vaguely recalled going fishing with his father. Twice. Edward was seven the first time. He didn't remember how old he was the second. Both trips were to a lake south of Chicago, just the father and his son riding the thirty miles south, in silence, his son's head cocked to the side resting against the back of the seat, staring out the window at the city garbage dump at 95th Street, the warehouses, factories and cement plants with colossal smoke stacks that belched smoke of all hues twenty-four hours a day, seven days a week. Scattered among this obese amalgamation of industry were destitute neighborhoods filled with tenements, all of them including the people who lived in them blackened by the soot that thickened the air, the buildings and the people crumbling under the weight of their own poverty—pockets of indigents, street people, unemployed. "Who lives there, Dad?" "Nobody you want to know." "Why do they live there, Dad?" "Don't know." Edward wondered. He stared at the squared off neighborhoods, enclosed by the monstrous factories, the smoke stacks as sentries, barriers to those who might wish to leave, alerting those who might make a wrong turn and enter those destitute regions. He wondered and he watched with amazement for the ten minutes it took their car to zoom past those neighborhoods. He tried to answer his own questions, the questions his father could not or would not answer. Maybe they liked it there, Edward thought. Maybe they worked in those factories and it was easy for them to get to work. He didn't know those people who lived there didn't like it there, that they could not get out, that they had no where else to go, that they didn't have the money to get out, or the right color. He didn't know at that age that color forced a person to do things they didn't want to do or allowed a person to do just about anything they wanted to do. He didn't know they didn't work in the factories and warehouses because they didn't work, no one let them work. When he was older, maybe twelve or thirteen, he knew the answers to his questions and, like his father, he didn't care.

At the city limits the suburbs rose from what once were fields of corn. Old communities at first, the pioneers of suburbia exploring new ground, finding new paths away from the neighborhoods that were changing, neighborhoods that were mixing in ways that went beyond simply ethnic qualities. Then the masses followed the path finders building newer homes and shopping centers, communities that were safe and comfortable, where people *did* like it there, where they *were* employed, where no one had to be alert to making a wrong turn or frightened if they did.

The southern suburbs melted into fields of corn and beans, mostly corn, bordered by inconsequential rows of trees providing respite from the wind for a farmer's home or edging fields and providing a haven for birds and small wild animals. Unplowed fields held a scattering of cows standing like statues in the grassy fields. The only evidence of life was the circular movement of their mouths chewing grass or the cud.

Then came the lake. A sudden upshot of trees, forests of trees a kid from the south side of Chicago never sees unless he travels away from the concrete and steel. Hidden among the trees was a small lake meant only for fishing. No motor boats, no skiers, no swimmers, only fishermen, serious fishermen, the ones who sit in a boat all day from dawn to just as dusk approaches, their lines probing the water, bobbers bouncing ever so slightly, then plunging out of sight. A bite, a fish, a shout, tugging and pulling and reeling, a fish on the end. Then it begins again.

Edward found out then that fishing has its code of silence. The first time he went fishing with his father he did not realize this code existed. His father was always silent. But Edward noticed other fathers with their children silently staring at the water, waiting. No one talked. The only voice heard was the brief shout when the fish was on the line, or the "Damn" or sometimes a word more offensive when the fish was lost before it could be hauled into the boat. Edward's father fit in perfectly in this environment. Edward did not feel uncomfortable in his father's presence when they sat on the lake and fished. He didn't have to talk. Neither did his father. Edward asked no questions. His father didn't have to answer any. It was the one time when, in the company of his father, Edward felt at ease.

After a day of fishing, eating liver sausage sandwiches while sitting in the boat still holding their fishing rods, picking parts of worms out of their fingernails, catching fish and throwing them back, they made the return trip home. That was when Edward's discomfort returned. His head again cocked to the side resting against the back of the seat. Out the window he watched the sequel to the puzzling documentary he witnessed on their way to the lake, but in reverse. The corn transformed into new houses, freshly paved streets, into old houses and rutted dusty streets, into tenements and factories with filthy, menacing streets, then the city garbage dump at 95th Street, then home.

That dump provided Edward with more memories than his father ever did. On weekends in the summer, when there wasn't anything better to do, Edward's friend from St. Clem's, Gus Morton, and he went to the dump to play. Gus's father worked at the dump and on the occasional Saturdays he worked there Edward and Gus tagged along. While Gus's father drove the bulldozer pushing one pile of garbage into another pile of garbage, Edward and Gus explored the workers' shanties that were randomly placed around the dump. That was where the workers took their breaks and ate their lunches. It was where Edward and Gus hid to watch for rats, and when they spotted the vermin crossing from one pile to another, the boys jumped out and pelted them with rocks. Every time Edward and Gus went to the dump there were always hundreds of piles of garbage. Edward never figured out what they did with the garbage. Each time he went to the dump it seemed like it was all the same garbage piled a little higher.

At Springfield, Illinois, heading north, Edward remembered his father barbecuing pork ribs on a homemade grill built near Edward's sand pile in the backyard at their old home. Three times a summer, always on a Sunday afternoon, his father brought up the grill from the basement, set it over a pile of wood, put some crumpled up newspaper under the wood and lit it. From around noon after he had changed from his church clothes, had his breakfast and read the Sunday paper, until about six o'clock, the ribs cooked over coals that had been blistering hot for hours casting the aroma of sizzling meat and barbecue sauce throughout the neighborhood. Edward would stand in the drifting smoke and inhale the aroma of barbecue sauce, wood smoke and sizzling fat. The smell was marvelous.

The wood had to stay at an even burn, no flame or the meat burned, the coals fiery red or the sauce did not penetrate the meat. Edward's father let him throw fresh wood on the fire but only the small twigs that burned quickly and kept the coals at the right temperature. When the meat was done Edward ran to the table to feast on ribs, vinegar slaw and corn on the cob. When he was older he was astounded that this man, his father, so innocuous, so meager in personality and style, could be so skillful at preparing barbecue ribs. What was the source of this anomaly? How did he develop such a talent where evidently there were no others?

The other oddity in his father's character came to Edward at Decatur, Illinois as he turned east toward Indiana. It wasn't really a talent, but an ability that Edward never expected his father to have, and one which he allowed Edward to access sparingly. Edward played baseball in Little League each summer and he was always looking for someone to play catch with to keep his arm in shape. Edward once asked his father to play catch with him, a recreation normally shared between Edward and Kevin until Kevin enlisted in the army, or between Edward and the neighborhood kids who, for whatever reasons, were not available on that particular day. Edward was reluctant at first to ask his father to play catch because he was not certain his father could throw a baseball. Edward had never seen the man participate in any sport except two fishing expeditions. He hesitantly asked his father, and only because Edward was unable to find anyone else to play with and had the urge to throw a baseball back and forth. Boys have these urges once in a while, throwing a baseball or a football around, riding a bicycle, throwing rocks at a fence. They emerge quickly and just as quickly pass after ten or fifteen minutes when the recreation becomes tiresome and a new urge sets in.

So Edward asked his father. Edward thought that his reaction, like every other time he had asked his father to do something with him, would be negative. But Edward's concerns were for naught. His father said yes. They played catch and his father was good at it. He was actually good at something that required exertion, that required some smidgen of concentration and therefore some interest in the activity. They played catch for fifteen minutes. No words passed between them. He threw the ball; Edward threw the ball. He caught the ball; Edward caught the ball. Edward was the one who actually ended the entertainment. He threw the ball and told his father he was tired and was ready to quit. His father nodded and the look on his face showed a trace of disappointment, or so Edward thought. His father simply placed the ball in the glove, handed the glove to his son and went inside. But the affability that Edward thought was developing between father and son for the first time was short-lived. Perhaps his father was just being charitable that first time, perhaps he had a brief pang of guilt, guilt that was fleeting. Perhaps there were no games on TV or he had run out of beer. The next time Edward asked him to play catch, a week later, he did but it seemed like he was put out by it, like it was an effort he cared not to expend. The third time Edward asked, his father said no, maybe another time. The fourth time he simply said no.

The hospital loomed in the distance, a brand new brick building in the middle of decaying homes and shuttered businesses. Edward parked and sat in the car for a moment trying to prepare himself for what he was unable to visualize inside that building. He focused on how he *would* react, not how he *should* react, for he knew he could not react the way people expected a son to react toward his dying father, not how the family or the general public, those who have been programmed to show certain emotions upon the imminent death of a family member, thought he should respond. At the entrance to the hospital stood Kevin. Edward had not seen his brother for two years. He shuddered when he first noticed him for he had aged considerably. At a distance he looked like their father.

Kevin hugged his brother when Edward walked up to him. "Glad you're here." he muttered. Edward knew he saw his presence not so much as a reunion of siblings but as reinforcements for any battle that may erupt, that most likely would erupt, between Roberta and the two sons. Edward saw his presence the same way. They were allies. They had to be allies.

"How's Dad," Edward asked trying to make his voice sound sympathetic for a man near death.

"No change. He's just lingering."

"Is Roberta here?"

"Of course she's here. What else would you fucking expect? She's been here since Dad came in, or one of her goddamn kids has been, just fucking waiting for him to die so she can get her fucking greedy hands on his fucking money."

"Shit," was all Edward could say. Another battle to be fought. Probably a bigger one than anything he expected to confront. But that was later. She had to get the old man in the ground first before the siblings locked in combat over his estate. He was sure she was upstairs waiting for death to come. Edward and Kevin headed inside.

When Edward walked into the hospital he became suddenly morose. His mouth dropped, his shoulders felt heavy and his walk slowed. Hospitals are dreary places, made even more depressing by the legion of aromas that have marinated the walls and floors and even the patients. Even if a person might be lucky enough to be confronted by a cheery lady at the information desk, or be approached by a cheerful nurse at the nurses station, or be greeted by a lighthearted smiling volunteer in the gift shop, it is still a dreary place. Hospitals are not meant to be lighthearted or cheery. As Edward and Kevin walked down the halls they heard moaning and gasping and coughing, sometimes sobbing, sometimes the sound of what might have been the final breaths of someone's life.

On their way to their father's room Roberta bolted out of a room behind them, a sitting room where, Edward imagined, all family members of patients who are near death go to contemplate the demise of that person. "Here," she called to us. "Come in here first." She quickly ducked back into the room.

On one side of a long scarred and mottled folding table sat Roberta, her daughter Rachel and her son Eric. Eric the Fuck looked down his nose at Edward and Kevin as they entered as if he were sitting in judgment of the errant brothers finally coming to watch their father die. They did not exchange greetings. Roberta poured a can of Coke into a frosted plastic cup. The foam slipped over the cup's rim and she caught it with her finger before the brown bubbles could reach the playing cards laid out before her. Edward noticed that she still colored her hair. It was the color of a tomato just beginning to ripen. Roberta began talking as if they had just recently finished a conversation and, after a brief respite, were preparing to begin another one. "I just talked to Father's doctor." She always called him Father, a designation she had used to identify him face to face and with family friends and strangers as far back as Edward could remember.

"And?" Edward said succinctly. Edward had sworn to himself that he would keep his conversations with Roberta as compact as was humanly possible.

"No change. It could be any time." She shook her head, more as if she were in pain than as a sign of despair. "It's just a waiting game."

Who's the doctor?" Edward asked.

"Nolan, a good doctor, very compassionate, very up front about Father's condition."

Edward made a mental note to contact the doctor. He could use an up front opinion. "Can I see him?"

Roberta gave Edward an odd look as if she didn't understand his simple request. "The doctor?" she asked.

"Dad!" Why, Edward thought, did he even ask for permission?

"Oh, sure. Follow me." Edward waved her back to her chair. "Not necessary," he said. "Kevin can show me." Edward and Kevin walked down the hallway in the original direction they had headed before Roberta had sidetracked them. Their father's room was at the end of the hall.

All hospital rooms look alike, antiseptic, restricting, the wall behind the bed full of an abundance of life monitoring devices flashing endless digital readouts and firing red lines that shoot up like a bullet with each beat of the heart and then abruptly flatten at the interim rest of that muscle. Entering the antiseptic room Edward felt like all the dirt he had collected during his lifetime was being sucked out of him and deposited in some huge chamber buried somewhere deep in the guts of the hospital.

Next to the bed stood the gleaming metal rod for hanging intravenous bags of sugar water or whatever other fluid they pumped into his father's body to induce the insufferable lingering before death. Edward quickly scanned the displays of life functions. He understood none of them except the heart monitor that indicated to him that his father was still alive. In the corner hovering next to the television was a helium balloon with a picture of Garfield grinning and pointing to the words "Get Well" inscribed in flowery letters and rainbow colors. *Get well soon* cards sat upright on the window sill. Even with this incursion of pleasant thoughts, the room was overpowering with a omnipresent feeling of doom.

Roberta entered the room behind her brothers and walked to the bed to smooth the covers over her father's anemic feet. She motioned Edward over to the side of the bed then left the room. Edward recognized that she was clearly uncomfortable with his presence as well as with his close proximity to the man she had worked so hard to alienate from him. She needn't worry. As soon as Edward looked at his father he realized the man was unable to talk or hear or perform any other life function except a shallow breathing. There was no difference between him fully alive and him near death. There was no way Edward was going to be able to reverse any damage Roberta had done to an already tenuous relationship.

Kevin stood behind Edward. He had his opportunity to view what was left of his father, to express his feelings of commiseration, if he had any, to show compassion for a dying man, if he knew what compassion was, to reflect on the past, to try finding meaning in the fifty-five years that this man had been his father, if he could think beyond his own present. Trying to put his life, his father's life and now his father's death in perspective, to build an immense panorama of mistakes and achievements, misfortunes and victories, pleasures and anguish, won and lost columns scratched on the brains of two men, one old and one middle age who shared the same fluid of life, the same biological qualities, much of the same history, the same appearance and demeanor, the same mannerisms. How was Kevin to do all of this, if he did any of it, to construct in a few moments a vista of two conjunctive lives and now one death that would shatter that connection, with a man who was on the verge of being comatose, of a man who appeared squeezed together in a painful fetal position, like he was trying to stuff himself into a container half the size it should be?

Was he able to do that? Was he able to attain a level of cohesiveness with a man where, over fifty-five years, the connection had become frayed and nearly torn to pieces? He stood in the shadows of the hospital room seemingly content with what had transpired between him and his father. Or perhaps resigned to being unable to conquer the wall that had been erected. Now it was Edward's turn. Was he able to do it? To find some commonality in a relationship that had been so uncommon, so indefinite?

His father lay on his side, the tube that sprouted from the vein in his arm spiraled around the bed frame and up to a pouch of clear liquid. Another tube ran from his nose to a jack in the wall behind the bed. There were more tubes growing out of the wall. The clear plastic tubes ran underneath the covers intended to assist his body with functions it no longer could manage.

Edward stood next to the bed. His father faced him. He was barely breathing, barely living. The skin on his arms was mottled with dark maroon blots like stains that someone had been unable to wash off. They had become hideous symbols of the storm of age and the siege of medical attention that had converged on him with such immediacy.

His feet again protruded from beneath the blanket that covered him. He must have moved ever so slightly, just enough to throw off the blanket but so insignificantly as to miss Edward's notice. His feet didn't have the pinkish color of healthy feet. The nails were long and jagged, the toes bloated and the color of old peeled whitewash. They were old feet, meager feet, much like the man they had supported, feet that had walked thousands of miles from home to bus stop, from bus stop to office and repeated again later in the day, each weekday, each week, each month, each year for forty-four years.

He always wore wingtips, the shoe of choice for men of his generation, black and brown wingtips with cleats on the heels and toes. Edward could hear the rasping sound they made when he walked to the bus stop as Edward was getting ready for school in the mornings. Cleats were a measure of his frugality. Whenever he bought new shoes, before he wore them the first time he took them to the shoe repair shop on Commercial Avenue, down near the Commercial theater Edward and his friends filled at numerous Saturday matinees, to have cleats applied. The shoes lasted much longer that way and the cost of new heels and soles was delayed. Many of the kids in the neighborhood wore cleats on their shoes, not as a means of economy, but to identify themselves as cool. They intentionally walked with a certain gait, a rhythm, so the cleats grated firmly and noisily against the concrete sidewalks. They periodically stopped and lifted each foot up one at a time to inspect the cleats and how worn down they had become. They made certain they were heard when they walked.

Edward called to his father. "Dad?" There was no movement, no response.

"He can't here you, Ed," Kevin offered. Edward knew that. He could see the lack of consciousness that filled his father's face, that gripped his entire body.

"Dad?" Edward called again. His father's lips quivered. His eyes opened slightly, barely revealing the darkness within, like slots of a casino slot machine where most everything pushed in was forever lost and rarely was there any payback, any jackpot. Did he hear his son? Was the feeble exposure of his eyes just an unconscious reaction, something he did not mean to do but his body forced upon him, like the movement of his feet that exposed them to the air? Edward knew his father really didn't see his son. He saw nothing. Nothing was emitted from those slits that were directed his son's way. If there was any sight whatever emerging from his eyes it was going past Edward, or maybe through him. It was eerie. Those eyes revealed nothing, no feeling, no acknowledgment, yet Edward felt his father knew it was his son standing next to his hospital bed. Edward thought he should have said something more, anything. But he didn't. He just stood there, his hand resting on the bed, trapped between his long-standing intense antagonism and benign absolution of all the sins he had recalled, sins his father had committed against him. Will he forever be trapped there?

Edward was relieved, though, that his father did not respond any more than with those narrow slits. Edward really did not want to talk to his father. He had too many things to say that a person does not say to a dying man. Perhaps he felt lucky he couldn't say anything to his son. He was able only to moan. But Edward was sure his father felt secure in the fact that he was unable to talk to his son because if he had been able to talk, with death looming so close, he may have felt he had to admit that he had left something undone, something of the greatest importance.

Edward left the room and headed back to the lounge where Roberta and her accomplices had congregated. Kevin was already there. He had left the room while Edward was staring at a man who had barely said a word to him for the seventeen years he lived in his household and now, when he stood over him, asking for some kind of response, some acknowledgment that he had driven four hundred and fifty miles to see him, again said nothing. When he was healthy and was able to talk, he did not. Now he was dying and unable to talk, but Edward still wished he had some words to say.

In the visitors lounge Roberta, Rachel and Eric sat on one side of the long folding table as a panel of judges would hunker together to hear the evidence against the accused and quickly pass judgment. "Well," Roberta said, briefly looking up at her brothers, mostly at Edward, then going back to the card game she was playing with her daughter. They were playing Hearts, a game their mother, when they were little, taught all of them to play to fill rainy nights or to keep them busy when they went to visit grandparents and became bored, a feeling that always enveloped them within the first hour of their visits.

"Well, what?" Edward shot back. Roberta laid her cards on the table and glared at her brothers.

"What did you think of Father?"

"I thought he looked great," Edward answered without missing a beat. "We had a great discussion about the upcoming elections, although our opinions of the President are poles apart. Of course, you know Dad and I have never been able to agree on politics. He said he thought maybe he would like to come down to visit me for a few days after he's rested from this horrible hospital stay. I really don't think he likes the hospital. Of course, who does. Oh, by the way, he said he would like you to bring him some ice cream, vanilla I think he said, or maybe chocolate. You might ask him yourself. We talked about Mom. He thought he might go out to Phoenix again this summer and visit her. Of course he better not drive when he gets out there. Not a good idea at all. He told me about the car wrecks. Yes, we got along famously, just had a grand visit."

"Why are you doing this?" Roberta asked contemptuously. "Why are you mocking me and Father?"

"I'm not mocking anyone, especially Dad." Edward tried to act as contemptuously as Roberta was acting, knowing all along that she really had no equal when it came to her arrogant and derisive attitude. "You asked an absurd question, 'What did you think of Dad?' and I thought what any reasonable person would think after standing in that room and staring at what is left of him. He's dying. He looks sick, very sick. He doesn't look like the father I knew when I was a kid, or as an adult." Edward realized he should not have said those last four words, but they were out and the dam quickly broke.

"You didn't know him as an adult." Roberta's volume steadily increased as she spoke. She stood and propped her arms on the table, her fists clenched. "You didn't try to know him. You didn't want to know him. Now that he's dying you think you can just right all the wrongs of the past. Well, you can't."

Edward stood there patiently waiting to see if any more condescending words came out of her mouth. She gathered up the cards in front of her and shuffled them indicating to Edward that she was finished for the moment.

Her daughter put her arm around her to console her. "You said you wouldn't do this, Mom." "I'm sorry, honey," she told Rachel patting her hand softly.

Edward moved to a padded folding chair in the corner, opposite the inquisition. Kevin left the room probably to go outside to smoke. He leaned back in the door and cocked his head indicating that he wanted Edward to follow. Eric shot one of his "You fuck" looks at Edward. Edward stopped and shot what he thought was even a greater one, a "You fuck who almost jumped out of a car and would be dead now if I hadn't saved your ass" kind of look. Before Edward exited, he felt compelled to get some last words in, despite how meaningless they might be. "He didn't let me know him as an adult. He didn't want me to know him as an adult. He didn't care." Edward didn't wait for a reaction or a response.

Outside in the cool autumn air Edward felt relief from the heated prosecution he had been subjected to inside. "Has she been this way to you?" Edward asked his brother.

"Are you kidding? No fucking way she's going to talk that way to me. She knows I'd fucking bop her upside the goddamn head if she came at me like that."

"Why's she doing it to me. What's it going to get her?"

Kevin lit his cigarette and took a long drag. "She's going to try to get you so fucking pissed that you'll just leave and won't ever come back to this goddamn place. She thinks if she fucking beats on you hard enough you'll want nothing to do with Dad, Dad's funeral, her or the fucking estate."

"The estate?"

"Yea, she wants all the money, or at least your share. She knows she'll never get my portion."

"Eric sure is a shit, too," Edward said as an aside.

"He's a fucking dick head."

"How much are we talking about?" Edward asked with some uneasiness for he felt uncomfortable talking about a person's estate before that person was even dead.

Kevin took another long drag. "Well, she had a long talk with me yesterday about the estate. Fucking laid it all out for me and she figures that after expenses there might be around two hundred fucking thousand dollars. She even got a goddamn lawyer already."

"She's already gone over it with you?" He nodded. "Who's the executor?"

Kevin gave Edward a grin that spelled disaster.

Edward headed back upstairs. Roberta appeared startled by her brother's reemergence into the fray. "I understand you discussed Dad's estate with Kevin yesterday." She nodded. Edward sat down at the table directly across from her. "Tell *me* about it now."

She looked at Rachel and Eric and made a motion toward the door with her head. They rose and withdrew from the room leaving the adversaries to discuss terms. "There's not much to tell," she began, her coldness toward Edward intensely displayed in her tone and the cock of her head. "He had . . ." "Has," Edward interjected. " . . . has a CD, a small savings account, and a checking account in Eastlake Bank and another small savings account in another bank."

"How much?" Edward asked.

"Not very much."

"How much?"

"Well, I don't know for sure. I haven't totaled it all. My God,

Edward, the man's not even dead yet."

"Don't give me that. I know you've already hired a lawyer. As soon as the doctor told you Dad didn't have long to live you went out and hired a lawyer. And I bet you checked every bank book he has. How much?"

"About one hundred fifty thousand dollars."

Edward looked at her with a mischievous grin. "More like two hundred thousand, I suspect. You better get your stories straight. You can't tell Kevin one thing and me another. Kevin and I talk you know. I won't sit back and let you cheat me out of what's rightfully mine. I can hire an attorney just as easily as you can. And I will."

"Go ahead," she said with a confidence that momentarily unnerved Edward. He will call her bluff, he thought. Edward left the lounge and headed to his father's room to continue his death watch. It was the only place now where there would be no one to interrupt his thinking or give him grief.

His father's position had not changed in the thirty minutes since Edward last saw him. He was still curled up as if he was shrinking and would in a short time dissolve. It was like this fragile body that lay before Edward was being deliberately siphoned by the seemingly endless miles of tubes that had been voraciously inserted into his body. Nothing will change for him now. He will die and Edward will go back home with no notion as to what transpired in this room. Had anything been accomplished by anyone who had entered this room to view this wasted man? Or had the damage of past years been so monumental that there was no possibility anyone associated with this man could rise from the wreckage and find comfort in his life or in his death?

For two more very long and exhausting days Edward watched his father's life end. What he witnessed in the hospital was a physical end to his father, a conclusion where Edward would no longer have a father present on earth. He died in all other ways many years before. Edward watched those deaths too. They were just as unpleasant as this one.

Edward, Roberta and Kevin worked out a schedule so they were able to have some respite from the long, grueling death watch. Kevin negotiated with Roberta on Edward's behalf. Edward had refused to say anymore to his sister. He was reserving any confrontations for a later time when they were needed for the task of salvaging something from what their father left after his death. They designated the hours each of them stayed at the hospital, shifts that kept Edward and Roberta apart and only required them to cross paths at the change of their shifts.

The next day Edward's tour of duty began at 8:00 a.m. It lasted two hours. Roberta was next and then Kevin, then the shifts started again. Though the short time periods when one of them was on duty at their father's bedside were meant to ease for all of them the burden of watching him die, two hours sitting silently at the bedside of a man wasting away and about to expire seemed endless. Edward hoped his father did not die on his shift.

Edward's game plan was to stay through Monday morning, then drive back home. Monday was his birthday and to choose which observance he would take part in was not difficult. He wanted to spend his birthday with a family, the people that cared about him, his wife and kids, and not with a family he felt little affection for and who felt no attachment to him. He planned to leave after his morning shift on the third day, drive the seven hours home and return when his father had died, or, if he decided to linger on a bit, he might drive back every so often to at least maintain a presence so Roberta could not claim he abandoned his father.

To keep himself occupied for the two days Edward stayed became a chore. He read magazines and newspapers supplied by the hospital. He read them more than once. He sped through a cheap novel he purchased at the hospital gift shop. He played cards, solitaire, two handed draw poker with an imaginary poker buddy who sat across the table from him. He learned how to play solitaire from his mother, but poker from his father. He didn't teach Edward. Edward learned from observing him and his poker buddies play at the dining room table. It was not so much the game itself that interested Edward, there were as many versions of solitaire as there were of poker, so the determining factor was not variety, but the gambling, the wagering, the risk. The more Edward contemplated the life of his father, the more he became astonished that he played poker. His father never took chances, never took risks, never ventured beyond what was certain and secure. Perhaps this was his one indulgence that took him beyond the safe life in which he had enclosed himself. Maybe poker became his insignificant transgression that for three hours every other Wednesday night gave him the brief respite from his life of imprisonment.

His father's card playing not only created Edward's penchant for poker but, as a youngster, before he started school, also taught him to count. When the five men almost glued to that table and their cards took a small break in the middle of their poker marathon to use the bathroom, refill their glasses with the bourbon Edward's father kept in the dining room cabinet or snatch another beer from the refrigerator or refill their plates with the sandwiches, chips and sausages his mother prepared for the gathering, Edward rushed up to the table, stood at attention, and began counting for them—*one, two, three, four, five, six, seven, eight, nine, ten, jack, queen, king, fourteen, fifteen.* They all laughed, especially his father who laughed the loudest. Edward's mother just shook her head and ran into the kitchen. Edward was never corrected by any of them and never was aware of the error he made each time he counted until he started first grade, and the first time he counted out loud in class Sister Mary Frances slapped his ear and told him to drop the face cards out of his counting routine.

Edward's father wasn't proud of him. He just thought what his son did for his poker buddies was funny, the half time entertainment. But it was the only time Edward remembered his father laughing. Other times, when he did something that young boys do, or learned something new that makes a kid feel like he is progressing toward adulthood, his father became annoyed, even agitated.

At age seven Edward learned to snap his fingers. He practiced all the time. He was proud of his accomplishment. His father became annoyed. He told Edward that only criminals snapped their fingers. Edward believed him and stopped snapping his fingers. At age eight Edward learned to whistle. He practiced a monotonous tune day and night. His father became annoyed. He told Edward that only sissy kids whistled. Edward believed him and stopped whistling until several years later when he figured out that it was not just sissy kids that whistled. At age nine Edward wanted to learn to play the drums. His parents said they couldn't afford to give him lessons or buy him drums. He practiced on pillows and buckets and empty cereal cartons in his bedroom. His father became annoyed. He told Edward only drug addicts played drums. Edward believed him and gave up his improvised jam sessions. At age ten Edward began to fart and belch like his father did. His mother became annoyed. She told Edward only disgusting people did those things. Edward thought it was cool so he continued. His father didn't say anything.

The two hour shifts next to his father's bed, staring out the window, staring at him, reading, covering his father's feet, smoothing the blanket, thinking, stirred up for Edward numerous memories of his father, recollections that he carried with him to the cafeteria to get a cup of coffee or to the bar each evening where he and Kevin went to try to shake off some of those memories, and as Edward sat in the achromatic hospital room watching him languish, his colorless body curled up in the disheveled blanket, there were numerous flash backs that brought with them acute pain.

Affection was hard for Edward's father. As he watched his father lying in his death bed it was hard for Edward to show any affection, to give the dying man something he never gave to his son.

The emergence of those disturbing recollections brought back to Edward numerous traumatic experiences of his adolescence, most of them minor compared to that first one when his father stood on the front porch of their house eating a sausage while a neighbor pulled Edward's mangled leg from the back wheel of a bicycle, and Edward realized his father was never there for him. Edward could not comprehend why he was not there at least to make a token appearance, a validation that "yes, this is my son and I am here so therefore I care, maybe minimally, but I care." Where was he? He had no social life, no hobbies. He had no garage to go to, no workbench where he was able to use his hands, to create, to build. He played no sports, no golf, there was no bowling league on weeknights, only his poker club, his every other Wednesday night, sausage eating, beer drinking, your son's leg almost got cut off, poker club. No baseball games on weekends. The Cubs and White Sox were television teams. He had no stories to tell. There had been nothing consequential or meaningful in his life to share with his son. He did not trudge off to war. There were no medals, no heroic acts, no strategic battles he could boast on. He had no tales of his empty life to pull Edward into his world.

He was Edward's father but he did not father him. There was little that could be told in the retrospect of a man nearly deceased about a life barely lived. Even less when that life left others untouched.

XIX

Edward drove back home to Missouri on a Monday morning, his birthday. His mind was full of the visions he had dragged along with him, images of his father lying in the hospital dying, of the sterile hospital room, of the quiet. Instead of the road, Edward vividly saw a man seventy pounds lighter than when he had seen him healthy, of rigid toenails, ashen feet, clear plastic tubes slowly and deliberately, drop by drop, pumping a colorless liquid into his ravaged veins; of nurses inspecting his condition every hour, fluffing the pillow that enveloped his pale, bald head, straightening the blanket, jabbing a needle in his leg dozens of times and then in his arm because his legs had been so poked by so many pieces of metal they no longer offered any space for the needles to poke again, prodding already collapsed veins to draw more blood to take more tests to find out . . . what? To certify that he was dying? For the pleasure of taking blood? To keep the lab at full staff—no lay offs this week, we got that old man in 202? He saw the nurses poking a thermometer in his ear to see if his temperature matched that of a normal, healthy human being; of emptying his catheter bag full of fluid that came from the body that had for days taken only that transparent fluid from the IV bag; of nurses' aids bringing in breakfast, lunch and dinner because it was paid for and of his children eating his last meals; of sitting still for hours next to him wondering why he never cared enough to be a father, then changing shifts and going out to a restaurant, or a bar, or Kevin's condo, or a park to sit idly alone on a bench to wonder why he never cared enough to be a father, returning for the next shift to again be besieged by those same unanswerable questions.

Those baffling questions that Edward recognized as being unanswerable followed him home on his birthday, a birthday that was at least temporarily successful in relieving some of the uneasiness and trepidation that had filled his last three days. But while those feelings filled him up as Edward's family sang *Happy Birthday*, the ominous ring of the telephone brought him to the realization that his relief was only transitory. It was Kevin. He called to say that Dad had died.

"Who was there?" Edward asked.

"Nobody. It was my shift but I had to piss. When I came back the goddamn heart monitor had . . . well, it just had that fucking straight line. I yelled to the nurses and they called the doctor and Dad was dead."

"Where are you now?"

"At the hospital still." Kevin sounded so solemn, (only two curse words; it must have really affected him.) even caring, a quality he was ordinarily light on.

"Is Roberta there?"

"Yea, she's a mess, a real fucking basket case." A relief for her, Edward thought. She had been discharged from her obligation of caring for "Father", a chore she at first thought noble, then tedious and wished for an end to so she could have her own life back, and his money to finance it. Edward believed Roberta truly felt her father owed her more because she volunteered to tend to him in his final years, but her acting as his nursemaid became more than she could bear and after a while she carried that burden because she saw the possibility of some financial gain.

"Who's taking care of the body?"

"Don't know. I suppose Roberta has that all worked out."

"Yea, I suppose she does." Edward had no more questions to ask. The answers to what he had asked were unimportant to him, but he felt compelled to make conversation with the person on the other end of the phone because Kevin sounded so uncharacteristically moved by the death of his father. "I'll come up in the morning. Meet you at your place." They hung up.

He died on Edward's birthday. Of all the days for him to choose. He probably died on that day on purpose, his final attempt to get even with his son for whatever it was he thought Edward had done to deserve revenge. Suddenly their prolonged silent quarrel was over and his father had gotten in the last word.

Edward left early the next morning, just after sunrise. He drove to his father's funeral hoping in the seven hours it took that he might hit upon a reason why he was driving to his father's funeral. Edward's family did not come with him. He had asked them not to. He thought this was one event he wanted to face alone. He needed to sort out the recollections of his past without questions or somber commiseration. They did not know their grandfather anyway. For them the trip would be meaningless. Perhaps for Edward too.

Early morning before sunrise was the best time to drive. Traffic was light, the sun withheld its brightness until Edward had driven most of the four hundred fifty miles to his destination. By the time he was within fifty miles of Kevin's house it was only eleven o'clock, too early for him to check in at his brother's and sit idly while waiting for Roberta's direction to do whatever it was they had to do. It had not been that long since Edward's mother had died, nine years, but he had forgotten all the preliminaries of burial, all the rites of passage from one world to the next. He had time before all that started, time to visit the only fragment of his past that still meant something to him, that still provided sustenance to his hunger for what once had been a valuable component of his life. He detoured from the route to Kevin's and headed for his old neighborhood.

Everyone remembers, sometimes cherishes, that portion of the planet where growing up took place. But when Edward entered the neighborhood where his boyhood had been forged and legitimized he found that what had been stored in his memory or catalogued in old photographs of the old houses, remembered playmates and friends, lively playgrounds, sedate, tree lined side streets where the huge cottonwoods tangled their limbs together over the concrete roads, was no longer identifiable as his mind had sketched it over and over again through the years. Nothing was the same. Nothing related to the past as it once was, as Edward thought it always would be.

Edward left his old neighborhood in 1968 when he was eighteen years old, never to return as an inhabitant, never finding the time or the motivation to return as a visitor. Since that time he made a half-dozen trips to Chicago, each time running into barriers that prevented him from paying his respects to the place where he grew up. But it had been postponed too long. He turned off the interstate just south of the city limits and headed into the deep recesses of the South Side. When he entered the side streets where he had played tag or softball with his friends, he suddenly realized he had come here not only to attend his father's funeral but to also pay his last respects to a neighborhood that had also died but, he discovered as he drove into it, was not resting in peace.

When Edward lived there the neighborhood was mature, sensible, at least as neighborhoods went in the fifties and sixties. Despite its diverse ethnic character, it maintained a dignity ordinarily associated with age and worthy of the respect that he and his friends held for it. It had been brought to its full flavor and richness by that aging. But, as with many venerable institutions advanced in years, the neighborhood also manifested traits that suggested an unfavorable perspective of old age: lack of vitality, resistance to change, fear, prejudice. It was these features that produced the weakness and frailty that, in the end, were no match for the circumstances that hastened its decline.

Edward stopped his car at the corner where he had learned to ride a bicycle, a service furnished to him by Kevin, not his father. To his left was a large open area where the Little League field once stood, where Edward had on many Saturdays and Sundays worn the knees out of his baseball pants, turned the pants and shirt and shoes a pale shade of brown with traces of green from all the running and sliding and falling in left field while chasing a fly ball sometimes caught and sometimes not, where he played his heart out and many times sobbed because the effort had not been enough. It is where he won a case, an entire case, of twelve ounce bottles of Coca Cola because he hit a home run, an in-the-park home run, but still a four bagger. In place of the field, its flat board bleachers, chain link fence and roofed dugouts, was discarded furniture and decayed automobiles so badly disintegrated that their model and color were unidentifiable. Somewhere beneath the heaps of scrap and rotted fabric were the remnants of what once was a finely manicured and well-used baseball diamond.

The fence over which he had never sent a ball but, nonetheless, had won a case of Coke, had been torn down; the chain-link backstop lay rusted and shattered. The whole field of competition resembled an archeological excavation, a discovery of an indistinct but violent culture, with which the diggers had become bored and soon abandoned it to be left to some future expedition that might find some worth in the rubble.

One block beyond the field were the railroad tracks, a main thoroughfare of trains hauling goods in and out of the city to and from destinations all over the country. Edward had been regularly warned never to go beyond those tracks, never to mingle with the people who lived on the other side. When he was very young, he and his friends sat on his front porch, their feet keeping uneven time with the squeak of the glider, and they stared at the railroad tracks. They thought of their mothers' warnings. Did the people who lived beyond those rails consider them as people who lived on the other side of the tracks, not to be associated with?

The streets that had once been void of trash, cleaned by the weekly run of a roaring, faded yellow street cleaning machine, were now wallowing in repulsive garbage that blanketed the gutters. Refuse, discarded tires and other scattered remains had become an indelible part of the landscape. The lawns, once bright green, cushioned playgrounds for adolescent games, now grew in patchworks of yellow and brown. The trees he climbed, immense trees that clearly, from their size, demanded that every child in the neighborhood must climb or be labeled chicken, were also ailing. The acrid breezes that seeped silently along the foul and dirty streets had taken life from many of them. The trees that remained, an assortment of ornamentals that had been planted as a final attempt at revival, and a handful of the stately cottonwoods that had adorned each and every street in the neighborhood, looked like they had lost their enthusiasm for life.

The houses that pressed close to each other along the now barren streets were built in the thirties and forties, sturdy enough, he thought when he was young, to withstand anything. But something had crept up on them after he had left and slowly eaten away at their dignity and strength. The once handsome structures had fallen into disrepair, many of them looked unsafe for any human to live in. A few had been burned out; all that remained were shells of blackened brick. The particle boards nailed up against the doors and windows to bar entrance were warped and weather scarred, evidence that the fires occurred years ago. The flames had left the decomposing structures to become a showcase of the aggregate neglect that plagued the streets of the old neighborhood. Of those houses still lived in by the immigrants that came after them, few maintained a full complement of unbroken windows. Edward had been told by a friend of his who once lived in a similar neighborhood in St. Louis that people who lived in neighborhoods that had become so diseased preferred to keep the boards on their broken windows instead of having the glass replaced. It is better that way, his friend told him, because it deflected the bullets that sometimes split the otherwise silent nights.

The porch steps on the other houses were cracked and gaping. Bricks that had lost their soundness had fallen from random weak spots in the porches and lay in scattered piles beneath the porches they once framed. Sidewalks that lined both sides of the street were buckled. Through the windows coated with a thick film of years of grime, soot and dust, there were faint glimmers of light from bare bulbs. When Edward lived in this neighborhood, anyone who passed by any house on any street at any time of the day or evening, was able to look through any window where the curtains had not been drawn and see into the house and clearly witness what might be going on, see the television flickering or a neighbor lying on the couch asleep after coming home from a days work at the mill, or the family sitting down to dinner. Now the curtains, if there were any, were thread bare and hanging at a slant. On one porch at a house three doors down from where Edward had lived, a woman sat in a lawn chair, the rusted metal frame was bent, the torn seat ribs were repaired with rope and wire. On her lap was a worn out rag doll child drugged into lethargy by despair and neglect.

When he came to the house in which he had lived, his reaction was not the quickening pulse and excited recollections of adolescent delight. As he drove up to it, his eyes first met the hedge that had once served as a barrier for hide and seek games and snowball fights but was now void of all greenery. Only the bare brown limbs remained. It was here at this palisade that he and his friends amassed all their forces on snowy winter days, assembled an enormous stockpile of snowballs, some filled with small stones pulled from the driveway of Edward's neighbor, and besieged the busses and trucks that passed by. The trucks kept moving for most of them were oblivious to what had hit them, some were uncaring. The bus drivers usually shook their fists at the attackers and drove on. When a police car was spotted coming their way, they crouched behind the bushes and waited patiently until it was out of sight, then they rose up again and renewed their assault.

Edward drove around the corner and entered the alley that

ran behind the house, the alley used by the rag man. In the large backyard where, as a boy, when not at the playground next to the elementary school or in someone's basement, he spent much of his time, the sand pile that served as his construction site and battleground, a preserve of adolescent games, the site of the summer barbecue ribs fest, had become a cemetery for decayed machinery. In place of the tunnels, roads and mountains he had built lay an old automobile rusted and lacking most of its movable parts.

He had the desire to enter his old house, to measure the extent of its injuries, to see if the odors that had once given the structure its character, that had lured a child home after a hard day at play or school had lingered over the years, to know if those odors and sights and sounds had refused to remove themselves from the interior. He needed to grasp at anything familiar to see if any of the intrigues, the adventures, the hiding places where he played and read and pondered those significant riddles that children, without parents to help them, try to solve, had been preserved.

He craved the chance to reexplore every fragment of this neighborhood, rediscovering structures and alleyways, every scent that gave him some identification, the coolness of dark places on hot summer days, the crevices and hideaways, all the commodities that could reestablish the connection he needed, all the objects and events in which children delight and adults find pleasure in remembering. But he knew he could not. Those experiences that long ago helped him acquire a sense of neighborhood were now indistinguishable.

He continued down the alley that ran behind his old house and behind the houses occupied by his former neighbors. He saw that the other houses had also suffered a similar fate as his house. A Hungarian immigrant family had occupied the house next door to where Edward had lived. It was an old man, an even older woman who was the old man's mother, and a younger man, though not too much younger, who was hunchbacked and bald and always carried an umbrella with him. At one time, long ago, their back yard had held an immense, prolific garden—half flowers, half vegetables. They frequently became angry with Edward when he carelessly shot an arrow or threw a ball into their yard. Whatever he had inadvertently sent over the chain link fence that separated their yards would not be returned for days, sometimes never, especially when the projectile damaged one of their prize plants. Perhaps there are arrows with rusted tips or baseballs with rotted seams secluded in that house still waiting to be claimed.

On the right side of the alley was the elementary school and its adjacent playground. That was where, under the protection of darkness and hidden beneath the shadows of the cottonwood limbs that filtered out the glare of the street lamp, the older boys in the neighborhood drank their whiskey, sniffed their glue and took advantage of the girls who were looking for excitement, who followed the tough guys, the gang members, the guys who found their pleasure in taunting the gangs from other neighborhoods, wreaking havoc in other neighborhood school yards when one of those gangs took the challenge. It was where they drank hard whiskey and filled their clean, neatly folded handkerchiefs with airplane glue to forget the pain from the chain or baseball bat that claimed them as a victim in that day's rumble, and then, at night, to delight in the pleasure that their girls gave them for being so daring.

They were older girls, girls beyond the reach of a younger boy, but Edward admired their looks, their free spirits, their tight sweaters and tighter pants. The intense, glistening makeup, fingernail polish that gleamed in the sunlight. The way they walked, their rear ends keeping a rhythmical beat that matched the throbbing of his heart as they walked away from him. He was only twelve years old when these feelings of longing came over him. He was embarrassed by it because he was heading for the seminary. He told it in confession but his contrition was unable to rid those fantasies from his mind. He was twelve years old when

Arlene, the ex-officio leader of the older girls that followed the older boys, placed a kiss on his cheek for finding her car keys lost in the grass and gave him a sense of excitement he had never experienced; not the same kind that Peggy Petrazak gave him but one that lasted most of that day as he ceaselessly thought about that kiss and what it could have led to had he been four years older. That experience brought on a susceptibility that raised serious questions about the vocation he had chosen, as well as biological explosions that he was not aware could happen. He could not go to his father about those sensations and their inevitable gratifying conclusions. He knew, if he was lucky, all he would get from his father would be some stammering and a vague, brief sentence about how Edward would just have to be careful. And then the volume on the television would be turned up. There would be no explanation, no layout of the entire sequence of sex, of how that first heart palpitation, that first heavy perspiration that was not a result of running or playing baseball, the sweat that didn't cool you off but made you hotter, that first erection could lead to . . . at that time he didn't know what it could lead to.

Edward had his first kiss under that swing set. On a summer night in 1963, long before his curfew and before he had told Father Healey over bacon and eggs that he wanted to be a priest. The older boys and their tag along girls were not there that night leaving the playground to those in the neighborhood who used it for the purpose it was designed—to play.

Edward didn't remember her name. Thirty-five years erases a lot of adventures that enter a boy's life. They were the only ones who remained at the playground after their friends went home for the evening. Edward had some stirrings for her, feelings that were stimulating in the sense that he felt compelled to be near her often. When he sat near her on the swings he had a constant smile on his face, his palms sweat, he felt pangs of excitement in his stomach. But never an erection. Even when he kissed her, that first kiss, each one sitting on a swing, her arms around his waist, his arms around her neck, even then it did not stir him like that simple peck on the cheek from Arlene several weeks later. Or like the thoughts he had after Peggy Petrazak's tongue attacked his lips. Arlene with the large breasts, the deep red lipstick, false eyelashes, tight shorts that made certain parts of her body distinct and identifiable. Arlene who's blond hair brushed against his face when she kissed his cheek. Arlene who at seventeen was already an experienced woman who gave a thrill to a boy who had no experience. His first kiss presented a fragment of what would be available to him later; Arlene's kiss showed him the power of even the slightest affection. He was never the same after Arlene. He suspected it was she, with her simple act of appreciation, who compelled him to maintain the momentum she had initiated even though his quest for girls became stagnate all through high school. Why else would he have become so intrigued with the girls that walked home past the seminary grounds. It may have been Arlene who was the cause of his quitting the seminary months after his encounter with her, and of the misery that ensued at home as a result of that loss of vocation. He could blame a lot of things on Arlene.

He turned onto another street that went past his old house, to view it one more time and to take one last look at all the ailing houses on this diseased street in the dying neighborhood. He saw in his mind what it had been and with his eyes what it had become. He longed for what it will never be again. The pictures he held in his head for so many years were now beginning to fade. The sounds were gone; the smells had dissipated. He drove away quickly, regretting that he had come this far, saddened by the fact that he had suffered the loss of a significant part of his past. He headed east to Kevin's home to bury another part of his past whose significance was not so consequential.

For Kevin, Edward was sure the connection to the neighborhood he was leaving behind was not as powerful as his own. He moved into that neighborhood at age nine when the family migrated from southern Illinois to the northern part of the state. Eight years later he enlisted in the army and never returned to call the neighborhood his home. Those eight years in between were simply a brief stopover on his tour of a spirited and sometimes defiant life. In those terms Kevin was not like his father at all, maybe that's why they clashed so often. Clash perhaps is not the right word; it implies a collision between two contrasting forces, a struggle of wits, between contrary principles. Actually, the contest involved a movable object (Kevin) who was never able to focus on anything for any appreciable length of time, opposing an immovable object (his father) who was never able to focus on anything beyond the television and beer and who did not have the interest to rein in a son who invited trouble to accompany him wherever he went.

When Kevin got into trouble it was never near his home because he was never there. He and his friends congregated on what was known as the east side of Chicago, a term of location that, for a person unfamiliar with that part of Chicago, could be puzzling. It was actually the southeast side of Chicago since it was on the south side as gauged by its location, but as far east as one could go and still be in the city. It was bordered on the east side by Whiting, Indiana, the south side by the city limits, the west side by the suburbs and the north side by anywhere the inhabitants of that enclave wished the boundaries to be. When and how it became the east side no one seems to know. But it has always been the east side as far as anyone who lived there or used it as a hangout can recall.

The east side is where Kevin hung out with a lot of boys whose names either ended in "ski" or began with "O". They were tough, everyone of them. They started fights with each other to demonstrate their toughness. They drank themselves into a stupor almost nightly to prove they were tough. They all went into the army, were shipped to Viet Nam and those who returned alive proclaimed they were even tougher. When the black kids from the southwest side of the city came to the east side to swim

in Lake Michigan, the east side boys again intended to prove
their toughness by throwing stones and beer bottles at the southwest side kids to keep them from integrating the east side boys'
park and beach, and to reaffirm that toughness by defying the
high pressure fire hoses trained on them by the police, and again
by being arrested and carried in paddy wagons to jail where the
police called their parents, if they had any, and told them to
come and get their sons, along with a few unwieldy daughters,
out of jail and take them home, and if they knew what was good
for them they would whack the shit out of them with a belt and
stick them in their room and throw away the key because if they
didn't and this happened again, they would be in jail for quite
some time.

They were tough. Being arrested made them tougher. Jail
would have been welcome because it would have given them a
toughness they had never before been able to proclaim. They
stole cars and went down into the Hispanic neighborhoods just
south of the east side and threw stones and beer bottles left over
from the southwest side black kids at the Hispanic kids who
chased them in their cars and threw bottles and rocks back at
them until somebody's car crashed and then they all got out,
beat on each others heads for a few minutes or until they heard
sirens, got back into the cars that still ran and hightailed it back
to the east side, where they drank more beer so they had more
ammunition for the next raid into whatever side of town suited
their tastes. They were tough.

Kevin was part of that toughness and his father did not like
it. Whenever Kevin got arrested it was his mother who went down
to the police station to bail him out of jail, or if the police brought
him to the house after a night of drinking and raiding, it was his
mother who intercepted the policeman before he rang the doorbell, brought Kevin around to the back of the house, through the
cellar door and put him to bed before his father was aware of
what was going on. Edward didn't understand why his mother
resorted to subterfuge to keep Kevin's exploits from his father.

The man did not care. There were times, many times Edward remembered when it was his father who took the call or answered the door, and he handed the phone to his wife and then sat back in his seat to find his place again in the boxing match on the television or the Garry Moore show, or Lawrence Welk, or leave the door open and walk back to the kitchen to make himself a sandwich and grab a beer, anything to distance himself from his son who seemed to be drawn to the wrong side of the law. If he had cared at all at any time, then Kevin probably would never have been in trouble with the law in the first place.

Edward attended high school on the east side. He wasn't tough, didn't want to be tough, but the toughness that flourished with Kevin and his young tough friends became Edward's curse. Because of Kevin's mischief, because he paraded his toughness all over the south side of Chicago, because he used police cruisers as a taxi service, because he sometimes came home late with bloody hands, bruised face and arms, beer drenched clothes, and slept until noon when he then got up, went to work on the second shift at the mill and after work headed out to begin another round, his parents resolved that, if not attended to in a decisive manner, Edward would end up the same as Kevin. A young tough, a brigand, a fugitive from the standards his parents thought they had instilled in their children.

So Edward's parents protected him and themselves from the agony that they were certain would result if Edward pursued the same sinister and corrupt life style that Kevin had adopted. While their motives may have been honorable and in their best interests, the means by which they sheltered Edward and protected themselves from another disastrous adolescent and young adult were contemptuous and caused quite the opposite of their intended objective: to keep Edward wholesome and undefiled. Kevin never knew how his life choices had limited Edward's, how his frequent brushes with the law and skirmishes with other young toughs had condemned his brother to an adolescence laden with agonizing regulations, absurd curfews and ludicrous stipulations on choosing his friends, his clothes and where to spend and where not to spend his free time. It was as if Edward would immediately begin raping and pillaging the entire city of Chicago simply because he had a brother who always seemed on the verge of doing just that.

It began in Edward's freshman year of high school, almost immediately after he quit the seminary and came home to what amounted to an ostracism, as if they had made a clear connection with his leaving the seminary and an instantaneous plunge into sin and debauchery. *Yes, mother,* (his father always called his wife mother) *I do see a distinct change in the look in his eye now that he is no longer learning how to be a priest. He could turn on us at any moment.* Peculiar how a person can change so drastically in only five hours. Five hours on the Illinois Central from St. Louis to Chicago and Edward had progressed from saint who would guarantee his mother's ascension into heaven, her assurance of eternal life with her maker, to a villain arising out of dormancy by virtue of his forsaking the priesthood and adopting his brother's miscreant ways.

First, and, of course, most limiting, there was Edward's curfew that superseded the official curfew of the City of Chicago. On weekdays, Edward's nine o'clock, the city's ten-thirty; on weekends, Edward's ten-thirty, the city's twelve-thirty. It was not a significant issue to his parents that this curfew they imposed reduced the amount of time their son had to spend with his friends and thus, at least in his mind, diminished his social skills. At age fourteen many, actually all, of the social events Edward's age group attended began at eight o'clock in the evening and ended about midnight. His time to mingle and learn the ways of a teenager was reduced considerably.

So when they adamantly denied Edward his choices in clothing he did not protest, at least overtly, because he had no basis for objection. He could not look out of place wherever he went because he had little opportunity to go anyplace. However, his reluctance to scream and carry on, instead of giving his parents pause to reconsider the error in their parenting, inspired them to tighten their hold on him. His friends became his parent's enemies; everyone was suspect. They could recognize calamity in the eyes and manner of everyone Edward claimed as a friend. Even telephone calls were evaluated for a hint of evil in the voice of the caller and messages were never given to Edward if his parents felt there was any suspicion the caller may lead their son into temptation. The rare times he took a girl on a date, mostly when he was a freshman in college, they were ridiculed and appraised for their looks, "Too much makeup," where they lived, "Is she Jewish, she lives mighty close to where the Jews live," their religion, "You will not go out with a Presbyterian, I will not allow it," their nationality, "My God, she's Polish, what are you thinking!" and again for their looks, "She's got a really big nose; are you sure she's not Jewish." After each insulting critique his mother added, "Date an Irish girl, Edward. Marry an Irish girl. I don't want grandchildren that are half skis and half some other European name that has no vowels."

Where was the Irish girl for which his mother longed? Kevin had failed her. He married first a Mexican and, when that marriage became a burden for him, he married a Hungarian Protestant. Both unions ended in divorce which his mother steadfastly attributed to the lack of Irish blood in either of Kevin's temporary spouses. And now Edward was failing her. Just one more sign that he was headed on the road to moral bankruptcy, just one more nail in her coffin. The fact was that there were no Irish girls in the neighborhood who measured up to Edward's standards of form and appearance. There were a few who attended the same high school he did, but they were even worse than the ones who lived in his neighborhood. As a teenager, as with most teenagers, the only criterion a girl had to meet to entice Edward was reasonably well-shaped breasts, legs and butt that contained no hint of fat, a face any man would die for and long hair. A pleasant personality was a plus but not essential. And if she was Irish, that was a plus, but that factor never entered into the equation that added up to his type of girl.

Irish, Hungarian, Mexican, Polish, it really made no difference. Since Edward was prevented from seeking entertainment during the same hours as his peers, and intimidated into wearing clothes that placed him in a class that caused him to be ridiculed and abused in ways meant to harass and embarrass him, he probably unconsciously avoided Irish girls just to be spiteful. It really didn't matter any more, Edward thought as he neared Kevin's condo. That was in the past. The end of that past was in the neighborhood that he had passed through hoping to recognize but unable to identify. The end was also in the funeral he was heading toward, the end of a past that had been forgotten, briefly brought to life and now, at least soon he hoped, again lost from memory.

XX

A man pees in the toilet with more forethought and more imagination than Edward's father ever put into his sons. That was what Kevin said to Edward soon after Edward arrived at his brother's condo. It was something he said as the brothers swilled beer on his living room couch while catching glimpses of a basketball game on television. It was a notion Kevin must have put a lot of thought into when he went to the bathroom after the first period of the game. The only difference between how he expressed it and Edward paraphrased it is that when Kevin said it he embellished it with a number of descriptive words. But Edward agreed with his brother and it sounded better without all his adjectives. What Kevin said, and Edward agreed with between beers, they concluded applied to their father's life. So it came as no surprise to them that their father had given no direction to Roberta, his obvious choice for making the final arrangements after his death, as to where, how and in what form of ceremonious finale he should be laid to rest. Since Roberta had found it advantageous to take care of her father's estate before he had even died, Edward assumed she had also made final arrangements soon after she had secured her financial advantage and while the body was still warm. So neither Edward nor Kevin felt compelled to offer advice or preferences for the funeral, particularly when any suggestions they had made regarding the staging of their mother's funeral nine years earlier were met with teary eyed appeals by Roberta to her father imploring him to side with her for she truly knew what mother wanted.

"I like the cherry casket," Edward had offered. "It's a beautiful hardwood, nicely detailed. Mother loved fine wood furniture. I think she would feel very comfortable in something so well made."

"Oh Father," Roberta countered, a tear rolling out of the corner of her eye, "would you really want Mother to be buried in a wood casket?" "Well," he began, on the verge, Edward believed, of agreeing with his choice, but cut off by Roberta's pleading whine. "Wood will rot and then mother will not be protected," she begged.

Edward wondered if he should respond to her nonsense? He began the slight inhale that is the prelude to blurting out a argumentative response. But in deference to his father (why, he didn't know), he held back. Mother will rot, he thought, no matter what she's in. What the hell difference does it make if she rots a few decades sooner in a cherry casket than later in a steel casket painted in four shades of gray with gold plated trim meagerly added to embellish what was a dreary, prosaic box to hold a dead person that probably just about everyone else chose because, like Roberta, they were afraid their loved ones might rot too fast. What is this protected crap? Protected from what? The worms and bugs that will make her rot? The casket will be in a steel vault for Christ sake. Edward's father looked at each casket, hardwood or steel, steel or hardwood. He looked at Edward. Edward hardened his stare hoping his mental arguments about rotting in her grave would pass the four or so feet that separated father and son. He looked at Roberta, more tears welled up in her eyes. He glanced at Kevin. Kevin didn't give a shit. He was running his hand over a satin pillow in one of the metal caskets. He had no idea what was going on over near the cherry casket.

Edward wandered over to a corner of the room where more caskets were crammed. Fiberglass. He glanced over to his father still being hammered by Roberta about his wife rotting in the coffin. Edward started to call to them, but then thought his sister would never go for fiberglass. Some of them looked like wood, some like brass. Some were emblazoned with logos of the lord, pictures of someone's impression of what God looked like. Edward thought, wood decays, metal rusts, but fiberglass is eternal. No way worms could eat through fiberglass, or water could flood his mother's eternal home. No, a fiberglass coffin will forever seal in the dearly departed. It would not be worth the chastisement of Roberta to say, "Hey, over here, how about fiberglass?" Roberta would gasp. Fiberglass is cheap, she would yell from across the room not caring at all about the feelings of the coffin salesman aka the funeral director. It's fake. How could you even think of such a thing? Edward's father would cup his ear and say, what, what did you say? And after Roberta ended her tirade, her father would look at her and say, what did he say?

Edward walked back over to where they stood. "Well, Dad," he said hoping to end the debate and move on to something not so grim, although it was difficult to find anything cheerful, or at least less than grim, in a funeral parlor.

"I think your sister is right," He turned to the casket salesman. He, as well, was ready to move on. "We'll go with the steel casket."

Edward hoped the "we'll" meant his father and Roberta, for as Edward considered how the remainder of their shopping tour was going to be monopolized by Roberta, his attitude toward the whole matter almost instantaneously shifted to what Kevin had assumed when they entered the funeral home. Dad had no idea what to do. Roberta was in charge. There was no reason to argue and there was no way in hell Edward or Kevin was going to clash with the grip Roberta had on their father, nor could their father or Kevin or Edward or the coffin salesman compete with her tears and her whine.

So with each little, although expensive, item the funeral home people presented to the family as part of the final goodbye—the remembrance cards, the votive candles, the guest registry, the candelabra—Edward bit his tongue on all of them, not so much on whether it should be the Virgin Mary or Jesus on the remembrance cards, an angel or cherub on the registry cover, a gold or silver candelabra, but that one dime should be spent on most of the merchandise that was being peddled. He left the room after the candelabra, joining Kevin outside where he had taken his attitude, the attitude Edward wished he had had from the beginning, to smoke a cigarette.

And so it was at their father's funeral nine years later that Edward and Kevin sat at his condo, watching television, eating donuts and drinking beer while Roberta was commanding the respect of the funeral home staff with her decisive choices for her father's farewell: casket—steel, remembrance cards—Jesus, guest registry—an angel, candelabra—gold. Why she made those choices Edward had no idea; if they were different or the same for his mother's funeral, he didn't recall; that she made them without her brothers was, the brothers thought, a rare benefit to the exile they had been subjected to for so many years.

Funerals are curious rituals for children. They are not suitable for them nor are they pertinent to their young lives. By the time people reach middle age, they are accustomed to attending them periodically for parents, aunts, uncles, coworkers, in-laws. The rituals are essentially the same no matter who the deceased might be: the person is viewed, eulogized, prayed over, cried over, sung over and covered over. But children, as rarely as they attend a funeral, have difficulty sorting out any connection the ritual has to their lives.

When Edward attended the funeral of his grandmother, on his mother's side, he found its relevance to the life of a seven year old missing. The funeral home where his grandmother laid in the casket was large relative to the size of a small boy. The building was made of brick, dark red brick. Inside there was hardly any light; most of it was from candles or wall mounted lamps with dim bulbs. The gloom frightened him. He remembered holding tight to someone's hand, maybe his mother's or an aunt's. It was a gentle hand, he remembered. As he was led up to the casket, the person guiding him said, "She looks like she's sleeping." Edward was too short to see whether grandma looked asleep. His guide picked him up. He saw an old woman that scarcely resembled the grandma he barely knew. She was not wearing the bib apron she always had on when the family visited. She did not smell like the talcum powder she sprinkled on herself each day. Instead she smelled like . . . actually she didn't smell, it was the aroma of flowers that filled the room, that stole from grandma the remembered smell from when she hugged Edward. He remembered pushing against the person who was holding him signaling that he wanted down, that he was done looking at his grandmother. He remembered heading to the back of the room and finding a comfortable couch where he stayed until it was all over. Grandma did look like she was asleep, although it was hard to say because Edward had never seen his grandmother asleep and he did not know what dead looked like.

When Edward was ten years old he went to his grandfather's funeral, also on his mother's side. He remembered staring at his grandfather lying in his casket and thinking back to his grandmother's funeral, her lying in a casket also. She had not looked like she was asleep. She had looked no more asleep than a felled log. She had looked dead. And so did grandpa, because by the time Edward attended his second funeral he knew what dead looked like.

The next funeral Edward attended was his grandfather's, on his father's side. He was thirteen and, although his life had progressed to a different plane, the notion of death, even of a person more than six times his age, was not something he, or anyone else his age, pondered, and if they did, their concept of death and dying had not ripened enough to enable them to grasp what it was, only what it looked like. Old people died, that was a given; young people did not, that was a tenet of youth. They could do anything, go anywhere, attempt the daring and, although there might be bumps and bruises along the way, death was not an alternative.

It was a Saturday when Edward was told his grandfather had died. Edward's father called him from the alley junction. Edward was up to bat, but his father's call was deeper, more pronounced than his usual blaring monotone, so Edward laid the bat down and said, "Gotta go." It was dinner time anyway, but Edward normally waited until the end of the inning before he headed home. The peculiar way his father called him told him he should call it a day at that very moment.

Edward's mother and father were already at the dinner table when he washed his hands at the kitchen sink and took his place at the table. Dinner began as always. His father laid his napkin on his lap. That was Edward's signal to say grace. "Bless us oh Lord and these Thy gifts which we are about to receive from Thy bounty, through Christ our Lord, Amen." Edward's mother always was able to say her amen at the same time as Edward. His father always mumbled something that sounded like "ahem" a few seconds later, as if he had items he silently added to the prayer, or maybe he had taken a quick snooze as Edward recited the prayer and awakened with the amens.

Edward sat on one side between his father and mother who sat at each end of the table. His father faced the window that looked out onto the vacant lot next door, a lot that surprisingly had remained vacant since all the other houses in the neighborhood had been built thirty years before. It was a corner lot, a lot that anyone in the neighborhood rarely used except as a short-cut from one sidewalk to the other. The path that cut diagonally through the lot was like a part down the middle of a shaggy head of hair. The lot was full of tall grass, milkweed and a few locust trees that never lived but a few years because the kids in the neighborhood chopped them down and used them as swords or rifles when they played war. There were piles of refuse that seemed to grow bigger each year. New trees grew where the old ones had been pulled out of the ground, and they grew so fast that the neighborhood kids had an ample supply of weapons each summer. It was the vacant lot where, nearly six years before, Edward had watched his father stuffing a sausage in his mouth while Edward's bloody ankle was removed from the back wheel of Kevin's bicycle.

He stared at that lot intently while sitting at the dining room table telling Edward that grandpa had died. Staring was common place for him at the dinner table. Ordinarily his gaze was vacant and not directed at any singular object. This night it carried some meaning. It was direct and Edward could see from the frown on his father's face that it contained thoughts that had never entered his head, or had been absent from his thinking for a prolonged interval. When he made the announcement his eyes never left the vacant lot, never gained the intensity that would have given meaning to what came out of his mouth.

They passed the food in silence after the death announcement beginning each dish with Edward's father, then to his mother, then to Edward. There was a system to eating dinner in that household, a compulsive procedure eerily resembling assembly line motion. First the meat, usually roast beef, fried chicken or, on Fridays, every Friday, fish, most of the time salmon croquets. Then the potatoes, boiled or augratin, a vegetable, corn or green beans, iced tea or water. Edward always had milk. His father picked up each dish, scooped out a large serving, passed it to his wife who took her share, then passed it to Edward. As his mother passed a dish to her son, his father presented another one to her. His timing was impeccable. He never held a dish while waiting for someone else to take it. There was never a lapse between passings. The salt and bread and butter were handled in the same way, passed with the precision of an automated assembly line.

He said it in rather solemn way, a trait he avoided. "Grandpa died today." He said it with no emotion, no feeling that Edward thought, at that age, any son should have upon the death of his father. Little information was offered. They would have to leave in the morning. His cousin was arranging the funeral. It would be a long, hot drive. When he was done eating he got up, grabbed a beer from the refrigerator and turned on the television. Edward was just beginning to understand the concept of death. People he knew had died, people who were younger than those whose deaths seemed to be within the logical scheme of living and dying. Old people died because they were old. But not the younger, those not quite middle age or barely at that juncture. Like the third grade teacher at Edward's grade school, Sister Mary Agnes, forty-one years old. Or the neighbor across the street, Mr. Francis, who was a drafting teacher at the public high school, fifty years old. When Grandma died, Edward was not old enough to grasp the meaning, the reasoning behind why she was no longer able to breath or walk or talk, why she was put in a huge box and carried to a grassy field, lowered into the ground and left there never to be seen or heard from again. He was older when his father, in his inconsequential manner, announced grandpa's death. Edward knew death came, not to him, at least for a while, but it came to people in surprisingly different ways and sometimes at uncommonly young ages. Edward was too young to formulate questions about death and its imperceptive components when his grandmother died. This time he had questions. He had a lot of questions. How did he die? Was he sick? He didn't know he was sick. Did he have a heart attack? Where did he die? At home, at a hospital? Did he have any family besides us and cousin Mabel? Who will be at the funeral? Edward asked a few of those questions and when he didn't get any answers but was simply ignored, he stopped. He wanted answers. He needed answers. His father didn't have to make up any tales. No lies, just simple answers to his son's very mundane but meaningful, meaningful to him at least, questions.

The drive to grandpa's funeral *was* hot. Five hours from Chicago to East St. Louis, Illinois, no air conditioning, no radio, just the entertainment afforded by the passing scenery, the three of them staring at his or her own piece of those distractions as the car sped by them.

At his grandfather's wake Edward was not led by the hand up to the coffin and forced to view the wasted remains of his father's father. Nor was he encouraged to touch his hand or fed the ludicrous presumption that the man looked like he was just asleep. Perhaps they thought Edward had reached the stage where he had acknowledged the validity of death, for they left him alone to do whatever he thought he should do when attending a funeral. "Everybody grieves in their own way," his Cousin Mabel told him as Edward approached the casket. She took his arm, squeezed it gently and followed him to where his grandfather was laid out. Edward did not recognize this man dressed in his bright red and black Knights of Columbus uniform. He seldom visited him, and when he did the old man was intensely aloof. When he spoke to his wife it was in German; when he spoke to Edward it was in broken English used only to discipline him in some way, for some minor infraction—tracking mud into the kitchen, sitting on a chair reserved for adults in the darkened living room, hitting the side of the house with a rubber ball he had dug out of the basement.

Edward looked at his grandfather, a man he did not know. He smiled at his Cousin Mabel who was wiping her eyes with a white lace handkerchief, and he walked outside and sat on the front steps of the funeral home. After a few minutes he walked across the street to get a root beer. He watched cars park in the lot next door and the strangers who drove them enter the funeral home. He did not know if they were related, if they would enter the funeral home and emit the artificial grief that all who attended were expected to offer. Perhaps, if they really did grieve, they grieved for themselves, mourning their own impending death.

Edward, despite his youth, offered to himself as he sipped his root beer the notion that people, especially adults over forty grieve not for the deceased or the wife or sons and daughters of the deceased, but for their own mortality. For Edward dying was not imminent, it was a benign abstraction that required no grief for himself nor for his grandfather who gave him no reason to grieve. It was a funeral that was preparing Edward for the one he would witness thirty-three years later.

When his grandfather's wake was over Edward and his parents drove back to the motel. Kevin and Roberta did not come to this funeral. Kevin was in the army, in basic training at Fort Knox; Roberta was pregnant with her second child and could not travel. They stopped at a grocery store where his father bought a six pack of beer. At the motel they watched Johnny Carson's monologue. His father drank one can before the monologue and one during. Then the lights went out. Tomorrow was the funeral. Edward had taken his Cousin Mabel's advice. He was grieving in his own way: not at all.

The funeral was ordinary except for the six pall bearers dressed in their Knights of Columbus splendor. Edward sat in the front row, watching the altar boys perform their chores. His mind wandered in directions that removed him from the final formalities of his grandfather's death, the rites that the small crowd gathered there believed were necessary for the deceased (and for them at some later time) to reach heaven.

Edward was an altar boy and had served many funerals since he had been inducted into that elite company. He critiqued every move the altar boys serving his grandfather's funeral mass made. The short, chubby one whose cassock and surplus were designed for a boy much slimmer, held the incense burner too low for the priest to fill. He didn't concentrate, instead he stared at the stained glass windows daydreaming of where he would rather be at nine o'clock on Wednesday morning in July. The taller one could not decide how to hold his hands, palms together pointing to heaven or fingers entwined resting against his chest. When he knelt he wobbled back and forth; when he rose he pushed himself up with his arms and did not rise with his legs. Too sloppy to serve Mass; no pride in their work. The altar boys' miscues and carelessness kept Edward's mind occupied for the hour it took to wheel his grandfather into the church, eulogize his life, pray for his soul and wheel him out to be driven to the cemetery and forever remembered as a good man who served God and his fellow man. Maybe so. For Edward, the end of that hour meant going back home to Chicago where he could resume the life of a thirteen year old, be troubled by death later when he relinquished his immunity to its consequences, and tell his fellow altar boys about the shoddy work he witnessed at his grandfather's funeral.

XXI

Their thirty-years war had ended suddenly and without the decisive battle that precedes the end of a conflict. Then again, maybe not. Perhaps Edward had made a strategic error. Perhaps the battles they fought were only a prelude of what was yet to come. He was beginning to feel that his father's death had not produced a permanent armistice. Certainly no peace had been achieved. To secure peace required some conciliation before the bombs stopped falling. He gave nothing; Edward gave nothing. Edward expected nothing; he did not know what his father expected.

Every person makes bad choices in the life he or she leads. Edward's father made no choices, or at least the choices he made were of little consequence, indiscernible, except two: to take no part in his son's life and to die on his son's birthday.

Birthdays were not given a great deal of significance in Edward's childhood household. A cake was baked and the candles on it were extinguished after dinner. No one sang *Happy Birthday* while the honored person eyed the cake and the burning candles. Edward sang happy birthday to himself in his room after everyone had gone to bed. Actually, he hummed the song to himself as he lay in his bed. Sometimes, when Kevin was living at home and he was still awake, he would tell Edward to "Shut the fuck up."

A gift was given as the smoldering candles were removed from the gooey icing. Edward received a bicycle on his fifth birthday, a baseball glove on his seventh, a ring on his fifteenth—a black star sapphire in a gold setting. There were other gifts, he was sure. There had to be, he just couldn't remember what they were. But this, this birthday gift was the most memorable of all. Death. Death on his birthday. Death wrapped in a wrinkled sheet, an eighty pound wasted body filled with tubes, the monitors silent, his children's and grandchildren's eyes staring at him, some blank, some tear filled. Death encased in a gray steel casket topped with roses from the grandchildren, roses saluting his eternal life, flanked by gladiolas, the flower of choice for death celebrations, and more roses and carnations and green plants that can be taken home, deposited on a table or on the floor in a corner where they are watered periodically and can forever be a reminder of that birthday. Death embossed on the remembrance cards, the face of Jesus on one side, "In remembrance of Alfred, loving husband of . . ." on the other. The ultimate birthday gift buried in a steel vault, forever hidden under ground in a cemetery two thousand miles away, eternally wishing Edward a happy birthday each time some vague recollection seeps out of storage and brings back the memory of that gift of death.

The funeral home where Edward's father was displayed was out of place in the industrial area of Dalton, Illinois, where it sat between a steel fabricating plant and a paint manufacturer. It was an old rundown one story building, older than the man who was exhibited inside. Roberta stood in the lobby holding the arm of her fiancee, Brent, a guy who was on disability from his manufacturing job and seemed to find his idleness quite productive and obliging. His tanned face and muscular body showed Edward how pleasant disability can be if just manipulated correctly. Roberta's three children from her first husband stood on each side of their mother, the entire family talking to persons unknown to Edward. Roberta acknowledged her brother's presence as he entered, nodding slightly and raising her eyebrow in the most articulated greeting Edward had received from her in nearly thirty years. Her hair color had been modified in the few days since he last saw her; it was still the color of a tomato but a little more ripe. Her son Eric, Edward was sure, said something obscene under his breath. Edward smiled at him. Her daughter Rachel continued listening to the conversation between her mother and a gray-haired man too young to be an acquaintance of Edward's father, too old to be a member of Roberta's generation. Roberta's grandchildren were scattered about the room, too youthful, too inexperienced at death, to be concerned or enlightened about what was transpiring.

Edward and Kevin walked in to where the casket sat against the wall. The steel, not cherry, casket was flanked by a dozen baskets of garish floral arrangements, mostly gladiolas, some carnations and iris and roses, other flowers Edward could not identify except to know that they were common at funerals— death flowers packaged in that special moribund way to honor the dead.

Edward sniffed the air. Flowers at a funeral smell different than they do in a garden or at a wedding. Perhaps it's just the difference between celebration and melancholy. On the lower half of the coffin, the half that was never opened, lay a small bouquet of roses from the grandchildren. Entwined in his father's hands was a rosary, an implement of prayer used to carry out the meager penance people are given when they confess their sins, repeating prayer after prayer as ordered by the priest and then stored away until the next penance is imposed. Edward's father did not own a rosary; he never saw him use one. If he prayed he did it as silently and as obscurely as he conducted the rest of his life. Roberta had bought this rosary especially for this occasion.

People intermittently entered the viewing room. They were friends of Roberta's or of Kevin's, each at his or her own turn softly uttering consoling words to the family, making the mandatory walk to the casket where each of them stared at the body, some for a few seconds, some for a few minutes, each one silently debating the proper amount of time a dead body should be viewed. Too short a time taken to stare at the dead person and the family and other visitors may think unkindly thoughts, too long and the visitor was cornered by family members and forced to answer questions about what relationship the visitor had with the deceased. Coffin time was also determined by that relationship. Did the visitor know the deceased personally or did the visitor only know a member of the immediate family? A family member was compelled to stand at the coffin whenever there was a need to answer questions or guide the visitor through the life of the deceased. For a close friend of the deceased, the amount of coffin time decreased to only viewing the person who had died and then to offer condolences to family members who approached. The remainder of the visit was spent at the back of the room talking to others who held various ranks in the hierarchy of visitors. The time requirements gradually decreased even more for those who were friends of the family but not of the deceased: coworkers of family members who knew the family members well and coworkers who did not, and down to friends of friends or friends of coworkers who were not even required to view the casket but did so anyway and then stood near the door and nodded in a sympathetic manner.

The time spent at a funeral is awkward even when the family members have an unsullied relationship, when there is no animosity shown or unkindness wished on other members of the family. But when there are feelings of loathing that pervade the site where the progenitor of those family members is being memorialized before he is laid to rest, where there is a malignity that lurks in every side glance, every covert glare that you can feel on your back, every time the antagonist talks to a patron who enters the parlor and you think that the words of their conversation, the gestures, the eye movements are directed at you, you try to find ways to retaliate for what you perceive to be an attack on your integrity, on your position as a member of that family told to strangers who have no business hearing it. Edward could not find a way. He stood near the back of the room watching Roberta greet the parade of her friends and coworkers, giving each one little snippets of her father's life that no one but her found interesting, praising his life as a human being and his accomplishments as her father. In between the adulation for the dead man for whom they had come to pay their final respects and her assault on each person in an effort to gain their undivided sympathy, Roberta cast a quick side glance to Edward's little corner of the room, her voice lowered and the people receiving her malicious tales of the errant son nodded with understanding and amazement. They then took Roberta's hand, or hugged her and offered more solace and walked over to the casket, shooting a fleeting glance toward Edward as if too frightened to look at him head on but wanting to make sure they could identify him for future reference. Edward felt he was a misfit they were fearful might infect their family too if they came near him, a desperado who instilled dread in them because the word going around was that he was not fit to be this man's son and should be horsewhipped or worse.

Edward stood in the back of the room for ten minutes then made his way to the casket for another look. Why he was compelled to inspect his father again he did not know. Perhaps he was simply tired of standing in one place and a change gave him the stamina to finish out the night. Perhaps he wanted to see if there was anything he could glean from the man in the coffin that he missed the first time, that he had not discovered in the past but that might jump out at him if he just took one more look. As he stared at his father's body, his final stare, if someone asked him at that moment how he would describe his father, he would describe him as meager. Just as he looked lying in his coffin. He did not run counter to anything. Not even against his own obsessive needs. He did not run. He was intensely obsessive. Everything by the clock.

Neat stacks of white dress shirts picked up from the cleaners every week, starched the same way with the same amount of starch or they were sent back to be redone. Dark pin-striped suits with cuffed pants hanging neatly by color in the closet, black and brown wingtip shoes complete with cleats arranged by color on the closet floor underneath the suits he wore with them. Out the door at six-thirty every weekday morning. Dinner at six every night. Up at seven every weekend. The same shows at the same times; the news and then Johnny Carson's monologue. The same beer drunk at the same time with the same peanuts. Everything the same. The same responses to Edward time after time and then when the responses stopped, the same disinterest and indifference. The same everything, all the time coming from a man, or not coming from a man, who had a meager and shallow life.

Many of the other visitors did the same as Edward. One by one, from time to time in groups of two or three, at random intervals, the visitors again ventured up to the casket. If alone, the person catching another glimpse of its occupant simply stared for a moment, maybe made the sign of the cross and then moved back into the small groups that filled the room. Those that went in groups stared the same way, then murmured words back and forth, "He looks good." or, "It doesn't look like him at all." or, "Lost a lot of weight." or, "Did he suffer?" or, if a child was with the group, "He looks like he's sleeping." Each group had its own opinion of the man's status as a dead man, how he got to this point and if he might be recognized when he arrived wherever that destination might be.

When Edward was young and attended his grandfathers' and grandmother's funerals, the time when the family and friends milled around the room and traded stories of the man or woman they came to visit, eulogized him or her, painted him or her in the best light, made somber overtures of melancholy to the family, was called a wake. It was the interval between death and burial when a vigil was kept and the finality of death was memorialized. At that time, to Edward as a ten year old, the word *wake* conjured up rows of waves churned up by a boat as it sliced through the water. The word had no other meaning for him. Nor did it this time. Certainly his father could not be compared to the upsurge of symmetrical mounds that rise behind the churning propellers of a boat. His life as Edward remembered it never experienced an upsurge, never churned like the life of a man who has had moments where he did something daring, something that showed he had balls, something that left a wake.

By the time Edward's mother and father had died the name had been changed to visitation. What it was called was not important. By either name they were teasers for the main event. For this family which had lost its last progenitor, it was a strenuous exercise in tolerance to see how long their patience with each other could be endured, how much tongue they could bite without bleeding, how many side glances and rolled eyes and shaken heads must be withstood. But each of them found his or her means to keep the others at bay for the evening. Roberta had her moments when her snide remarks to her friends, exchanges that caused their eyes to hastily roll Edward's way, then give an understanding nod, gave her satisfaction. Kevin slumped in a deeply padded couch at the back of the room never moving until the last visitor had exited and the undertaker was ready to close up shop for the night. Edward found that the best way to avert a showdown with Roberta, if a showdown is what she had in mind, was to never stay in one place for more than a few minutes. He walked at least ten miles from back to front and around the chairs. Outside then inside. It was a circuit he found to keep him a moving target thereby making it difficult for anyone to take aim.

Edward's log of funerals attended was not lengthy. He only attended a few and at those he had at least a discernible relationship with the person who had died. He always thought that it was quite hypocritical, even irresponsible for a person to frequent funerals where knowledge of the person who had passed was wanting. This funeral was one of those.

So why did he attend? To attempt some closure on a relationship that had never opened? Doubtful. He had tried before, when he was young and when he was older and never had any success. To protect his interests? Probably. He knew Roberta would try anything and everything to eject her brother from the family after his father's death. To bring back memories? Yes, in a way. When Edward got the call from Kevin, the first thing that came to his mind was the chance to visit his old neighborhood and rekindle some of the great memories he had from growing up there. After he went through the neighborhood he was sorry he had made the turn to head in that direction. As for his father, there were no memories worth rekindling.

So Edward bided his time as the visitation droned on, and again the next morning as the funeral mass droned on. Oddly there was no luncheon after the funeral with little old women from the ladies' auxiliary scurrying about to prepare a cheap lunch of bologna and stale bread. But that was a given now. When his mother died, the money to pay for the post burial lunch came from his father's pocket. This time the money would come from his father's estate, or, as Roberta viewed it, potentially from her pocket.

The funeral mass was the same he had experienced when his mother died. There were not enough people young enough and strong enough to carry the casket, so the family carried it. Edward and Kevin in the front. Eric the Fuck, and Rachel's husband in the center, Kevin's son and Roberta's fiancee in the rear. The coffin was light. But Edward didn't know what to expect. He had never carried a coffin before. He had never carried his father before.

The priest, a young, athletic man who, based on Edward's estimate of his age, had been recently ordained, conducted the funeral mass as if he and Edward's father had been friends for years, like he knew every intimate detail of his father's life. Certainly Roberta had fed him a lot of what he said, but most of it Edward was sure he made up because he said things, generic funeral remarks, that he assumed were true for all fathers. Maybe true for the priest's father, but not for Edward's. He said things, many things, that were the opposite of what Edward's father was like. He told the gathering what a great father he had been, and a great husband, and a devoted Catholic, and how well he served his community. The priest talked as if he had baptized him, confirmed him, heard his every confession, tossed thousands of Eucharist wafers on his tongue and maybe even hoisted a few with him. They were comments that sounded like the priest had a set funeral discourse about fathers, and probably one about mothers and daughters and sons and uncles, and just rattled them off hoping that some of them might hit the mark. What did he care if he was wrong some of the time. He would never again see the man he spoke of, nor would he see most of the people who sat in front of him and listened to his speech.

He said nothing that really identified Edward's father. Nothing that was indisputable. Kevin mused about the one important item left out as the priest droned on. The priest said nothing about his father's flatulence. How could he overlook that? Apparently Roberta had not filled him in on everything. It was the most significant characteristic he remembered about his father. But this distinctive attribute was not mentioned in the short eulogy the priest, a man who never knew Edward or his father, gave to the few friends and family that cared to listen. It was not mentioned in his obituary where families exalt the dead kin by listing all of the great deeds and lasting impressions the departed had endowed to the world. It never was mentioned at the visitation where people extol the virtues of the departed. Well, this was a virtue, or at least an art. If anyone at the visitation or the funeral had asked Edward what he remembered most about his father, he would have had to say, "He farted well." And as they immediately became horrified by such an irreverent accusation, Edward would immediately go into an explanation as to why he thought this was so. But nobody asked and, even if they had, they would have never stayed around for the explanation. What they missed.

After the funeral mass Edward stood on the church steps and said goodbye to Kevin. He said nothing to Roberta. She was soon on her way to the airport with the casket holding "Father" to bury him next to "Mother" and the bishop in Phoenix. Edward had nothing to say now to Roberta anyway, but there would probably be plenty to say later. He drove home in silence.

This visit was different from the last two. This visit was not one where his father just vegetated in front of the television while his son and grandchildren tried to talk to him. When Edward stopped for lunch on the way home, he called Teresa. He briefly told her what went on and then he asked her a question. "Do you think they buried a *TV Guide* with him?" Edward didn't laugh. Teresa didn't either. It wasn't funny. It wasn't supposed to be.

XXII

On his way back to Missouri Edward had seven hours to think about what lay ahead for him with Roberta and Kevin and his father's estate, particularly Roberta. Although Edward knew Kevin was eager to get his hands on any cash that might be available, when it came to asserting his claim on equal shares, he would be inclined to take what he could get without raising a stink. Edward tried to come up with strategies aimed at keeping his interests alive and well. As he mulled over what devious plans Roberta might have, his thoughts kept being interrupted by reflections on the man who they had just sent to his eternity. For forty-five years he never had anything of consequence to say to his son and, because of his reticence, Edward never had any reason to respond or to offer any words to him since he was never inclined to respond to Edward.

But he wanted to say something even though he was dead. As he drove the flat highways of Illinois, he mentally devised a letter to his father between Decatur and Springfield. He did not say things that he had thought over the years. He invented words he wished he was able to say to his father, things he might have said to him had he been a real father. He began it with, *Dear Dad.* He wished he could have really meant the "Dear."

*I feel like my life has been successful, not only in my
job but in the wife I have chosen and the family I have*

13298-STIC

*raised. People have often asked me where I get my skills
and talents. I say, "My Dad."*

*I know what kind of dad you've been and I am forever
grateful for the involvement and time you put into my life.
I have so many memories with you. I am flooded with
wonderful memories of my childhood. You are one of the
few dads who got down on the floor and played with me;
spent countless hours building block forts and destroying
them in battles with my soldiers or playing with my train
set until we realized it was so late that you missed the late
news. You drove me to countless lessons, were always there
to help me with my homework even after a hard day at
work, and gave up so much so I could accomplish so much.*

*I remember that evening you drove through the blind-
ing snow to get me to play practice for our high school
play. It was South Pacific that year. What a production to
have in the middle of winter. And you sat in the front row
of the auditorium and patiently watched rehearsal and
then drove me home sliding on icy streets all the way. And
you came to the play and clapped harder than any parent
in the audience.*

*Even through college I was amazed at your devotion
to me despite all the stupid things I did and some of the
bad grades I got. But you were always there to support me
and guide me. Your advice to me through all those forma-
tive years, on sportsmanship, on studying, on girls, especially on girls, on how I should be careful about who I
hung out with, especially the older boys in the neighborhood.*

*And all those fishing trips and baseball and football
games, and camping trips. We had some great times, didn't
we?*

*And my children, your grandchildren. They adore
you and all the ways you have spoiled them as they grew
up. They never stop talking about their grandfather.*

*I am incredibly lucky to have been able to be so much
a part of your life. Thank you for being there for me, for
traveling great lengths to give me the very best, to shell out
all that money to give me the best advantages. Thank you
for understanding and for sharing your life with me. Thank
you for your presence.*

Your son,

Edward

And when he arrived home he felt the need to put something
down on paper about what he had experienced the last three
days, the last forty-five years. He sat down at the desk and wrote
another letter to his father.

Dad,

*You're cold now and in the ground. Are you any colder
than you were when you were alive? I feel like my life has
been successful without you, in spite of you, particularly
in my marriage and family because I have given the time
and devotion to my wife and children that you never saw
fit to give to me or the rest of your family. I know what kind
of dad you have been and I am grateful that I have had
the balls you never had and actually did something with
my life. I have so many memories of you now that you are
dead and I wish I didn't have them. I wish I could encase
them in something impenetrable. I am flooded with memories of my childhood and some of those memories are so
consuming I do not wish to have them.*

*You never got down on the floor to play with me no
matter how many times I asked. Then I stopped asking.
What was the use? Your television and beer were more
important than taking any time with your son. While I*

*spent countless hours building block forts and playing
with my plastic soldiers and my train set, you stared at the
boxing matches and football games and the Welks and
Moores and Sullivans. I remember the night I forgot to
pick up some blocks after you told me to. The next day I
looked for them and mom told me you had thrown them in
the trash.*

*You never drove me to lessons because you never al-
lowed me to take any. Too expensive, you said. I remember
one evening I went to a dance in Whiting, Indiana and
missed my ride home. You didn't come to get me when I
called. Too tired, I guess. Or maybe one too many beers. Or
maybe you just couldn't find the way. And all those fishing trips and baseball games and football games you
never took me to, and the camping trips we never went on.
There was never an opportunity to have great times with
you because we never had times.*

*I was incredibly unfortunate to have you for a father.
I was never a part of your life. Thanks for nothing.*

By the time he pulled the car into the drive he had dismissed
from his mind the letter he had written in his head while heading
home. The words he put down on paper, he tore up and tossed in
the trash. Teresa entered the room as he pitched the last shreds
in the waste basket. "What ya doin'?" she asked. "Nothing that's
worth doing anymore." He went to bed.

The next morning when he went to work there were twenty
sympathy cards laying on his desk, twenty cards from people at
his office signed by a total of forty-seven people. Twenty cards
costing a total of thirty-five dollars plus tax. The time and effort
choosing a card and passing it around for others to sign could
not be priced. There was more effort exerted by forty-seven people
in the simple choice and transmittal of sympathy cards than his
father had ever shown in his son. Forty-seven people who did
not know his father. And why did they do it? Because they all

thought all sons and fathers and all daughters and fathers had relationships that were worth something. They figured Edward had a relationship like that. Had they known the relationship Edward had with his father, they might not have gone to the trouble. The people at work, people who did not know his father, unlike Edward, appeared genuinely grieved.

He thanked those forty-seven people and put the cards in his desk drawer. A week later he threw them out when no one was looking.

XXIII

When Edward's grandfather, his father's father, died, Edward never thought about what property he had left to be doled out to the clamoring relatives. Actually, he didn't think he had much and he did not have many relatives to complicate its distribution. Edward's parents, as they often did, discussed family affairs late at night when the children were asleep and they felt comfortable talking about those things they believed children had no business knowing. After Edward's grandfather's funeral, discussions of his grandfather's estate were infrequent, but what he could hear, at least on those nights when he had trouble encountering sleep, was very informative.

His grandfather could not have had very much in the way of value when he died. He had no property. He, like Edward's father, flaunted his frugality. He did not own a home. Neither did Edward's father. He rented. So did Edward's father. He did not own a car. They were different there. He walked or occasionally used public transportation. Edward's father walked to the bus stop or the train station to go to work. The car was used to go to church and to the bar on Wednesday, Friday and Saturday nights. For three or four years before he died Edward's grandfather had a room at the Knights of Columbus home in East St. Louis. Edward's father was not a Knight of Columbus. It was a tiny room, pitifully furnished with a metal bed, a metal table and a metal pole lamp, much like the room Edward's father had at Roberta's house after he moved in with her. On the table was a radio and a hot plate.

Edward vividly remembered the room for a few years after his grandfather died, but lost touch with its memory as he grew up. It was when Edward first visited his father at Roberta's home that the memory of that Spartan chamber in the Knights of Columbus home was restored.

As Edward's parents talked in the darkness of their bedroom about his grandpa's estate, Edward's mind captured glimpses of the room at the Knights of Columbus home. What in it was so valuable that his parents stayed up nights debating how to get a hold of it? Was there something he had missed? Was there a mass of money his grandfather had accumulated over the years? Buried under a floorboard? Stacks of stocks and bonds stuffed in a drawer, investments that had doubled and tripled since they were purchased. Edward doubted it. Even at twelve years old he was able to recognize when a person had been able to sock away some spendable cash. His grandfather had none. All his life he worked as a telegraph operator for Western Union. When his wife died he was not able to afford a head stone for her. Edward's father paid for it. He had no car, no valuable jewelry or furniture or expensive antiques or valuable collectibles that people display ostentatiously in their homes in polished hard wood cabinets. He rarely spent money on modern conveniences that people spend their money on whether they have it or not. He wore no clothes that proclaim if a person feels comfortable about spending hard earned money to buy them. Whatever he had left when he died, however, Edward's father wanted it and he was determined to fight for it.

The primary obstacle to his father getting this unknown wealth of Edward's grandfather was a cousin who lived in southern Illinois. Edward never knew this relative existed until those late nights when he laid in his room, his head at the foot of the bed, his ear cocked toward the hallway that connected his room with his parent's and heard his cousin's name mentioned in the most loathing tone. What he was doing was criminal. He was a conniver, a cheat, a greedy little. . . . Edward's mother shut their bedroom door before his father finished the phrase, a precaution made not to shield Edward, if he happened to be awake, from bad language should he be listening, but to prevent Edward from witnessing what she thought he would perceive as disharmony in the family. As if he had not repeatedly witnessed it by then. But he imagined what was being said. He inserted words whenever the door was closed. Bastard, asshole, and others that, at twelve years old, he was just beginning to gradually hear in his friends' vocabularies.

This went on for several months until the late night discussions suddenly changed and were of different subjects and used subdued language. Edward presumed the battle for his grandfather's estate had ended. He never found out what his father received from it, if he received anything or whether it was worth all the fuss. And so it was after Edward's father was buried, that the late night discussions began again, this time between Edward and Teresa, but now Roberta was the greedy evildoer and their father's estate became the target.

Edward called Roberta the same names, even more since language such as that had become common place in most persons' vocabularies. Discussions with Teresa though were not as secretive as those that took place between Edward's mother and father. Edward's indictments of Roberta, that she was conniving, greedy, overbearing, shady, deceptive, were made whenever he had the inclination to express his opinion about her latest scheme to deprive Edward and Kevin of their rightful share of their father's estate. It was when name calling dominated the accusations, when words were used that a person tries to prevent children from hearing and taking back to their friends and classmates, or use them in public in front of strangers who then spread tales of the moral decay of our youth, that the discussions occurred at night with the door closed after the children had gone to bed.

The scheming by Roberta began a few days before Edward's father died. The tangible scheming, that is. Her conspiracy to rob Edward and Kevin of their share of whatever remained after he died began many years before. It began about the time Edward departed the nest, or was discarded from the nest, and became an outlaw. Roberta had made the substantive run for the money while his heart beat feebly and his breath was near its last. How much there was he didn't actually know. Kevin told him one thing; Roberta told him another. Whatever the amount, she wanted as much as she could get.

It all began innocently enough in the waiting room of the hospital when Roberta told Edward and Kevin she had hired an attorney to handle their father's estate. At the time Edward thought that was a reasonable and not out of the ordinary move. He didn't know for sure because he never had the opportunity, nor did he ever want it, to handle everything that comes along after a person's death. It was a simple chore to handle his mother's affairs after she died. Everything she had was her husband's. When Kevin called Edward to tell him their father was in the hospital, they knew he would be dead in a few days. Planning for what comes after a death was not really out of the ordinary. Later, however, after his father was under the dirt, Edward discovered that retaining an attorney was only one of Roberta's many assaults on all three thirds of the estate, and the most benign.

When the eulogies for his father were completed, the anecdotes relived, the sympathetic greetings and smiles and arm squeezes forgotten and the funeral home closed and locked for the night, Roberta approached Edward and handed him a box. "I thought you might want this. I gave a similar one to Kevin." No other remarks, no "glad you came" or any other comments that might be appropriate after the burial of a father. Not even a "Why did you have to come?" Why don't you leave now. Kiss my ass." Nothing that even appeared to be a suitable salutation from Roberta. Only a three inch by three inch white box shoved in his hand, a few empty words and then off, Edward presumed, to begin counting her money.

Kevin came up behind him on the steps of the building, carrying his box. "What was in yours?" he asked. Edward opened it. A watch, his father's watch that he remembered him wearing when Edward was a child. An old watch. And as he examined it, a watch that did not work. In the corner of the box was a ring. It looked expensive—gold setting and what looked like a diamond in the middle—but, knowing his father, to him jewelry was a waste of money, a luxury for which the money paid for it could be better spent, or not spent at all. It was probably worth twenty-five dollars at the most. "What about you? Edward asked Kevin. "Same" he answered irritated. "You know she's going to try to get it all. Fucking bitch," he added.

Edward tucked the box in his jacket pocket. He wanted to get back to his hotel and he started to cross the street to get his car and leave. Long conversations with his brother had always been annoying. He could not complete a sentence without throwing in at least one and usually two or three four letter words, a trait that caused the listener to strain to find the substance of what he was saying somewhere among the obscenities. "What exactly is 'all of it'?" Edward asked reaching for the car door handle. "I mean, what is the total of Dad's estate?"

"Like I told you at the hospital, I think it's about two hundred fucking grand."

"You really think it's that much? Roberta told me hundred and fifty."

"That's because she wants the fucking fifty she ain't telling you about. The way I fucking figure it, she stashed some away while Dad was alive. You know, like maybe he paid her rent and chipped in for food and maybe even just fucking signed over his entire pension and social security checks to her for all I know. For all I know, she could have put a vice on his balls and twisted it every fucking time a check came in the fucking mail. I mean, goddamn it, he had a shit load of money when Mom died. I think at least a hundred and fifty fucking thousand back then and that's been nine years."

"You really think it's that much?" Edward said again. The word "fucking" gave the amounts Kevin quoted a much loftier interpretation of the assets their father had. Edward did not doubt his appraisal of his father's worth either now or at the time of his mother's death. He could easily see how the man could sock away that much considering how stingy he was. Even being the primary source of welfare for Roberta during her fertile years would not have severely limited the amount of funds he stashed away. Edward could not grasp why his father saved all that money. His lifestyle after retirement was barely a step or two above squalor, a small apartment on the edge of the seedy side of Tempe, furniture they had since their move to the upscale side of South Chicago, unreplaced, unrepaired and uncomfortable. Edward's father spent only on necessities and a semi annual trip to Las Vegas so Edward's mother could glue herself to the slot machines with all the other blue, gray and white haired ladies that frequented that city, and his father could sit in the lounge and dream of Vanna when not ogling the young women who moved sensually through the casinos. Whatever amount remained, Kevin was sure Roberta would make a strong effort to keep the two sons from getting any part of it. Edward was sure of the same thing. Kevin shook his head. "Fuck, Ed, I don't know. What I do know is that she ain't gonna fucking get away with it. I'm gonna fucking fight her until I get every cent I deserve."

Edward nodded heartily. "Yea, yea, me too. I'll fight her with you. With the two of us together, there's no way she can cheat us out of our share." Edward started toward the car. "We'll talk. I'll call you," Edward told him. He nodded, shook his brother's hand and stood on the curb as Edward drove away. The forlorn look on Kevin's face told Edward that his brother wished he were driving four hundred miles away from Roberta and did not have to live in the same city as she. Edward smiled to himself. How lucky.

Four weeks after Edward returned home from his father's funeral, he received a letter from the attorney Roberta had chosen. From the start he sensed something about the whole process was not right. The way his sister had manipulated their mother and father, particularly their father as he exhibited such helplessness and naiveté after their mother died and exposed himself to his sister's conspiring manipulations left a very bad taste in Edward's mouth. Edward was convinced she had played a significant role in inciting his parents to break their relationship with him, to, in effect, disown him, because of what she termed his "outrageous disrespect toward their authority." But the repulsive flavoring of loathing Edward carried with him for many years had become even more disgusting.

That loathing became even greater after he discovered that what he had told Kevin on the steps of the church after their father's funeral mass and what Kevin told Edward at that same time was wrong. Roberta did get a larger share of their father's money. Somehow, sometime, she had conspired with their father to build her own nest egg that her brothers could not touch after his death. Their father and Roberta had a joint savings account that amounted to just under ten thousand dollars. He had put money in trust for her that was hers and hers alone after he died. That trust totaled eighty thousand dollars when he died. What was left? Sixty thousand dollars which Roberta, Kevin and Edward split three ways. Roberta was right. One hundred fifty thousand. So Kevin couldn't fight her and Edward couldn't be behind him every step of the way, because everything Roberta did to cheat Edward and Kevin out of a fair share of their father's assets, she did legally. Even the glassware and dishes and furniture and knickknacks their mother had collected over the eighty years of her life had been sold and the money socked away in the joint savings account.

When Edward found all this out he called Kevin. Yes, he knew about the trust fund and the joint account. Yea, he knew she was ending up with more than five times as much as they were and that they ended up getting screwed. "Fuck her," he said. "Yea," Edward agreed, "fuck her."

XXIV

Ultimately, even after Edward's father died and was buried, he was still a significant force in his son's life. A significant force, but not a positive one. Even though everything he heaped upon Edward was contrary to what should have been heaped upon him, what he piled upon him never left him even after his father died. The memories never passed with his passing.

While Edward tried to forget all those memories he had of his father, recollections that had been stirred up after Edward went to visit him in the hospital, he never was able to fully rid himself of them. Edward will forever be, until his own death greets him, surrounded by the shadows of his parents, particularly his father.

So it was with some misgiving that those shadows that had haunted him after his father's death increased in all possible dimensions when Edward was scheduled to attend a business meeting in Phoenix.

Edward's boss asked him if he would go to Phoenix in January for three days of meetings with some clients of the company Edward worked for. Edward thought he could handle three days in Phoenix, Arizona, in the middle of winter. Sure, he told his boss. Fine. He'd love to go. As Edward left his boss' office it dawned on him what was in Phoenix besides the warm weather and the desert. He stopped in mid stride and wondered if he should go back to his boss and tell him he changed his mind. "Why," he would ask. "Well," Edward would respond, "my parents are buried there and I don't. . . ." "You don't what?" he would ask with a confused look on his face. And as Edward would try to explain to him the reason why, a reason Edward could not articulate himself, his boss would get that look on his face that told Edward it was a bad idea to back out. So he returned to his office.

"What am I going to do?" Edward asked Teresa that evening, pleading for some direction. She gently rubbed his back. "You're going to do the same thing you did the last two times you went to visit your father when he lived in Indiana."

Edward looked at her with a mix of relief and bafflement. The back rub brought relief. Her statement brought confusion. "What the hell do you mean?" he asked. She rubbed his back harder but still smoothly. "I mean that you're going to go to the cemetery just like you went to your sister's house. You're going to say a few words to him just like you did then. He won't respond just like he didn't respond then. And then you're going to leave. It will be over and done with." Edward smiled. Wonderful Teresa, he thought. "Don't worry about it," she said, "you won't get anymore out of him in Phoenix than you did in Indiana. And if you're lucky, this final visit will rid you of all the tormenting memories you have of him." Edward doubted that. He laughed at her argument, then he rubbed her back.

On the way to Phoenix, Edward still had misgivings about visiting his parents' graves. Unfortunately, he had more than ample time between meetings to drive the rental car to the cemetery. He put it off as long as he could. The first afternoon, when he had some free time, he took a jeep ride in the desert with three strangers, tourists out to the desert southwest to find some definition in their lives that they had been unable to discover back home, and the tour guide, a young man with a master's degree in zoology and an acute knowledge of desert flora and fauna, but with little direction in his life.

The second afternoon, with more free time, he sat by the pool. The third afternoon, the day before he was to go back to

Missouri, he had no more excuses or diversions and he had plenty of free time.

Edward asked the hotel desk clerk for directions to the cemetery. He didn't write them down. He should have. The longer Edward drove, the more he became lost. The more he became lost, the more his gut and his head reacted to his decision to even make the visit. He stopped at a convenience store to use the bathroom, buy some aspirin and ask directions. This time he wrote them down. He bought some coffee to go.

In ten minutes he was at the cemetery entering under a wrought iron arch way, the kind that might be found at the entrance to the double bar ranch. But this one had cherubs, not the ranch's brand, staring down as visitors drove beneath it. Fat little angels welcoming both the dead and the living.

It had been nearly fifteen years since Edward's mother died and the family brought her to this place. It quickly came back to him. Too quickly. The first road to the right, then the second left to the other side of the mausoleum. There under two aging cedar trees were the head stones—*Loving Wife* and *Loving Husband*. And next to both of them, their protector, the bishop.

Edward sat in his car, unable to lift the door handle, reluctant even to look toward where they were buried. He stared straight ahead, then to the right, but not at their graves. He looked for other visitors as if he must be cautious that no one see him lest they think he cared about the two people he came to visit. He had to make a decision. Either get his ass out of the car or get his ass out of the cemetery.

Edward opened the door and stepped from the car. The sun was hot; the wind was hot. The sweat crept down from his forehead and filled his eyes and mustache. It dripped onto his sunglasses. He wiped his forehead with his shirt sleeve, but that seemed to only give the sweat more incentive to rush out of his pores. He walked to the cedar tree that shaded their graves and sat on the bench beneath it.

Every man has a refuge somewhere, a shelter that protects

him from everything that may be perceived as dangerous or intrusive. Edward's father had such a retreat when he was alive, a hideaway that was unassailable. It was his television, his *TV Guide* and his reclusiveness, his lack of interest in anything that might touch him and ignite some kind of feeling in him. The television was his medium of silent desire. Edward thought his father was always searching for that life he wanted, envious of those lives that flashed before him, lives he could not have, lives he was never able to emulate. He never had feelings, never wanted to have feelings. No compassion, no concern, no regard for anything or anyone that might touch him and make him a normal human being. In his grave his refuge was the metal and dirt that forever concealed all the flaws that should have given Edward cause to not be in this place trying to find things that never existed. He simply sat and wondered.

It was peculiar what entered his mind as he sat near their graves. Perhaps it was the unyielding heat that forced thoughts, old thoughts, thoughts that had been archived for decades and had not been retrieved even when his father's death had brought many others out of hiding.

Edward thought of the family Christmases as a kid growing up in the old neighborhood. Christmas morning, about six hours after getting home from midnight mass, sleeping restlessly, getting up and rushing to the living room where all the presents for Edward, Kevin, Roberta and their parents were stacked in neat piles in front of the Christmas tree. It was a metal Christmas tree that simply required removing the stand and limbs from the box, bending them back into shape, sticking them in the holes on the metal trunk and, with little cheer, adding the few drab decorations.

Each person opened one present at a time beginning with their father. Edward always got him a carton of cigarettes, Chesterfield, and Kevin always got him a bottle of Old Spice after shave, and Roberta always got him a tie that their mother picked out. After their father, it was their mother's turn, then Kevin's, the oldest child, then Roberta and finally Edward. After each present was unwrapped and examined, and the wrappings put in a trash bag that hung on the handle of the front door, the privilege of opening a present passed to the next person. There was no playing with a gift, no trying on of brand new clothes, no taking new toys out of the boxes until all the presents were open and all the wrappings and empty boxes carried away to the trash. So they stacked their opened gifts in another neat pile next to the assemblage of unopened ones.

Edward sipped his coffee and looked around at the cemetery. The grave stones were flat, even with the ground. The grass, what little there was, was yellowing from the intense sun and lack of water. It was well kept but uninteresting. His mother liked well kept places. Her home was always neat and tidy. It really could not have been any other way. Strangers may have thought his mother a tidy housekeeper, but she really had nothing to keep. The biggest mess was the Sunday newspaper scattered about the coffee table, a coffee cup emptied a few minutes before which was quickly snatched up and carried to the kitchen lest it leave a ring or get knocked over and dribble the few drops of the brown liquid it still held. Perhaps there might be a pair of slippers from the previous evening neatly set in front of the couch.

Edward got up from the bench and walked between their graves. He stared down at his father's head stone. He didn't talk like a lot of people do when they visit a parent's grave, telling their dead loved one how the grandkids are doing, how much they are missed. Edward didn't talk at all because he had nothing to say, and even if he did, and they could hear what he said, they wouldn't listen.

He didn't talk. He just thought. How had all this started? Was it worth the anguish to try to figure it all out now? It had been a tremendous waste of years, a drawn-out time that could have been put to better use, a time when conflict in a family, in a country, in a world full of conflicts could have been avoided. Now that they are dead and other people might grieve for them,

Edward had never been able to find gratification in grieving nor in not grieving. So there is no point in either. Grief, or lack of it, wouldn't change a thing.

Life may have been much easier if he had simply moved out without writing that letter. The letter is what did it. That and quitting the seminary. He had felt imprisoned.

He wanted to be a ten year old again and start over, and learn all the things he wanted to learn and do all the things that fathers and sons do together. Or maybe younger when he got his ankle caught in the spokes of Kevin's bike, and have his father come running from the porch, no, jumping off the porch to save him. He wanted to be all the ages of his childhood and have his father think it is important to give quantity time to his kids. If he had given Edward the quantity, he was certain the quality component would have emerged so that they could have developed a fantastic relationship. He wished his father could have understood that a father has to say things to his children occasionally, nod at their childish insights, smile when they act silly, rub their heads once in a while just for the hell of it, definitely say "I love you" to them.

Edward sat for a few more moments on the bench next to the graves until the sweat began to drench his clothes. He was done. He got in his car and drove away looking for a place to buy some French fries.

End   ᵎ

Printed in the United States
2951